Karl Schroeder won early [...] his short fiction. The fantasy novel he collaborated on was similarly well received and *Science Fiction Chronicle* named it "The best first fantasy novel of 1998." But it was only with his first solo novel, *Ventus,* that he began to truly come into his own as a masterly writer of science fiction epics. *Locus* described *Ventus* as belonging "in the company of recent work by Poul Anderson, Greg Bear, Gregory Benford, Greg Egan, Paul J. McAuley, and especially, Vernor Vinge." High praise, which Schroeder now validates with another grand hard SF adventure, *Permanence.*

"*Permanence* starts in the tradition of a Heinlein juvenile, then takes off across the universe into the realms of Gregory Benford and Vernor Vinge. Schroeder has hidden a philosophical novel in action novel clothing. . . . Schroeder isn't afraid to stagger the reader emotionally or intellectually, and the ratio of ideas to pages here is high enough to satisfy the curiosity of any science fiction reader. *Permanence* is a fast-paced, adventurous ride."   —*Bookpage*

"The author of *Ventus* showcases his gift for panoramic story-telling in this story of a young woman's struggle to find her place in a world where trust and friendship are rare treasures."
          —*Library Journal*

"By turns exciting and thoughtful, pitiless and romantic, Schroeder's excellent novel is the best kind of coming-of-age tale, one that seizes the imagination and the emotions as it presents a fully realized future society, fascinating technology, and believable characters."   —*Booklist*

"A complex, conceptually satisfying story of interstellar intrigue, cosmology, theology and nanotechnology. . . . The narrative fairly bursts with interesting ideas . . . the author packs in enough material for several volumes. Yet Schroeder knows how to entertain and should continue to build an audience across a broad range of SF fans."
          —*Publishers Weekly*

Also by Karl Schroeder
from Tom Doherty Associates

Ventus

PERMANENCE

Karl Schroeder

TOR®

A TOM DOHERTY ASSOCIATES BOOK
NEW YORK

This is a work of fiction. All the characters and events portrayed in this book are either products of the author's imagination or are used fictitiously.

PERMANENCE

Edited by David G. Hartwell

A Tor Book
Published by Tom Doherty Associates, LLC
175 Fifth Avenue
New York, NY 10010

www.tor.com

Tor® is a registered trademark of Tom Doherty Associates, LLC.

ISBN: 0-765-34285-5
Library of Congress Catalog Card Number: 2001059652

First edition: May 2002
First mass market edition: March 2003

Printed in the United States of America

0 9 8 7 6 5 4 3 2 1

Acknowledgments

Writing is not really a solitary activity, so thanks are due to many people who helped make this book happen: my editor, David Hartwell; my agent, Donald Maass; Moshe Feder and Rob Stauffer for production help; and as always the clever and relentless critics of Cecil Street. Thanks to the unruly mob at OpenCola for indulging my unusual lunchtime conversations. And especially, thanks to Janice for putting up with the uneven and sometimes bewildering creative process that is novel writing.

It is expedient that there be gods;
therefore, let us believe in them.

—Ovid

Prologue

THE DISCOVERY THAT made interstellar travel possible and an interstellar civilization inevitable, was made in 1997; but at the time no one recognized its significance.

Maria Teresa Ruiz, an astronomer at the Universidad de Chile, was searching for white dwarf stars when she spotted something unusual. Thirty light-years away, in the constellation Hydra, a very faint red pinprick of light lay adrift. Its spectrum didn't show titanium oxide, which would have marked it as a red dwarf star. Instead, Ruiz found the unmistakable signature of lithium in its atmosphere—an impossibility for any real star. She named the object Kelu-1, the first free-floating brown dwarf ever seen.

The first brown dwarfs, Gliese 229B and Teide 1, had been spotted two years before, within weeks of one another. Too small to be stars, but too large to be planets, such galactic oddities glowed faint red from the heat of their slow gravitational contraction. Young dwarfs were hot enough to sustain Earthlike conditions on planets that might orbit them. The first dwarfs spotted had orbited around known stars, but Ruiz's find was different. Kelu-1 floated free of any stellar influence. It was a place in its own right, an invisible sun between suns.

Astronomers had theorized the existence of such interstellar solitaries; what they hadn't imagined was just how common they were. True, some astronomers had an inkling: in 1984 Bahcall declared that "about half of the [galactic] disk material at the solar position has not yet been observed." Some of this material would be stars whose distance had not yet been determined correctly—tiny red dwarfs, for the most part, which were close but looked remote. Still, he estimated that about a hundredth of a solar mass per cubic parsec was unaccounted for—was not, in fact, embodied in the Lit Stars.

Within a year of Ruiz's discovery astronomers were finding brown dwarfs all over the place, prompting J. Davy Kirkpatrick to declare in 1998 that they were "the most common spectral type in the galaxy." In a press release he went on to add that "They are so commonplace that there is a good chance that we will discover one which lies closer to the sun than Proxima Centauri, the closest of the known stars."

He was right: Nemesis was discovered several years later. But even those astronomers who had come to suspect that the galaxy held more brown dwarfs than lit stars still failed to grasp the implications. Like everyone else on Earth at this time, when they thought about the future expansion of humanity into space, they pictured colonies on single, Earthlike worlds orbiting Sunlike stars. And since there were only six G-class stars within twenty light-years, their dreams were spare and even forlorn—of six tiny settlements huddling on worlds separated by generations of travel time. Such settlements would only be reached using colossal, expendable starships capable of carrying a mere handful of people at some small fraction of light speed.

But the brown dwarfs each had their retinue of planets— the *halo worlds*, as they came to be called. And though they were not lit to the human eye, many of these planets were bathed in hot infrared radiation. Many were stretched and heated by tidal effects, like Io, a moon of Jupiter and the hottest place in the Solar System. And while Jupiter's magnetic field was already strong enough to heat its moons through electrical induction, the magnetic field of a brown dwarf fifty times Jupiter's mass radiated unimaginable power—power enough to heat worlds. Power enough to sustain a population of billions; enough to launch starships.

Did Dr. Ruiz ever step outside and gaze up at the stars and think that for every star she saw, there were five she could not see? Did she realize that the moment she discovered Kelu-1, she had taken star travel from dream to possibility? For although the stars were as far away as ever, with her discovery the known distance between planetary systems had been halved.

PART ONE

Ediacara

1

RUE PAUSED JUST long enough to catch her breath. She had reached the outer station now, far from her bedroom, and was breathing hard enough to use up a day's ration of oxygen. *Add that to my bill*, she thought sourly.

Jentry and the others couldn't be far behind. She had been unbelievably stupid, she knew; but this time Jentry had gone too far. She reached up and absently stroked the small stone disk that hung on a thong around her neck. Jentry could insult her; he could restrict her access to vital parts of the station; he could poison the minds of the workers against her. But to steal her birthright—no, if she had to do it again, she would still have gone to steal it back. Maybe more carefully, though . . .

Her uneven breath frosted in the dim weightless air. The outer shells of the spherical station were a maze of corridors and cells, relying on what little warmth trickled out of the core for energy. This corridor was one of the rarely used ringways—a long hexagonal tunnel outside the Earth-G centrifuge, intermittently lit and lined with filmy shipfur. As she rapelled from handhold to frosted handhold she looked for signs. In the Core, especially the centrifuge, everything was labelled: Mom's poor substitute for the baroque carving that covered every surface of more wealthy stations. Out here, the only markings were the ones Rue had made for herself over the years, during the hours and days she spent hiding out from Father and Jentry and the others.

There—she spied interlinked triangles scratched near a bulkhead door. They glittered faintly with hoarfrost and for the first time she shivered. Rue knew that the temperature beyond that door was little more than 250 degrees Kelvin. She had come this way many times partly because she knew the others wouldn't venture down here. The halls beyond that bulkhead were unusually cold for this level and unless you knew to dress for it in advance, the cold would ward you away. She'd used that fact to her advantage many times.

The only problem was, she wasn't dressed for it herself tonight. She wore only the light thermals she had donned in her bedroom.

"There she is!" Despite her years and independence, Jentry's voice still had the power to freeze Rue. A flashlight beam jiggled crazily over the frost on the walls and blinded Rue for a second. She shook herself and spun away, groping for the handle of the bulkhead door.

"Come back here, you little leech!" Jentry had called her that for so long that the insult had lost its force years ago.

"Suck vacc!" she shot back.

Her knuckles rapped the door handle and she grabbed it. The cold hit her palm like fire, but she ignored it as she yanked on the door. It groaned open and the puff of air that emerged made her gasp. She let go of the handle, leaving skin behind and dove into the dark opening.

Talking back to her half-brother was the quickest way to a beating, but this time Rue had worse things to worry about. Mom was dead three weeks now; the last roadblock in Jentry's plan to sell Rue was removed. She knew a cometary cycler would be passing the station in two weeks time and Jentry had sneeringly told her that there was a man on it who needed laborers for his station. Allemagne's tiny ecology couldn't support Rue, he'd said. She just wasn't productive enough. She would have to go— one way or another.

There was no time to shut the bulkhead door behind her. Rue dove shuddering into the cold. Her thin shipfur jacket was no protection at all here. She clamped her mouth firmly shut and breathed through her nose, feeling a ring of fire around her nostrils every time she did so. A single full-mouthed intake of air could freeze your lungs here; she had to be careful. And she avoided touching the snow-covered walls with her skin, using taps of her boots to keep herself moving forward.

"She's crazy! Rue, get back here! You'll freeze your sorry little ass down there." Shadows from Jentry's head moving in the doorway loped ahead of her. He wasn't dressed for this part of the station either—her only advantage at this point.

"Rue, come back here this minute or I'll send the miners after you." He'd adopted Father's tone of authority of late and seemed to relish using it on Rue. She snarled but didn't succumb to the temptation to talk. The skin of her face and hands felt tight from the cold; the air here was perfectly dry and she'd start to dehydrate soon. Scraping snow off the walls would not satisfy that thirst; the finer whisks of that frost were made of carbon dioxide, not water.

At least her frost-burned hand no longer hurt. She came to the end of the long corridor, where another ringway started. The walls here were nearly cold enough to liquefy nitrogen. To breathe was to drink fire; she held a hand over her face so that the weak heat of her fingers would help warm the air. She probably had less then a minute to live if she didn't find what she was after.

Years ago, there had been an accident on a visiting rendezvous shuttle. It had slammed into the half-mined comet that loomed next to Allemagne and bits of hull and debris had flown everywhere. Jentry and the other favored lads had spent the better part of six months rounding up all the flotsam that had drifted away into interstellar blackness. Rue, who was never allowed outside, had instead used some miner robots—probably the same ones Jentry was about to send after her—to patrol the outer hull of the station looking for breaches.

She had found one—a hole punched by a section of the ship's hull. In the zigzagging lamp light of her miner's headlight, she had beheld a rough triangle of wall, torn and peeled along the edges, wedged into a gap of broken fullerene spars. Clouds of shipfur floated everywhere. In the very center of the triangle was an airlock door.

Before she reported her find, Rue had pried open that door, to find an almost intact cylindrical airlock beyond it. Its lockers were filled with treasures.

Now she raced down the leftward arm of the ringway, hands held in her armpits, breathing shallowly while her ears and face went numb from the gentle movement of air past her face. She was shivering uncontrollably now and her back was dangerously close to spasm. Rue tried to calm herself; she had calculated this distance quite carefully when she stashed her discoveries all those five years ago. She should have time.

She bounced herself to a stop over a frost-rimed door. The only illumination here was a single blue tube ten meters down the corridor, but Rue knew where the doorplate was and she used a corner of her jacket to wipe it free of frost. Then she breathed on her thumb to warm it and tapped the plate.

Nothing happened. Rue cursed; she didn't want to hold contact with the thing for more than a split second, or she would freeze to it. She prodded the plate again.

This time it flashed and the door grated open, light blooming from inside. She couldn't breathe and her hands had gone completely numb by the time she maneuvered herself around the icy metal doorjamb. Here, though, was her treasure: a storage room containing three EVA suits, reaction pistols, rolls of fullerene cable, and bundles of shipfur. Also, an addition that she had stolen from Father's stores a week after stashing this stuff: an emergency thermal pack.

She dove for the thermal pack and looped her unresponsive fingers through the big ring on its side. One good pull and it began to throb with warmth, stronger every second.

For a while she just huddled around it, soaking up the warmth. After a minute or two she heard a faint hissing coming from all around her: some of the frost on the walls was evaporating.

Rue had rehearsed her next moves a thousand times in hopeful daydreams. Her fingers were waking up and felt like they had been burned to the bone. Her ears were still numb, but her face was starting to hurt, too. As soon as she could move her fingers enough, she pressed the thermal pack against one of the EVA suits, then grabbed the warmed fabric and pulled it free of its hook. She worked in stages, putting the thermal pack against each item before she touched it: diagnostic panel, thermal controls, zips. She started the suit's heat cycle, then began attaching her meager supplies to its belt loops. When it was warm enough inside the suit, she wormed her way into it.

With the suit enfolding her like a second skin, Rue made herself stop and just breathe for a while. She had done it! From here things got easier. She popped open the door to the ringway and exited it hand over hand. The suit had been perfectly preserved in the cold and worked like new.

She pitched the nearly spent thermal pack down the corridor. Hopefully Jentry's miners would fixate on its infrared signature and go after it rather than her. The insulation in Rue's suit was efficient enough that her main problem was overheating. Back to the intersection, then past it, and soon she had reached another bulkhead door, beyond which the cold was an order of magnitude more deadly. She rapelled confidently through it and down two more levels as the outside temperature dropped closer and closer to absolute zero. By the time Rue reached the outside hatch she sought, all air had frozen out of the corridors and the meager heat radiating from her suit made the snow on the walls flash into vapor.

Her skin was all pins and needles; her hands ached and she curled them arthritically. It was a familiar pain. Rue had felt such cold many more times than Jentry, she'd bet. He never had any reason to lurk in the outer rings of the station, after all.

She pried open the outer hatch and for only the third time in her life, stood on the outside of Allemagne station. Starlight didn't illuminate the great black curve of the sphere; there were no running lights. She could see the station only by how it blotted the stars. Much clearer was the comet to which Allemagne was parasitically attached; it formed a bulky scab-colored mountain above the sphere's black horizon.

Rue was on a mission, but the temptation was too strong to look up. She thought only to glance at the stars to orient herself, but ended up gaping. They were brilliant points here, hard as diamond and so distinct as to be three dimensional—ranks and sheets of stars behind stars, clouds and swirls like the frozen breath of the unimaginably titanic All.

All her life, Rue had seen the stars on screens and twice in glimpses as she stood on the hull of Allemagne. They were the homes of wonders, those stars, and tonight she was finally on her way to visit them.

It took a while to psych herself up, but finally she kicked off from the hull. Long ago, when they were friends, Jentry had shown her how to maneuver using a reaction pistol and she blessed that memory now as she fired hers to wobble in a long loop around the station. After a few minutes the dark rectangle of the docks came into view. Long gantries jutted out into space and here the station's ships and shuttles were silhouetted against the stars. She picked out the largest of those black forms and jetted toward it.

Any second now miners would come out of the dark at her, claws out, carapaces shielding the nested purple curves of the camera eyes through which Jentry would be watching. She would fail and be dragged back—or he would just kill her on the spot. It didn't matter. She had made her bid and, for Rue, that was the first and last unshakable fact that declared who she was.

She grinned tightly when she found herself touching the hull of the cycler shuttle—safe and unsuspected. Maybe the miners were still rattling around in the ringways, thwarted. She would pretend they were, anyway, until rude reality stopped her.

The miners didn't arrive in time to stop her from locating the airlock to the cycler shuttle. They didn't reach to stop her from turning the emergency handle and nothing was waiting for her in the red-lit airlock that opened for her.

Rue entered the ship with a sense almost of disappointment; certainly of anticlimax. She had been afraid of Father and Jentry all her life; nothing that she'd done in defiance of them had ever gone unpunished, except for the tiny actions, like making her own safe refuges in the outer ringways, that were symbolic to her and utterly unimportant to the world at large.

She undogged the suit's helmet and said, "Ship, awake."

Light bloomed around her, inside a ship that was as much hers as Jentry's (according to the inheritance) but where she had been only a few times in her life. She quickly stripped off her gloves and reached to touch a tapestry on the wall. The walls and floors were done in complex, quilted fabrics in dark earth tones and crimson, lit by unobtrusive spotlamps. This airlock opened near the galley, which glowed with suspended holos; a central well with a ladder led up and down to sleeping quarters and games rooms. There was no control room; everything was voice and inscape-controlled. The shuttle was designed to keep its occupants comfortable—and amused—for the weeks that it might take to rendezvous with a passing cycler.

It was the most luxurious place Rue had ever been. No wonder Jentry had forbidden her to visit it. She remembered there were fish tanks and a tiny arboretum with green plants in it. There were lots of places she had never been, as well. She wanted to explore right now, but first she had to finish her escape. She dove down the central well of the ship.

As she entered the main cargo hold she shouted, "Ship, cast off. Set a course to rendezvous with the next cycler."

"Nice try, Sis."

She caught herself on a cargo net and looked around. Jentry hung in the open airlock that connected to the docking tube. "I thought you might try something like this," he said. "So while you were pulling maneuvers in deep space, I sailed up here. After all, the others could find you if you went anywhere else. This was your only option—too bad you're so predictable." He grinned insolently and launched himself at her.

Jentry had hit her so many times that Rue's instinct was to raise her hands when he came for her. This time, though, she found one of her gloves still held the reaction pistol.

The look on his face when he saw it was priceless; Jentry was in midflight and couldn't stop himself or turn away. She levelled the pistol and shot him in the face.

He vanished behind a puff of white vapor; the pistol kicked back, nearly tangling Rue in the cargo net. Jentry shrieked, limbs flailing as he tumbled past her and hit the wall.

His face red and blistered, Jentry groaned as he drifted back into the center of the hold. For a second Rue felt a deep pang of remorse, because she had never wanted to hate Jentry. He had driven her to it.

"I'm sorry, Jentry," she said and she meant it. She jumped, rolled in midair and planted her feet in his midriff. Kicking off, she ended up back at the cargo net while Jentry sailed precisely through the middle of the airlock door. She watched him recede down the docking tube for a moment, then dove to the doorway and pressed the close button.

"Ship! Cast off!"

"I recognize you, Meadow-Rue Rosebud Cassels," said the ship in its liquid voice. "Jentry Terrence Cassels has issued an order that I should remain in port."

Rue felt a shock run through her, like the premonition of a blow. "I have authority over you. Mom gave you to both of us."

"Yes, Meadow-Rue."

"So . . . what's it to be?"

"According to law, when equal ownership applies to a ship, authority is held first by the one who is physically aboard the ship. Your order takes precedence over his."

"Then go! *Go*, damn you!"

Then suddenly she was moving, drifting toward the floor—no, the floor was drifting up as the ship left dock. She alighted on the soft surface and gradually over the next few minutes her weight increased to full.

It took Rue a full hour to convince herself she was really on her way. When she finally believed it, she curled up in a corner and cried. Then she slept and didn't wake for almost a full day.

BEFORE CREEPING INTO Jentry's quarters to retrieve her heirloom, Rue had visited the few places in Allemagne that had meant something to her. She needed to say good-bye, but with Mom gone there were no people she wanted to say it to. But all her memories were here—her whole past—so she went to the gardens and sat for a while sniffing under the coal-black leaves of her favorite air tree. It was very bright here—as bright, Grandma had told her once, as a full-moon night on Earth. The black trees and black grasses were much more efficient light-gatherers than the green wildflowers Mom kept in her blinding hot terrarium. As a child Rue had lain back in the grass, feeling the faint heat of the ceiling lamps a dozen meters overhead, seeing a slight glow through her eyelids. She imagined she was on Earth or some exotic alien planet in High Space, baking in sunlight.

The gardens took up nearly a third of Allemagne's two hundred meter centrifuge; the rest of the circle was taken up with fish tanks and other recycling equipment and sleeping quarters for the hundred or so residents and transient workers who struggled to keep Allemagne livable.

They were roughnecks—rejects of the cometary halo worlds, criminals, misfits, and failed profiteers. These men were Rue's "uncles" as she was growing up and a few had been kind. The rest had trained her to a caution and cunning that ran as deep as her marrow.

From the gardens she had gone to the observatory. Things here were shut down. Father had declared last year that every mineable object within half a light-year had been spotted and claimed, mostly by other stations with better telescopes. No scrap of ice bigger than a fist had escaped the prospectors' attention. Hence there was no reason to look outside anymore.

The observatory enchanted Rue, as it had when she first discovered the place. Although it was deep inside the station, outside the centrifuge and near the fusion generator at Core, a mirrored screen twenty meters across brought in the glow of the stars via light pipes. Rue loved to hang weightless in the center of the observatory, with her entire field of vision taken up by sky. The Milky Way was a ghostly band that twisted diagonally across the black. Everywhere were stars. She knew many of them by name. She could order the computer to rotate the view and look anywhere and by the time she was twelve Rue had learned to orient herself by merely glancing at those stars. Quite an accomplishment, she thought, since at that age she had never been outside the station.

After visiting the observatory she had rapelled her way to the newsroom. Information feeds too complex for inscape were presented here. Mom had shown Rue programs from many halo worlds in this place and even broadcasts from Earth. The big octagonal chamber flickered with multicolored holos, even now with no one present to see them.

Here she had learned to dream of faraway worlds, aliens and exotic men from High Space. When Jentry began to turn bad, she'd started coming here to launch herself into a universe of adventures and romance where he could never follow.

These rooms had been Rue's refuges. Jentry and the other station rats never visited them, preferring the telepresence locker where they operated mining robots and had them race or fight in off hours.

Finally she admitted to herself that she was procrastinating. It was a short run to the docks, there to steal a rendezvous shuttle and escape. Before she could go there, though, she had to rescue her heirloom.

She went back to the centrifuge and dawdled outside Jentry's apartment for a while. There was no traffic in the halls this late at night, nor any sound coming from inside his rooms. He always locked the door at night, but one of the first skills Rue had taught herself in idle hours was lock-picking. She had a small pad of shipfur on which she'd reproduced his thumbprint and after taking a deep breath she pressed this against the door plate and waited. The door slid aside without trouble.

Jentry's main room was dark; next to it were the head, his bedroom, and the kitchenette, all luxurious compared with her own single room with fold-down toilet. In theory Rue had never been here and would have no idea of the place's layout; in fact she had visited these rooms many times while Jentry was busy playing telepresence games or pursuing any women unfortunate enough to be visiting.

She walked quickly, sweeping her toes ahead of her to scan for unexpected obstacles. Here was the couch and here the dining table. Make a left turn, take four steps, reach out carefully . . . she felt the cool smoothness of the small display case where Jentry kept her inheritance. A pulse of anger burned in her as she pictured him impudently displaying what Grandma and Mom had declared to all was hers.

Lifting the glass cover off with both hands, she flipped it onto the palm of her left hand and lowered her right to the surface of the dais. The cool siltstone disk of the pendant was right where it should be. She scooped it up and turned back to the door in one motion.

"Whooz' ere?"—Jentry's voice, thick with sleep and in all likelihood drugs. Rue started involuntarily at the sound and dropped the glass cover.

It shattered. She cursed and ran to the door. Behind her Jentry swore too and she heard bedding being thrown aside. She was in the hall before he got the light on, but Rue knew he would know who had stolen the pendant. There was only one person in Allemagne who coveted it enough to risk his wrath.

"Come back here, you little beggar!" She made it to the elevator that led out of the centrifuge, but by the time Rue reached the weightless corridors outside Core, Jentry had roused the entire station and locked down the doors to the docks with the command codes he'd inherited from Father.

OF COURSE JENTRY had called: a little inscape diamond was hanging in the air above her when Rue awoke. She ignored it and went to freshen up. Her new quarters were sumptuous and she took full advantage of the water shower and sonic cleaners. She ordered a new fullerene EVA suit from the ship's assemblers and made herself eat a full and complete breakfast before she finally sat down to review his messages.

Never once in all his ranting did he *ask* her to come back. "You will come back, I'll make you," he said at first. Then, later, "I see you're trying to hook up with a cycler. Well, guess what? I've called them and told them you're a criminal—that you spaced a man here. The instant you board that cycler, you'll be arrested and they'll extradite you right back here. Enjoy your holiday while you can, you little shit. 'Cause the instant you get back you're dead."

She laughed at that—he'd given himself away. There was no way any legal body was going to believe his story over hers, once they reviewed the messages. It was quite possible, though, that his deal with the cycler was more pragmatic. He might just be buying her back from them.

Rue had heard stories—more and more of them in recent years. Anarchy and despair were leaking into the stations, year by year. One couldn't hang around the rough types who filled the labor force at Allemagne without listening to tales of cannibalism, neural-lock slavery and mass suicide from the far fringes of the cometary zone. Some of those stories had given her nightmares when she was younger. Some of them, she had later learned, were true.

Cometary cyclers were supposed to be above petty disputes. They made their slow rounds between places like Allemagne, gossamer magnetic sails turning them ever so gradually to a new heading every time they passed within ten billion kilometers of a station. Light cargo ships accelerated out from the stations, docked at the cycler and disembarked at later stops. The cyclers were supposed to be bastions of stability and civilization in the halos, like their cousins the great interstellar liners.

Well, when a cycler came within hailing distance of a major halo world such as Erythrion they sure acted civilized. But out here, beyond law and sanity, Rue knew they had begun to deal in slavery and vice—whatever their customers desired so long as they made the trades that kept the cyclers supplied.

Rue had been reviewing the messages in the galley, which might well become her favorite place in the shuttle. Now she gripped the table and stared into the starfield she'd called up in inscape. The stars shone in their indifferent millions and floating before them were hundreds of tiny strings of red numbers: all the stations, comets, and ice chunks within half a light year.

She still had plenty of fuel for the shuttle's fusion engine. Normally cyclers were the only practical way to ferry passengers the huge distances between the halo worlds, but that was partly because people tended to save their trips up and take them together. This shuttle had life support enough to keep a hundred people alive for a month. Rue used only a fraction of that and the life support system was designed to be scalable; only a little of it was switched on right now.

"Ship, how long can I stay alive without resupply?" she asked after a while. Her finger strayed from one little address to the next and mentally she put names and faces to some of them—considering, then rejecting each.

"I can keep you alive for two years, Rue," said the ship.

She took a deep breath. "How long would it take us to reach Erythrion?"

The ship's voice showed neither surprise nor concern. "Minimal or maximal-burn?"

"Maxi."

"Four months."

She started. "Is that all? Well, shiz, do it!"

The ship started a stomach-flipping turn. *Four months.* To someone else, sixteen weeks of solitary confinement might have seemed an awful prospect, but all Rue could think was, *Peace and quiet for four months.* It was perfect.

Exactly halfway into her journey, Rue received a hail from Erythrion. The shuttle had filed a flight plan unbeknownst to her and now the great halo world was replying. The reply was mostly numbers.

Navigation Fee	40 dites
Docking Fees	1500 dites/day
Oxy/Food Per Diem	10 dites/day
Visitors' Card	75 dites

Rue had no money on her at all.

The shuttle was worth a million dites easy, but selling it required both her and Jentry's thumbprint. She supposed she could sell some of its fittings and furniture, but when Rue totalled it all up her assets came to a meager two thousand dites, enough to let her dock for a day at one of Erythrion's colonies, but no more. She would have to set the shuttle on a slow-burn return flight to Allemagne and find work right away.

The prospect was depressing. She would have a few days at most before she was in debt and debt could mean deportation. Maybe Jentry would have the last laugh after all.

Finally, after considering all the angles, she reluctantly brought out her pendant and shone a little crafts light on it. It wasn't much to look at—just a dark gray disk five centimeters across. In the center of the disk was a slightly upraised circle with a rough three-armed spiral in it. She traced the arms of the spiral carefully with her fingertip.

"What's so special about that old rock?" she'd asked when Grandma first showed her the pendant.

"You must never tell anyone," said Grandma. "It's a secret, but this 'old rock' is the most precious thing I own."

"Why?" Jentry had asked belligerently. He had been sitting next to Rue on the floor of Grandma's apartment.

"Because," she had said, dangling the pendant for Rue to see, "this stone is from Earth!"

Rue picked it up and sniffed it. There was no smell, but she imagined she inhaled a few molecules of old Earth. Maybe there were dormant bacteria or spores trapped in the pores of the rock. Dropped on a fallow world, it might seed a whole new biosphere.

"But there's more," Grandma had said. "See this design?" She had held the siltstone so that the trefoil pattern caught the light.

"It's a galaxy," Jentry said. "Isn't it?"

Rue had reached out to trace the shape with her finger, just as she did now. "No it isn't. Is it a *fossil*?"

"Yes, Meadow, it's a fossil and not just any fossil, but the oldest kind of Earth fossil. This is an *Ediacaran* and it dates back to the very beginning of life. This is the first thing bigger than a microbe that lived. And it is ours."

"What's a fossil?" Jentry asked, annoyed.

Rue smiled at the memory. It was probably that single display of ignorance on Jentry's part that made Grandma decide to bequeath the pendant to her alone, instead of both of them.

It was all she had left of Grandma or her mom. And if she was going to make a life for herself in Erythrion, she was going to have to sell it.

Rue took a photo of the pendant and then sent a message ahead to inquire what a siltstone fossil from Earth, six hundred million years old, might be worth. She was pretty sure it would be a lot.

She traced her finger over the faint design on the stone. As an adolescent Rue had been sure the pendant held the key to understanding time. There was a mystery to the thing, because caressing it you could feel its age: life had turned to stone here without the intercession of Medusa, just by lying in deathly repose for sufficient aeons. Yet Rue could go outside Allemagne and scoop from their captured comet snowflakes that had formed three billion years before the little fluttering Ediacaran was born.

To have such a snowflake end its unimaginable life span by melting in your hand left no impression; somehow it still seemed younger than the pendant, since for over three billion years nothing whatsoever had happened to it or near it. The stars had changed. That was all.

During the ever-so-more-brief life of the Ediacaran fossil, on the other hand, comets had smashed into the Earth, trilobites and coelecanths had arisen. Mountains thrust up and wore down around the stone cocoon that held the Ediacaran. The planet's continents had collided and subducted numerous times. Dinosaurs had fought above the fossil's resting place; later men had missed it while blowing up cities and overturning mountains in their fight for resources. The Ediacaran had survived all these adventures unscathed, to be finally dug up and shot halfway across the universe. It was still in one piece.

Now *that* was *time*.

As Rue was turning the stone over in her hands, becoming increasingly depressed over losing it, the ship *pinged* to get her attention.

"What? Is it dinner time already?"

"The prospector scopes report an anomaly, Rue," said the ship.

She sat upright, forgetting she was in freefall. The pendant bounced through her fingers and drifted away.

"Show me!" She slammed her hand on the tabletop, bringing up the external view. There were the stars and the hundreds of little addresses; lately Erythrion had appeared among them. One of the little strings was flashing green.

"The prospecting scopes have spotted an object that is not registered with the Claims Bureau," said the ship.

"Is it a ship? A cycler?" For a moment she wondered if Jentry was following her—but that was preposterous. She had Allemagne's only shuttle.

"All ships in halo space are accounted for, and there are no more interstellar cyclers on this ring," said the ship. "This anomaly is not in the database."

"H-how big?"

"We will not know until we get a parallax view of it, Rue, but based on its spectral signature and occultation pattern it may be a kilometer or more in diameter."

"A kil-" She sputtered. There hadn't been a kilometer-sized comet discovered in the halos in half a century. "I'm rich! I don't believe—Wait, wait a sec, are you sure nobody else has staked a claim on this thing?"

"The maximal-burn course you asked me to take has brought us far from any stations. It is quite possible that their scopes have not picked it up, even though they are larger."

And if they're as gob-stupid as Jentry, they've all turned their scopes off to save power, since everybody knows all the ice in the area has already been found.

"Stake me a claim! Right now! I don't want to risk a single second. If that thing is as big as you say it is, we've got it made!" She wouldn't have to sell the pendant—quite the contrary, she could buy a box full of fossils. Speaking of which, where was it? Rue dove across the room and retrieved the siltstone from where it had drifted against an air grate.

"Preparing the claim form, Rue . . . claim sent."

"That's it? That's all you have to do?" The ship said yes and Rue proceeded to turn somersaults through the galley, screaming her relief. When she finally settled down, she fell to waiting nervously for the reply from the Claims Bureau. By the time it came—seven hours later—she was frazzled with nervous exhaustion. But the message was clear:

New object verified. Designation number 2349#MRRC, staked by Meadow-Rue Rosebud Cassels July 23, 2445.

She had escaped. She was going to see civilized society for the first time in her life. And she was rich.

2

THE MATRONLY WOMAN in the inscape window smiled broadly. "Meadow-Rue, you don't know me, but I'm your mom's sister—your aunt Leda!"

"Yeah, right," muttered Rue. She could see the family resemblance—but Mom had never mentioned a sister. "We heard that you're coming to visit Erythrion," continued the matron, "and of course you're family, so you can stay with us! We don't have anything special in the way of houses, just a little place in Treya. Here's my number. Call me right away and we'll arrange things. Oh, you're going to have such a good time here! I can't wait to meet you after all these years."

Rue had been cynically examining the woman, noting her brow tattoos and the jewelry studded around the lobe of her ear—symbols of wealth, surely, but she could still be a scam artist. But when she heard the name *Treya* Rue's mind went blank. The name was almost mythical. It was the most amazing place in all Erythrion, or so she had heard. And here this woman—her aunt?—said as casually as anything that she lived there. And that Rue was invited!

If this woman was really a long-lost relative, Rue might finally find a real home—one where she was loved and accepted. She doubted that. On the other hand, if this woman wanted to scam her, Rue was confident she could take her on. She hadn't gotten an education from roughnecks for nothing.

Either way, her opening gambit was the same. As soon as the message ended Rue was composing a reply. Surely Mom must have had a good reason for not talking about sisters if they existed, she mused, even as she was saying, "Of course I'd love to come stay with you, auntie! I didn't even know I had relatives in Treya. Tell me all about the family. And where do you live? Is it a *city*? What's a house? Does Treya really have a sun, like they say? Can you look at it or is it too bright? Heh, listen to me. Hey, how did you hear I was coming?" She didn't have to fake the enthusiasm; it would be so wonderful if Leda turned out to be for real. And as she asked how they'd heard about her, Rue's heart flipped when she pictured Jentry calling long-lost relatives, spreading poisonous slander about her.

There was still a significant time-lag on messages to Erythrion, so while she waited Rue brooded over the other piece of news she had received this week. A museum at Treya had finally replied to her query about fossils. It was a fake. Apparently somebody had shipped in a cycler cargo of the things thirty years ago, along with gems and carved wood, all purported to be from Earth. The fellow who had ridden down the beam with the cargo had sold it all for a fabulous sum and left on the next cycler, rich. It wasn't until years later that it was revealed the fossils were fake and the stones came from an Earthlike but fallow minor world in High Space. To this day, despite the publicity, not everyone knew that what they owned was worthless.

The news had hit Rue hard—she had risked her whole future to recapture the thing, after all. She had cried and stuffed the pendant deep into her kit bag so she wouldn't have to see it anymore. She almost threw it out the airlock, but even if it wasn't real, it was still her last link to Grandma. It just hurt to think that Grandma could and had been deceived. Rue felt more vulnerable for knowing that.

This aunt, if she really was one, could be the *real* link Rue longed for. But she couldn't allow herself to believe it.

Aunt Leda's reply, when it came, was straightforward: "Of course we know you're coming, dear! Everyone in Erythrion knows about your claim. They're doing a parallax on it now and they've verified that it's there, but it's so far out and so faint they're having trouble resolving it. But if it's as big as the readings say, you're going to be rich! And when that happens all manner of bad people are going to be sticking their oars in" (a term that made no sense to Rue) "trying to wingle the wealth out of you. So we thought, you need allies. We don't care what you do with the money, dear, we just want to make sure you keep it!"

And: "Your Mom and I had a terrible fight when we were young, dear. It's sad that she never mentioned me in all those years. I don't know what to think. But it was certainly my fault, you know and I don't blame her. I've regretted the things we said every day ever since—but I never got a chance to tell her so! And now she's passed on. All I can say is that I'm terribly, terribly sorry and sad that we never got a chance to make up. But clearly, any fights we might have had were between us. You're my niece, Rue! How could I turn you away for something that happened between your Mom and me years ago?"

At this point Rue's cynical inner voice said, *Then why didn't Grandma mention you either?* She wanted to ignore that voice, but decided, to be at least partially sensible, that she wouldn't say a word about Grandma until Leda had talked about her—just to see what she would say.

Caution aside, the idea that she had family waiting for

her was a great comfort to Rue as the days of her journey passed. Feeling more settled and confident now, she caught up on local news and played some of the latest books from the halo world. She consulted the fashion newsgroups and tried to get the ship's assemblers to reshape her clothes so they looked a little less provincial. She even tried out the Erythrion accent, with some success.

Occasionally she called up an inscape view of the outside. Erythrion itself was visible now, a gigantic red eye in the night. The halo world was a brown dwarf, sixty Jupiters in mass, too small to be a sun and too big to be a planet. Like countless billions of others it moved through the galaxy alone in the spaces between the lit stars. So small and invisible were the halo worlds that they hadn't even been known to exist until the end of the twentieth century. But to Rue, Erythrion was huge and magnificent and all the civilization she hoped to ever see.

There were three major nations at Erythrion, one of them in the oceans under the ice surface of the Europan planet Divinus, one visible as scattered sparkles of light— orbital habitats scattered throughout the system—and one on Treya. As Rue's ship made its final approach through Erythrion's radiation fields, she swung the prospecting scope around to look for Divinus and Treya. Erythrion's dull red glow wasn't enough to make them shine; she spotted Divinus after long searching when it eclipsed a star. That absence was a planet. Treya, though—she could actually see it, a diffuse oval of light, like a fuzzy star. She stared at it until her eyes were sore.

Closer to hand, brilliant filaments of light illuminated dozens of O'Neill cylinders. Each cylinder was twenty or more kilometers long, home to nearly a million people. They utterly dwarfed the tiny station where she was born and raised and she gaped at them as they slid silently by.

Even the colonies were dwarfed by their surroundings. They swarmed like insects around incandescent filaments hundreds of kilometers in length. Each filament was a fullerene cable that harvested electricity from Erythrion's magnetic field. They were kept in orbit by vast infrared sails, visible only as a shimmer of reflected stars. The power running through the cables made them glow in exactly the same way that tungsten had glowed in light bulbs for billions of people on twentieth-century Earth. These cables were vastly bigger, of course; the colonies concentrated the light to provide "daylight" for whole populations with the waste product of electricity production.

The glowing cables had been built to provide power for launching starship cargoes. To see them serving merely as lamps was somehow saddening.

Erythrion flared one morning; Rue watched in wonder as the whole planetary system blossomed with light. While there was no nuclear fire powering the dwarf's internal heat, its prodigious magnetic fields occasionally kinked together and created vast arches of brilliant fire that overwhelmed its normal dull glow. The flare was just over the dwarf's horizon, so for a few hours Erythrion became a crescent of royal purple and mauve, from which sprang an incandescent filament of white. Now Rue had no trouble finding Divinus, bathed as it was in this temporary radiance.

She really wished there were somebody on board with her to share these sights with. Time and again she would go, "Oh!" and want to say, "Look at that!" to someone next to her. She even caught herself longing to know what Jentry would make of things.

She and Aunt Leda spoke regularly now that the time-lag from distance had reduced to nearly nothing. Leda told Rue about the "house" and sent photos when Rue had a hard time understanding her. It was the sort of structure she'd seen in books and movies about Earth—ancient, simple, and perfect. Leda continued to assure Rue that the family didn't need her money, they were just happy to see her. Rue wanted to believe her and despite herself, she found that her hopes were growing by the hour. When she went to bed she imagined living in a house, with dozens of people, all her relatives, breathing the night air in neighboring rooms. A family.

Leda was not the only one calling, though. She had received mail from all over Erythrion, from government bureaus and lawyers, tour guides and investment counselors. Now that she was on final approach to Treya the news hounds started phoning, too. She had nothing to say to any of them, so she eventually told the ship to screen all calls except those from Leda. The only indication of the incoming stream of messages became a flashing counter in the corner of the inscape window.

All those messages did point out a central problem, though: If she couldn't trust Leda, who else could she trust here? The thought made her laugh. Oh, the problems of the rich!

After several days' travel through the system she finally reached the orbit of Treya, the greatest and most troubled nation of Erythrion. There had been a coup recently, she knew; the place was in the hands of isolationists and had she not had family waiting, Rue might not have been able to even land.

Rue didn't care about the coup; she could hardly contain her excitement and spent the entire morning on the scope staring at the place. Treya was about Earth-sized and had an atmosphere, oceans, and tectonic plates like Earth. There the similarity ended, because Treya had never known the light of a real sun. It orbited just outside the Roche limit of Erythrion, and kept one face turned toward Erythrion at all times, just as Luna did for Earth. Enough infrared leaked out of Erythrion to heat the surface of Treya to livable temperature, and tidal and induction heating kept it volcanically active. But without a sun, life had never developed here—or rather it had developed and died out a number of times. When humans came to the Erythrion system Treya was in a lifeless phase, its dark oceans lit only by the constant surging aurora from Erythrion's radiation belt, and by an occasional flare.

As she orbited it now Rue could see a faint filigree, red-black on black, that might be a coastline. Smudged clouds overlaid it. Every now and then long bands of iridescent color flowed past, but the aurora wasn't strong enough to show the planet's surface. Dark though it was, Treya was the most hospitable world Rue ever expected to visit. After all, it had an oxygen atmosphere, though that was artificial, not the product of life as on Earth.

The atmosphere was the least of Treya's wonders, as far as Rue was concerned. She held her breath as a glow appeared on the horizon. Any minute now Treya's new sun would rise.

As she was waiting, Leda called. "You're due to dock in three hours, Rue! We'll all be there—the whole clan. We've got your landing ETA from the flight controllers, so don't you worry about a thing. Oh, I'm so looking forward to seeing you!"

A pinprick of light appeared on the limb of Treya and quickly grew into a brilliant white star. This seemed to move out and away from Treya, which was an illusion caused by Rue's own motion. Treya's artificial sun did not move, but stayed at the Lagrange point, bathing an area of the planet eighty kilometers in diameter with daylight. The sun was a sphere of tungsten a kilometer across. It glowed with incandescence from concentrated infrared light, harvested from Erythrion by hundreds of orbiting mirrors. If it were turned into laser power, this energy could reshape Treya's continents—or launch interstellar cargoes.

A flat line of light appeared on Treya's horizon. It quickly grew into a disk almost too bright to look at. When Rue squinted at it she could make out white clouds, blue lakes, and the mottled ochre and green of grassland and forests. The light was bright enough to wash away the aurora and even make the stars vanish. Down there, she knew, the skies would be blue.

She could have stared at that beautiful circle of earth and sea all day. Reluctantly, Rue closed the inscape window, which was flashing to show yet more messages received. She needed to rest, she knew, so she strapped herself into bed and turned out the light for a while. She couldn't sleep, but at least felt slightly refreshed when they finally landed at a beanstalk dock three hundred kilometers above the clouds.

"You'll be fine, you'll be fine," she told herself as the airlock slid open. She was dressed in a skirt for only the second time in her life, had her kit bag firmly over her shoulder, and had rehearsed a dozen opening lines to use on Leda, depending on what happened. Light speared her, she squinted behind the "sunglasses" the assemblers had built her, took one last deep breath, and stepped out.

Rue was momentarily blinded by the brightness; she hadn't counted on that. "H-hello?"

No one answered.

After her eyes had adapted enough that she could make out shapes, she looked around herself. She stood in a round windowed lounge about twenty meters across, paneled with eye-hurting colors and ringed by elevators. The windows gave glimpses of gantries and catwalks suspended in space above the azure horizon of Treya. Cables stretched above her all the way to the "sun" and below her all the way to the surface of the planet. Through the windows she could see other round lounges like her own, most of them swirling with people greeting or parting. The one she was in was empty.

Leda had been very precise about the lounge number and had said she'd be waiting. She'd also warned that reporters and camera crews might be there, since Rue was famous now. All Rue saw was a single humanoid serling, which flickered insouciantly behind a counter near the elevators. The silence was complete.

Rue dropped her bags, chewed her lip, and after a minute walked over to the serling.

It bowed to her. "Meadow-Rue Cassels?"

"Yes. Where is everybody?"

"I'm sorry, I can't answer that. I have some forms for you to fill out. Docking fees, stowage, per diem . . . How long are you planning to stay?"

"Um . . . I'm not sure. Listen, was my flight plan changed? I'm not sure I've landed at the right dock."

"Let me check." The serling paused for a moment, then said, "Your flight plan was finalized one week ago, Ms. Cassels. There have been no changes."

Maybe they're waiting below, she told herself. "Where are these forms?"

The serling pointed her to some inscape windows where she was to place her hand for signing. She read them carefully. "Wait—I thought my credit was good. This says there's a lien on the shuttle if I'm not able to pay within sixty days."

"That is correct. You have no other collateral."

"Yes I do. I have a whole comet's worth!"

The serling smiled. She could see the wall through its holographic face. "I'm sorry, but I have no record of that."

"Wait. I arranged to pay the docking fees on loan against my claim on comet . . . um, 2349-hash-MRRC. Right?"

The serling nodded. "Ah, yes, I see the cause of the confusion. That claim has been overturned."

Rue suddenly felt sick. "Overturned? How? Why?" *A prior claim? But surely they'd have told me . . .*

"Apparently the object you staked your claim against is not a comet after all," explained the serling.

"Then what is it?"

"According to my news feed, it is a ship. An interstellar cycler, to be exact."

She stood there for a while, unable to think. The serling waited patiently, inscape forms gently bobbing in front of it. Eventually Rue stuck out her hand and the red forms turned green. *So much for the ship,* she thought. *Jentry's going to come out here and personally kill me for this.*

The serling directed her to an elevator and she went without speaking. Throughout the long descent she kept her eyes shut against the light. Her head hurt.

When the elevator doors opened Rue found herself in the tall glass lobby of some kind of house. *Building,* she corrected herself, since this was obviously not a residence. People were bustling to and fro, ignoring her which was good because there must be hundreds of them here and she had never seen that many people in one place before. Rue stood there for a while, totally derailed. She had been all ready for a verbal fencing match with strangers who claimed to be kin and now she had no idea what to do.

The air was thick with water and scents. And it was very warm here—hot, in fact, and brighter than she had imagined any place could be. Rue took a few steps, but had to stop as a wave of dizziness assaulted her.

She took a few deep breaths and started walking again. The kit bag was heavy on her shoulder and she was sweating by the time she had passed through the huge archway at the end of the lobby. The heat enfolded her with as much intensity as the cold in the ringways of Allemagne. She forgot about it as soon as she looked up, though. For the first time in her life, Rue stood under a sky.

It went on forever, bigger and more beautiful it seemed than the stars. Gigantic white clouds were piled up all over. She craned her neck back and saw that one sat directly overhead. It must be kilometers away, because she saw the threadlike black lines of elevator shafts pierce it before disappearing in the blue.

Everything was huge and spaced far apart. A road ran by the building she had just exited and vehicles festooned with garish paintings and carved detail zipped past at reckless speeds. Everywhere there were green plants like the ones in Mom's terrarium only huge. There were many trees, real ones like she'd seen in books.

But the sun . . . Rue staggered and finally had to sit down. Nobody seemed to care; the only people standing on the steps were a dissolute looking fellow in rumpled clothing, who glanced at her sidelong but said nothing, and a woman in hospital greens who was talking on a ring phone. The light was blazing hot, the sun impossible to look at. The air was full of dust and other irritants; it was hard to breathe. Was this what Earth was like? How could these people stand it? And where was her welcoming party? Where was Leda? Oh yeah, they weren't coming. Rue was poor after all, they had no need of her now.

"Meadow-Rue Cassels?"

She looked up hopefully. A nattily dressed young man wearing a newsvid monocle stood several meters away. He smiled. "It is you, isn't it?"

"Rue. It's just Rue." She watched him step up and stick out his hand. She flinched, remembering Jentry, but when he just stood there, hand out, she realized he wasn't going to hit her. What was he doing, then?

"Help you up?" he said.

"Oh." She took his hand and he drew her to her feet.

"Would you like to comment on your discovery of the first cycler to visit Erythrion in ten years?" His voice had changed subtly; he was in newshound mode now. Suddenly self-conscious, Rue stammered and blushed.

"Don't worry," he said, "this isn't live. We can edit you however you want. If you don't want something to go out, just say, 'off the record.' Is that okay?"

"I don't know," she said. "I just—"

"Get away from her, you parasite!"

It was the fellow in the rumpled clothes, who had approached and now waved at the news hound as if he were some kind of irritating insect. He was in his late thirties, had greasy hair and a paunch and dark circles under his eyes. His clothes were rumpled, Rue realized, because he had probably slept in them. "Shoo," he said to the news hound, "there's nothing for you here."

The newshound raised one eyebrow (the one opposite the monocle). "And who are you, sir?"

"Maximilian Cassels," said the rumpled man, drawing himself up to his full meter-and-a-half. "And I'll not have you leeching off my cousin."

"I just want an interview," said the newshound. "Look, all the other guys ran off to the Permanence monastery when they learned your comet's really a cycler. They're all trying to interview the abbot; a new cycler is a much bigger story than a new comet. But . . . I think there's a human-interest angle here, with her." He turned back to Rue. "I understand you're probably upset and tired right now. Can I leave you my number? You can call me later when you're ready for an interview. And listen, it'll probably be a good idea for you to do one. Get you the sympathy of the public, you know?"

"Well, I—"

"She doesn't need sympathy," growled Maximilian. "She needs her family." He went to take Rue's arm; she stepped away from him.

"What about my family!" she said. She took another two steps back. "They were supposed to meet me. Aunt Leda and the whole clan, she said. Not that I believed it really, but then . . . who the hell are you?"

The rumpled guy put his hands on his hips and cocked his head. "I really am your cousin," he said. "Leda really is your aunt and she did come to meet you. They all did. I came by myself since none of 'em will have anything to do with me. When the news came down that you'd staked a claim on a cycler, they all threw up their hands and left. No money in you, so why hang around?"

There it was. The humiliating truth. "And you stayed?"

"Damn right," said Maximilian. "You're family."

"Oh. I don't know what to . . ." Rue was seeing spots. Without warning she found herself on her knees. The sunglasses had flown off her face; blinded, she waved her hands and cried out. Everything was turning around her. She must be feeling Treya's rotation, she thought crazily.

"Hang on," said somebody, "I'm a doctor." She felt a hand on her shoulder. People were arguing over her head. One of them, she realized, was the woman in green who'd been talking on her phone a few minutes ago.

"She's got heatstroke," she said. "Probably lived her whole life in one of the stations. Never been above ten degrees before."

"She stays with me," said her cousin.

"We'll let her decide that," said the doctor. "Right now, the only place she's going is the hospital."

3

THE DOCTOR'S NAME was Rebecca France, though as she admitted, she wasn't quite a doctor. "An intern," she told Rue the next morning when she came to visit. "I was actually practising back on Terisia, but licensing is much stricter here. I had to go back to med school when I emigrated."

Terisia was a deep colony three light-days from Allemagne: Rebecca was from the stations too, which, she explained, was why she had known what was happening to Rue outside the elevator building.

"They're supposed to mail you a package on how to adapt to Treya. I take it you didn't get it."

Rue shrugged. "I missed a lot of important mail."

She had awoken to find herself in a hospital bed, dusk light brighter than Allemagne's gardens at mid-day glowing through heavy drapes. The nurse who came in when she buzzed had shivered. "I can't believe you need it this cold," she'd said.

The nurse, like Rebecca and everyone else here, was deeply tanned. "You'll get like this, too," said Rebecca now as she put her wrist next to Rue's for comparison. "After a year or two. Believe it or not, this is still considered pale by Earth standards." Rebecca had black hair like Rue, but she kept it up in a complex braid. She was slim like Rue as well, but much taller. They shared the wide gray eyes most station people had, but that hardly implied any family resemblance, as there was genetic engineering way back in most people's lines. Where Rue had an oval face that she considered far too fragile-looking, Rebecca had a square jaw and wide cheekbones, implying a different racial origin, though it was hard to tell nowadays.

Rue nodded absently. She thought it was probably gauche of her to ask, but she'd been brooding on a problem since she awoke. "Thanks for helping me out, Rebecca. But . . . who's paying for my stay here?"

Rebecca looked surprised. "I don't know. I assume they're charging it against your credit.—Except that you're still on a visitor's visa, I guess. I understand you thought you'd come into a lot of money and now it's all gone. Do you have any money?"

Rue shook her head. "No." she said. "But I can work. How soon can I start?"

Rebecca laughed. "You're getting ahead of yourself. First you have to adjust to the heat here. That'll take some time."

Rue opened her mouth to object that she wouldn't have that time if she got deported as a debtor, but decided it was too ugly a discussion to have with someone she'd just met. "Then how do I adjust as quick as possible?"

Rebecca sat back. "Well, there's three ways. First, you can buy a cool suit and go nocturnal. That's the easiest, but the only jobs you can get for that shift are service jobs. Not a good start. Or, you could move to the mountains at Penumbra North. It's much cooler in the alpine biomes; that's what I'd do if I were you."

"What's the third way?"

"Well, that would be to ingest some medical nano that can protect you while your body adjusts. It would fix you up instantly, but the problem is they're expensive."

Rue frowned at the beige ceiling. "The mountains it is, then."

"So, you're planning to settle down here?"

"Yeah. I guess so—I've got nowhere else to go."

Rebecca gnawed on a thumbnail for a while, then said, "Since the coup, they've raised the bar on citizenship requirements. You know, isolationists." She rolled her eyes. "Okay. Here's what you do. You've got to apply for citizenship and to do that you've got to put in your quota of eco-work. It's usually a minimum of planting twenty trees and seeing them through at least two seasons. There's always plenty of eco to do in Treya. Then, you've got to pay off your debt. That means getting a job, which will be hard to do while you're doing eco-work. So, you get something part-time to convince the bureaucrats that you're sincere in paying them back and spend the rest of your time on the eco. Make sense?" Rue nodded. "You'll also need bribe money from time to time," added Rebecca.

The prospect was daunting. "Um, Rebecca . . . could you help me with that stuff? Just a wee bit?"

The intern laughed. "Sure. Look, I've got to go, but I'll pick up a reader and find pointers to some immigration brochures and maybe stop by later?"

"Yeah!"

Rebecca rose and walked to the door. "Why?" Rue asked impulsively.

"What?"

"Why are you helping me?"

Rebecca made a moue and shrugged. "I'm from the stations too. It's hard here for us outsiders. We have to stick together."

Rue nodded and lay back. She soon slept again.

When she awoke it was to find the newshound sitting in the corner of her room, reading. He wasn't wearing his monocle today. Out of the light of the blinding sun, she could see he wasn't much older than she was, though it was hard to tell since his skin was so dark. He was dressed perfectly, though, in a burgundy suit that must have cost a small fortune. Even his hair was perfect.

He looked up, saw she was awake and said, "Hello again. I'm Blair Genereaux, we met at the elevator yesterday?" His voice was smooth and pleasant, like an announcer's.

Rue nodded guardedly.

He cleared his throat. "We seem to have gotten off on the wrong foot somehow," he said. "You see, I didn't know . . . that you didn't know . . . about the cycler. I guess it was an awful shock for you."

"Yeah." Despite her natural caution, Rue felt grateful that he should be sensitive enough to notice. Or comment. Not at all like Jentry, this one. "Thanks."

"You'd become something of a *cause celebre* before you docked," he continued. "I thought it would be fun if I could get an interview, so I came down. The other hounds were all after the smell of money. I wanted to know how it had all affected *you*. That's why I was still there when you came down."

Rue's caution reasserted itself. *Nice story.* "But why? I'm just a girl from the stations."

"Well." For the first time he looked uncomfortable. "The fact is, Rue, I'm new at this. I don't have a byline or good representation on the Web. I've been breaking in slowly by doing pieces that . . . well, frankly, that nobody else bothers with."

Rue laughed.

"What's so funny?" he asked.

"I'm relieved, that's all." He stared at her in obvious puzzlement.

"Sorry," said Rue. "Look, the last thing I want is publicity. You scared the crap out of me when you popped up begging for an interview yesterday. You were the first sign other than messages on the screen that this fortune thing was real. And then . . . I'd just had the fortune taken away before I even got to it. So why should you be interested? I *know* I'm a nobody without it."

Now it was his turn to grin. "Fame doesn't work that way, Ms. Cassels. There's probably a million people out there today wondering how they would feel if they were in your shoes. Yesterday they were all daydreaming they were you. Now they have a chance to contemplate the twists of fate that fortune brings us, using you as the exemplar. I think they'll want to hear the story and I think both you and I could make some money off it."

Money. There was that . . .

"I'm not going to say yes," she said at last. "But I'm not saying no either. Can I think about it?"

"Sure. You've got about a day before this becomes stale news." He rose and came over to the bed, extending his hand. She shook it, surprised by the warmth of his skin.

"You're like ice," he said, concerned. "They told me outside that you're doing fine . . ."

"I am. Thank you, B—Mr. Genereaux. I'll seriously consider your offer."

"Good. I'll call you again tonight."

He left and Rue snuggled back into the covers, thinking about the interview, then thinking about Blair Genereaux's pleasant face and the warmth of his hand.

"ARE YOU PACKED?" These were the first words cousin Max spoke as he strode into her room after dinner that evening. Rue was sitting in a chair by her bed, reading the brochures Rebecca had brought and waiting for Mr. Blair Genereaux to call.

"Packed? Why?"

Max looked like the bouncer at Allemagne's bar had shaken him down for contraband. He was carrying a large plastic-wrapped bundle under his arm. His hair was matted as if he hadn't combed it since he'd slept and the heel of his left shoe flapped open as he paced to the closet.

"It's checkout time, couz," he said. "They say you're fine."

Indeed, the doctor had told her that at lunch time, but

Rue had put off thinking about it. "I don't have anywhere to go," she said. "Except back to the ship."

He smiled brightly. "You can stay with me."

"What about the hospital fees?"

"Paid." He shrugged. "It was the least I could do and never let it be said that I didn't do the least I could do. Ha. This yours?" He held out her bag.

"Give me that."

"Put this on," he said, tossing her the package he'd entered with. Rue puzzled over it; it appeared to be clothing, but all wrapped up and folded for some reason.

"It comes like that," he said. "From the *store*."

"Oh." She fumbled for an opening; there was none. After a moment Max came over and unceremoniously tore the plastic open.

"Oh," she said, "How . . ." Thoughtful? He seemed to have bought her some spacesuit underwear.

"It's a cool suit," he said. "Top of the line. You'll want to have it on when we go out; it's still about twenty-six out there and muggy."

"Oh." She went to the bathroom to change and there she anxiously examined her own face in the mirror. She looked every bit as worried as she felt. She wanted to tell Max to go away, but she'd never had the power to do that with Jentry and truth be told, she didn't know what control Max might have over her here on Treya. Helplessness was a familiar sensation; she let it guide her hands as she dressed, then emerged to find Max stuffing the last of her things into a bag.

"Ready?" He grinned at her.

She was frightened. Was he abducting her? What did he want?

From somewhere Rue summoned the memory of herself shooting Jentry with the reaction pistol. She was not helpless. She wouldn't let herself be.

Still . . . she had no where else to go, unless she phoned Rebecca, but she didn't want to impose on her either . . .

She sighed. "Okay, Max."

"Great! These are yours," he said, handing her a small card and a ring phone. The card had a hologram of her on it and proclaimed her to be a probationary citizen. The phone consisted of two rings, a big one worn on the wrist and a small one, the speaker, which went over her middle finger. "Keep the card close to your skin for the next couple of days; it has to learn your scent. I've put a hundred dites in it for you." Without another word he left the room. She hurried after him.

"Thank you, Max. But how did you get the card?" It was very bright here in the hall so she put on her sunglasses. They still felt weird, like having a tiny clamp around her temples.

"Your aunt Leda had it made up," he said as they entered an elevator packed with serious-looking people. "I stole it from her last night."

Rue tilted down the sunglasses and looked him in the eye. "You really are a Cassels," she said.

He laughed. "Oh, Leda hates me! But she'd never deny me the hospitality of her home."

"Why not?"

"Because she's my mother."

The doors opened and people surged out while Rue was trying to think of something to say. Max hurried her through the lobby and out into roaring heat. The light was a bit more tolerable now. Diffuse, somehow . . . She looked up and shrieked.

"What! What is it?" Max clamped a hand on her arm and stared hectically around.

"Rainbow! That's a real rainbow!"

He groaned and put a hand over his face. "My cousin, the rube. Come on."

"But Max, I've never seen a rainbow before."

"Yes and now everybody within earshot knows it." He towed her along the roadway toward a large flight of stairs that led into the ground. Rue didn't want to go underground, she was too busy cataloguing all the strange and wonderful objects in the near and far distance: trees, grass, hills, buildings, many of them familiar through inscape or movies, but all wonderful.

"You've got to get a grip," Max grated. "We've got a lot to do and you're going to have to have your head screwed on right for it."

"What are you talking about?"

He let go of her arm. "This is the way to the subway. We need to get you home; all this exposure isn't a good idea. Listen, haven't you been paying attention to the news?"

"No. Should I?"

"Yes! Your cycler is the talk of Treya."

"My cycler?" She allowed the bitterness to show in her voice. "It's not my cycler, Max. And I don't want to hear another thing about it."

"But couz, it's not responding to hails! And it's coming in from a very strange direction; there's no known cycler ring on that radiant."

People were funneling down the stairs into the subway. The press carried Rue and Max along. People were dressed in all kinds of ways, with way more variety than she'd expected from her investigations aboard the shuttle. The walls of the stairwell were festooned with garish screens advertising all manner of wonders; the people behind her were discussing a publishing venture of some kind. Compared to this, Max's news was just a bothersome reminder of things past.

"I do not want to hear any more about the cycler! Is that clear?"

"But until they've got a positive I.D. on the thing, you've got to be circumspect, Rue, don't you understand? That means no going out without an escort for now; you can't look for work yet and most of all, no talking to anybody! Especially the media."

Rue stopped walking, but was immediately pushed by somebody behind her. "What are you talking about?"

"I know that newshound was poking about the hospital again today. Rue, he's bad news. The best thing for you right now is anonymity."

They had emerged onto a huge underground platform. She recognized it as a subway from movies. There was a train sitting there and people were cramming themselves into it. Chimes filled the air and Max dashed in its direction just as the doors closed.

"Damn! That was our train." He walked back. "You gotta understand, Rue, you can't trust anybody."

Another train was pulling in on the other track. Rue kept her face neutral, eyeing it as the doors opened and people poured out.

"How's the cool-suit?" asked Max after an awkward silence.

There was the chime; Rue spun on her heel and sprinted for the closing doors of the train. "You're right, Max!" she shouted back. "I don't trust anyone!"

She barely made it in as the doors hissed shut. Max pounded on the glass, but the car was already in motion. Rue stuck her tongue out at him, then they were in a tunnel painted blue and dotted with long lozenge-shaped beasts that could be fishes. Rue let out a shaky sigh and turned to catch about a dozen people looking away quickly.

"It's okay," she said, a bit loudly. They all studiously ignored her.

She groaned; Max had been nice and he'd paid her bills and bought her the cool suit. Maybe he really meant well—how was she to know? Jentry was the best example of the male species she knew and he'd sure sounded like Jentry there, ordering her not to talk to people. But how was she going to get anywhere if she couldn't trust anybody?

She wanted to cry, but she'd be damned if she would do it in front of an audience. Instead Rue took a seat demurely at the window and after watching the painted fish flit by for a while and calming her breathing, she phoned Rebecca.

.   .   .

THE APARTMENT HAD a window that opened on dusk. There was a lot of Rebecca's personal memorabilia scattered about: pictures on the walls, little sculptures she appeared to collect, and real folio-bound books. It was the window that attracted Rue, though. It faced the Penumbra, the edge of the sunlit realm of Treya. Rue thought the subtle fade of bright to dark blue toward the northern horizon was beautiful. She stood there for a while, impressed, until Rebecca told her, "This is what the poor people get to see." Rebecca's side of the building was much cheaper to rent than the south-facing side, precisely because of this view. On the other side of the building, the southern penumbra was over the horizon and so according to Rebecca the illusion of being on Earth was nearly complete, except for the fact that the sun never moved in the sky.

"If I had any money at all I'd be living on the south side." Rebecca plumped some pillows on her small couch. "You can sleep here tonight. I don't know what we'll do with you in the morning."

"I'm really sorry to impose on you," said Rue. She sat down.

Rebecca glanced at her, then did a double-take. "Rue, how did you come to be in space alone, in that shuttle?"

"I . . . sort of, well I didn't steal it, I half own it. But I ran away. From my brother."

The intern nodded slowly, looking at her. "I thought there was something like that. You've got the mannerisms of the abused, like the way you're sitting now scrunched into one corner of the couch."

"I wasn't abused," said Rue. "I always fought."

Rebecca didn't smile. "Is that why you ran away from Max? You thought he was like . . . ?"

"Jentry. Yeah. That was it."

"You were probably wise to do so." Rebecca disappeared into the apartment's tiny galley kitchen. "Tea?"

"Sure." Rue fidgeted for a while. Her gaze kept returning to the window—an actual window! Such things didn't even exist on Allemagne; here it symbolized Rebecca's poverty.

"What about you?" she asked. "You're not so poor, surely. You're studying to be a doctor."

Rebecca poked her head around the corner. "To tell the truth, I don't know where I'm going from here," she said. "There've been no offers. You know, people from the stations who train here generally end up back on the stations. And you know why? It's because nobody'll hire them here on Treya."

"Oh." Rue thought for a while. "I guess it comes down to which do you want more: to be a doctor, or to live in Treya."

Rebecca muttered something. Then she said, "I want them both, Rue. Both."

"Oh. Um, listen, remember that guy I told you about? The newshound? He wants to interview me. Tonight. I'm, well, kind of nervous about it. Can I trust him?"

"Do you want me to go with you?"

"Um. Can we invite him here?"

Rebecca's head appeared again. "What? Have an actual man in my apartment? It'll be the talk of the corridor!"

"Come on, Rebecca."

She laughed. "Of course you can. I'll play mother hen just this once. Then tomorrow, you start looking for you own place. And a job. Deal?"

"Deal."

The water boiled and Rebecca carried out a little china teapot in the shape of a half-melted station. "Cute, ain't it?"

"Yeah."

"Rue, do you like this newshound?"

"Blair? Yeah. He's really cute."

"Ah." Rebecca nodded pensively. "Just wondering. Drink up."

AWAKE AGAIN. THIS was the third night in a row that Rue had awoken in darkness, unsure of where she was or what was happening. This time it only took her a minute or so to recognize the ruffling sound above her as the fabric of her tent rippled in the breeze. In the distance the wind made a soughing sound along the hillside. On the first night, she had been terrified by its lonely music—an alive but inhuman thing stalking the dark, unlike the wholly man-made sounds that permeated sleep-shift in Allemagne. Last night, she hadn't been afraid, but wonder had kept her awake. Both times, she had ended up sitting outside the tent for hours, staring up at the shimmering, restless aurora. Every now and then she could see stars through it and once or twice made out the cloud-smudged disk of Erythrion. She could feel the warmth of Erythrion on her face, even when she couldn't see it.

The publicity from Blair's interview had paid off in a modest way; the very day it was posted to the net, Rue had received nine job offers—plus a hurt-sounding message from Max to which she had not replied.

None of the jobs were high-paying, so she had chosen one that fit well with Rebecca's advice to her on how best to fulfil her eco responsibilities. She was planting trees.

Over the past few grueling days Rue had often thought of her mother; she would be so proud of her daughter. At the same time, whenever she paused to gaze out at the vista of hills and towering mountains that made up the North Penumbra, Rue felt a deep sorrow at the memory of her mother's tiny garden of green things. In retrospect, it was pathetic, that little terrarium. Here, Rue walked kilometers of rock near the alpine limit of the mountains, guiding the planting machines to pockets of soil and tiny barren meadows where trees might grow. The center of Treya's lit circle was all green, but neither green plants nor the aurora-adapted night grasses grew here in the twilight. The same wind that sighed around her tent tonight moved over a hundred kilometers of barrens and through rocky uplands where only lichens had taken hold. On the other side of these mountains was permanent night, where a man-made

ecology of low-light plants covered the rest of the hemisphere. Seeds were regularly dumped from the air onto the
penumbral lands, but in some environments this was a
wasteful exercise; the vast majority of seeds that fell in
Rue's zone landed on rock. Her job was to optimize the
planting so that a true subalpine forest would grow here
eventually.

She smiled and stretched. A week ago she'd never been
in a true forest and certainly had no idea of the startling
contrasts between the lush foliage of the valleys and the
hardy, tiny plants that thrived up here. She had moments of
acrophobia and agoraphobia as she walked the mountain-
sides, but so far she'd been able to transmute the fear into
exhilaration.

She had also spent a fair amount of time worrying, because her pay wasn't enough to cover the docking costs of
the shuttle; instead of saving to pay for her citizenship, she
was getting further into debt. She might have done all right
if she'd known who to bribe, but her skills in that area were
minimal. Jentry had refused to send any money for the
docking fees; she suspected he was planning to break her
financially and get her deported back to Allemagne. Then
he would pay the fees and recover both her and the shuttle.
It was a grim prospect.

Because it was so grim, she had been refusing to dwell
on the future. The mountains were gorgeous, all limpid
shadow and fogbound majesty and she found it easy to forget her problems here. Sheer rock walls rose from the
plains to ice-capped peaks, sunlit on one side during the artificial day, long shadows sloping into apparent nothing-
ness on the other side. Half the sky was a gorgeous bright
blue; the other half, azure fading to black. She could actually see the clean boundary of the gigantic shaft of light
coming from the "sun"; it was as if she stood by the wall of
a sky-sized glowing crystal, with bright clouds, forests,
and towns embedded in it. Penumbra seemed like the end

of the world in ancient myth; if she walked into the darkness, Rue fancied she might fall off the edge into space.

Working in such an Olympian landscape might have made her lonely, but Rue's supervisor kept tabs on her. He phoned once an hour to monitor her progress and that of the other planters working other slopes. In between times he e-mailed spirit-building slogans like KEEP UP THE ADEQUATE WORK and WE ARE ALL COGS IN THE WHEELS OF INDUSTRY. It was all in fun and when she wasn't chatting with him, Rue often spoke to Rebecca and even Blair.

Blair had taken her out to dinner two days ago; who knew where this might lead? If she only had a month or two before she had to leave . . . No, the money would come, she would think of something. Rue snuggled down into her sleeping bag and let herself dream about Blair and his ready grin, hoping the nice thoughts would let her get back to sleep.

The distant wind called out her name.

Rue opened her eyes wide. She saw nothing but the billowing blackness of the tent above her. It must have been her imagination.

"Rue . . ."

She sat up, heart pounding. Now she could see a faint glimmer of light through the tent wall. It came from downslope.

"Oh, shit!" She fought her way out of the sleeping bag and dressed hurriedly. It was cool but not cold; the nights here hovered around freezing, which to Rue felt just fine. She unzipped the tent flap and stepped out into muttering wind and the distant cracking noise of a glacial avalanche.

Some kind of air car was parked about two hundred meters down the valley. Between it and her was a little bobbing light.

"Rue!"

"Max?" She could see pretty well by auroral light, so

Rue jogged down to him without bothering to get out her own flashlight. Her cousin was waving a lantern around, peering myopically into the gloom; he jumped when she padded out of the dark to stand before him.

"Max, what are you doing here?"

"Thank Permanence I found you," he said. He was panting, probably from the thinness of the air. "Your phone was turned off."

"No . . ." But it was probably buried under clothing and gear; Rue's tent was pretty small.

He waved a hand. "It doesn't matter. They'll be here any minute, we've got to go."

"They? Who's they?"

"The government—military types who work for the generals of the Coup. They're about ten minutes behind me—look!" He pointed at the sky. Sure enough, a little knot of lights way up there was drifting in their direction.

"Come on! Grab your gear and let's get out of here!"

"I don't understand. What—"

"The cycler! It's the cycler, Rue, don't you get it? Your claim has been upheld. The cycler's a ghost ship, or non-human, which means your mining rights are automatically converted to salvage rights."

"Salvage rights . . ." She stared at the incoming air cars.

"Rue, if you thought everybody wanted a piece of you before, just wait! As of this moment, cousin, you are the only person in Erythrion to own a starship!"

4

RUE CLUTCHED HER kit bag and watched the mountain slope fall away below them. Max was apparently piloting the air car himself, because he held a control stick and as he moved it the car swooped and dove. "Wish we could turn off the running lights," he muttered. "Maybe if we stay low they won't see us." They shot over a mountain saddle and Rue's stomach flipped as they dropped to nearly treetop level over the slope below. She felt giddy, but wasn't sure whether this was due to Max's piloting or the news he had just dropped on her.

"Who are those people?" She pointed to the aircraft that were even now touching down on the black soil below her newly abandoned tent. "Newshounds?"

"The newshounds are the least of your problems," said Max. "Believe me, I know."

"Then . . . Max, talk to me."

He glanced sidelong at her. "You're not still mad at me?"

"Max, I was never mad at you. I just needed to do things on my own. I—I'm really grateful for your generosity and of course I'll pay you back for the hospital fees and the cool suit and all, it's just you were taking over the way my brother used to. Oh, I can't explain! You were pushing. I had to get away."

"I just wanted to protect you," he said sullenly.

"I see that now. Now, please tell me who those people are and why they're all coming after me in the middle of the night."

Max let out a long sigh. He looked like he hadn't slept and his clothes were disheveled as always.

"I've been following the attempts to contact the cycler," he said. "Which you should have been doing, too. Between times I talked to my lawyer and verified that if it proved to be a relic, that you would have salvage rights according to the laws of the Cycler Compact. Well, they won't announce it officially, but a guy I'd been paying off at the ministry just told me that they can't raise anyone on the cycler. Long-range telescopes show minimal energy signature except from the plow sail, so either it's a very efficient heat radiator or it's dead."

"Dead? But it's moving fast, isn't it?"

Max grunted a laugh. "Fast, yeah—point eight five lightspeed. It'll pass Erythrion in a little over two days. If it was manned, we would have received a message from it months ago offering cargos and asking if any passengers wanted to rendezvous with it. Takes that long to set up the braking beams and allocate power for acceleration beams, normally. So normally speaking, 'round about now there'd be a magsail or two braking into the system with passengers and cargo and the monks at Permanence would be getting ready to send an outbound magsail to catch up to it on the way out. There's none of that."

"So maybe it's a cargo packet, not a cycler." Cargo packets were small, weighing only a few tonnes; they were used to send nonliving cargoes between adjacent stars or halo worlds. Even they were rare, these days—and nobody launched a cargo packet without first arranging for its deceleration and capture at its destination. Max confirmed that none of Erythrion's neighboring colonies had announced that they were sending a packet. Anyway, whatever it was that was coming was far larger than any packet.

They swung out over the foot hills and Max leaned back from the controls. He slumped back in his seat. "It looks like we lost them."

"Max! Lost *who*?"

He glanced behind them. "Government officials, newshounds, the military . . . who knows? Whoever they are, they're after you for the same reason I came: the cycler."

"But . . . they don't even know it's a cycler," she said incredulously. "Maybe it's a ship from High Space. They don't use cyclers because they've got faster-than-light ships, right? So if they visit us in the halos, they do a direct flight."

Max shook his head. "Yeah, but when they visit, they come in faster than light. They can come here that fast, Rue, they just can't start the FTL engine again for the trip home; halo worlds like Erythrion don't have enough mass for that. Anyway, this thing's not on a direct trajectory to us; it's nudging itself into a course correction. It's not stopping here, it's using a ramscoop to bend its trajectory, like any cycler would. It's come from nowhere, Rue and where it's going we don't know—though if its new course holds, it'll be passing close by Chandaka in about two years."

"Chandaka!" She had often gazed at that star in the observatory at Allegmagne. It was the nearest star in High Space—once part of the Cycler Compact, now a habitation of the mysterious, despised Rights Economy.

"The point is, Rue, the thing behaves like a cycler; it's alive but seems to have no life support right now."

The last cycler to pass Erythrion had come twenty years ago; once, Rue knew, there had been at least one every month. But that was fifty years before, when all inhabited worlds—lit stars and brown dwarfs alike—were part of the Compact.

Then faster-than-light travel was discovered; unfortunately it only worked between massive enough worlds. Chandaka and the other lit stars had joined the FTL Rights Economy and stopped maintaining their parts of the cycler rings. Cycler traffic to Erythrion had dwindled over the years and finally stopped.

Cut off from the rest of the universe, Erythrion was turning in on itself. The coup at Treya was the latest symptom of the slide.

"That cycler may not be manned," Max continued, "but it's at least partly operational, because its plow sail is doing a course correction.

"And you, cousin of mine, own it."

The aircar skimmed above fields and forests and a black snaking river. Auroral light reflected off the water. In the distance inhabited hillsides glittered with lights, the way the docks of Allemagne had. As they approached Rue made out dozens of huge, sprawling mansions—not mere houses, certainly—each with its own grounds and pool. Private roads snaked through the forest. Private air cars sat on pads or roofs.

"I'm a billionaire," she whispered.

"Multi multi," observed Max laconically. "But it's not a done deal yet. The next few days will be critical."

"Why?"

Max didn't answer; he was concentrating on spiralling them down toward a big sprawling villa with red roofs. He hovered the car over a broad landing pad, hit a switch and lights bloomed around the pad. Apparently on automatic pilot now, the car settled slowly down, landing with the barest thump.

Max pumped a fist in the air. "Yes! I am so good." He banged open his door and hopped out. Rue followed reluctantly. This was not the sort of place where one just dropped in; even a bumpkin like her could recognize that.

"Max, whose house is this?"

He was halfway around the pool. Glass doors were sliding open before him. Max turned, scratched his head and said, "Well, whose place do you think it is? It's mine, Rue."

He went in, while she stood there with her kit bag at her feet.

"THERE IS ABSOLUTELY nothing like a good drink at times like this," said Max. He handed her a tumbler with some dark liquor in it.

"Times like this?" Rue could hear a slight tinge of hysteria in her own voice, but there was nothing she could do about it. "You've had other days like this, then?" She stood in a living room of such opulence that she was sure the characters of her favorite star serial would emerge from the corridors at any second. The carpet was a self-cleaning biomimic, the walls held paintings on real canvas and there was even a little fountain in the corner. At the same time, there was no possible way Max could have been lying about owning the place, because every surface was covered with gaming scrip, empty bottles, dirty laundry, and ragged balls of plastic packaging. One of the paintings was askew and some sort of primitivist electronic device, with vacuum tubes and knobs, was upended in the fountain.

"You'll be safe here," declared Max as he turned and let himself collapse onto a sock-festooned couch. "Drink up."

Rue took a sip, then a stiff shot of the scotch, which tasted like soil and smoke. She kicked a shoe off the armchair opposite the couch and sat down, back straight.

"Oh, I've had days like this," said Max. "The first was when I was sixteen and I won the Treya lottery. Didn't that newshound friend of yours tell you? I won twenty-seven million dites. It tore my life apart. Mother would have taken it all, you know . . . The second time was when I won my first Penrose Go tournament. I'm the world champion. Shit, I just started playing because I was bored." He threw an arm across his face, seemingly intent on sleeping here with one foot on the couch and one on the floor.

Overwhelmed, she just sat and drank until the scotch was all gone and she felt ten kilos lighter. Max began to snore.

"What do I do?" she blurted.

"Wha?" Max blinked and sat up. "You get a good night's sleep, that's what. Tomorrow we have to face the wolves."

"What do you mean? I'm a billionaire now, aren't I? Doesn't that give me . . . anything?"

Max scowled. "Not really. You see, according to the laws of the Cycler Compact, you own the salvage rights to this starship—provided you can take possession of the cycler."

She remembered now—there had been all kinds of legal stuff when that shuttle collided with Allemagne. Rue had been more focused on what she could get out of it herself, but her brother had talked about the salvage rights. "You normally establish your salvage on a wreck by going out to get it," Jentry had gloated. "But this time it came to us!"

"But—" She got up unsteadily and headed for the bar. "That's crazy. I can't claim salvage unless I fly out to the thing."

To her dismay Max nodded. "You've got to physically visit the wreck to establish your claim. If you don't within a reasonable amount of time, it'll go to whoever gets there first. And *that* is why you are in trouble. The cycler's going to be beyond our reach in a matter of days or weeks. Anything that's done has to be done now.

"It gets worse, too. Think of it—this is a cycler! A cycler! We haven't seen one in . . . what? Twenty years? If it really is a ghost ship, its value is incalculable. Since the lit worlds abandoned us, the Compact is in trouble anyway; but as long as the remaining cyclers are loyal, it controls travel between the halo worlds. A cycler in the control of the Treya government means they could challenge the Compact itself. In other words, this cycler is valuable enough to kill for.

"Since you're completely impoverished, there's two possibilities: either somebody funds an expedition for you—and uses you as a powerless figurehead—or they block you from going somehow, leave you scrabbling in the muck—or dead—and go out there themselves. Which is by far the better option from almost anybody's point of view. That's why they were converging on you earlier—the wolves smell blood and it's more likely to be yours than anybody's.

"So drink up. Tomorrow's going to be a mess."

Rue had uncorked a bottle of sherry, hoping it would taste better than the scotch. She resealed it and put her glass down. "This somebody who's going to fund the expedition," she said. "Would that happen to be you?"

Max scratched under his chin. "Maybe."

"So I'd be your 'powerless figurehead,' then?"

"Oh, look around you, Rue. I *have* money. I don't do anything with it. Why should I want more? Truth is, I've never found much worth taking it out of the bank for."

"Then why help me?"

Max didn't answer for a long time; he just sat on the couch like a broken doll, staring straight ahead. Finally he said, "Mother has started a court case against me. She claims I was still a minor when I won my money. It's not strictly true, but true enough . . . This time she's got the best lawyers and . . . I don't think I can win. You see, Rue, I expect I'm going to lose all of this to her and sooner rather than later. So it's a case of using it while I've got it.

"And frankly, I can't think of a better way to thwart Mother than by making you rich beyond your wildest dreams."

RUE HAD STAGGERED off to sleep shortly after Max made his proposal. She lay in bed for a while thinking about what was involved in catching a ghost cycler and concluded that the whole thing was impossible. First, the starship was retreating almost as fast as light itself and for all they knew it was just a tangle of dead radioactive metal—except for the plow sail, which was an electromagnetic ramjet and presumably too hot to get near anyway.

Whatever expedition was able to catch up with the thing would need to bring it under control and turn it. She wasn't too clear on how starships turned, but knew it was a gradual thing. It might be thirty years before they "cycled" back to Erythrion. She'd have to be crazy to throw away the best part of her life sitting in a cold metal can in the middle of nowhere; that was the existence she'd just come from, after all.

No, it would never happen. Consoled by this thought, Rue found sleep came easily at last.

Morning was different. She awoke to find Max already up and bustling about. He wore the same clothes as last night and hadn't showered, but otherwise he was being frighteningly efficient.

"I've verified that there's an emergency shipbuilding order been put through by the Treya Provisional Government," he said as Rue came into the kitchen, knuckling her eyes. "They've applied to the Order for power to accelerate a cargo to point eight-five lightspeed. Seems they're acting already."

"Oh," said Rue as she peered into the fridge. "I guess that settles it, then. They got to the Compact first."

"Doesn't work that way. Your claim has priority. If you apply to the Order for beam power, you'll get it."

"How much would that cost?" she asked as she reached for some fruit juice.

"Four million dites, I reckon."

Rue nearly dropped the juice container. "Four *million*! You can't be serious!"

Max looked insulted. "I'm good for it. Besides, you're going to pay me back."

"No. No, Max, this is crazy. I just got here, I'm not going back to deep space and exile myself for half my life just to get rich. If that cycler can't sustain life anymore it would be suicide to go there anyway! Let's just drop it."

"Admittedly we need to send a bigger than usual cargo," said Max. "Life support for several years, tools, repair equipment . . . But it's still doable. And what's this about exiling yourself for half your life? Look, the cycler's going to pass Chandaka in two years—that's one year cycler time. All we have to do is alter the cycler's course to bring it back past Erythrion, then climb back in our cargo magsail and coast to Chandaka. Then we're in FTL space. A holiday among the lit worlds, just think about it! You'll have enough credit at that point to afford an FTL ship to come back here. So you could be home and rich in two years, Rue!"

"Oh." She hadn't considered such an option. "And if I can't change its course?"

"Well, shucks, then we're just stuck in FTL space, on a Rights Economy world. We'll get by."

"You said 'we.' Are you coming on this . . . hypothetical expedition?"

For the first time since she had met him, her cousin looked completely serious. "I wouldn't send you into something I'd be afraid to do myself," said Max.

"Think of it this way," he went on. "I'm proposing we

visit the stars. That's a once in a lifetime offer, Rue, you're not going to get it again. We'll just happen to be riding alongside, or maybe in, a cycler we've found."

"When you put it that way . . ." Of course she had dreamed of visiting FTL space all her life, like anybody else. A realm where people could travel freely between the stars at unbelievable speeds, leaving the crawling cyclers of the halos behind . . . You could see a hundred different worlds in your life, even visit Earth. It was an unreachable fantasy for almost anyone in the halo; and the Rights Economy was nominally the enemy—it had abandoned the halo worlds, because travelling to them was so expensive. Still, the allure was intoxicating. Rue had never expected to be able to go anywhere except Erythrion, unless she emigrated to another of the orphan planets drifting in interstellar space between Erythrion and Chandaka.

She still didn't really believe what Max was saying; maybe because of this, she said, "Okay. Why not? Let's go to Chandaka."

"That's my girl!"

She held up a finger. "One condition. The cycler is mine." She pointed the finger at herself. "My cycler. Mine mine mine. And my expedition. I'm the captain."

"Fine by me. I'm not the leader type."

"Okay." She was being reckless; it felt good. "Shake?"

Solemnly, Max held out his hand. "Shake."

"First thing I guess we do is apply for the beam power, right?"

"No. Rue, that would tip our hand. Hopefully they don't know where you are right now and I don't want to let them in on it until the last minute. We do all the other essentials before they know you're even in the game. Then we pop it on them."

Rue watched as Max transfered an unbelievable amount of money into the accounts of a dormant, numbered company he'd created years before. With a casual shrug he erased the debt Rue had accumulated for docking her shuttle and sent an offer to Jentry to buy the shuttle. Jentry would jump at it, Rue knew; the offer was absurdly high. Max's logic was that they would do best with a proven shuttle, rather than something right off the shipyard. After all, there would be no shakedown cruise for this expedition.

This activity took most of a day; Rue might have thought it a sufficiently huge accomplishment for that amount of time, but Max had compiled a long list of things to do. By the time Jentry accepted the offer it was after six in the evening, but Max had already hired a crew to gut the shuttle and refit it for interstellar service. "Double pay if you get it done in forty-eight hours," he barked into his phone. "Rue, we need schematics and repair histories for all the major cycler designs. Download 'em out of inscape, could you? Also, we need to know how to turn a cycler if it's unpowered. If we have to separate the cycler from the plow sail, so be it. A smaller cycler is still a cycler."

The Allemagne shuttle wasn't designed for interstellar use, but as a deep-range craft it was the next best thing. Interstellar shuttles were built as lightweight as possible, so much of what they had to do was strip mass out of Rue's, while beefing up the life support system. Among other things, this meant removing the engines and most of the fuel tanks and installing a plasma sail loop. All they would have left were some small maneuvering rockets. They would be at the mercy of the Cycler Order's particle beam launch and capture system for acceleration and braking. This was normal for interstellar travel, because a little shuttle like Rue's could never accelerate to eighty percent lightspeed on its own, no matter how much fuel it carried.

Max spent a great deal of money keeping mouths shut at the shipyard; he seemed quite adept at this sort of thing. When Rue asked him about it, he looked pensive for a while, then said, "I used to trust people. Implicitly. It's still a hard habit for me to break. But I learned to cultivate suspicion, after I got money." He didn't elaborate.

Rue understood somewhat, because Max's mother Leda had started nosing around, being quite solicitous and friendly toward Max. Rue kept out of sight during those visits.

Lying in Max's guestroom, she stared at the ceiling and daydreamed about cyclers.

REBECCA OPENED HER door and blinked in surprise. She was dressed in a housecoat and her hair was frazzled.

"Aren't you going to invite me in?" teased Rue.

Rebecca laughed and embraced her. "Come in, come in, I'm just so surprised, you dropped out of sight and the rumors!" Rebecca closed her apartment door and leaned on it. "Do you think you were followed?"

They both laughed. "Probably," Rue said. "But it doesn't matter. I'm leaving in a couple of days."

"So it's true. You're going after the cycler."

She nodded. "What about you? How's the job hunt going?"

Rebecca grimaced. "Not great. But I'll survive. Tea?"

"Sure."

They sat for a while and got caught up. Rue spun stories of her time as a tree planter and others about Max. "Ah, I thought he might be your anonymous benefactor!" Rebecca exclaimed when Rue told where she had been staying.

"So we're not committed to staying with the cycler for its whole cycle," Rue finished. "All we have to do is set its course and then disembark at Chandaka. If we can prove the cycler's following our course, we're rich. We should be able to afford to fly directly back here. Max thinks we could be back in two years!"

"Incredible. Oh! The tea!" Rebecca jumped up to get it. "I'm insanely envious," she said from the kitchen.

This was the opening Rue had been waiting for. "You don't need to be, you know," she said as distinctly as she could.

Silence—then Rebecca poked her head out. "What?"

"I said you don't need to be envious. I didn't come here to say good-bye, Rebecca."

Tea forgotten, Rebecca came and stood over her. "Don't be coy, Rue. I hate that. What are you saying?"

She smiled. "We're going to need a doctor. What if one of us gets sick a year from Chandaka? I also need somebody I can trust. I want to get to Chandaka alive, Rebecca, not die conveniently so that somebody else can take the claim. If I'm going to do this at all, I have to have a doctor. And you're the doctor I want."

"But . . . I don't have my license yet! It wouldn't be legal for me to practice—"

Rue waved a hand negligently. "I'm prepared to fund you getting your license at Chandaka. Do you think they'd refuse you a position here if you had that?"

Rebecca sat down, hands clenched in her lap. *So this is what power feels like,* Rue thought as she watched the flight of emotions across the other woman's face. It was delicious.

"Hey, you know this makes sense," she continued. "You grew up in the stations, you'd make a far better cycler crewman than any of these pudgy Treya types. You won't be afraid of the emptiness or the cold. I need that. And I need a friend."

Rebecca looked down. "You don't know what you're asking."

"I think I do. Will you come with me to Chandaka? I've thought about this a lot and I want you to come."

When Rebecca looked up her eyes were shining. "Well, yes, Rue. I'll do it."

"I THINK WE'VE covered our tracks pretty well," said Max as he banked the aircar in the direction of Penumbra West. "There's nothing we've bought in the last few days that wouldn't be normal for a comet-mining company that's come into town to restock. It's not like you need anything special to rendezvous with a cycler."

"Except the G-beds," Rue pointed out absently. She was watching the ground go by; it wasn't frightening, just bewilderingly detailed; she knew she would never get used to the sight.

He shrugged. "By this time tomorrow everybody's going to know."

The visible wall of shadow that was the Penumbra reared up ahead of them like a translucent cliff. Bright clouds drifted into it and turned gray, then black as they merged with the eternal night beyond. Far away in that night was the monastery of Permanence. Such monasteries could be found on every halo world; they were owned by the great religious order who controlled the launch and return mechanisms for the interstellar cyclers.

The western Penumbral lands weren't mountainous like the north. Way down below, where shadow met rolling fields, Rue could make out wide bands of alternating light and darkness. "What're those?"

"Interference pattern. You probably didn't notice it when you were standing under them; they're pretty wide. But they shift back and forth during the day."

She nodded. That explained why the light had brightened and faded in ripples as she'd walked the hillsides doing her tree planting.

"You want to see closer up?" Max put the aircar into a dizzying dive. He followed a strip of highway as it exited the green splendor of sunlight. In the shadowlands, houses still dotted the sides of the road, but they became fewer and fewer as the interference bands became sparser and fainter.

"The strange thing is," said Max, "that the houses start up again about fifty kilometers along. Not too many, mind you, but they're there. They belong to people like you who're sensitive to the light and heat. Some people just prefer the aurora light."

The last dim band fell behind and they entered a land of permanent night. Here, in the deep twilight, someone had built a glittering glass-and-wood house on the top of an escarpment. White fungus grass grew long in the yard and no vehicles sat on the overgrown landing pad out front. It gave Rue a funny feeling to realize she was seeing a real abandoned building. Historically, the only abandoned structures in the halo were in colonies that had failed. Treya was such a vibrant, exciting place—was it possible that the seeds of collapse had been sown here?

When she was born the cyclers had still come, though fewer and fewer. As a child she hadn't associated their loss with the drop in immigration and rise in crime among the Stations. Cyclers didn't carry enough cargo to directly affect the economy or population of a developed colony like Erythrion.

The effects of maintaining contact with other worlds might be subtler than money or birthrates could account for. Maybe they were no less important, though.

"Damn the government," she said.

Max laughed richly. "Spoken like a true Treyan," he said.

They flew on and the glow of the sunlit lands gradually fell over the horizon behind them. Timidly at first, then with graceful confidence, the aurora revealed itself in the sky ahead. Behind the aurora, the stars attended like an enraptured audience.

There was no shred of green left below. Rue's eyes adjusted quickly and she could soon make out the riot of color that had replaced Earthly tones on the land. Most of the grass was black and it rippled like velvet in the wind. The trees were dark shades of purple and red, but here and there furz and heather dominated and this was rainbowed with shades of lilac and lemon-yellow. These plants used a pigment more efficient than chlorophyll and tuned to the frequencies of light the aurora produced. They absorbed blue-green light, unlike chlorophyll which absorbed red. Hence, they appeared in any color but green itself. They normally grew with agonizing slowness, but whenever Erythrion flared they would undergo brief, explosive growth spurts.

The aircar was still following the road, which snaked between low hills and past rivers but maintained a westward
tendency. After a while Max pointed ahead. "I think that's
it," he said.

On the horizon Rue could make out a glittering building,
tall as any she'd seen in the lighted country behind them.
Rows of windows high on its flanks lit the hillsides around
it and she could see that it sat on the edge of a cliff, above
a lake or ocean that stretched out to the horizon. More than
that she couldn't see, except that this building was the terminus of the road they had been following.

Rue rehearsed the arguments she'd been preparing. She
was the legal owner of the cycler; she must be given a
chance to assert her ownership . . . she was good at defend-
ing herself verbally, she knew. She'd done it all her life.

Beside her Max heaved a sigh and she was about to say
something about his sounding relieved that they'd made it,
when sparks flew up the canopy beside her. Rue shrieked
and jumped back, catching up against her seat belt. The
aircar dipped woozily.

"What's happening?"

A bright vertical line of light appeared, jittered around
crazily outside, then vanished. It left spots in Rue's eyes.

"Laser!" shouted Max. He put the car into a hard turn;
light flashed outside again. "They hit one of the jets!"

"Are we going down?" Rue figured she should be
afraid—didn't objects pick up a lot of speed when they fell
on a planet? The fear didn't come naturally, though; freefall
was a sensation she associated with safety and stillness, not
danger.

"They build these things with multiple redundancy, so—"
Sparks flew again and all kinds of inscape windows appeared around Max—most of them flashing red. "There
goes another jet."

Okay, now she was scared. There came another flash and
then they were falling.

Max sat numbly staring at the instruments, which were

now complaining of a computer failure. Rue looked around herself. Freefall itself felt natural—it was the idea that they were being shot at that scared her.

Off to the right was the sky and off to the left the planet was closing fast. Three of their jets were down, but according to Max's instruments they had a fourth.

She reached past Max and hauled on the control stick. The aircar responded by flipping over several times. The rotation was very similar to the spins you did when playing freeball and she was good at freeball. Max was screaming now, but Rue had a good idea of how the aircar was responding to its only remaining jet. She put the car into a tight, blood-pounding spiral and threw all power into that jet.

They seemed to be slowing down, but it was too late. The ground came whirling up at them and then everything flew apart.

5

"I DON'T BELIEVE it," she heard Max mutter. Rue seemed to be squashed between a number of giant pillows, which were making various rude noises as they deflated. She pulled herself free, to find herself standing in black grass, shaken but unhurt, next to the aircar's crash bags.

Max clawed his way out from the bundle of neon-green balloons. "Don't believe it," he said again. Then he laughed. "Love the way they design these things."

The rest of the aircar was a mangled wreck lying some meters away. The car must have ejected the cockpit at the very last second.

"Gods and Kami, when we went into that death spiral I thought we were dead," said her cousin as he inspected himself for damage. "You okay?"

The spiral had been deliberate: Rue had needed to stabilize the aircar so that she could keep their one remaining jet pointed down and that was the only way to do it. It seemed petty to bring that up now, though. "I'm okay," she said. "Have you called for help?"

Max looked around himself uneasily. "I tried. I can't raise the inscape net out here. Signal's jammed . . . Look, we should get out of here. They'll come to make sure we're dead."

"Then you're going the wrong way," she said, taking his hand. "The monastery's this way."

His hand was shaking. He clasped hers tightly. "I can't see it," he said. "Too dark."

"I can see perfectly well," she reassured him. The aurora lit the land with a flickering, inconstant ghost light. Still, Max wouldn't move until they'd rummaged through the wreck of the aircar and found a flashlight he kept stored there. "I know we don't dare use it," he said. "I just need to have it, that's all."

They had crashed in an area of mixed grassland and thickets. In the light of a flare the tall bushes might have been a bright orange color; in this diffuse green glow they appeared deep brown. The air was warm; Rue could feel heat from Erythrion on her face when she looked to the east.

Luckily the brown tangles were big enough that they afforded some cover. Rue and Max wove their way around them for a hundred or so meters. Then they had to stop, because an unmistakable sound reached them through the clear air.

"It's an aircar," said Max. They both dove for cover among the thorny stalks of an orange bush tall as a house. "It's coming in low."

Rue could see it now, a dark blot against the aurora. The car showed no running lights, which was supposed to be illegal. This had to be the people who'd shot them down.

"But who are they?" she asked. She hadn't been afraid when their aircar went down; that had been more of an exercise in soft docking than anything frightening. This, though . . . that circling car reminded her of the brutal men who'd frequented the bar at Allemagne. She knew what such men were capable of. She kept very still as the car passed directly overhead, but her heart was pounding like it would burst.

"It's landing at the crash site," said Max. "Quick, let's get some distance between us and them."

"Yeah." They ran, with Rue leading, weaving a drunkard's path around the thickets, which blocked their way like the walls of a maze. Every now and then, Rue would catch a glimpse of the distant lights of the monastery. Several times when she did this, she found it was way off to the side and once, behind them. She suspected they were making little progress in its direction, but she didn't have the heart to tell Max.

He was busy anyway, speculating about who their pursuers were. "Gotta be government thugs," he decided. "But which faction? The isolationists won't want anyone to catch the cycler. On the other hand, the generals at the core aren't isos, never have been. They're probably falling all over each other to go after the thing."

Rue was panting from the heat and exhaustion of running. It was just lucky she'd spent all those days walking up and down mountains, otherwise she'd have collapsed after just a few minutes. Max wasn't looking so great, though. He had to stop more and more often.

Every now and then they heard the aircar in the distance. Once it flew overhead again, but the thickets were good cover and their pursuers didn't seem to be using any sophisticated sensing gear.

Just when Rue felt she was at the end of her strength, they crashed through a particularly tall and dense stand of orange bushes and found themselves at the base of a stone wall.

"Safe!" cried Rue. "If we can find the door . . ."

"Actually . . ." Max examined the dark stone doubtfully. Rue ignored him and ran along the wall. "I don't think we're there yet," said Max, just as Rue reached a spot where the lichen-encrusted wall had tumbled down, revealing a gap. She searched the sky for the aircar and when she didn't see it, clambered up the rock fall to look at what lay beyond.

They were nowhere near the monastery. Its lights still glowed kilometers away and above them. Between her and it sprawled the dark and overgrown streets of an abandoned city.

"What . . ." Streets, plazas, hundreds of tall dark towers and treed suburbs spread for kilometers around the base of the monastery's hill. The city was huge, but Rue saw no movement in its unlit streets. Grass sprouted through the sidewalks and vines were slowly covering the windows of the house nearest where she stood. A young tree arrogantly blocked its front door. Only at the far end of the city, near the monastery, did she see the twinkle of lights.

"This is Thetis," said Max as he climbed up next to her. "The old capital. They abandoned it when the sun was built. Everybody moved into the light. Well, all except a few holdouts, hermits and assorted misfits. They live in the mansions on the slopes now." He pointed to the distant lights.

"Why didn't they just aim the sun here?"

"They had originally planned to build more suns—one for each of the big cities." He shook his head. "The one we've got now was originally an experiment."

"What happened?"

"We lost almost all our trade with Chandaka when the Rights Economy conquered it. No chance of attracting immigrants anymore, when they could go elsewhere faster than light. It was political bickering over things like the sun funds that finally led to the coup."

"So." She waved at the broad streets. "How are we going to cross all that without being seen?"

"I've got an idea." Max led the way into the deserted city. Rue wouldn't have taken a step into this place on her own; it was unbelievably creepy, like the graveyards she'd read about in old books. All desolate, the buildings like crystallized despair. Many of their windows were broken and some doors yawned open like waiting traps. She kept imagining she saw movement there—and maybe she did, maybe the killers who'd shot them down were closing in. She clutched Max's hand tightly as he pulled her along. He was looking for something.

"There it is!" He broke into a run. Rue followed, groaning. As he reached a flight of stairs that led straight into the ground, she heard the rising whine of an approaching aircar behind them.

"Hurry!" They stumbled down the overgrown steps and into a space so black even Rue couldn't see anything. Then Max clicked on his flashlight, revealing a long empty chamber with some kind of trench running down its center. With difficulty she deduced the place must be a subway station.

Rue shied away from the black tunnel mouth that gaped at the end of the trench. "I don't know about this . . ."

"No, look." Max pointed the light at a dusty map on the wall. He traced the routes with a finger. "We're here. All we have to do is go down Line Five, which is this one and it takes us straight to the monastery. They'll never find us."

"Unless they saw us come in here."

"In that case, we're out of luck anyway. Come on, couz, it's not much further."

She sighed and followed him down onto the tracks and into the mouth of blackness.

"WELL, I GUESS this makes sense," said Max an hour later. They were crouched in a narrow space under the ceiling of the tunnel. The way was completely blocked up ahead. "The rain must have been washing silt in here for years," he said. "It's a miracle we got this far."

Rue was near tears. They had walked for ages through tomblike darkness, past side tunnels where the phosphorescent eyes of something glowed suspiciously; stepped over slick trails of slime that crisscrossed the floor and ran straight up the walls; kicked through weird pillars of fungi that stood as tall as a man and were twisted into tortured shapes that seemed to move in the weakening glow of the flashlight. Sighs of wind like distant voices echoed constantly through the long tunnel.

"We'll have to go back to the last station," said Max. "I hope the flashlight lasts long enough." He put a hand on the slick wall of the tunnel and looked down miserably. "Rue, I am so, so sorry that I got you into this."

"You got us into this?"

"Yeah." He turned dejectedly and they began walking back down the tunnel. "I convinced you to go after the cycler."

"Well maybe, but I could have changed my mind, couldn't I?"

"Well, I suppose, but . . ."

"I'm not a child, Max. It was my responsibility to say no and I didn't."

He grimaced. "So now what? Do we hide out until they leave and then try to sneak home?"

"No," she said hotly. "They're trying to steal my cycler."

"Is it really that important to you, Rue? It wasn't before. Why the change?"

She thought about it. "Maybe . . . it's because nobody was actually trying to take it away from me before."

His look told her he didn't understand. "Look. If the government had offered me a finders' fee or something I would have jumped at it. But they didn't; Blair told me they didn't even try to find me through him. They figured that a woman like me would never be able to reach the cycler herself, so they just ignored me. Like Jentry used to. And now they're trying to use violence to beat me down— like Jentry used to."

That reason seemed petty; it wasn't right. "But that's not actually it, either," she admitted. "I guess there's two things. The night before I ran away from Allemagne, I had this bad moment when I thought: I can live like this. Allemagne's not too bad. I can cope. I'm an adult now, I can learn to stand up to Jentry. I can carve out my own life like Mom did."

It was pretty hard to resist that urge.

"It's the same now. We *could* sneak away. Let the government have the cycler. Just make do. And Treya's not terrible, like Allemagne, even with the provisional government and all. I might never have much here, but I would have enough.

"You know what?" She grinned at him. "I resisted that urge on Allemagne. I took the mad chance and here I am! And now, another mad chance comes along. I could resist. Or I could jump."

They had reached the platform. Dim auroral light glowed at the top of the steps. They went up cautiously, watching the skies for any sign of the aircar. Nothing was visible; there was no sound except the sighing of the wind through the streets.

When they reached the top of the stairs, Max said, "Maybe we won't have to turn tail after all." They stood at the foot of the hill upon which perched the monastery. From here the place appeared mountainously huge and Rue could see that nearly all its windows were dark. Only a band near the top shone defiantly. Once, Rue supposed, when the cyclers came every few weeks, this would have been a very busy place.

They jogged through the shadows toward the long sweeping roadway that ran up to the monastery's gates. Max pulled Rue into a doorway just before they reached the road. "I don't like it," he said. "This is too perfect a place for an ambush."

"Well, what do we do?"

"Watch and wait, I think. What we need is to find cover where we can see if anybody's moving down here."

"How about there?" She pointed to a building across the street. It had wide archways leading into a courtyard and a tower with prominent balconies. Max squinted through the gloom at it. "Perfect. You'll have to be our eyes and ears, though."

They checked the road; nothing was moving so they darted across and into the courtyard.

"Right," said Max. "Now all we have to do is—"

"Don't move! Put your hands up." It was a woman's voice and it came from behind them.

Rue's heart sank. She exchanged a stricken look with Max, then they both raised their hands.

"Turn around."

The woman who stepped out of the courtyard's shadow was dressed in a black skinsuit; her hair was tied back to cascade down her shoulders. She was pointing a snub-nosed pistol in their direction.

"Who are you?" she asked. "Answer quick."

"Uh, we live here," said Max.

"That's not what I asked."

"Look, we don't want any trouble," said Max. "I—"

"Kami!" shouted the woman. She levelled her pistol and then Max was tackling Rue and they went down as she heard the pistol fire. "Run!" Max shouted in her ear, as Rue tried to get to her feet.

Rue stood up and practically ran into the dark-clothed woman. "This way!" the woman said, grabbing Rue's arm.

"Wha—"

"Do you want them to kill you? Come on!" Then Rue was being hauled into the darkness of the building. Max stood gaping for a second, then jumped when another shot sounded from somewhere nearby. He ran inside too.

Only now did Rue realize that the woman had fired past them, not at them.

"You're the two whose aircar got shot down east of here," said the woman.

"Yeah . . ." They were moving deeper into the place and it was now too dark for Rue to make out more than an outline of the stranger. Max's hand found Rue's shoulder and he held on tightly as they went. Behind them light welled up in the outer rooms.

"My name's Corinna Chandra," said the woman. "I'm with the search team that's looking for you."

"Who do you work for?" asked Max suspiciously.

"I'm a nun with the Permanence Order," she said. "I work for the compact."

They found some steps and went down them. When they reached the bottom, Chandra let Rue and Max go by, then closed and barred a heavy door behind them. There was a moment's silence, then bright overhead lights flicked on. Rue had to close her eyes against the glare. She heard Chandra saying, "This is Green Two. I've got them. We're coming in."

Rue opened her eyes a squint. They stood at one end of a long corridor that stretched away, apparently to infinity. Chandra grinned at her; Rue was amazed at what she saw. If not for the catsuit and the pistol, Corinna Chandra might have been anybody's aunt or older friend. She had iron-gray hair, and the wrinkles around her eyes and mouth suggested she was in her late forties. She looked like she would have been at home in a library—certainly not in a gunfight.

"Come," she said, gesturing down the tunnel. "These utility ways don't go all the way to the keep. We'll have to rendezvous with our team and get up there before the soldiers find out we've taken this way." She started to jog away down the tunnel.

The lights overhead flickered; a cloud of dust suddenly appeared far away down the long tunnel and moments later a loud *bang!* left Rue's ears ringing. Then the lights went out completely.

Another series of loud reports made Rue crouch with her hands over her ears. Then bright lights reached through swirling dust and pinioned her and the others.

"Hands up!" shouted a man from somewhere behind

those lights. Rue saw Chandra reluctantly drop her pistol and raise her hands.

THEY WERE MARCHED back into the courtyard, where at least a dozen men dressed as soldiers waited. Rue, Max, and Corinna Chandra were ordered to kneel, their hands clasped behind their heads. The whole scene seemed a bit unreal to Rue; it was like something out of a movie.

The leader of the squad walked up and inspected each of them in turn. Satisfied, he nodded to his men. "It's them. Let's make this quick and get out of here." He stepped aside and the men raised their weapons.

"Remember, this is live!" said a strangely familiar voice from somewhere overhead. The soldiers reacted to the words as though they'd been shocked, jumping back and raising their lights and weapons.

Rue craned her neck to look up and behind her. Perched on the wall of the courtyard, monocle gleaming in his eye, was Blair Genereaux. Beside him on the wall sat a powerful looking portable inscape transmitter. Its indicators glowed warmly.

"Yes, folks, it's a real paramilitary execution and it's happening live and on the inscape net!" continued the newshound, seemingly unperturbed at all the guns aimed in his direction. "If you're really lucky, you'll get to see this reporter killed as well. But before this happens, let's shed a little light on the killers. Let me open up our recently declassified military personnel database . . ."

Rue glanced back down in time to see the blood drain from the squad leader's face. Then the man cleared his throat, turned to his men and said in a stilted voice, "These are not the criminals we are after." A moment later he was fast-walking out of the courtyard. His men stared after him for a moment, then followed in confused haste.

Blair hopped down off the wall and brushed dust off his pant leg. He grinned as Rue ran over to hug him.

"Well, folks, seems there's no story here after all," he

continued in his announcer's voice. "But stay tuned to the visual feed, just in case.

"Hi," he said in a more normal tone. "Glad I found you guys."

"But how?" asked Max.

"It wasn't hard, actually. I've been camped out in the monastery for days now. I figured you'd have to come here eventually, so I'd wait and interview you when you arrived." He grinned. "When the alarms went off and a bunch of people dressed in black started running out the gates . . . well, let's just say I came to a logical conclusion and followed some of them."

"Well, good for you!" She kissed him on the cheek. Blair's smile grew even broader.

"I can't believe they just left," said Corinna Chandra, staring after the departing troops.

Blair laughed. "Power of the press. The provisional government couldn't get away with overt murder. These guys know they'd have been the patsies if they'd gone through with it and it got onto the net."

"Come on," said Max. "Let's get to the monastery before those goons come back." They left the courtyard and began marching up the road to the distant, open doors of the giant building.

Blair matched his pace to Rue's. "So, you'll give me another interview before you leave?"

Rue laughed. "I'll do better than that! How would you like to be the official chronicler of the adventure?"

"You mean . . ."

"I mean crew! I mean come with us. We haven't got all our crew together. You too, Ms. Chandra."

Blair looked stunned. "I . . . I yes, that would be . . . Rue, this story would make my career."

Corinna Chandra appeared to be thinking. Finally she smiled. "I would be honored," she said.

"Then it's settled."

Blair had seemed calm staring down the barrels of a

dozen guns. Now he looked dazed. "Blair Genereaux, author of The Chronicles of—" He frowned. "Chronicles of what?"

"Huh?"

"Rue, haven't you even named your cycler?"

Rue pretended to think about it, but a name for the cycler had popped unbidden into her head the instant Blair asked and she knew it was right. "You want a name? How 'bout *Jentry's Envy*?"

Max laughed. "If you want. You're the captain."

Yes, I am, Rue thought and then she had to stop and sit down for a while.

6

RUE KNEW ALL about cyclers.

She had read cycler romances, watched movies about cycler captains, participated in sims about them ever since she could remember. They were a matter of practical fact in her life. They were also unbelievably romantic.

In sims, she had walked the decks of interstellar cyclers that were more like grand hotels, some even modelled on old Earth styles, with sweeping staircases and statues in niches and stained-glass windows that looked out on Mother Night. Only the richest, most important, or most talented could afford to travel between the stars: delegations of diplomats, eccentric billionaires, mad scientists, and artists from many different worlds were thrown together here and asked to get along for months or years at a time. Naturally, there was intrigue.

How you got to and from cyclers was itself a study in legend. So when Rue awoke on her last morning on Treya, grabbed her carefully packed bag and dumped it in the back of Max's aircar, she had all kinds of embarkation stories in mind. You rode particle beams or microwaves, or used a pion drive to rendezvous with passing cyclers; that was the trite truth. But there were thousands of gripping tales of how that rendezvous might be accomplished. One that was on her mind as she waved away the column of midges flittering above Max's car and watched him lock up his house, was a movie where some bad guys inserted their magsail into the beam behind the hero's. This cut off his acceleration and boosted theirs; they had stolen his beam and would reach the cycler while leaving him stranded. This kind of piracy was known as beam-stealing and it had been known to happen. The monks couldn't turn off the beams if it happened without dooming both crews to die adrift.

The various envious powers of Erythrion—ranging from Max's mom to the government—seemed to have decided on letting them go, which considering recent events seemed very suspicious. As they flew out to the orbital elevator she constructed frightening scenarios for herself about the government secretly beam-stealing their power and riding out to claim *Jentry's Envy* while they died in interstellar space.

She had barely shaken hands with the last member of their crew, a shy man named Evan Laurel, before they were all shooting to orbit. Her dark fantasies had no time to properly germinate.

As they rode up the elevator, Rue stayed glued to the window, watching the people, then the streets, buildings, and towns, dwindle below. The world resolved itself as a giant sunlit disk with blackness beyond it, and they ascended the center of a well of light that descended from impossibly far above. Clouds drifted to the wall of this well, faded and vanished. Beside Rue, Blair was doing a report, describing the crew and their impending adventure. He seemed so serene and engaging when he talked, it both calmed and infuriated her. Did he not realize what they were getting themselves into?

They managed to avoid several ships' worth of other newshounds and made it to her modified cycler shuttle. She barely recognized it; Max had removed nearly everything made of metal, even the hull, replacing it all with lightweight alternatives. It was a testament to his fanaticism that what little metal had been in the shuttle before had been lightweight beryllium alloys; even that was too much for him in his determination to cut mass. The hull was now a balloon-skin coated with shipfur, pale against the black sky. Several windows gleamed in the short cylinder; that was all. Nearby, Max's second shuttle hung like a brooding cloud. That one held life-support stacks and supplies. It was all they could afford to bring—and the total mass of both shuttles was under sixty tonnes.

The shuttles had small nuclear power packs which doubled as maneuvering engines. They had no other drive source, but coiled around their waists were some kilometers of superconducting cable. Charged, they would spring out to form rigid magnetized rings attached to the ships by tethers: plasma sails, they were called. Rue knew the principle, but wouldn't get to see the famous acceleration aurora those wire sails would kick up; she would be asleep in a life-support tank when the million or so particle-beam accelerators orbiting Erythrion turned their baleful gazes on these two little ships and pushed them at three gravities' acceleration on their way. For a few weeks, a significant portion of Erythrion's immense magnetosphere would be tapped and transmuted into these beams and yet those tens of trillions of watts were barely sufficient to boost sixty tonnes up to relativistic velocity. Halo worlds like Erythrion had power to spare for their colonies, but couldn't afford to launch something so gigantic as an interstellar cycler. Only the lit worlds could muster that kind of energy, and the lit worlds had abandoned the halo. Since its colonization, Rue's world had maintained its tenuous contact with the rest of the universe only through cargo packets and the rendezvous shuttles that met passing cyclers. The cyclers were gone; only the occasional packet came and went. Hers would be the first passenger shuttle to rendezvous with a cycler in twenty years.

Beyond the halo, millions of FTL ships of the R.E. might be winging to and fro between the lit stars. Perhaps—but no one at Erythrion could know, except from the evidence that there was less contact with the lit worlds every year, as their economies shifted away from launching expensive cyclers. As existing cyclers were decommissioned, they were not being replaced. It was becoming impossible for humans to travel between the halo worlds. It was this fact that made *Jentry's Envy* priceless.

They cycled through the airlock; when the inner door opened, Rue said, "Shit," very quietly. She had been expecting the familiar, cozy interior of the shuttle—but the interior had been gutted.

"We've got everything we could possibly need," said Max, waving expansively. "Even a few kitchen sinks thrown in for thoroughness."

Corinna Chandra and Evan Laurel were the least known of Rue's new crew. She watched them as they settled in; they had similar appraising looks in their eyes as they went through the supplies, occasionally tossing questions back at Max. Rebecca had gone to put her luggage in her little stateroom; Blair drifted around, recording everything.

In cycler romances, the key figure was always the captain. The cycler captain was the prime mover of many stories; he or she was the epicenter of intrigue, the judge, jury, and executioner of villains. He was frequently a rogue, or a perfect gentleman—but the captain in his jet-black uniform was always in godlike control of events.

Rue supposed she was, or soon would be, such a captain. The idea was ludicrous. Still, here was her crew, all looking nervous in one way or another. She had intended to give a stirring speech to them before they all entered the cold sleep tanks. Now that they were here, though, her mouth was dry and she couldn't say a word, until Max came over and took her hand.

"It's real now, isn't it?" he asked. Rue nodded quickly.

The others gathered around. They looked expectant. Rue

cleared her throat. She knew they could see the fear in her eyes and the knowledge shamed her. Indeed, her motley crew did not look like a band of adventurers, but like a random group of citizens pulled out of their ordinary lives and condemned by unknown powers to senseless exile.

"I'm scared," she said. Corinna and Evan glanced at one another. "But I'm only scared because I haven't done this before," Rue continued quickly. "We're doing something that our people have been doing for centuries. We're going out to meet a cycler. Nothing unusual there. We don't know what we'll find when we get to it, but we're well supplied and ready for a long trip." She wracked her brains, trying to think of something inspiring to add. "I-I'm glad you've put your faith in me and Max and . . ." Her mind went blank.

Rebecca came and took Rue's hand. "Let's focus on one thing at a time," she said gently. "What's next?"

Rue tried to pull herself together. "Cold sleep," she said. "Let's get ready for it."

Her crew went to check on the cold-sleep tanks, all except Blair, who stayed by her side. Rue tried not to cry, but she was really, really scared, in a way she had never been on Allemagne. And she couldn't hide it from these people who now depended on her for their lives.

COLD SLEEP WAS not really sleep, but more like a long half-waking nightmare. Rue hadn't appreciated that before and nothing prepared her for the experience. She felt suspended in timelessness, comfortable and cocooned. Dreams came and went, some beautiful, some terrifying. Every now and then, a cold brittle voice she later realized belonged to the shuttle rattled off statistics. She would rise almost to waking, pondering those numbers until she realized that they represented the shuttle's status: acceleration, heading, integrity of the cold sleep capsules. When she knew all was well, she would drift away again.

Sometimes her body roused and she dimly knew she was flailing about, limbs under the control of a nervous system shunt. She was exercising. At other times she heard her own voice, croaking or singing aimlessly. It sounded like a stranger's voice.

There came a time when she really did sleep, then woke slowly to hear voices—real ones, this time, murmuring nearby. The feeling of huge weight that had pressed down on her for so long was gone. She had survived a month at three gravity's acceleration and they must now be approaching the *Envy*.

As this awareness dawned Rue struggled to sit up. It was surprisingly easy; she had expected stiff joints but everything seemed supple. Her eyes, though, wouldn't focus properly. A flesh-colored oval hovered in front of her. A familiar voice emerged from it. "Do you know who I am?"

"Re-Rebecca."

"Do you know where you are?"

Rebecca asked a few more questions, apparently satisfying herself that Rue was sane. Then she wrapped her captain in a blanket and towed her to the galley. "It'll take your eyes a few days to fully recover," she said as Rue groped for a coffee bulb she could dimly see floating in front of her. "You haven't used them for a month and the muscles have loosened up."

There was a gray bulk to Rue's left. She gradually realized it was Evan Laurel. He and Corinna had been roused before her, according to Rue's own instructions. Medical staff, engineering, and avionics first, that had been her decision. Blair and Max were being decanted now; all seemed well with them.

"Are we there?" Rue asked. After the health of the crew, it was the first and most important question on her mind.

The gray oval shook in a shrug. "Not sure," said Evan. "Corinna's checking now."

"I feel so . . ."

"Helpless, yes," said Evan. "It'll pass. I've done this a few times. It's always like this."

Another blob swam into sight, above and to her left. "Bad news," said Corinna.

Adrenaline had Rue instantly alert. "What?"

"The radar didn't make it through accel. We can grow new parts with the custom nano we brought, but it'll take weeks . . ."

"So we can't see where we are?"

"We've got the scopes," said Evan. "We'll manage. Right, Cor?"

"Yes," said Chandra in her usual neutral tone.

"Great," muttered Rue. As the adrenaline passed, she felt infinitely weary. She supposed that this weariness was on her now like a mantle; she was a captain, or at least had to pretend to be. The weariness was doubtless part of the job.

"We'll wait, then," she said. "When our eyes are up to it, we'll see where we are."

IT TOOK SEVERAL days before their eyesight came back. Evan stumbled around, his hair mussed, checking the stability of their life support and power. Every now and then he would glance out a window at the starry blackness and look longingly at the telescope. But the necessities of life had to be established before they could investigate where they were.

They huddled like invalids, growing stronger slowly; Blair was chatty as always and Rebecca efficient and kind, but Corinna maintained her aloof silence, Evan seemed perpetually nervous . . . and Max had sunk into himself. Rue was to learn that she had never before known him in his "normal" state—that is, surly and introspective. It was as though he had switched on some hyperactive part of himself in order to get them out here and once that was done he sank back into himself, reserves of charisma and genius exhausted. He hovered in a corner, blanket around his shoulders, playing Penrose Go with the computer. He seldom spoke.

Blair set about interviewing them on the third day and they perked up, all except Max. Blair started with Evan, sitting him in front of the window and chatting. The conversation became imperceptibly more focused and at a certain point Rue realized the interview had begun—but Evan himself either hadn't realized it, or was just very relaxed with the process. She smiled proudly at Blair's cleverness.

"I was born and raised in the Rights Economy," said Evan, "so I'd never been on anything like a cycler before I enlisted in the Cycler Order. A cycler's like a station, I guess, only moving. They're a lot like this shuttle, too. The first one I was on, the *Martine*, was pretty opulent, I guess—but small. There were fifty staterooms, a small garden, a banquet hall. It had several annexes which were separate balloon habitats floating next to it. One of those had a spherical swimming pool."

After several years with the *Martine* (amounting to three stops in its cycle) Evan had transferred to another cycler, the *Xao Li*, when for several months their circular but perpendicular cycles ran parallel.

"The *Xao Li* was amazing. It was an old cycler and I can see where you might get romantic ideas about them. Its main hab was in a bolo configuration—a crystal palace connected to a dead weight of supply sacks by a two-kilometer cable. The crystal palace was mostly one big garden, full of trees. Staterooms were under the garden, but you spent ninety percent of your time among the trees; some people even slept 'in the open.' They had artificial rain and a little sun; in the very middle of the garden you could almost imagine you were on Earth."

To be a brother of the Cycler Order was to adopt an uncommon religion, one that had as its ideal Permanence: the creation and maintenance of a human civilization that could last a million years. The Order was all about discipline and spiritual purification, requirements for people who trained to plan operations that lasted centuries.

"You have to understand, the Order was a lifesaver to somebody like me from High Space, where everything's disposable. And being a part of it had meaning while I was in flight. But I made the mistake of volunteering to accompany a cargo down to Erythrion. We got . . . stranded. I thought I was stuck in the halo forever. Things got bad; I left the Order . . . And then I heard about you and posted my résumé to the net on spec, thinking what the hey, they might be putting a crew together . . . and Max called me."

Corinna came next, but she was much less forthcoming than Evan. She had been an engineer, she said; her husband and children had died; after that she had entered the Order, to try to find some sense in life. Her voice was flat as she related these facts. A little animation entered her eyes when Blair asked her what she expected to find at *Jentry's Envy.*

"Another life," she said firmly. "A new life."

There was nothing more to be said after that. Blair thanked her and Rebecca took her place. Rue watched with satisfaction; Blair was distracting them from their isolation and uncertainty and bringing them together at the same time. This was great team-building.

"You come from the stations, like Rue," he said to Rebecca. "She's told us all about Allemagne. Did you grow up in a comet like her?"

"Next to one. No, actually my station was totally different from hers. For one thing, it had a population of almost a thousand; for another, we had trees and grass and stuff; the whole habitat was lit up by starlight."

"Starlight? You don't wear sunglasses all the time like Rue."

"No, this was concentrated starlight—gathered in a molecule-thick mirror the size of a continent. Bright as a sun. When you looked up at the axis mirror," she said, waving up at the plastic ceiling as if to indicate a window there, "you saw the Milky Way like a blazing bar across the sky. It was almost too intense to look at, but the overall effect was a soft, shadowless light, not like the harsh pinpoint they say you get at a place like Chandaka."

Rue thought about it and found the image utterly enchanting: a garden lit by the Milky Way.

"We mined gas straight from empty interstellar space, using some low-powered ramscoops." These giant wire wheels were invisibly far from Rebecca's home cylinder, but she described how the laborers at Terisia would clip themselves to a cable and leap out, flying thousands of kilometers into darkness to where the cable joined with a collecting tank, there to reap a harvest of hydrogen, helium, and other frozen elements.

"We made money by firing cans of frozen gas on trajectories that cyclers and other passing ships would intersect. We had a lot less raw material to work with than Allemagne, but Terisia's better placed, so we did good business."

One thing that Rue would always remember about Rebecca's home was her description of vacuum painting. It seemed that a talented vacuum painter lived at Terisia and every now and then he would unveil a new masterpiece. He used tiny drones carrying canisters of garbage material, such as argon, and these he would send back and forth and back and forth, drawing a complicated grid pattern in three dimensions in some far distant region of space. The volume would be huge, thousands of kilometers on a side; and in that volume his drones would deposit small frozen beads, one every kilometer or so.

After a few weeks the whole ensemble would drift between Terisia and its colossal mirror—and the little beads would vaporize, at different rates according to their sizes and composition.

"Then," Rebecca said, "we would all gather around and look at the sky mirror. The Milky Way would dissolve into something else—a beautiful face, maybe, or an animal like a horse. And it would *move*, because his little beads were vaporizing in sequence and diffracting the light from the mirror as they did it. For a while our little colony cylinder would be lit by the glow of dancing angels, or swarming bees, or the cloudy gates of heaven. It was the most gorgeous thing I ever saw, more gorgeous than anything I've seen since, even on Treya."

The interviews dissolved into an impromptu party. Max perked up a bit and they told each other stories and laughed until they were all exhausted and then they went to bed. Rue hung weightless in her sleeping bag listening to their various snores, thinking that they were her family now and, in a new cocoon of faintly heard breaths, she slipped into her best sleep in months.

The next day, everyone's eyes were pretty much back to normal and Evan eagerly turned to the telescope.

Rue hovered at the table, eating breakfast with Blair and Rebecca. They tried to ignore Evan, but all knew how much was riding on what he saw in the scope. Conversation started out jovial, but eventually trailed off as Evan hid behind the scope's inscape display for one hour, then another, making noncommittal grunts whenever anyone asked how things were going. Finally he said, "Damn," and kicked himself away from it to the real window. He hung there staring.

Rue flew over to him. "What is it?" she asked quietly.

"I can't find it," he said. "It's the damn scope—it's the wrong type."

"Explain.—Wait," she added as he opened his mouth, "everyone should hear."

Rue whistled, a sound she'd discovered would immediately bring people from the far corners of the shuttle. Max and Corinna appeared from their staterooms and sailed over.

"The scopes at Erythrion picked up several cargos attached to the plow sail," said Evan when they were all there. "I can't find them." He held up a hand as Corinna and Blair both started to speak. "Just because we can't see them right now doesn't mean we're not close. You installed the wrong kind of telescope," he said to Max.

Max huffed indignantly. "This scope's got ten times the power of the one she had before," he said. "I bought the top of the line."

"Top of the line for distance viewing," said Evan. "That's part of the problem." Beside him, Corinna rolled her eyes.

"How much of the sky is the scope looking at?" asked Rue.

Evan frowned. "At any given time? . . . half a degree." This wasn't the prospecting scope that had originally been installed and which had first seen *Jentry's Envy*. Max had upgraded it, something Rue had given no thought to at the time. A true prospecting scope could scan at least twenty degrees at a time.

"So the problem isn't that there's no cycler out there," said Rue. "The problem is, it might be right beside us, but we can't see it. Is that correct?"

"Yeah. That's right." Evan fidgeted as he talked, like he did constantly. It didn't fill Rue with confidence about anything he said.

"So what're we going to do?" Max asked.

Rue looked around, thinking. Despite yesterday's closeness, everybody's nerves were frayed, except perhaps Corinna's, as she didn't seem to have any.

Rue thought about it for a minute, then smiled as she realized what to do. "It's not a big problem. Back home, Jentry and the other boys used to take some of the mining bots out and play hide-and-seek with them around the comet. They wouldn't usually hide on the comet, because they'd be visible there. They'd just drift off into space and try to present as small a cross-section as possible. Jentry'd have to shine a light out and look for a reflection, or wait for an eclipse."

"Eclipse?" said Blair. "What do you mean?"

Rue jumped away from the table and rapelled her way

over to the airlock. "I'll show you," she said. They watched as she pulled her suit out of its locker.

"Ah," said Corinna, dead-pan. "I get it."

"Get what?" Evan seemed insulted. Rebecca had settled back, smiling secretively.

"Come on," said Rue. Evan didn't move. "Suit up! That's, uh, an order. We're going to find out where we are. Why don't you come too, Blair? You'll like this."

She waited as the two went through their suit checks, then cycled them through the airlock into a yawning abyss of stars.

"Gods and kami," said Blair. He backed up. "Gods and kami."

Rue was a bit surprised by his reaction. "Here, I'll clip a line to you," she said. Evan was a bit bolder, but he kept one hand on the edge of the airlock. Rue simply turned and stepped into the darkness.

It was just like the night at Allemagne, the billion angelic stars in their wreaths and coils. As soon as she was out here, in fact, Rue calmed right down. What had she been so worried about? This was just like home—only moving ten thousand times faster, a fact that the eye could not discern.

"It's beautiful," she said. "Look at it."

"Great Rue, now can I go back in?" said Blair.

"Okay, I want you guys to each pick a part of the sky and watch it," she said. "You don't have to leave the airlock—just look around."

"What are we looking for?" asked Blair. His breathing was shallow, but he seemed to have gotten control of himself. These guys were from planets, she reminded herself. They weren't used to being out in the real world.

"Just rest your eyes and watch," she said. "You're looking for a star to wink at you."

This was just basic prospecting technique, though usually done by automated full-sky telescopes. Rue hadn't realized when she let Max upgrade the scope that he would replace it with an instrument more suited to delving deeply in one narrow field of view. No wonder they couldn't see where they were.

Hanging in space and watching the stars was very calming. Soon, both Blair and Evan were into it; they began chatting in a more friendly way than they had to date. Rue looked for familiar constellations—they weren't that far from Erythrion yet—and then just let her eyes rest on the scene. Waiting for one of those billion stars to blink. The problem was, the eye played tricks. Things on her peripheral vision were constantly shifting. There were lots of false alarms over the next hour.

At last Evan said, "I think . . . I think I see it."

"Where?"

He pointed. "Four or five stars have disappeared over there."

"What's the constellation?"

"The Horologium."

"Okay. Corinna? Did you hear that? Aim the scope at the Pendulum Clock."

Ten minutes later, they had a confirmation: something was occluding the stars of the Horologium, in a line that paralleled their own course. When Corinna broke the news, they all cheered and Rue allowed herself a little grin of satisfaction. She had not let them down.

"NOW THAT WE know where to look, it should get easier," said Evan. "We can aim spotlights at the Horologium and see how many habitats we're dealing with."

"What do you mean?" asked Blair. "We found the ship, didn't we?"

"Yes and no." Evan summoned the telescope window and began adjusting controls. "Most cyclers are built as constellations; you never keep all your life support in one basket, so to speak. If a cycler habitat hits a rock going at point-eight lightspeed, the whole thing'll vaporize. The plow sail takes care of gas and small particles, but there's no way to avoid anything big. So we distribute the living quarters and cargo among several independent habitats and separate them by up to thousands of kilometers. We use jumpers to travel between them. So if I'm right," he said as he made a final adjustment, "the spot should find at least one more object out there."

Everyone gathered around and watched. The spotlight was programmed to track lines across the sky like an old-style cathode-ray tube. It had only been on for a few seconds before there was a pinprick flash of light in the window. "Got one!" shouted Evan. He reversed the spot and increased the magnification. And there it was.

Rue had studied cycler designs in the days leading up to their departure. What she saw looked a bit like Allemagne and didn't surprise her; a sphere was the best shape for retaining heat, an important consideration in interstellar space. Still, she felt her heart leap as she saw a silvery ball swim into focus, framed in stars.

"It's real," she whispered. All this time, she had been afraid to believe it.

"I'm fixing the distance," said Evan. "Then we'll move on to the next one. . . . Sixty thousand kilometers. We're practically on top of it!"

The sphere disappeared as the spotlight moved on. Another sphere appeared, then a rusty cylindrical shape. "There's no lettering," said Corinna. "Or painting. Cyclers are often covered in murals," she explained. "These habitats are plain."

"It's new?" speculated Evan. "Look, there's another! How many habitats are there?"

They counted eight more. Then, the spotlight found something odd—a dim red glow. "Magnify that," said Corinna. Evan fiddled with the controls. Some blurry red lines filled the window, faded in and out and resolved into . . .

"Words. There's something written on that one."

The sphere itself was black, but scrawled across it was spikey lettering utterly unfamiliar to Rue. There were about a hundred words, she guessed, in a discrete paragraph. No way to tell how big the letters were, although the scope indicated the object they were written on was thirty thousand kilometers away.

"Do a capture and run it through the computer," said Corinna. "I don't recognize the language."

They waited while Evan did as she'd suggested. After a while he looked up. His face had gone pale.

"The computer doesn't recognize it either," he said.

"Strange," said Max.

"More than strange." Evan took a shaky breath. "The computer knows every human script in the halo or High Space. This isn't any of them; it's not even *derived* from any of them."

"What are you saying?"

"All I'm saying," said Evan, "is that this isn't a known human language."

That wasn't all Evan was saying and they all knew it.

"Gods and Kami," breathed Corinna. "It's an alien ship."

THEY'D ARGUED BACK and forth all day, while Evan exercised the scope and mapped out the dozen visible habitats of *Jentry's Envy*. Now, exhausted, they retreated to their staterooms. Rue and Max were in his; he was drinking, as usual.

"We should have guessed," she said. "It came from an area of space we haven't colonized."

He shrugged angrily. "I still don't believe it. All the aliens we've heard about use the FTL drive. There's no such thing as an alien cycler."

"But it's there, Max. You saw it."

"I saw something. I don't know what."

"So what are we going to do? We can't go home," she said. "We'll have to try to make contact."

Max put the heel of his hand to his forehead. "No. We're

just not in a position to do that. We've got no defenses, no recourse—"

"Max, we have no *choice*!"

He glared at her. "Do you know anything at all about how to do a first contact? I know I don't. No, Rue, we're totally out of our depth here. I still say we lay low, don't approach and just ride until we get to Chandaka. If they come to us, well then, there's nothing we can do about that. But we can't go out to them. It'd be suicide."

She turned away. There was no discussing this any further today. She would have to wear Max down—or else finally act like a cycler captain and just command it to be done. Rue wasn't ready for that yet.

"What have we gotten ourselves into," she murmured. Rue's gaze fell on the public inscape images Max had arranged on his wall. These were the same photos he'd had at home—family and friends, mostly, plus a few landscapes of Treya.

They all looked so homey and sensible; how could they be light-months behind, inaccessible now for years? Rue rubbed her eyes, fighting weariness and fear.

She looked up—and her grandmother looked back at her from one of the photos.

"Max, are these of the family? Hey, there's my mom!"

"Yeah, I brought everything in my data accounts. . . . I've got more pictures, if you want to see them; I guess we've been too busy, I should have shown them to you."

"Oh, that's okay, I . . ." Rue peered more closely at the photo. "What's that?"

"What?" Max joined her. She pointed to the little dot on the throat of the woman standing next to grandma.

"Ah, the famous lost heirloom. There's quite a story to that," said Max distractedly.

Rue felt a flush spread from her toes up through her scalp. "Heirloom?"

"Yeah. An ancient fossil—from Earth, no less. Worth millions. It was brought out on the first cycler by your great-great-grandfather. Mother expected to inherit it, but when your grandmother disappeared she took it with her. Nobody knows what became of it."

"Oh." Rue had never told Max that Grandma had lived with them on Allemagne, simply because they hadn't had a chance to really talk about family. Neither had she told Aunt Leda, out of suspicion. Her omissions had been well-chosen, she thought wonderingly.

"This heirloom. It was worth a lot?"

"Priceless, really. Mother was always going on about it, that if only she'd gotten it like she was supposed to, she could have been the lady she was destined to be. Not like she isn't well off anyway, but that's my dear old ma, never satisfied."

"Hm. Interesting. 'Scuse me, I have to go to the bathroom." Rue sailed away, not too quickly she hoped, and when she was safely inside the shuttle's tiny bathroom, she strapped herself onto the toilet and started to shake.

Then she got up and went to her own stateroom and dug through her pack. There it was, the little brown-black disk with its embossed galaxy-shape. The delicate little Ediacaran, who really had journeyed through a billion years of adventure to nestle now in her hand.

Rue began to laugh. Oh no, it would not do to tell Max that this whole trip had been unnecessary, that she had been rich all along and not known it. Still, she looped the heirloom around her neck and let it nestle out of sight inside her blouse. Then she wiped her eyes, coughed past the lump in her throat and flew back to Max's room. She had to tell him that, fearful though he might be, they could not hide here, but tomorrow would announce themselves to whatever waited at *Jentry's Envy*.

PART TWO

Household Gods

7

MICHAEL BEQUITH SORTED through a cloud of public in-scape windows his employer had left open and floating over his bed. Usually Michael's eyes and hands were on his task—everything he did was done with meticulous perfection. Today, his hands went about their task, closing, nesting, and arranging insubstantial windows with the usual precision. His mind was elsewhere.

Dr. Herat's room was bigger than Michael's, but that was not saying much. Laurent Herat, Ph.D., had inhabited a metal cell four by five meters in dimension for the last three months. Michael's room was three by four. There was no decoration in these living quarters, beyond a failed attempt at wood panelling on some of the walls. The lights were harsh, the air recycled and flat and there were no physical windows because they were twenty meters underground.

Twice a day the walls shook with the force of a tidal bore thundering overhead. Dr. Herat was always in the control room during the tides, so Michael had taken that as the best time to tidy up after the professor. The rest of the day was his own, for there was precious little he could do for Herat in a research station as minimalistic as this one. He struggled with the vagaries of interstellar e-mail, trying to keep up with the academic debates raging back home, but his summaries for Herat were meager these days. They both knew where the discussion was going to leave *them*, anyway.

He finished arranging the windows and looked around for any other untidiness. Dr. Herat always left a half-glass of wine on the bedside table from last night. It was his habit to sip that while reading his mail and jotting notes on the day's research. Today the glass was there, but it was still full.

That was odd. Dr. Herat was in a glum mood lately; Michael had read the exobiologist's last report and knew it was doomed to explode like a bombshell back home. It was, in fact, an attack on the whole endeavor that had sent Herat and his research assistant to this and dozens of other worlds. It called into question the grant expenditures of a hundred top scientists. The first casualty of the grant application process was truth; Herat was going to be pilloried and he knew it.

Maybe he was just tired. Dr. Herat wasn't as young as he'd been when Michael first sought out his patronage. (Neither was Michael, but that sort of consideration never entered his mind.) Herat usually worked fourteen-hour days and slept only five hours. He had been operating on this schedule, machinelike, for ten years now. Small wonder that he should finally start nodding off before reading his mail.

Michael took the wine and dumped it in the metal sink. Then he took one last look around and left the room.

On other worlds he would have had a full day ahead of him. There was much organization to be done, sometimes behind Dr. Herat's back. Michael knew the supply clerks on thirty stations and understood the vices and habits of a dozen starship pursers. He could usually anticipate Herat's need for equipment or supplies and more than once he'd acquired pieces of equipment from half-legal sources that no amount of pleading with the Panspermia Institute had been able to produce. Dr. Herat proclaimed Michael's talents uncanny, but it was merely that he spent all his time learning the human side of bureaucracy and working it to their advantage.

Kadesh was not their usual research destination. Herat had a great reputation and several times in the past had been called in to examine priceless relics of ancient extinct civilizations. On those occasions the skies of the "dig" planet had swarmed with ships—news media, other researchers, guard ships, the yachts of the rich. There were no ruins on Kadesh; there was no swarm of ships, only the supply ship in orbit and this lone station buried under the tidal flats of a northern continent.

The tides were such that Michael couldn't even go out for a walk if he wanted to.

By his watch it was about fifteen minutes until the next bore. He stood in the narrow hallway for a bit, debating where to go. Finally boredom drove him back to his own room.

He sat on the bed and studied the walls. It was good to be leaving this place, even if they didn't know where they would go next. It might be time for Herat to resume his long-neglected teaching practise on Noctis Regina. Certainly Herat needed to do some hard thinking about his future. For the first time in five years, Michael knew he needed to do the same.

A chime sounded in his mind: an inscape call. "Dr. Bequith! Please call up."

He stood, relieved that he was wanted. "Bequith here," he said.

"Get your ass up here now, man, your boss is still out on the flats and the bore's coming in!"

For a second he just stared at the bed; then Michael was out the door and running.

The station was shaped like a can, buried on end. He raced up the zigzagging stairs from the living quarters, through the exercise level and the galley level and to the control room in record time. The research associates were crowding around a screen there, babbling and pointing.

"Where is he?" Michael demanded of Hart, a young and insolent RA who usually haunted the control room because nobody tolerated him anywhere else. Hart's face was twisted in a sneer.

"He's wading," said Hart. "Won't come back in. Says he wants to watch the bore."

"We've all done it," said Meline, a planetologist Herat had worked with before. "But you don't go down to the shoreline! You stand at the top of the ladder. That way you can slam the hatch before it gets too close." Her voice slightly emphasized the word *it*.

"All right," said Michael. "I'll fetch him in." He clattered up the next flight of steps, to the suit room. It took two precious minutes to get into his quarantine suit, then another to walk through the scouring jets that removed all trace of Earthly microbial life from the suit's surface. He paced clumsily to the airlock and when it finally released him into the bottom of the ladder well he wondered if he was too late. The bore would arrive any minute now.

He pulled himself out of the well into Kadesh's sunshine.

Kadesh's one moon was much bigger and closer to the planet than Earth's Luna. The tides here were orders of magnitude higher; there were few coastal areas that had not been pounded into gentle inclines by millions of years' worth of tsunamis. Here at the shoreline of the largest continent, Michael could have waded two kilometers out to sea before the water came above his waist. The flat vista was deceptively calm, the air blue with towering pillow clouds.

Any second now a wall of water three hundred meters high would come racing over the horizon, carrying with it a froth of boulders as big as houses. Michael had seen it on video; it was over almost before your eye told you what it was.

The scientist was hunkered down in the very shallows, a gloved hand swishing in the water.

Michael jumped as horns sounded from behind him. The sound was urgent, the kind that might have heralded an attack from the air in centuries past. "Doctor Herat?" Michael's voice sounded loud in his own earphone, but somehow he couldn't bring himself to voice the urgency he felt. It would violate the pact of propriety he and the doctor shared. "You'd better get in here, sir. Tide's almost on us."

"I know." Dr. Herat sounded tired. He stood up slowly (reluctantly?) and began walking along the shoreline. He was a tall, rangy man, his angular frame somewhat softened by the quarantine suit. He didn't look at Michael, but continued to gaze out at the regular pattern of rounded shapes half-visible beneath the waves.

It looked from here like gray diamond-shaped bricks, each about forty centimeters across, paved the coastal floor for many kilometers. Long tongues of the same substance reached up the sandy shore. Herat's team had been observing them for weeks and they had seen the transformation that was about to take place, but only on-screen.

Michael watched him warily. Dr. Herat *was* coming back, but slowly. Maybe he just wanted to see the transformation with his own eyes.

Dr. Herat walked up the low rise that led to the bunker and paused when he was close enough to dash to the entrance, but far enough away that he had a good view of the shore. Then he sat down on a rounded boulder.

Michael loped down to stand over him. "Sir! What are you doing? It's almost on us!"

"We can make it in time from here," drawled Herat. "I just want to see it come in."

This was so totally out of character that Michael found he had nothing to say. There was a brief silence, as they both stared out over the ocean.

Michael forgot the tidal threat momentarily as he saw the well-ordered tile pattern beneath the water swirl and change. In the space of a few seconds a tumult of activity rolled in from the deeper sea; some of the "bricks" retracted into the sand, while others rose. The pattern was different every time, but it always involved long walls and trenches whose exact spacing and orientation was determined by the strength and velocity of the incoming tidal bore.

Dr. Herat sighed. "We know *what* is happening out there, and we know why; but we haven't got a clue *how*."

He squinted up at Michael. "I never really believed it before, but you know, Michael, I don't think we'll ever fully understand that."

He turned back to the strange vista. "But it is beautiful," he said quietly.

Outside the narrow frame of the video, the full sight was astonishing. The entire ocean floor had come to resemble an Oriental carpet, its detailing done in raised or lowered shells. The photosynthesizing creatures known as Kadists—neither animal nor plant—that grew these armored domes had acted as one entity over an area of many kilometers. What's more, they had crafted a diffraction grating out of their own bodies. The tidal bore would hit this and shake itself to pieces because of the resonances it set up. Nutrients that would otherwise have been carried many kilometers inland to be deposited on the lifeless deserts of the continent, would instead fall straight down to nurture the living plain that had stopped the tidal wave.

Something glinted in the distance. "Doctor! Now!" Michael took Herat's arm as a white line appeared on the horizon. It thickened by the second. So far, there was no sound.

Herat looked up, sighed and levered himself to his feet.

Michael took his arm and they ran for the bunker's hatch. It was farther away than he'd estimated. As Michael ran the last ten meters he could hear a rising roar behind him. Still, he did his duty and made sure Dr. Herat was first down the hatch. Michael himself didn't look back until he had his hands on the ladder.

A cliff of white water rose above him. Deep inside it emeralds shone.

He ducked down and slammed the round hatch. The next instant, the hatch was hit by something massive. Michael nearly fell down the ladder. Dr. Herat was waiting for him at the bottom.

"That was idiotic, sir. What were you thinking?"

"I knew what I was doing." Dr. Herat, who seldom

smiled lately, was grinning like a fool. Michael glowered at his employer, but he was too puzzled right now to say more.

Above and around them a deep vibration rattled the fixtures. Still smiling, Dr. Herat put his hand on the wall. They could always feel the strength of the tidal bore through the metal of the station.

"It's got a rhythm to it," said the scientist, "an almost musical one. The AI can't figure out how the Kadists know what patterns to craft: those gray lumps have a better mental model of local conditions than we do."

"Sir, why did you stay so long?"

"I thought . . . maybe we've been missing the essential experience by just not being out there. We hide in our holes and poke our instruments out and then we try to imagine what it's like for them." Herat shook his head as he walked to the decontagion chamber. "We're not learning anything."

"This isn't about the Kadists, is it," said Michael to his retreating back. "It's about your report to the High Commission."

Herat didn't answer, but his pace faltered for a second as if he were about to turn and say something. He kept going into the bleach shower, where further conversation became impossible.

By the time they met in the station's observation lounge, Meline, Harp, and the others were well into their analysis of the latest bore. The station was now drowned under several hundred meters of ocean and, outside, the Kadists would be sifting through the flotsam that had settled on them. When the tide went out, they would funnel the excess mud and stones into the deep sea again.

"Welcome to the Topside Club," Hart said to Dr. Herat with a grin. "And you even managed to get Bequith to join you." He smirked at Michael, who simply crossed his arms and watched Herat.

Dr. Herat was looking very tired. He didn't return Hart's smile, but spoke to Meline. "Any word on the supply ship?"

"It's in orbit," she said. "But it's got company—a military cruiser."

Dr. Herat sent Michael a puzzled look. He shrugged in reply; this was the first he'd heard of it. "That's funny," said Herat. "Um, any reply to my report?"

"Not yet."

"Okay." Dr. Herat stretched and nodded at Michael. "Let me know when the lightning bolt hits. Meanwhile I'll be in my quarters."

Michael nodded. "I'm sure they'll see the logic of your argument, sir."

"I'm equally sure they won't. Would you care to bet on it?"

Michael shrugged. "I only bet when it's my idea."

"You're a wiser man than I, Bequith."

Michael couldn't summon a pithy reply in time, as Dr. Herat walked away. He'd never heard Herat talk like this. But then, this wasn't the first time the professor had surprised him.

Alongside the professor, Michael had walked the ruined streets of ancient races who travelled the stars before the dinosaurs died; had floated in deep space outside the wrecks of ancient star ships whose shattered sides glittered mirror-new in starlight. He had taken mining elevators through a kilometer of stone to look at the fossilized remains of an alien nuclear reactor. Michael was shocked with awe at each new discovery. He was inspired; the NeoShinto implants in his cerebrum made it easy for him to find the *kami* of each place they visited. The monks of Kimpurusha, who had sent Michael with Dr. Herat, believed that humanity could perceive the Divine only in the familiar environment in which the species had evolved. In deep space, surrounded by machinery and on worlds whose scale and physical laws were literally inhuman, the human heart quailed. Human spirits shriveled. In order to survive, the NeoShintoists believed, humans had to learn to find the Divine in each new place and the Divine presented itself in endlessly different ways.

In the dying days of their Order, Michael Bequith was a message they had cast into the ocean, hoping their teachings would live on through him.

For years, it had worked. Michael sent his encoded kami templates out to the galactic data net, using the best and most current tricks to maintain his anonymity. He heard that thousands if not millions of people were aware of his work and that it was a great comfort to them.

Then Dr. Herat's investigations turned to much more alien species and more terrifying places and Michael's courage began to falter.

Today he just felt restless. Apart from the gym or the galley there was only one other place to go in the station and that was back to his room. As he walked he wondered about Laurent Herat's state of mind.

Inside his room Michael flopped down on the bed and frowned at the gray ceiling. His own mood had been black lately, although for reasons other than Dr. Herat's. Herat had his faith in science and that was unshakable, even if it led him to conclusions that broke his heart. Up until a very short time ago, Michael would have said that he had a similar faith. But then they had visited one world too many and on Dis, he had finally run into the limits of his own beliefs.

He sat up and faced the little table in the corner, where he had placed a curved, half-broken piece of basaltic rock taken from the shoreline. This was a symbol of the kami of this world, chosen by Michael in consultation with the NeoShinto AI implanted in his skull. He and the AI had found this stone on the third day of his visit and at that time he had tried and failed to derive a mystical experience from it; he had not tried since. Now he drew the room's one chair next to the table and sat down to contemplate the stone again.

He placed his hand on the stone and closed his eyes,

conjuring in memory the sight of the tidal bore coming in. He tried to recover every sense from that moment and wished again that he could have smelled the breeze and felt the cold air on his own skin. Because no one could go outside without a quarantine suit, touching this sterilized piece of basalt was as close as he would ever get to contacting the kami of Kadesh itself.

Still, touching the stone should awaken the proper reverence in him. He remembered the awe that he'd felt, seeing that wall of water rolling toward him. And he remembered the depth of it—the emeralds.

Emeralds . . . He called up the mental discipline of NeoShinto contemplation, let go of verbal thought and tried to become pure awareness.

The AI took over smoothly; no need for the constant discipline of meditation here. Michael felt his consciousness expand to fill the stone. He heard a sound like the tide, only deeper—the music of the Kadists, perhaps. He let it carry him away.

For a few moments he felt a reverberating awe, as if he were in the presence of some mighty being. He waited for the sensation to translate into something more, but it didn't happen. Missing was the sense of understanding. Also missing, the feeling of acceptance. Most of all, where was the sense of kinship-with-place that he had always been able to find before?

He stared at the stone, straining, for several long minutes. Then he shook his head, let the AI fall dormant again and flopped back on the cot. Rather than feeling elevated, it seemed he could feel the weight of Kadesh's ocean settling onto his shoulders.

He lay there with an arm flung over his face, thinking about the worlds he had seen and whose kami he had captured. Few people would ever have the luck to visit as many exotic places as he had in his service to Herat. After all, Herat was one of the vanguard of the Panspermia Institute—one of the select few who spent their careers in the field trying to identify and contact new intelligent species.

Michael remembered multiple star systems, worlds with suns scattered like diamonds across the sky; cold Galilean planets where they drilled hundreds of kilometers into the ice to find hidden oceans; he had walked in the ruined cities of a dozen extinct starfaring species. Everywhere, he had been able to find the spark of the Divine, hidden though it might be. Dr. Herat left these worlds with a greater understanding of humanity's relation to other species; Michael Bequith left each knowing what kind of religious observations would permit someone's spirit to thrive in that place, or alongside that species.

And then he and Dr. Herat had come to Dis and found things that whispered doubt into both their souls—so that now, Dr. Herat no longer believed in the ideals of Panspermia and Michael could no longer summon the kami of the worlds they visited.

He sat up and entered full lotus position. The hollow echo of Dis was sounding in his mind; he had to clear his consciousness, or he might fall into despair again. Just as he was beginning to gain control of his thoughts, an inscape daemon chimed.

"There's a message from the cruiser for Dr. Herat," said Meline; she was one of the few on this remote station who regularly remembered to notify Michael first about things. Michael's role was mysterious to these technicians, who mostly came from the oldest worlds of the Rights Economy and viewed the idea of service without remuneration as silly, if not criminal.

"Thanks, Meline. Route it to me and I'll let him know."

He opened his eyes—inscape would not write its images across his sensorium with them closed. The inscape window looked into some lounge aboard a starship; the only way to tell that this was a military craft and not a luxury liner was the row of high-gee couches along the wall and the uniform of the man who faced Michael now.

"Dr. Laurent Herat. This is Rear Admiral Crisler, you may remember me from my days at the Institute. You're being temporarily relieved of your appointment here, sir. I'm authorized to take you to a new assignment. If you'd join us aboard the *Spirit of Luna*, we'll debrief you at twenty-hundred hours." The window blinked out of existence, revealing the stateroom's gray wall.

So, it's happened. He sat up and looked around his tiny room glumly. It was early afternoon; they had a few hours to pack and say their good-byes.

Dr. Herat should never have written that report.

Michael could have called him through inscape and simply forwarded the message, but that wasn't polite. He went and rapped on the scientist's door instead.

We have spent trillions on the search for our equals in the galaxy, Herat had written. *What we have found has caused us to change our tactics, our goals and ultimately our ideals. The search as it is now proceeding is on its last legs. We must accept that and understand why.*

Herat opened the door. "Yes?"

"The cruiser has signaled us. They want us aboard for a debriefing tonight."

"Ah. I see. Forward me the message, will you?" Dr. Herat turned back inside, leaving the door open. He had been packing, Michael saw.

Michael concentrated for a second and saw Herat purse his lips as the message arrived.

Over the past four decades we strove to find other starfaring intelligent species with whom we could communicate. Our goal was the creation of a galaxy-wide, multispecies civilization, because we knew other species were out there and we had the evidence of past galactic-wide civilizations to inspire us.

"You knew the cruiser had come for us?" Michael asked. Usually it was he who arranged transportation and who knew the starship routes and schedules. Michael knew nothing of the military, but Dr. Herat had his connections.

Herat shrugged. "Nobody else on this planet is worth the effort. Although . . . I knew Crisler slightly, he used to be a scientist, back in the innocent old days. Now he's a rear admiral? Still doesn't explain why they sent him in particular. I wouldn't think I'd merit more than your average captain."

Michael hadn't thought of that. "Maybe they were the closest ship?"

"That could be. Help me with this stuff, would you? You always could pack better than me."

Our well-funded and highly public search for our equals has turned up none. We have found some intelligent alien species, even a few that travel between the stars. We have not found a single race that shares our ideals, or even comprehends them.

"You know, I can't in all honesty say I'm sorry it's ending like this," said Dr. Herat later as they piled their few belongings in a transit capsule at the bottom of the freight elevator. A few of the staff were fluttering around, upset at the suddenness of their departure. Herat was generally well liked.

"How can you say that?" asked Meline. She stood with her arms crossed, scowling at the doctor.

"It's better go out with a bang than a whimper," said Herat. "We've been reduced to studying lumps of gray rock on tidal flats—have you thought about where it goes from here?"

They had made their inscape public, as was polite, and now Michael saw Dr. Herat summon a clock, which hung in the air above them like some ancient ghost, translucent and dire. "Ten minutes until the tide goes out," said Herat. "I'm going to miss the sound of it."

Michael summoned a video image of topside events. The water above was choppy and low; scintillations of sunlight could be seen through it. He made the image public and placed it near the clock.

The dream of Panspermia goes back to Teilhard de Chardin and his vision of ever-increasing sentience in the

universe. We were brought up on this faith without even re-
alizing it. The many assumptions behind it only became
apparent when we began searching for a real counterpart
to the vision. Then we learned the truth.

Finally the waters parted, revealing late-afternoon sunlight and a few clouds. They said their good-byes and entered the egg-shaped transit capsule. The door slammed
and Michael and Dr. Herat sat looking at one another in
pensive silence.

The truth is that we are intelligent animals, but ani-
mals just the same, subject to the inescapable laws of our
evolution. Our first theories about alien intelligence were
providential: *we believed with Teilhard de Chardin that*
consciousness is a basic characteristic of complex thinking
entities. When we developed the FTL drive, we burst into
the galaxy in search of beings more "evolved" than our-
selves, in the belief that a universal Reason would unite us
with other species at the same level.

What we found instead was that even though a species
might remain starfaring for millions of years, conscious-
ness does not seem to be required for toolmaking. In fact,
consciousness appears to be a phase. No species we have
studied has retained what we would call self-awareness for
its entire history. Certainly none has evolved into some
state above *consciousness.*

The Panspermia Institute was formed out of the disap-
pointment of this discovery. We sought to uncover the con-
ditions that give rise to sentience; if we could not find
aliens like ourselves, perhaps we could guide candidate
species into our mode of experience.

With the faintest shudder, the platform began to rise.
The darkness of the station fell below and sunlight stabbed
through the capsule's window. Michael and Dr. Herat
leaned over as one to look at the shoreline of Kadesh one
last time. It was beautiful under the sunlight; you wanted
to run into the water every time you saw it. Michael could
make out the faint checkerboard pattern of the Kadists un-

der the water. They were just as mysterious now as when he and the professor had arrived.

A shadow flitted overhead, then the capsule rang as something took hold of it. They were lifted gently and silently skyward by Kadesh's only skyhook, which normally reeled itself back to avoid the churning water when it passed over this spot. In seconds they had climbed above the lowest clouds.

Studies on hundreds of worlds have turned up no pattern to the development of sentient life. The idea that Nature somehow instructs or guides species into sentience in a repeatable way also appears to be wrong. There is no discernible policy for the Institute to be gleaned from the evidence of past civilizations. We can neither predict the rise of sentience in a species, nor predict its ultimate course, not even in our own.

We are left with a selectionist *theory of sentience: consciousness and space-faring toolmaking ability, arise by chance from countless combinations of traits that in the vast majority of cases fail to produce results. Our studies have turned up thousands of species that "might have been" like ourselves. One, for instance, has all our traits, except that it lacks a tolerance for remaining stationary for long. Its people roam across the plains of their world, incapable of creating tools larger than they can carry.*

Countless other species are similarly close, but also miss the mark, some for want of a single trait. Records from extinct starfaring races show that some of our forerunners tried to genetically engineer such candidate species, to no avail: Even a single genetic alteration cascades unpredictable changes throughout culture, language and thought. Only brutal trial-and-error produces results. That, we do not have the moral courage to attempt.

So we are alone. The existing starfaring species of the galaxy are not able to be our companions. We cannot find nor create a companion species. Indeed, the only way we could create a pangalactic civilization would be to exter-

*minate or enslave all potential competition, as the Chicxu-
lub did.*

MICHAEL HAD LEFT behind many worlds in his travels
with Dr. Herat, but as they rose above Kadesh he was reminded of his very first leave-taking, the day he left Kimpurusha and his family. That time, he had sat and stared out
the porthole as white cloud swallowed the city of Manifest
and then even the stark mountains that rose above it; he
had watched as the horizon became a curve and the whole
vast glacial plain of the northern hemisphere came into
view. He remembered being astonished at the beautiful and
subtle colors that played along the planet's terminator. His
life was about to change forever, yet he felt confident and
not alone, because he had embarked on this journey as a religious pilgrimage. He was taking Kimpurusha with him;
how could he be lonely?

It was hard to believe that was only five years ago.
"We've seen a lot of worlds," he said as both he and the
professor leaned back again.

"Yes." Dr. Herat looked older than ever. "It's a rare priv-
ilege. I'm glad . . . I'm glad you're the kind of man who
appreciates nature, Dr. Bequith."

Compliments from Dr. Herat were rare. Michael smiled.
"Thank you, sir."

"I've never felt that you would be reluctant to accompany me on any of these jaunts," Herat went on. "Though
some of them have been . . . well, insane."

Michael grinned. "Like Ember?"

Herat laughed. Ember was a fast-eroding planet recently
swallowed by its red giant sun. Its surface was immersed in
faintly glowing red fog, a single giant flame; the human
settlers had dug their cities deep into the rock and there
they claimed to have found artifacts of alien origin, fossilized in the limestone. Herat and Michael had joined a
party of archaeologists on the surface, living in thick-
walled refrigerant tanks, venturing out only by proxy using

telepresence robots. Ember had strained their normally serene relationship almost to the breaking point.

"Very different from Kimpurusha," said Herat. "You've seen fire and ice, now. Something to tell your grandchildren about."

Michael nodded. "Have you heard from yours lately, sir?"

"Yes, I was meaning to tell you. Mina is buying a house! Can you believe it? She's almost thirty years old now. Still single, like you." They shared a grin; it was an old ploy of Herat's to try to marry Michael off to his granddaughter. "And Jackson's completed his second tour for the service. They're actually talking about an expedition to the galactic center, can you believe it?"

Dr. Herat sighed, looking, if possible, somewhat bewildered. Outside the blue of the sky had turned to black. The skyhook would release them soon on a trajectory to intercept the *Spirit of Luna*. That point of release—when they were briefly weightless—would be the moment when Michael felt he had really left Kadesh.

They talked a bit more about Dr. Herat's family, but when weightlessness came they both fell silent. This was it; the long journey from Kimpurusha might be over today. Dr. Herat had insulted his colleagues by exposing the truth they'd sought to hide for years. He was sure to pay for it. This summons away from an active research project could only mean one thing: dismissal or downgrading in the Service. Oh, Herat would never be disgraced and he would never want for work. In all likelihood, though, their next stop would be Noctis Regina, Herat's homeworld. He had a mansion and a tenured position waiting for him there and if Michael remained in his employ he would likely be housebound, with no opportunity to use his talents for discovering and capturing kami.

Michael had always felt that when the time came for them to part, it would be because Michael was being arrested because his religious activities had been found out; or because Herat was done wandering and Michael had found another way to seek out the spirits of the stars. Never had he imagined that he might lose his own faith and have nowhere to go himself once Herat retired.

The mirrored sphere of the *Spirit of Luna* appeared and minutes later they were pulled inside it. Gravity returned abruptly and shortly thereafter the hatch undogged itself.

The capsule stood alone in a gigantic hangar. Several uniformed men approached from the far end; one saluted. "Dr. Herat, welcome. I'm Chief Petty Officer McNeill. Here, let me take those bags, sir. We'll just run them through the scanner for you."

Michael had handed over the bags before he realized that his black market kami storage unit was in one of them. It was too late to do anything; he would just have to hope they didn't find it.

"Admiral Crisler is waiting to see you. You can visit your quarters to freshen up if you'd like . . . ?"

Herat waved away the offer. "No, I'm fine. Here, my man can take care of my things. He'll get me settled."

"Good. If you'll come with me?" McNeill and Herat walked away, leaving Michael with several enlisted men. This was their usual pattern; the professor would do the high-level negotiating and Michael would become invisibly part of the local culture. Except in this case there was no way to fit in; he was a civilian.

One of the men ran a wand over the luggage and whistled. "Lookee here, guys. A Mark 820."

That was the offline datapack for the Shintoist AI. Michael folded his arms and watched as they zipped it out of its pocket.

"Uncle of mine had one of these," said the soldier. He hefted it and squinted at Michael. "You realize that neurasthenic storage devices are illegal, sir?"

"Yes, I do."

"Where you from?"

"Kimpurusha."

"Ah, well." Kimpurushans were reputed to be eccentric; Michael found this prejudice sometimes let him get away with things others couldn't.

"Well, I'm going to have to confiscate this, sir. Now normally I would write a report specifying exactly what it is, before we put it in storage." The soldier grinned at his friends. "If we say it's a religious AI you'll never get it back. But I could just as easily mark it down as a porno unit, which are only prohibited on military ships. Then you'd get it back on the way out."

"I see." Michael knew this game. "What would motivate you to do that?"

"Well, you see, we have absolutely no idea where in the *hell* we are, or where in *hell* this ship is going. This is unusual . . ." From their expressions Michael saw that it must be pretty much unheard of.

"You tell us what this sneaking is all about and I'll make sure you get this baby back safe and sound whenever we get to where ever the hell it is we're going."

Michael hesitated. These soldiers looked uneasy; was there combat happening somewhere?

"We've been out of touch," he said after a moment. "Is everything all right, back home?"

"Rebel attack on Kavya," said another of the soldiers. "The fleet's headed there."

"But we're not," said the first. "Instead we come three thousand light-years out of our way to pick up a scientist, under blackout no less. So what's it all about?"

Michael shook his head. "I . . . I have no idea," he said. "We thought . . . we thought Dr. Herat was being retired."

"Well then," said the soldier with exaggerated patience, "can you tell us what it is that your Dr. Herat studies?"

Michael felt a sinking feeling: they had been recalled for a reason that had nothing whatever to do with Dr. Herat's report.

"Aliens," he said. "Dr. Herat hunts aliens."

8

"BEQUITH, GET UP here!" Dr. Herat's voice sprang out of nowhere. It was the emergency inscape channel they'd established years ago and rarely used. The soldiers shouldn't be able to intercept it. They were still mulling over Michael's statement.

"Dr. Herat wanted me to join him as soon as possible," he said. "About that . . . ?" He pointed to the AI.

"You haven't given us anything yet," said the soldier.

"I'll tell you what I find out," he said. It was a small price to pay to keep the AI.

"Good on ya." The soldier stuffed the AI into a black case. "Just dial 4330 to get me. Nice doing business with you."

"Right. Now where . . . ?"

"There's only one way to go," said another of the soldiers. "You'll see."

Michael did see. The military neuro interface had effectively taken over his inscape sensorium and it laid its own version of the ship over his vision. He knew there were side corridors and doors because every now and then he saw someone walk out of what looked like a wall; but the edited view of the place he saw had only those doors and stairs that took him in the direction of whatever briefing room they wanted him in. It was disconcerting and he had no idea how far the illusion went; the walls and ceiling themselves might not be real. The eeriness of the effect added to his apprehension.

Because there was only one way to go he quickly found the lounge where Dr. Herat and the admiral sat at a large teak table. Rather, the admiral sat; Herat was pacing, a look of intense excitement on his face.

"Bequith! There you are. Sit, man, sit."

"What's this all about, sir?" There were two other men

and two women seated with the admiral. The lights were low and a public inscape window near the far wall showed a blurry gray something surrounded by streaked stars.

"We were just showing Dr. Herat some pictures of the artifact," said the woman to Michael's left. She smiled at him and gestured to the window.

"Why is it named *Jentry's Envy*?" asked Dr. Herat.

"The owner named it that. We don't know why," said the woman. Michael retrieved her name from inscape: Linda Ophir, Ph.D.

"Owner?" Herat looked down his nose at her. It was an intimidating professorial gesture that would stand him in good stead if and when he returned to teaching.

"The artifact has been claimed by a certain . . ." She paused, accessing something in inscape, " 'Bud' Cassels. A halo worlder."

Michael felt a bit at a loss as to what was happening; but he looked up at the inscape window as he sat and nearly missed the chair. Kimpurusha had traded with the halo worlds until the early days of his childhood. Michael had faint memories of a time before the FTL ships regularly stopped at Manifest—a time when the stars had been infinitely far away and when his heroes had been the brave cycler captains.

"Does this fellow have any idea what he's doing?" Herat was outraged. "Only the state can own rights to an alien artifact!"

"Here in the R.E., yes," said the admiral. "The halo's different. In any case, this is not only an alien artifact, it's a working starship. And you can claim salvage rights to a ship, even here."

"That's ridiculous. And if it's a working alien starship, where's its real crew?"

"The *Envy* appears to have been abandoned. In any case, we have to clear all our activities with this Mr. Cassels," said Ophir. "It's something you'll have to get used to. At least until we can buy it or expropriate it."

Intrigued, Michael made a private copy of the inscape window and blew it up. What he saw was a blurry gray cube, streaks of stars behind it. There were several tabs above the window so he flipped through them. The next picture showed nothing but a perfectly round hole in the starscape—a black, spherical object? The next showed two gray cylinders. He recognized the final image; that round, bluish glow with the black circle and bright white dot in the center had to be a ramjet sail, viewed from an unguessable distance away.

"What are these," he asked, "or have you gone through this already?"

"No, we were just getting to that part, Dr. Bequith." He dismissed the private window, just as Ophir was tiling the public ones so that everyone could see the grainy images.

"Whoever they are, they've designed this cycler remarkably like our own," she said. "Humans tend to build cyclers to consist of a number of habitats, separated by tens or hundreds of kilometers, as here. That's part of the normal redundant safety design; if a habitat were to be hit by anything substantial travelling at half lightspeed or more, it would simply vanish in a puff of atoms, so you distribute your cargo and passengers among a number of separate containers. But see with this cycler, yes there are a number of habitats, but they appear to be of wildly differing designs."

"Different species?" asked Dr. Herat. He stood, head cocked, staring at the window.

"Cassels reported he and his men opened several of the habitats and they were definitely designed for different life-forms."

"The implications . . ."

"Are enormous. But we've saved the best for last." Ophir swept away the tiled images and replaced them with a single picture. This was another shot of the black sphere, but in this one some light source had illuminated what looked like faint writing, drawn in thin red lines on the side of the sphere. The characters were geometric, spikey, and woven together in a way that made Michael's eye hurt to follow them. The shapes were instantly recognizable.

Dr. Herat sat down. "That's impossible," he said, very quietly.

"I see you recognize it," drawled Dr. Ophir. "Few people would."

"What do you think that is, Dr. Herat?" asked Crisler.

"That language," he said, waving his hand at it. "It hasn't been used in the galaxy in two billion years. That used to be the script of a species that dominated the whole galaxy when the only life on Earth was bacteria. We know the Chicxulub were obsessed with them; we see reproductions of ancient texts in Chicxulub records—never translated, though. Maybe some modern race has managed to translate it?"

"What were they called?" asked the admiral.

Herat shrugged. Ophir said, "The usual problem—they have a thousand names. The Chicxulub called them the 'lamp bearers' or something like that."

"We call them the *Lasa*." Herat waved away the question. "We know they existed and that they were everywhere, but almost nothing else. The Chicxulub made a particular point of obliterating all evidence of them. Nobody's sure why, since they predate the Chicxulub by almost two billion years."

"If these really are habitats for multiple species, that might explain why," said Ophir. "A galaxy-spanning civilization encompassing many species—that's the Chicxulub's worst nightmare."

"And now somebody's taken up the torch again?—So to speak?" Herat bounced in his seat like a boy.

"Then why haven't we met them?" asked the admiral. "Why haven't they signalled us? If they're multispecies, surely one of them would have developed the FTL drive.

So why aren't they here? You don't mean to tell us, Dr. Herat, that your institute's careful and meticulous search of the galaxy over the past twenty years has missed a civilization that at the same time was searching for you?"

Ophir shook her head. "Above all, why should they send a cycler to contact us? An empty one at that. Unless the contact was accidental, even unwanted."

Michael felt he had to make the point: "From what you're saying, they didn't contact us, they contacted the halo worlds."

"Technically, yes," someone else said. "This Cassels fellow and his crew picked up the *Jentry's Envy* as it passed a halo world called Erythrion. They rode it into cometary space near Chandaka and then begged beam power to disembark. The cycler's on its way back into interstellar space and Cassels's crew are at Chandaka now."

"That's our next stop," said the admiral. "We will interview Cassels before going on to the cycler itself."

"Um . . . I assume we have Cassels's permission to do that?" asked Michael.

"Absolutely," said the admiral, a bit too forcefully.

"Beyond what we've just told you, we know almost nothing," said Ophir. "The cycler must have a point of origin within sixty light-years of Chandaka; once we determine its age and isotopic constitution we should be able to close in on its origin. We'll be visiting all the stars in that volume; meanwhile, we need to put a research team on the cycler itself. That is where you come in, Dr. Herat."

"Of course," said Herat. He didn't take his eyes off the image of the cycler. "Of course."

"Nobody can think of a reason why a multispecies civilization would use cyclers when FTL travel was available," said the admiral. "But it's possible that one or more of their homeworlds are substellar in size. So they could only use cyclers to leave their homeworld. Obviously there can't be four or five spacefaring species within sixty light-years of

Chandaka, though! There's only twice that in the whole galaxy."

"Yes . . ." Herat frowned. "The more I think about it the less it makes sense. Something's wrong with this picture."

The admiral nodded. "That's partly why this expedition is being undertaken as a military operation. There's also the fact that we don't know the cycler's origin. We don't want to alert the rebels to this find, lest they stumble on the homeworld first."

"Yes, I understand," said Herat.

"Then, welcome aboard," said the admiral. "We leave immediately for Chandaka. Make yourselves at home."

"WHAT JUST HAPPENED?" asked Michael later, as he and Dr. Herat settled down in the professor's quarters for tea.

"As they used to say, I think we've fallen down the rabbit hole," said Dr. Herat. "My head's still spinning. To think that I had given up hope! And committed the fact to permanent record. Now this cycler comes along." He shook his head and sipped pensively at his tea. "A cycler! Who would have thought they'd arrive in a cycler?"

"That's not what disturbs me," said Michael. He waited until Dr. Herat's eyes focussed on him. The professor raised a polite eyebrow. "Who's in charge of this expedition?" asked Michael. "It's certainly not the Panspermia Institute."

"What do you mean?"

Michael waved a hand. "This. We're on a military ship, commanded by a rear admiral—even if he was once a colleague of yours, he's military now. Sir, have you tried to send any mail or voicemail since we boarded?"

"No . . ."

"I can't get an outside link. Something about galactic security. We should be talking to the Institute about this find, but I can't get to them. And I checked the credentials of this Dr. Ophir and the others against our local database.

None of them are listed as members or affiliates of the Institute."

"What are you saying?"

"He was at the Institute when you were. How well do you know him?"

Herat sighed. "Not well. There were a lot of us, back in the old days. Let me think . . ." He frowned at the wall. "Crisler was trained as an evolutionary technologist, I believe. Studied how different technologies are selected for in different species. He published some good papers, if I recall. Which means he understands the issues involved in a find like this one. That could make him unique in the R.E. military." He looked at Michael. "You know, this expedition could well be his initiative."

Michael nodded. "So why did he leave the Institute?"

"Don't know. Could be he became disillusioned, like a lot of them did. I don't remember when he left." He sighed and stretched. "Well, it's late. Could you try to track down some wine? I'd love a glass before bed. Got to go over the records about the cycler."

"I'll see what I can do." Michael turned to go.

"Bequith?" Herat sounded puzzled. Michael looked back from the doorway.

"Something else is bothering you, isn't it?" said the professor.

Michael hesitated, then stepped back into the room. "Actually, yes," he said.

Dr. Herat was examining him as if he were a new specimen. "Do you know what I did before you met me?"

Herat frowned. "Your father told me you were in seminary school."

"Did he tell you why?"

"No." Dr. Herat looked nonplussed. "I always assumed . . . That is, Kimpurushans are known to be devout. And you've always shown yourself to be."

Michael sighed. "Another boy died because of me. I was

in the seminary because the alternative was jail, both for me and my father."

Dr. Herat reached for his tea cup, frowning. "What happened?"

"The rebellion. It came to Kimpurusha, I don't know if you knew that. I was a student at the Polytechnic, studying xenology, and . . . I got involved with a rebel cell at the school. I was a courier. I got caught, because my cell commander betrayed us. People got arrested because my message was intercepted and one of my friends . . . was killed. I was sent home with a tracking wristband on. This was four months after your first visit."

Surprise was written eloquently on Herat's face; he said nothing.

"I hated what the Rights Economy was doing to our world. But while I was under house arrest I realized that the rebels were just as much a product of the R.E. as the other aspects of it that I hated. I decided that fighting the R.E. would just drag me further and further away from what Kimpurusha had once been. If I wanted to protect my world, the best way would be to perpetuate the values that made us what we were. Those were the values of Permanence. So I went into the NeoShinto seminary."

"You never told me any of this."

"I buried it. I did finish my xenology degree, and when you came the second time I saw a chance to get away from the poisonous atmosphere that had taken over at home. Rigorous discipline was my way to salvation. Besides, I came to admire you and the whole Panspermia project—once I learned to separate it from the Rights Economy."

"And we all admired your critical mind," said Dr. Herat thoughtfully. "They don't teach your skills anywhere in the R.E.—geneaological philosophical analysis and differential deconstruction. You can look at a scientific paper and find the flaws in less than a minute." He laughed. "You know most of the younger academics in the Institute hate you? They call you the Voice of Doom."

"Yes, I know, I'm your secret weapon; you've said that before." Michael poured more tea for the professor, a reflex of Service. "What I'm saying is that entering your employ wasn't the adventure for me that I think you've always thought it was. I went with you in order to survive and to try to find some peace for myself."

"Oh."

"Service was the glue I needed to keep myself together."

"I see. And now that glue is coming unstuck?"

Michael smiled at the overextended metaphor. "Maybe. Yes. Service is no longer enough."

Herat sipped at his tea, then put it down. "It's cold." They sat in silence for a while, then the professor cleared his throat. "So you won't be coming with us on this trip?"

It had been said; Michael sighed, and took the teacup from Herat.

"I don't know," he said. "I feel that I'm still searching for something, but I don't know anymore if I can find it out there." He gestured at space, invisible beyond the metal walls.

Herat sat musing for a while, then smiled wryly. "All that may be true," he said. "The one thing I do know, Bequith, is that in order to find something, you first have to know what you're looking for."

Michael had no answer to that.

IT TOOK SEVERAL weeks to get to Chandaka, even going at the several thousand *c* that the *Spirit of Luna* could muster. Each FTL jump took them about a hundred light-years, but it took time to maneuver the ship close to a star to initiate the next jump. There was enough time to thoroughly study the meager findings about the cycler, enough time for Michael to insinuate himself into the confidences of several crewmen and enough time to worry. The rebels were indeed on the march; they had more ships and guns than ever, defying all the predictions of the government. The rebel economy was far more efficient than the Rights Economy, Michael knew, simply because the rebels didn't pay a royalty for every single transaction they made. They were fighting against the crushing weight of the Rights Economy and Michael and most people he talked to admired that idealism. But nobody thought they could win.

The rebels were Crisler's explanation for the tight security. Under pressure from Herat he did produce a document from the Panspermia Institute releasing the professor into military contract. They still weren't allowed to contact the Institute and when pressed Crisler admitted that the Institute hadn't been told the nature of the find.

"Come on, professor," Crisler had said after Herat harangued him for an hour about it. "You don't seriously think that something of this magnitude is going to just bypass the sole government organization set up to deal with it? It'll all fall into your people's lap eventually. And you'll get the credit. Hell, I'll even sign a paper saying we shanghaied you if you like. Meanwhile, this is a military matter."

Dr. Herat wasn't happy about that, but his excitement about the find completely eclipsed his political sense. — Perhaps that wasn't quite fair; Michael knew the professor trusted him to ferret out such details. But Michael had precious little to go on himself.

The whole situation was troubling and not just politically. A few days ago, Michael had been thinking that their long wandering was finally coming to an end. He regretted it; at the same time, he knew it was past time that he face some issues of his own. Now this cycler artifact had come along and it looked as if he and the professor were about to be flung off on another extended jaunt. Stuck in some balloon habitat next to an alien starship, surrounded only by the military and under radio silence, he would be left to wrestle his own demons. Even now, sitting alone in his cabin while Dr. Herat pored over the cycler photos and chatted with Dr. Ophir, Michael felt restless and unfulfilled. He had no focus for meditation and he was, frankly, afraid to use the AI. That which should have comforted him most had become terrifying to contemplate; he could not close his eyes without the shadow of his revelation at Dis creeping up on him. At times he felt like he was falling; at other times, like a sleepwalker going through the motions of his life.

He tried to focus onto minor interests, such as the prospect of meeting some halo worlders—but there was a troubling aspect to them as well. Thinking about the halo worlds always took Michael back to his childhood.

If he lay back on his cot and closed his eyes, he could summon some inscape images of his home. It was as if he stood in the marble-floored atrium again and he could turn and look out the tall leaded-glass windows to where the sun was turning distant peaks gold and mauve. Memory supplied the rest: The air was crisp and thin, even in the innermost chambers. His family's house adjoined the Permanence seminary and at certain times of the day he could hear the faint sound of the chants that drifted down from its distant windows. The music was ever present during his childhood, a reassuring and peaceful counterpoint to the rising tide of chaos outside the town walls.

He remembered one day running up the street to his house's door and his father shouting. That was the beginning and end of his personal experience of the Reconquista, when the FTL ships from the Rights Economy took the government of Kimpurusha.

When he thought about the Reconquista, he always did so through the lens of another, singular memory:

There was a chair in his home. It was unique in the household—made of rosewood, large and with an embroidered seat and splat, where the other chairs were more utilitarian and factory-made. The legs were carved with intricate floral designs. Michael's toys scaled it and it was the biggest mountain in the world; his dolls sat along its front edge and they were steering it, a cycler, through the deepest spaces between the suns. He built constructions of blocks around the crosspiece between its legs and it was a generating station. For the youngest son of the Bequith household, this chair could become anything, with a simple flip of the imagination.

One day, not long after the running and shouting, a strange man came to the house. He was tall and pale and seemed nervous as he paced through the rooms. In each one he took a canister and aimed it at the furniture and fixtures. A fine smoke puffed out and fell slowly to vanish as it touched things.

"What's that?" he had asked his father.

"Nanotags," said Father, as if it were a curse.

The man entered the hall and puffed smoke on the rosewood chair.

Other men came and Michael had to go with them. They took him to a hospital and made him sleep. When he awoke he could feel the distant roar of inscape in his head, like an unsettled crowd. He felt grown-up, because he knew you weren't allowed to get inscape implants until adulthood and he was only ten years old. The men took him home and his mother cried and it was at that point that he realized something was wrong.

He didn't know what for a while, but the inscape laid its own version of things over his sight and hearing. He would learn to tune it out, he was told; but for the moment, he couldn't.

Now, when he looked at the rosewood chair, all he could see was the matrix of numbers superimposed on it, that told the monetary value of its parts and whole. And so with the drapes, the walls, windows, and the rice as he picked it up with his chopsticks.

He imagined—and he knew it couldn't be so—that the people of the free halo worlds still saw things like the boy before they had put nanotags in every object and inscape in his head. As if a chair could be a mountain or a starship and not just a collection of values and registrations.

To think this way was to miss something he hadn't even known was his when he had it.

He would have paced the halls of the cruiser, except that the inscape illusion limited him to a very few sectors. Instead, he exercised in his room, or tried to read, and most evenings when Dr. Herat didn't need him he ended up lounging on his bed, staring at the blank ceiling, longing for home or something more fundamental.

They entered orbit around Chandaka and Crisler lectured them about not talking to the locals. Michael tuned out and summoned a window to look at the planet. Chandaka was bigger and warmer than Kimpurusha; he looked first for polar ice caps, his habitual metric for judging a world. Chandaka's were tiny, almost an afterthought. It was a wet and blue planet, its seas captured in crescents and circles rimmed with volcanoes—the typical Coronae alternative to plate tectonics. Michael felt his spirits lift at the prospect of walking unsuited in the air and feeling a real sun on his face.

After Chandaka, his future was cloudy. He resolved to experience this world to its full, while he could.

MICHAEL TRACED THE lines of intricate carving that ran along the wall, a legacy of Chandaka's history as a halo world. Hovering on the edges of his vision were tiny lines of text and numerals, inscape tags which named the Rights Owners for this place, as well as its value and history. He tried to ignore them and imagine the carvings as they had originally looked, unsullied by inscape.

This giant building, the arcology known as the Redoubt, was apparently the oldest inhabited structure on the planet. Michael and Dr. Herat had been flown here immediately on landing on Chandaka. They had arrived at night local time—morning, by Michael's circadian rhythms. He wasn't ready to sleep, so Michael wandered the vast echoing corridors of the Redoubt in the wee hours.

The halo-worlders who had boarded and named *Jentry's Envy* were billeted somewhere within the Redoubt's thousands of rooms and corridors; Michael hadn't caught a glimpse of anyone since he and the professor were shown their rooms.

There had been a hurry-up-and-wait quality to the flight out here. The *Spirit of Luna* had picked up a number of other researchers on its way. Everyone seemed eager, almost frantic to be gone after the cycler. Yet, until Crisler had all the pieces in place, there was nothing to do.

Michael had done his usual work and made friends among the new scientific staff that Crisler was building. He had learned nothing new about their destination or the reasons for Crisler's urgency and secrecy in assembling the team.

Everyone else had turned in, so Michael wandered, thinking. At the end of one carven and frescoed corridor, huge pressure doors stamped with infinity signs stood open to what looked like an open courtyard or garden. The doors would once have kept the air in before Chandaka's volcanic carbon cycle was kick-started with deliberate meteoric pounding. Michael could smell the new air as he approached the door, and unconsciously walked faster. The breeze tasted wonderful—green and fresh.

He stepped out onto a gravel path that led under dark trees. This garden was very extensive, but the cyclopean walls of the Redoubt reared up on all sides to enclose it. Somewhere in those tapering black towers, the rest of the expedition was asleep. Tomorrow they would be meeting the halo worlders and settling their plans. Michael didn't feel a part of that. The problem was, he didn't feel there was a place for him outside the redoubt either, unless he returned to Kimpurusha.

He heard the crunching sound of someone walking up the gravel path and, turning, discovered it was Admiral Crisler. The admiral was walking meditatively, with his hands behind his back. He looked up and smiled at Michael. "Nice night, isn't it?"

"Yes, sir."

"I see you're of like mind to myself, Dr. Bequith. Soaking up the feel of being on a planet while you can, eh?"

"Well, I just spent the past few months able to look out my window at places like this, but never touch them."

"Yes . . . I remember that sense of frustration, back in the days when I was a respecter of planetary quarantines myself."

Michael sensed an opportunity; it was time to be direct. "Sir? Why did you leave the Institute? Was it to join the military, or was that a later decision?"

Crisler arched an eyebrow at him. "Why the curiosity? Are you thinking of leaving the good professor?"

That hit close to home; Michael shrugged. Crisler looked away, grunted, and said, "It's never one thing that changes the direction of your life, you know. I began my scientific career believing that the aliens we studied were fundamentally like us. But they're not. Humans alone are conscious. We really are special, Bequith. Once I realized that, I realized just how precious and fragile that made us. I mean, just for you and me to be standing here talking in this garden . . . how rare a thing that is. It was a short step from that to wanting to protect that rarity."

"From what?"

Crisler stared at him. "The rebels. Son, you must know that they use alien technology. Some of them have been practicing genetic engineering on their children. They're abandoning humanity. The Rights Economy exists to keep humanity together; they want to pull us apart into a million warring species. I won't have that. Not on my watch."

"I see."

"I hope so." The admiral looked away, sighed heavily. "Now, if you'll excuse me, I think I'll continue my walk, and try to store up as much of this fine night air as I can."

They nodded their goodbyes, and Crisler walked away.

To the right lay a jungle-thick garden. Michael walked that way, listening to the titter of tiny lives around his feet, drinking in the strange spicy scents of the garden. Here were all the sensations he had been cut off from on Kadesh. Being here felt like a release from prison.

Maybe in this place he could summon the kami. He looked about for a sheltered place to sit. As he did, movement caught his eye.

She walked with her head down, hands behind her back. He might not have seen her at all had the faint light from Chandaka's starlike second sun not caught her oval face as she passed through a clearing. Her hair was black and she wore a jet coverall that made her face and long hands seem to float among the shadowed bushes.

The young woman hadn't noticed him. She was humming quietly to herself as she drifted through the darkness. She paused in a dark bower and said something he didn't catch. For a moment Michael thought she was speaking to him and he was about to answer when another voice spoke from nearby her.

"You know, it's funny." It was a man's voice. His accent was more familiar. "I'm out of the halo. I thought it would be simple—we'd learn to control the *Envy*, become millionaires, and I'd head home."

"I'm sorry it hasn't worked out," she said. Her silhouette bent, perhaps to embrace the man. "You risked everything to trust me, Evan. I won't forget that."

"Well . . . I just wanted to get back to High Space," he said gruffly. "But I thought I'd have something to show for it when I got here."

"I know," she said, almost inaudibly. "I'm sorry. What are you going to do now?"

"I don't know. Max and I were going over the terms of your agreement with this admiral. That's when it really hit me: I can't stay here, not as it stands. R.E. laws are so . . . draconian. You realize that you still don't own the *Envy*?"

"I know," she said with a sigh. "Crisler knows it, too."

"He could move to expropriate it," said the man.

Michael tried to stay perfectly still, and breathe as shallowly as possible. This was *very* interesting.

"By R.E. law, someone has to own the rights to the *Envy*," continued the man. "If it isn't you, then it's the state. And until you're able to control the *Envy*, you can't complete your claim by Cycler Compact law. So I don't get paid."

"It's why I made this deal to go back, Evan. It's a deal with the devil, I know that. But what else am I supposed to do? I'm responsible, Evan, I know that. I can't just wash my hands of you or the others. I couldn't live with myself if any of us ended up in indentured labor somewhere."

He laughed humorlessly. "What are we going to do about it? Crisler only needs your permission as current claim-owner to visit the *Envy*. Once he's there, he can expropriate it for the R.E. Then we're all sunk."

"Believe me, I've been thinking about that a lot, Ev. But look at it this way: if we discover that she can be turned during this expedition, my claim is upheld. If we can't turn her, but it turns out in ten years that she's swung about on her own to pass Erythrion again, then my original claim is upheld. So Crisler can't expropriate until he has some idea of where she's going."

"Hmm." The man turned to look at the stars. "Yeah, you may be right. At the *Envy*'s velocity, even if they try to orbit her around Chandaka they'll have to do a constant expensive course correction and the orbit's probably gonna be big enough to include Erythrion. Light years in radius."

"Right," she said. "I may have to give them what they want, but not necessarily at the expense of what I want." She sat down next to the man. "Evan, come with us. You're the only one of us who knows these people—their culture, I mean. We need you."

"I . . . don't know, Rue. I spent years on the cyclers and that was fine. But when I got stranded on Erythrion . . ." He looked down. "I couldn't stand to be stranded again. I know myself too well. It would be the end of me."

She hugged him. "Sometimes," she said, "you have to jump right back at whatever just bit you. And bite it back."

Michael turned and walked away as quietly as he could.

Later, he lay in bed and fought with himself. Although he didn't know that man he'd overheard in the garden, Michael felt for him. Stay or go? It was a dilemma he understood.

There was no life for him with Dr. Herat anymore; he could no longer find the sacred in Service or, it seemed, in the landscapes that the NeoShinto AI was supposed to attune him to. He was adrift.

As they flew toward the Redoubt, Michael had seen glimpses of Chandaka, and they had been depressing. On the outskirts of the city they were building a glittering wall that would eventually become a geodesic dome. Michael had asked the local information service what the dome was for. "There's no money for the terraforming anymore," it had told him blandly. "Chandaka is losing its artificial atmosphere." After they landed, Michael had asked their guide at the Redoubt about this. He had grimaced unhappily. "When we joined the R.E., the politicians and businessmen who grew up here became Rights Owners of the lands and industry," he said. "Now they live in luxury on Earth, and they've decided it's too expensive to keep up the terraforming. They've passed on the problem, so the city council is building the dome just so we can keep breathing. Which sucks up money, so there's even less to go to the Rights Owners." The guide made a downward spiral motion with his finger. "It's all going to hell."

Michael knew he could return to Kimpurusha. He didn't want to find out what had happened there since he left.

The only thing that swayed him one way or the other, was the memory of that young woman in the garden tonight. She was of the halos, hence exotic and wild. No inscape indicators hovered over her. Yet she seemed well grounded. He had liked the sound of her voice.

Most of all, he remembered what she had said. "Sometimes, you just have to jump right back . . ."

In his imagination, the alien cycler was an awesome place, full of mystery and unguessable age. Dis had been like that. Michael sometimes wondered if things had been different, if he had been more prepared at Dis, more wary.

He couldn't go back to Dis; couldn't recover a moment that was lost. But just maybe, at *Jentry's Envy*, he could still try to capture and accept the infinite one more time.

"THIS WHOLE COMPLEX is amazing," said a habitat designer walking with Dr. Herat. "It looks like it was built by hand."

Herat nodded, looking around at the vast corridor they were in. "The detailing was done by monks of the Cycler Compact."

The designer ran a hand appreciatively over a wall carving. "It's beautiful. Intimidating. But almost . . . obsessive. Inward-turning, you know?"

"Alien to us, yes. It challenges our notions of time. Maybe that was the idea."

"Why do they call it the *halo*, anyway?" somebody else said. "That implies light. Those worlds are all dark."

Herat laughed. "There's a story about that. They originally called them *orphan worlds*, but try to imagine encouraging people to emigrate to the orphan worlds! So they renamed them the halo worlds. Just so people would find them attractive to visit." There was a general chuckle at this.

Admiral Crisler awaited them at the doors to what looked like a ballroom. Just inside was a short line of people: the halo-worlders.

Dr. Herat was the first in line to greet them. He shook hands down the line, followed by the man he'd been talking to—a Dr. Katz, it seemed. Then it was Michael's turn.

"Michael Bequith."

"Blair Genereaux." He was surprisingly young, sharply dressed in the latest Chandaka fashion. Michael wondered if he was one of the halo-worlders or a liaison.

"Michael Bequith."

"Dr. Bequith, nice to meet you. I'm Corinna Chandra." She was tall, of indeterminate age, with dark, shadowed eyes and dusky skin. Her iron-gray hair was tied back and cascaded in a fan down her back. She wore a simple red jumpsuit, and the only adornment she wore was a stud in her left nostril. Her gaze was direct and businesslike.

"Max Cassels. How ya doing?" Someone had made an attempt to dress Max well, but he wasn't having any of it. His shirt was untucked and his hair uncombed. He looked distracted.

Was this the famous "Bud" Cassels?

"Rebecca France, M.D." Tall and slender, with gray eyes and broad cheekbones. She seemed secretly amused by something.

"Evan Laurel." This was the man from the garden last night; Michael recognized his voice. He was tall and blond, with lines of care around his eyes, about forty-five years old. He had the sigil of the Cycler Order on his jacket. And standing next to him . . .

"Ah, yes, the man from the garden last night," she said before Michael had a chance to introduce himself. He felt his face grow hot.

"I'm Rue," she said. Her eyes were hidden behind black pince-nez sunglasses today. "And you are . . . ?"

"Bequith," he stammered. "Michael Bequith."

"Pleased to meet you, Mike." She smiled distantly.

That was the end of the line. He stalked into the hall, still smarting.

They'd set up a long table at one end of the hall. This place was sumptuous beyond belief—the scenes painted on the walls were neither inscape illusions nor copies done by mesobots. The ceiling showed scenes of planetfall and the conquest of nature here on Chandaka, with fabulous beasts and vines carved into the native stone that formed the arches. There was even design in the parquet flooring. Hot coffee and a good Martian breakfast was waiting for Michael as he sat himself.

Once all the members of the expedition were seated, Crisler walked to the end of the table. Where he stood, his head was framed by the baroque jaws of a dragon on the far wall. He said, "Welcome everyone. This is the first assembly of our full scientific crew. There will be seventeen of us, plus the halo worlders and a support staff of forty-five on the *Banshee*. Today I'd like to go over the mission profile we've developed.

"We're going to rendezvous with *Jentry's Envy* one point-seven light-years out from Chandaka. That's farther from an inhabited star than most of you have ever been." He smiled woodenly at the halo-worlders. "Since the *Envy* is receding at eight-five percent c, we can't use a conventional starship to catch up to her. If you'll check your inscape, you'll see the ship we'll be using."

A public inscape window opened over Crisler. It showed the golden limb of some gas giant planet. Clouds swirled below.

"Where's the ship?" asked Cassels.

"Patience," said Crisler. "Here it comes."

As they watched, a dark rectangle, translucent like a fine gauze, moved across the face of the planet. It resolved into a black cylinder of indeterminate size. There were some mirrored spheres at one end and a set of black rings of consecutively larger sizes appeared to be drifting behind it.

"You can't see a lot of the *Banshee*," said Crisler, "because it's mostly thin spars and cable. There's sixty kilometers of line played out behind the engine you see here. It ends," the image changed, "here." This was a more familiar sight: two standard balloon habitats, joined by a V-shaped elbow at their tops. It seemed to be floating alone in space.

"*Banshee*'s state of the art: a fullerene-wrapped super-conducting magnet with a field radius of eight thousand kilometers, a pion drive, and a courier class fast hyper-drive. The drive unit normally tows the habitats, so don't worry about radiation, we'll never get near the thing."

"It's a ramjet?" asked Cassels.

"Hybridized to use antimatter from an onboard supply instead of doing straight fusion. *Banshee* is very, very fast. We'll approach the *Envy*'s velocity in a little under two months. We'll use the hyperdrive first to get near the *Envy*, so we can accelerate in empty space. We'll come out of jump three light-months behind her and accelerate up from there. We'll have a six-week window to bail out once we get there. Then we'll have reached a point where it'll be just as worth our while to stay with the *Envy* until its next stop. So the mission is a five-week exploratory phase, fol-lowed by a possibly extended mission of a year and a half. Luckily the *Envy* is on a course that will take it near the K-class star Maenad in two years. Maenad has no planets or colonies, but it's a massive enough star to start our FTL drive. We can jump back to Chandaka from there."

Dr. Herat was shifting impatiently in his seat. "That's fine. What about the cycler? All we've seen of it so far has been a set of photos. What are we going to find when we get there?"

The admiral smiled. "Well, to answer that, I think we should defer to the owner of the cycler, Mr. Cassels. Max?" He turned to the rumpled halo-worlder, who glanced around and stood up.

"Actually . . ." said Max. "I'm Max Cassels, all right, but I'm not Bud Cassels and I'm not the real owner of the *Jentry's Envy*."

He was met with a puzzled silence.

Just as Admiral Crisler opened his mouth to speak, Max said, "We decided that while we were here, the real owner would let me play the part because I've got a bit more ex-perience dealing with . . . people in powerful situations.

She's confident she can take over now and frankly I think the deception really annoys her." He smirked at the other halo-worlders. "So, then, let me introduce the real owner of *Jentry's Envy*, Rue Cassels."

Michael squirmed in his seat. He was as surprised as the others at this turn of events, but even more embarrassed now than ever that she had seen him eavesdropping last night.

Max sat down and the young woman stood up. Max had made the introduction like a toastmaster and the lack of applause that greeted her was jarring. She stammered. "I . . . I'm from a station in the back of beyond, you know. Self-confessed rube. When we came here we didn't know whether we'd be conned out of the ship. I didn't know what to do, so I put things in Max's care for a while. Sorry for lying to you all."

Michael glanced around the table; the others were surprised, but not offended—except, perhaps, for Crisler, who was scowling at Max. Michael himself was completely enchanted.

This Rue Cassels was utterly unlike the one Michael had seen in the garden last night; there, she had been poised, confident, even eloquent. This Rue was a shy, barely adult young woman. She seemed to be hiding behind her dark sunglasses. Some of that might be real—but it came to Michael that she might be acting and if she was, she was superb at it.

"I know, Dr. Herat, that you want the facts and figures about *Jentry's Envy*," she said. "You'll get them. But I had a real hard time thinking of what to say today and I didn't know why for a while. Then I realized it was because the whole experience of being there at the *Envy* was so . . . huge, so wild, that I didn't have the words for it. I mean, I went into this whole thing without a clue what I was getting into. The *Envy* was a shock. I don't think it's fair to any of you to let you think that this is going to be like anywhere else you've ever been.

"Admiral Crisler and his aides have told me what star travel is like in the R.E. You get on a ship, eat some fine meals and use the exercise facility, hobnob with the other passengers for a couple of days, and then you're at your destination. It's seamless.

"Well, cyclers aren't like that." She glanced at Evan Laurel, who chuckled silently.

"To go to a cycler is not to go from one part of your world to another," she said. "To go to a cycler is to leave everything that you know and see it dwindle into specks and disappear in the hugeness. It's not like visiting somewhere, it's like leaving home for good."

Crisler cleared his throat. "With respect, Ms. Cassels, we're all experienced travelers. I think we know what to expect from your kind of travel."

Rue stammered. "Yes, of course . . ."

"What about *Jentry's Envy?*" asked Herat mildly. "What did you find when you got there?"

She smiled at the professor. "Well, that's just it. We'd arrived, but not at what we'd expected, and not at anything we could figure out. Radar showed a bunch of spheres of different sizes. There were other things, too—big half-empty gasbags that barely showed up in radar and little dense packets obviously made of metal. They all had thin lines trailing off them, joining up and ultimately connected to the plow sail. Most of them were at ambient temperature—a few degrees above absolute zero. A couple, though, were warm."

"You explored them," said Dr. Herat.

"Well." She adjusted her pince-nez. "We started to. But while the cycler was doing its turn, there was a slight pull on everything. If we parked our little habitat next to something, that something would drift away. If we used fuel to follow it, we were, well, using up fuel. So we found the warmest sphere in the whole collection and we attached a line to its line. Then we were hanging with the other cargoes, like some kind of weird chandelier."

"Surely you did some exploring," coaxed Dr. Herat.

"At first we thought the cycler was going to finish its turn in a couple of months. But it didn't, it kept turning; it was still going to pass Chandaka, but on the other side of the star from what we'd expected. We'd explored Lake Flaccid while we waited, then afterward I decided it wouldn't be wise to waste too much fuel, so we only explored one other—"

"Lake *Flaccid*?" Dr. Ophir was trying to keep a straight face.

Max gave a long-suffering sigh. "Our Rue has a talent for naming things," he said. "And, as captain, it's her right to name stuff however she wants."

"It *is* flaccid," cried Rue. "The name is perfect and you know it."

Dr. Herat held up a hand, a pained expression on his face. Michael could see that the professor didn't think much of Rue Cassels. He would never name a priceless alien site so irreverently.

Michael had to smile.

"What is Lake Flaccid?" asked Dr. Herat impatiently.

Rue appeared puzzled. "We took photos. You didn't . . . ?"

Admiral Crisler half stood. "We decided to withhold the key pieces of evidence until we had everyone committed to the mission. Sorry, Dr. Herat, but we couldn't show you everything before."

"Ah." Rue frowned at Crisler. "Well, let's take an inscape look at it now, if you want."

The picture of the *Banshee* was replaced by another image. This seemed to be a shot down the length of a round tunnel. Evan Laurel stood balanced on one toe near the camera. He was grinning behind his suit's faceplate and he was brightly lit by a light source near the camera while everything behind him faded into shadow.

"That's the rotational axis of one of the midsize habitats," said Rue. "It's huge by cycler standards—sixty meters across, easily. The axis is about seven meters across, so the bulk of the place is 'under' this cylinder. The habitat rotates, so gravity at the outside would be about two gees. At the axis, it's micro."

"This isn't the habitat that has the Lasa writing on it," Crisler said to Herat, who nodded slowly.

Rue paused, staring at the image. "At first we thought we might set up camp here. The atmosphere's pure nitrogen and though it was about minus twenty, we were going to hook up some heaters and oxygenate a tent. Do some real exploring. But when we got to the lake we got too creeped, so we ended up back at the ship. Well, all except Evan and Corinna. They seemed immune to the creeps."

Evan shrugged. "Needed to get off the ship for a while, that's all."

"What is this lake?" asked Ophir.

"You can see it in the picture," said Rue. "See that dark line?" Behind Evan in the picture, a broad expanse of darkness ringed the cylinder. Michael had taken it to mean that most of the length of the cylinder was surfaced with some dark material. Now he could see that that surface was indented some centimeters below the white metal Evan balanced on.

"We shone lights into it," said Evan. "Couldn't figure out what it was. Some liquid, we figured, but if it was water it would have massed an incredible amount and you just don't ship that much water up to lightspeed. Costs way too much."

Rue shrugged. "We only visited one other place—and it was even weirder than this." She shook her head. "I'm afraid we don't have much to tell you, Doctor Herat."

"Which brings us to the reasons for this expedition," said Crisler. "Obviously it's a huge undertaking and none of us would be doing this if we didn't expect to reap great reward from it. We all have our agendas and it's time to make those clear. Let's start with yours, Rue."

"I've been up front about it all along," she said. "I own the *Envy*. It's impossible or at least prohibitively expensive to slow it down to sub-light speeds—like it or not, it's a cycler and therefore the only issue is its course and ability to serve as a habitat for travel between planetary systems. I want to make sure it services the halo worlds. I also have to make sure that its course really is a 'cycle'—it has to pass by Erythrion again eventually. So this time out we're looking for ways to live off the habitats that are already there and change its course if we have to."

Dr. Herat sputtered. "That's . . . criminal. Well, no not criminal but I'm sorry, this is a priceless artifact, you can't turn it into a floating motel—"

"*Doctor* Herat," barked Crisler.

"Our civilization is held together by the cyclers and nothing else," said Rue coldly. Her shoulders were hunched now, as if she were anticipating a blow. "There are very few cyclers now and fewer every day, thanks to you people. Anything that can bring back a little of what you stole from us is to the good. If your precious investigation has to suffer so that billions of my people can continue to communicate, then so be it!"

"There is also the fact that not even the Cycler Compact has the systems in place to decelerate something as massive as this starship," said Crisler. "The *Envy* is not something you can tote home to a museum, Professor Herat. It will continue on its course until it erodes away. Ms. Cassels's plan is only sensible, provided we establish a permanent scientific presence aboard the cycler to investigate it during its occupation."

"Ah." Herat looked chastened. "I apologize, Ms. Cassels. Your people do deserve to benefit from this discovery." Michael could tell he was genuinely sorry for his outburst—but also knew that Herat would still feel the exploitation of an alien artifact for personal gain was wrong. "Of course, if we have a permanent presence on the *Envy*, in the long run . . ."

"You'll have to pay for that yourselves," said Max Cassels. "The halo cannot afford to subsidize the Rights Economy."

"So," said Crisler, "one of our priorities is to secure the *Envy* as a viable cycler for use by the halo worlds. Dr. Herat, what are your priorities?"

"Where to start?" he said. He cracked his knuckles under the table; Michael winced. "This is a find of unknown importance. We have no idea what we're going to discover there. It's imperative that we not make any course corrections until we know what the cycler's programmed course is. We need to find out how old it is, who made it, where it comes from. We may be on the verge of contacting an entirely new civilization. I think Ms. Cassels would agree that this is at least as important as securing a single cycler for the halo—especially if this alien civilization is friendly and also uses cyclers. Imagine what it would mean if they cooperated with the halo worlds to build more!"

Rue, who had sat down, arched an eyebrow.

Crisler ticked off points on an inscape scratch pad. "Origin. Makers. Course. Of course, any technological advances that result from the investigation will be shared by the halo and the R.E."

"So what is your interest, Admiral?" asked Michael.

"It's very simple," he said. "If there really is a hidden civilization out there, one that comprises more than a single species, we need to reach it before the rebels do. I hardly have to tell you that our attempts to create a unified galactic parliament have failed; the other spacefaring species are too alien for us to deal with. The whole construction of the *Envy* hints at a multispecies civilization, which has been humanity's dream since before we even had space flight. If such a civilization exists, the first faction to make an ally of it will inherit the galaxy."

Michael glanced across at the halo-worlders. Crisler seemed unaware of it, but he had just driven home a deep insult that they must all feel: The people of the Cycler Compact had seen themselves as the inheritors of the galaxy before the Rights Economy had burst out from Earth to steal the lit suns from them. Cyclers had been the essential glue binding the original interstellar human civilization. In thinking only of the polarity of rebels vs. R.E., Crisler was openly relegating Rue Cassels's people to the ash-bin of history.

No hint of this showed on their faces. They politely listened as Crisler set about negotiating the hierarchy of priorities. But as Michael looked around the table, he could clearly see what others might not: competing interests and old wounds ignored for now, but perhaps not forever.

They worked through more details of the expedition. When the formal meeting wound up, everyone remained to shake hands and proceeded to snack on the breakfast that had been provided—everyone, that is, except Max Cassels, who begged off and practically ran from the room.

Michael found himself avoiding the other Cassels. He felt embarrassed about eavesdropping on Rue last night. As he was skulking by the drinks table, Linda Ophir appeared next to him.

"I'm a great admirer of your and Dr. Herat's work," she said, hiding a smile behind a tumbler of orange juice.

"Thank you." He wracked his brains for a suitable complimentary reply.

"Listen, Dr. Bequith, before we get all formal in our roles, I was wondering . . ."

He reached for a drink. "Ah . . . ?"

"There's some . . . anomalies . . . in the data that you should know about," she said quietly. "I'd like to discuss them in a less crowded environment. Would you like to take a walk in the garden later this morning?"

"Oh. Well, sure. Uh, what anomalies are we talking about?"

"Nothing special. But please don't mention this to anyone. Okay?" She smiled winningly at him, and walked quickly away.

Michael realized he was standing holding the ladle to the punch bowl like a weapon. He put it down, shook his head, and went to join the knot of people talking with Dr. Herat.

LINDA DIDN'T SHOW up at the gardens. Michael wasn't sure whether she had been trying to pick him up or talk business, so he waited around for a while, increasingly annoyed. Finally he decided to abandon the wait, and went for a walk. As he stepped through the giant gates of the old Compact fortress, he smiled at the feel of warm air and sunlight on his face.

The sky was blustering today, but it was warm and muggy. The air smelled like cinnamon. Chandaka's star was G-class, like Earth's; the skies were blue here and full of big puffy clouds, and the light seemed natural. He knew that this world had not always looked like this; centuries ago, Compact engineers had blown off the planet's old atmosphere using directed cometary impacts, and had imposed a carbon cycle by force. Free atmospheric oxygen was a new factor in Chandaka's environment; in many places, apparently, deserts and rivers still spontaneously burst into flame now and then. Oxygen was absorbed out of the air almost as fast as it was introduced—sucked into iron-rich rocks and into the oceans for the most part. Though the hills that rolled away to the horizon on both sides looked green and peaceful, the terraforming effort required to keep them green was massive. And expensive.

The streets and towers of the city that sprawled in the valley below the Redoubt at first looked like fabulous confections spun in glass and chrome. Michael tuned his inscape to full realism, and the illusion vanished: Now he saw the buildings and streets of Chandaka's capital as they really were. The older towers were of carved stone, beautiful and baroque; everything new, though, was made of gray concrete, undecorated in reality. Looming beyond the blocky cityscape were giant stacks belching out oxygen; Michael had swallowed some mesotech scrubbers to remove the extra CO_2 from his bloodstream, otherwise he would die in this air.

There were no physical signs to designate shops or public areas—or rather there were some, but they were old and faded almost beyond recognition. The people were likewise unadorned, mostly dressed in utilitarian pant and shirt combinations. This spareness was typical of colony worlds that had little real money or resources; real wealth was siphoned from the citizens to the offworld Rights Owners through thousands of daily microtransactions.

Ironically, it cost Michael money to view the city without inscape filtering. He flipped his inscape back to full representation and instantly the streets became canyons of light, full of virtual pennants and floating holographic ads. The gray concrete walls became marble, a thousand kinds of music sprang up around him and what had been bare stalls along the side of the road turned into a carnival market. There weren't that many kinds of item for sale here, but they were presented in thousands of different inscape wrappers. Even buying vegetables became an adventure when you had to choose between the microspirits in each farmer's stock, each of which strove to be entertaining or wise or salacious as it danced upon the potato or breadfruit that housed its broadcast nano. You paid for this wrapping; you paid just to breathe in this place.

Some of the citizens who had been visible a moment ago were blurred out, edited by their own choice from this version of the street. Those that remained were now dressed brightly, even outrageously, in jewels or light or flame or swirling TV images.

There were other versions of the city, though not as many as you'd find in the inner systems. Michael tuned to a religious view and the hawkers and stalls turned into rows of bronze silent Buddhas. The light changed to something limpid and clear and overhead graceful white forms flitted between the clouds. There were very few people visible in this view, most replaced by ghostly cloth-wrapped figures so you didn't walk into them. Once upon a time there would have been NeoShinto shrines here, physically present along with all the other sects of Permanence. But it was illegal for a religion not to charge for its services in the R.E. There was in fact a Church of Permanence here—the bastardized version whose doctrines and rites were "owned" by a cabal of fallen brothers back on Earth. Michael would have had to pay just to walk through its doors.

This view was so crassly deceptive that he couldn't stand to look at it, so he tried a few other views of the city, finally settling on a garden view that emphasized the bowers and fountains that really did dot the streets. He found an outdoor cafe and sat in the sun sipping coffee while gene-adapted finches sang to him from their perches among the crimson leaves of bright bamboolike trees. With some judicious tuning he was able to bring the brightly clad citizenry back into this view and he watched them go by for a while, enjoying the ambience.

The expedition would be leaving for *Jentry's Envy* in a couple of days. Dr. Herat had given Michael the choice: He could come along or stay behind. The offer was made with seeming lightness, but both knew the implications. This investigation was not like any of the others and it would likely last for years. If Michael stayed behind, he would be leaving Dr. Herat's employ.

Common sense told him it was time to leave. He had to resolve his own problems; he couldn't put it off.

And how would he do that? He could return to Kimpurusha—but the monasteries had become gaming houses and he didn't know if he could find any of the brothers if he tried. Anxious and depressed, he finished his coffee and went walking again.

His footsteps seemed to naturally lead him into the older quarter of the city. Here he was able to switch off inscape entirely, and merely enjoy the architecture for its own sake. Human hands had crafted the stones here for the eyes of generations yet unborn, but not unimagined.

As he was crossing a plaza that had once had an active fountain at its center, he heard a distant clap of sound. At first he took no notice, since the city was full of noises. Then the clap came back to him, from the buildings across the plaza: an echo of a distant and apparently powerful explosion.

Michael shaded his eyes and looked up. A twisting contrail rose up from outside the city, vanishing almost directly overhead. That looked like a rocket launch.

Another bang came from the opposite direction. He turned, and this time he saw the thing rising from somewhere in the suburbs. Michael had time to realize that he shouldn't be standing where he was before the one directly overhead exploded.

The flash was insignificant, merely making him blink. With it came a loud clicking that seemed to come from inside his own head. And the bone behind his right ear felt hot suddenly. That was all: But throughout the plaza, people who had been walking like him only seconds ago were falling to the cobblestones, like dancers obeying music he couldn't hear.

And that was it, of course. He felt behind his ear. The skin there was quite warm—and that, of course, was where his inscape antenna was located, inside the bone. He didn't need to try accessing inscape to know his implants had been fried by the microwave bomb that had gone off a kilometer overhead.

Those who were using inscape at the time—nearly everybody—would have had their world go mad for an instant. There were too many fail-safes in the implant system to permit real brain damage, but these people were as stunned as though lightning had hit right next to them.

Michael took a few steps toward the nearest person, some vague notion of helping in his mind. Then he noticed how the few others who had not fallen were jogging purposefully across the plaza, in the direction of downtown. As he watched, one drew a pistol from inside his tunic.

Only now did Michael start to feel afraid. He was caught outside in the middle of a rebel attack. Common sense told him he should get indoors before real missiles—the explosive kind—started flying. It wasn't the fear that paralyzed him for long seconds, though, but simple déjà vu. He had seen this happen before.

Nor was it fear for his physical safety that had him turning in his tracks, looking for another exit from the plaza, but the realization that if he were caught up in a mass police sweep, they would find his rebel history. Herat might be able to vouch for him; then again, he might not.

Michael ran away from the city center, leaping over people who lay groaning and clutching their heads. He crossed an avenue full of cars, all stopped in orderly lines, drivers slumped in their seats. As he ran he remembered that other time years ago, when he had run through similarly silent, shocked streets carrying dispatches on foot because inscape was down, wire and fiber had been cut, and microwave bombs continued to go off, regular as a metronome. He remembered the echoes, which had bounced between tower and mountain over and over until the louder thunder of government lasers cutting down from orbit had drowned them out.

The rebels would use the current confusion to finish what the microwave bombs had started. They would go on an orgy of destruction in which not a single stone of the city would be damaged, but the values in every nanotag would be wiped clean. Ownership, credit histories, monetary value itself resided in the physical objects traded in these streets. There were no central records, as there might have been in centuries past. In the Rights Economy, information was immanent, and by the time the rebels were done, the citizens of this city would no longer own anything, not even the shoes on their feet. Whole inscape domains would be erased, taking with them jobs and pensions.

Any object that lost its nanotags automatically became government property, so hard-working people and those who had lived for generations in ancestral homes here would see their properties expropriated. The farmers who had brought their produce to sell no longer owned that produce. The government knew this would drive people into the rebel cause in droves, but they had no alternative. Their orders came from Earth, after all. Earth was very far away, and the Rights Owners there would not be sympathetic.

As people climbed to their feet, they would begin to realize all this, and then the rage would come. Within an hour, the city center would be a riot scene. Anyone identified as a rebel would be lynched, but that hardly mattered because resentment against the government economic hardship would drive those who had done the lynching into the rebel fold eventually, in weeks or months.

Michael circled the city, panting with exertion after the first few minutes. People were getting back to their feet, cursing and helping one another up. Some watched him go by suspiciously. And in the distance, he heard the sound of aircars droning low over the buildings.

New echoes came: "R-r-r-remain calm calm calm." Police cars spun in fans of dust ahead of Michael. Officers were leaping out into a milling crowd of workers who were locked out of their office building because its AI doorman no longer recognized them. Michael tried to hang back, but the growing crowd behind him was pushing him forward. Before he knew what was happening he was in a sea of running people, and he heard guns firing. Someone started screaming.

Somehow he managed to make it to an alley, and from there to an underground highway used by automated freight vehicles. Light came from ceiling grates; the vehicles were all frozen in place, and so he wove among them, and by this means made his way back to the streets near the Redoubt.

A few minutes later he paused at the top of the hill to

look back at the city. Smoke was rising from a dozen places in the towers, which were now all unrelenting gray, the illusion of faerie riches ripped away. Michael stood still for a minute, letting his breathing slow as he tried to compose himself. Then he walked through the gates into the Redoubt. Just inside the doors, he let himself slump against the walls. He'd made it.

"Dr. Bequith?"

He looked up. A slim figure clad in black stood before him. Rue Cassels was inscrutable behind her black sunglasses, but her forehead was pinched in the suggestion of worry. "What's happened?" she asked. "You look like you've run a marathon!"

"I have." He turned and put his back to the cool stone. "Rebel attack—on the city . . ."

"You were there?"

He started to nod, but a commotion from deeper inside the Redoubt caught his attention.

Rue Cassels pointed. Someone was shouting at the gates to the garden—several people, one yelling, "Help!"

They ran that way. The entrance to the garden was one of those giant valve doors that were the only egress from the Redoubt. A woman crouched there. "Gods and kami, gods and kami," she was saying. A small knot of people was clustered around her and something lying on the ground. These all looked like local people, Michael noted—townsmen come to trade to the large transient population that stayed in the Redoubt.

"They're on their way," said a man as he stood. At his feet a woman lay in a position that couldn't possibly be comfortable; Michael's scalp crawled as he realized she was dead.

"Linda!" Dr. Herat had appeared from somewhere. He knelt beside the prone figure and only now did Michael realize who this was. His vision dimmed for a moment from the shock.

"Dr. Ophir," whispered Rue. "What happened . . ."

"Shot," said the young man who had just stood. "I found her like this—it was just a minute ago! Whoever it is . . ." He gestured vaguely at the entrance hall, which was the way Michael had come.

"No, they must be gone by now." The woman who spoke looked around herself nervously.

Michael felt sick. Had he not gone walking in the city, he might have been with her and able to shield or hide her from the killer. Or he might have been killed as well . . .

He had to distance himself and so looked clinically and closely at everyone in the small crowd. Then he turned his attention to the body. Dr. Ophir's eyes were open, but her face was expressionless. She lay on her side, one arm flung back, and there was blood all over her chest and back. There wasn't much blood on the ground where she lay, but a splash of it stained the great doors that towered above her. Only a weapon could cause such a wound and not the sort of trifling rat-shooter you could buy from standard black market sources. This had punched a hole right through her chest.

Yes. This was just like that other time, when having been caught, Michael was marched through the streets by troops of the Reconquista, his message pack in the hands of the squad leader. They had passed Michael's designated rendezvous point and there in a doorway a man had lain crumpled like Dr. Ophir, with a hole in his neck and the same expression of dull surprise on his face.

And standing next to that dead man . . .

He turned away.

"It's the rebels," someone said. "Look, they didn't touch her satchel."

"Who is she? A visitor?"

Dr. Herat took Michael's arm and led him inside. Herat's other hand encircled Rue Cassels's arm.

"I've called Crisler," said Herat. "We'll tell him all about it. But from what you said to me the other day, Bequith, I don't think you'd fancy having to explain ourselves to the local authorities." Captain Cassels pursed her lips for a second, her head turning almost imperceptibly in Michael's direction.

"But who could have done such a thing?" she said. "Why?"

"The rebels?" It took a moment for Michael to realize Dr. Herat was asking him. He felt a surge of resentment at the implication that he might know.

He shook his head—not to deny it, but in confusion. "Why would rebels do this?—shoot one person, then run? It doesn't make sense. Unless . . ."

"What?"

"Unless the rebels know about the expedition."

"People know about *us*," said Cassels. "We got interviewed and everything."

"They don't know about *Jentry's Envy*, do they?" asked Michael.

"Well, we said it was a wrecked halo cycler. Nobody knew the alien bit except the people we contacted—the ones who got us in touch with the admiral."

Michael and the professor exchanged a glance. "Somebody knows," said Herat.

The captain wanted to talk to her people, so they escorted her back to her chambers. Then Dr. Herat and Michael went to find Crisler.

On the way, Dr. Herat said, "Does any of this make it easier for you to decide?"

"Decide what?"

"Are you coming along on this trip, or not?"

"I can't leave you now, after what's just happened."

"That's ridiculous, son. I can take care of myself."

Michael shook his head. It was shameful, the bombs, the people falling, and his own race through the streets—all this had made him feel alive in a way he hadn't felt in years. Something fundamental had happened today, and memories were flooding back of his brief time with the rebels: the excitement, the feeling of commitment.

There was one other memory that he could not deny, though. On the day when they had made their attack and Michael had been captured, he had been marched through the streets and had seen the body of a friend, shot like Linda Ophir had been today.

Standing next to that body, laughing with a colonel of the security forces, had been Michael's commander, Errend. Errend, free and relaxed, watching Michael being marched past after having betrayed all his comrades to the army.

"I'm going with you," Michael said firmly.

PART THREE

Jentry's Envy

1 0

WAKING CAME SLOWLY. For a while Rue drifted, wondering why the sounds around her were so like her habitat on the *Envy* and yet different—pumps whirred, voices muttered through the plastic walls, but not the pumps she was used to; and these voices were different. She blinked at the ceiling for a few seconds, realized she was on the *Banshee*, then groaned, rolled over, and tried to bury herself under the pillow.

Her alarm chimed again. In the past she'd been able to ignore such things; even if Jentry yelled at her for being late, nothing was really riding on her shoulders. Now, she had her people to think about. And Creepy Crisler and his band of merry men and those oh-so-serious scientists who were sharpening their knives even now for the dissection of her cycler.

Which they were going to do today, she realized. They had been at the *Envy* for two weeks now, four full days out of cold sleep. Everything was set to start exploring.

The thought of them going out without her supervision galvanized Rue. She threw off the covers and hurried to the bathroom. *Tomorrow*, she thought as she sat staring at the fake wood paneling. *Tomorrow I will sleep in.* She knew if she repeated this mantra once every day, after a few hundred repetitions it might come true.

The habitat balloons of the *Banshee* were palatial compared to her shuttle. Together the two balloons totalled twelve decks of large rooms and ample private space. There were labs, garrisons and weapons lockers, a complete medical facility and a gym. The lights were kept at Earth-normal most of the time, so she wore her sunglasses everywhere; luckily she had finally adapted to higher temperatures, so the twenty degrees Celsius air no longer made her wilt.

Her crew were awake now, though not entirely up to speed; despite their loginess, today would be their first EVA.

Rue's stateroom had a window, another contrast to her first time out. She turned the lights off to watch the stars wheel by. They looked no different than they had from Allemagne; she even recognized some constellations. In Rights Economy terms, she was still next door to Erythrion—and only two dozen light-years from Earth.

She turned away from the window with reluctance. There had been a couple of times when she'd had panic attacks standing here; looking out at the stars had been the only thing that had calmed her. Now, looking out had become a ritual.

After taking a couple of deep breaths, she fixed a confident smile on her face and stepped out into the curving hall of B Dormitory. A few of Crisler's people nodded to her in passing; the soldiers had a habit of checking her out, pushing the envelope of propriety, but they were always faultlessly polite when she spoke to them. Everybody radiated confidence; they were at the *Envy* and ready to start investigating its secrets.

They weren't like her—they were graduates of the finest universities, disciplined military minds. She was just a woman from the middle of nowhere, yet they treated her like an equal. It made her want to scream.

She entered the galley and immediately Corinna waved at her from an otherwise empty table. Blair had a tray and was headed that way too and she saw Max talking to the chef. Good. She nodded at Corinna, but before heading over there she took a detour.

Crisler sat with Dr. Herat, the lead scientist, at a table in the back of the room. Rue clenched her fists, loosened them and walked up to the two men. "How are you gentlemen this morning?"

They both nodded and greeted her courteously. Max had a term for guys like these: alpha males. Both men were instinctively dominant. They reminded her a lot of Jentry and having that frame of reference helped her. Alphas couldn't be coerced, but they could always be tricked; before Max had revealed that she owned *Jentry's Envy*, she had let him serve as foil with Crisler while she nosed around on her own. Now that he knew about her, Crisler was wary. She had been trying to appear young and naive around him, but lately was regretting that strategy. *You become what you pretend.*

Dr. Herat was a lot harder to figure out than Crisler. He seemed utterly relaxed, as usual. Being at the cycler seemed to have no effect on him, except maybe to increase his already considerable enthusiasm.

She remembered how she had been before her first EVA to Lake Flaccid. She'd thrown up. It wasn't the environment that had wrought her nerves that time—from the outside, Lake Flaccid bore a remarkable resemblance to Allemagne. It was no colder here than where she had grown up. No, it was a fear that hied her back to old stories about robbing graves. The cycler was cold and silent, after all: It was likely that it was in fact a tomb. She still felt uneasy whenever she thought about all the places here that they had yet to visit.

Still, she needed to be present on this first sortie. Herat was on the EVA team, at his own insistence. So were Corinna and Evan. Three other scientists and two soldiers rounded out the team.

"We're all set," Herat said sunnily. "The fellows on the EVA team are pacing like caged tigers."

"Remember, anything you find that might be a way of controlling the *Envy*'s course, you hand over to us. I invited your people on this trip to help me uphold my salvage claim."

"Yes, I know. But may I point out, Ms. Cassels, that we may not be able to identify the controls when we see them. How can you tell an alien inscape crown from a toilet? It could take us months. Then to understand how it works—"

She had learned to just interrupt him if she needed to get a point in. "I expect you to approve anything—but I also expect to understand everything you investigate. Look at it as a challenge; the fun part will be explaining it all to me in layman's terms."

He laughed. "I usually get paid to do that."

"You don't think having free rein on the *Envy* to be payment enough? When all your colleagues are sitting on their hands back at the Institute?" She smiled sweetly at him.

He stammered something.

"I'll see you gentlemen in the control room at ten o'-clock," she said, then hurried on while she still had the momentum.

"Oh, I'm sorry!" Michael Bequith had nearly run her down. He had a tray with two tiny bacon strips and a piece of toast on it.

"How do you survive on that?" she asked.

He blushed. He did that a lot, she'd found; she couldn't decide whether it was endearing or annoying. He was good looking, though, tall and lean, with dusky skin like Corinna and eyes so dark you usually couldn't see the pupils. He generally dressed severely and today was no exception: He was in a black jumpsuit with an equally black utility vest on it. A small, but not virtual, book lay on the tray next to his meager breakfast.

"I never eat much before a spacewalk," he said. "It's a sensible precaution."

"Oh, so you're on the team?" She already knew this, but wanted to keep the conversation going. Rue had a connection with him; they had both been there at the discovery of Linda Ophir's body, after all. She wasn't sure yet whether she liked Bequith, but she wanted to find out, and he seemed hard to get close to.

He grimaced at her question. "I'll be in charge of enforcing the quarantine precautions," he said. "Dr. Herat gets the fun work; I do the digging, he picks up the treasure." He grinned almost imperceptibly.

Interesting; she hadn't known he had a sense of humor at all.

"So spacewalks make you nervous?" she asked.

"Spacewalks into alien spaceships do." He shrugged. "Shouldn't they?"

"No, no, you're quite right. It's funny . . . nobody else is admitting to being nervous."

He registered a faint smile. "That's because most of them haven't got the faintest idea where we are."

"Oh? And you do?"

He peered off into the middle distance for a moment. "One thing I've learned in this job is, we never get used to the alien. Looking at something that's of alien manufacture is like catching a glimpse of God—no, don't laugh. What I mean is—well, ask yourself this question: What's the difference between holding an object, say a cup, made by alien hands and a cup created out of nothing by the universe—by the ineffable?"

Rue might indeed have laughed at this strange analogy, were it not that she remembered quite vividly how her scalp had prickled when she first looked through the telescope, saw one of the *Envy*'s habitats, and knew it was not man-made.

"An alien speaks, or a stone speaks—what's the difference?" said Mike. "The experience is similar."

"Rocks speak to you?" she said in a mock-indulgent tone.

"Not as such. Ask me about NeoShintoism sometime," he said.

"Uh . . . okay." Bequith was religious! She should have realized it before; he was very much the priest type, now that she thought about it.

"Don't worry," he said. "I don't bite."

"So you're from, what, the Vatican?" she asked.

"No, actually, I'm from Kimpurusha. It's not far from here—"

Rue's stomach did a flip. "Oh. If you'll excuse me, my crew's expecting me."

Even as she walked away, Rue was thinking, *Go back— keep talking to him!* She'd wanted to have some polite chitchat with the man and here she was running away instead. But if he really was from Kimpurusha, he was from one of the lit worlds that had betrayed the halo. In the years before she was born, there had been hundreds of embassies and trade centers around Erythrion, each representing one or another cycler ring. The jewels in the vast Cycler Compact were the lit worlds, places like Kimpurusha that had nearly Earthlike planets basking in the glow of G- , K- , or even M-class stars.

When the Rights Economy burst into the galaxy, visitations from the lit worlds had dwindled. It took as much to maintain one cycler as it did to maintain ten thousand FTL ships. Kimpurusha, once the spiritual capital of the halo, had turned its back on Erythrion and the rest of the unlit worlds. Rue had seen the former Permanence monastery at Treya; it was now a sports facility.

She was surprised that she felt so strongly about a decline that had begun before she was born. But then, this whole trip had been a series of revelations about just how much of a halo-worlder she really was.

"Good morning!" Blair waved her to sit. Max was already tucking into his food; he acknowledged her indifferently. Corinna sat herself next to Blair, just as Rebecca entered the room and looked around. Rue waved vigorously; Rebecca grinned and headed over. She seldom ate breakfast.

Max had focused his attention back on his meal and would probably not participate in the upcoming discussion; he was Bad Max again, after briefly being Good Max while they were on Chandaka. At times like these, Rue leaned heavily on Rebecca for support.

Evan was the last to arrive, which was typical. It was hard for him to drag himself out of bed; she had come to realize that he had horrible self-esteem. Rue wasn't surprised that he'd signed on again after loudly protesting that he couldn't. The crew of the *Envy* gave him the only meaning in his life right now.

"Sorry I'm late," he said, in exactly the tone he always used.

"Let's get down to business," said Rue. "The EVA's in an hour. First things first. Did you guys find the cache?"

Evan nodded. "It's right where we left it. Seems intact, from what I could see in the telescope."

"Good. Blair?"

"They don't know it's there. I checked the logs and talked to some of the techs. Like we predicted, the plow sail hasn't gone into ramjet mode since we left, so there's been no significant radiation on it. Parking it right next to the sail was a stroke of genius."

"We'll leave it where it is for now. What Crisler's people don't know can't hurt us. Are they still doing the radar survey of the habitats?"

Blair nodded. "It's supposed to wrap up tomorrow, though. Then they'll just do an occasional ping to make sure things don't move unexpectedly."

"Crisler will lose it completely when he finds out we're holding out on him," said Rebecca.

"Crisler is in charge of the *Banshee*, not the *Envy*," Rue said, with as much confidence as she could muster. "Leave him to me."

They nodded. Everyone was looking alert, with an undercurrent of excitement—except for Bad Max, who was indifferently stuffing his face. Rue had to smile.

"We're back!" she said. Everybody laughed; even Max grinned.

"We're back and we're going to find out how to control the *Envy*," she continued. "We'll handle this bunch of space marines and mad scientists and send *Envy* on her way back 'round to Erythrion. Then we go home and we're going to be heroes. Is everybody up to that?"

They all raised their glasses and cheered; the rest of the people in the galley turned to look. Rue laughed again.

She was thinking, though, that she had told a little story

to them: Capture the flag and return as heroes. It worked, it was a goal to shoot for.

She couldn't help remembering that they'd had no script to follow the first time they explored this place. Staring at the tiny dark crescent of an alien habitat through the scope, she had felt cold terror at facing a complete unknown. They had all felt it.

In talking to Crisler's people about their first trip out here, Rue had not revealed that they had huddled inside their shuttle for a week, debating and staring at that little crescent, before they'd summoned the courage to explore the lake.

It was so different this time around. But was it different only because, in bringing the *Banshee*, they had brought a comforting new set of stories to use in relating to this place?

The idea was too abstract to hold her attention; she turned back to her grinning crew and set about discussing plans.

MICHAEL HAD TRIED five times to compose a letter to his scattered brothers; he had deleted each one before sending it and now that they were at the *Envy* he couldn't hope to send an encrypted message out. Nonetheless, this morning he had felt compelled to write, so after breakfast, but before suiting up for his first trip to Lake Flaccid, he sat down in his tiny wedge-shaped room to compose.

He was more restless and unhappy than ever. Herat had forbidden him from performing any of the domestic duties he had always given himself. Those duties had been a kind of devotion for Michael—a palpable form of Service. Herat, the old bastard, knew that Michael needed to confront his demons, so had taken Michael out of his safe routines. Michael spent long hours in the gym and when he wasn't doing that he was getting to know the *Banshee*'s crew and Crisler's staff. He was now on a first-name basis with everyone except the enigmatic halo-worlders, who mostly kept to themselves. Michael could joke with the highest and the lowest and everybody thought he was a nice guy.

When he sat by himself in his cabin, he felt a black depression he'd not felt since the insurrection on Kimpurusha. It was as if the past five years had not happened.

He moved a private inscape window to easy view and subvocalized words: a greeting, a short summary of his expedition to Kadesh. He would not speak of *Jentry's Envy* here; it wasn't yet time and the risk was too great even if this message was encrypted.

"I have told you that something happened to me on Dis, but have not answered your inquiries as to what it was. I won't describe the actual events here, because they wouldn't convey to you the magnitude of the experience. Our goal has always been to become one with our environment—to absorb its particular character, which we call the kami or spirit of a place. That experience is always an experience of *union*, of joining with the world that we're otherwise alienated from. I've experienced it on a hundred worlds, in places humans can only timidly tread. On Dis, though . . . On Dis I experienced not union but annihilation: my consciousness expanded and at first it was ecstatic, but the kami of the place were too alien and too strong. I could see myself, infinitely small and vulnerable, a stranger to this place and then even that was gone; I was swept away, becoming one with Dis and lost to my Self.

"I tried frantically to find my way back, but I was lost in the vision. Dr. Herat found me and shook me awake, but the kami were still there, like a ringing in my ears, denying me my own reality.

"We have always believed that our religion was a real union of the transient individual soul with the eternal Absolute of the universe. But the kami of Dis are dying, slowly, in a paroxysm that will take a trillion years. Their light is fading; all light will fade, they tell me, and no one can hold back the darkness of individual and species extinction for long.

"What I am saying to you is that on Dis, I became one with the world and remained in that vision and am there still. And the vision is not what we thought it was; I am lost in it. I am truly lost."

He closed the window and rubbed his eyes. Beyond his little cabin, he could hear people moving up the stairs nearby; the *Banshee*'s balloon habitat was so small that the whole place bounced whenever anyone took a step. Michael knew he should be getting ready for the upcoming EVA, but he was so weary; all he wanted to do was sleep.

He popped the window open and reviewed what he had written. His brothers might understand his imagery, but to anyone else it would sound crazy—*wacko*, his friends back home would call it. Bitterly, he snapped the window closed. Enough self-indulgence. There was work to do. He stood and stretched and began to inventory his tools for the EVA.

1 1

"No, THERE'S NO chance this thing could be two billion years old," said Dr. Katz to one of the marines. "It would have eroded in this environment long ago."

They were all crammed into an inflatable airlock at the axis of the spinning habitats. The lock was transparent. Michael had trouble focusing on his suit checklist, because his gaze kept drifting to the infinite expanse of stars surrounding them. It was nothing he hadn't seen before—but to say that was to completely miss the point. There were few sights more awesome than space itself, devoid of worlds.

He tried to concentrate on the nasal twang of Katz's voice. "Any dust and debris we encounter comes at us as high-energy cosmic radiation. A few thousand years of that and even the best structure will deteriorate. No, this ship can't be more than a century or two old, if that."

"Yeah, what about this radiation thing," said another marine. "We're going so fast now, if we hit anything bigger'n a pin, we're vapor, right?"

"Maybe so," said Katz, "but you and I can't begin to comprehend just how empty it is out here. Every second each one of us is passing through about a million and a half times our own body's volume worth of space. In all that volume, we're only hitting a few stray particles—the rest have been cleared out of the way by the plow sail and there weren't that many to begin with."

The marine didn't look reassured. Michael couldn't say he blamed him.

"The stars don't look any different," said the first marine, who now had his suit check completed and his helmet dogged. Michael was still struggling with his gloves. "Isn't there supposed to be some kind of 'starbow' thing happening?"

"Popular misconception," said Katz. "Nope; you'd need a spectrograph to figure out our velocity. We might as well be standing still as far as I can tell."

Michael glanced behind him. Rue Cassels was already in her suit and was chatting with one of her crew. There were three of the halo-worlders on this jaunt, plus two marines and four scientists, Michael included. His scientific qualifications were pretty thin compared to some of the others, but he did have the benefit of five years spent with Dr. Herat.

The professor was suited up too. "Snap to it, Bequith. Here, let me help you." Dr. Herat settled the helmet on his head. "Nervous?"

"Of course. What kind of a fool do you take me for?"

Herat laughed. "There! You're all set. Not a second too soon, too—they're evacuating the airlock."

Michael looked around, expecting to see the transparent balloon crumpling in around them. It took him a few moments to figure out that since there was no air pressure out-side it, it wouldn't collapse even when all the air inside was removed.

"Load up! Four to a cart!" shouted the lead marine. Space suited figures began jumping up to the waiting EVA carts; these were little more than I-beams with clips, spare oxygen, and supply nacelles and a motor at the back. Michael clipped his safety line to one and found himself face-to-face—or more properly, faceplate-to-faceplate—with Rue Cassels.

"Mr. Bequith," she said brightly. "I'm sorry for my be-havior in the cantina this morning. It was rude."

"No offense taken," he said, a little stiffly to his own hearing.

"It just threw me when you said you were from Kimpu-rusha," she said. The cart lurched into motion and Michael grabbed for a handhold. Without missing a beat, Rue con-tinued, "I didn't realize I felt so strongly about it."

Michael tried not to look beyond her to where the translucent habitats were rapidly receding. They seemed the only objects in all of space.

"I feel pretty strongly about it, too," he said. He quickly checked to ensure that she had opened a private channel between them; then he said, "I was involved in a rebellion against the R.E. when I was seventeen."

He couldn't see her face now; she was a silhouette against the diamond-hard stars. She didn't say anything for a moment and he thought he must have revealed too much. Then she said, "I feel like an idiot."

"What do you mean?"

"Here I go knowing just how different all us halo-worlders are from each other and it never occurred to me that people from High Space might be diverse, too. I just assumed you were all one big happy family."

"I remember before the Reconquista," he said. "It was only twenty years ago."

"I guess so," she said. "We only heard about Kimpurusha four years ago. I grew up thinking that of all the worlds, it, at least, would never give over to the R.E."

Now that he thought about it, it was plain that news about Kimpurusha's fall would not even now have reached the farthest outposts of the Cycler Compact. Dispatches from his brothers at the monastery, sermons, and theological abstracts were still winging their way at lightspeed to the struggling colonies around isolated Jovian planets and methane dwarfs hanging in the silent darkness between the lit worlds. For them, the events of his childhood had not yet occurred.

"Turnover in five seconds," said the marine flying the cart.

"Hang on," said Rue. "No, like this." She drew his hand to a ring he hadn't known was there. "And watch the stars—it'll keep you from throwing up."

There was a stomach-lurching moment as the cart flipped over; watching the stars turn seemed to work, though, since that way Michael knew the feeling was real and not the phantom-falling sensation that he always had when weightless. "Deceleration in five," said the marine.

"There it is," said Rue. Her silhouetted arm pointed almost straight down. "Lake Flaccid."

Somebody had a floodlight and was roving it over the structure; there was no way to tell where the light was coming from, of course, since there was no air here to show a beam. Michael could see a disembodied oval of illuminated metal, which zipped to and fro dizzyingly, sometimes sliding off the giant sphere and disappearing completely. The first time that happened, he thought the light had been switched off, the effect was so total. It didn't help that the habitat rotated, so the vision of metal sliding through the spotlight made it seem as though the beam itself was moving, even when it wasn't.

"First time we came here," said Rue, "I was so scared. The place looks like my home, you know—like Allemagne. But it wasn't. It could hold anything—monsters, maybe, ghosts. I swear I have never been so frightened in my entire life as I was when we went to open the airlocks of the lake."

He laughed shakily. "I can believe that."

Whoever held the spotlight switched it to broader illumination and the whole habitat appeared, a ghostly white metal sphere covered with zigzag seams. A little vapor hazed off it; the marine, his voice flat, said, "See a bit of hydrogen evaporating from the heat of the lamps." They were probably still half a kilometer away and the light was not very strong. Michael decided he would not ask what the local temperature was.

The other cart blinked into existence below them; simultaneously its shadow appeared, hugely distorted, near the limb of the sphere.

"Knock knock," said someone; it sounded like Katz. "Anybody home?"

"There's two hotspots," said Corinna Chandra. She was on the other cart. "Opposite one another. Last time we found a hatch by one. Maybe there's one by the other."

"Did you mark the hatch you used?" asked Dr. Herat.

"We clipped a line to a ring there. You can see it at four o'clock."

It took a while for Michael to see it, because Corinna's four o'clock was his ten o'clock. A thin thread of white hovered just over the habitat's horizon; that must be it.

"We'll explore the second entrance later," said Dr. Herat. "Today we're going to follow your original route in. This time out we're interested in the lake, not the external structure."

Michael stared at the sphere, which was fast becoming a giant wall below them. "Decel burn," said the marine. Michael held on as weight reappeared for a second. Then they were drifting ever so gently in the direction of that dangling cable.

People from the other cart were grabbing for the line; Michael hardly noticed. He couldn't take his eyes off the sphere. He did not need the NeoShinto AI to help him feel awe of this place.

He imagined diminutive Rue Cassels floating here with her companions. Just them—alone, unknown to the rest of humanity and about to open an inhuman door. His admiration for her kept growing.

"Go, Corinna," said Rue. One of the anonymous space suits began to pull itself hand over hand up the line. Corinna stopped at a broad disk of ribbed and spikey, slightly purple material and began digging at an indentation near its edge.

"The airlock's a magnetic liquid; right now it's frozen so the magnets aren't on," said Corinna. "This switch turns on the heat and magnets at the same time. Watch." She withdrew her hand and the purple surface suddenly roiled and shimmered like an oil slick. Corinna reached over and her arm disappeared up to the shoulder in the material. "See?"

"Wait for us," said the lead marine. Both carts were at the cable now and Michael watched as they reeled themselves in.

"What's fun," said Rue, "is that the air pressure inside wants to pop you out like a grape seed. It's easier to get out than in, which doesn't strike me as too safe."

"On the other hand," said Dr. Herat, "there's no moving parts."

They were clustered around the disk now. "There's a bar just inside the edge here," said Corinna. "Just grab and do a flip—like so." She reached into the disk, somersaulted, and disappeared into it. The marines followed.

The material of the disk was denser than Michael expected—almost a meter thick and lens-shaped. It resisted his passage like a strong wind. When he completed his roll, though, he found himself floating inside a cylinder about four meters long and three across. It was brightly lit by the marines' floodlights and lined with ordinary-looking rectangular locker doors.

"You inspected these?" Herat pointed at them.

"Yeah," said Rue. "Nothing in them. Spotlessly clean, too. Like they'd never been used." She was undogging her helmet. "It's just nitrogen in here, so monitor your mesobots to make sure you don't come down with nitrogen narcosis. And keep your nosepiece in." She demonstrated the oxy clips, which promptly made her sound congested. Michael pulled up an inscape readout to watch the nitrogen scrubbers in his own bloodstream. He situated it down and to the right in his peripheral vision, so it wouldn't get in the way.

"Next is the strap palace," said Rue. She was obviously enjoying playing tour guide. "Come along, don't dawdle."

The far end of the cylinder had a two meter-wide opening in it. This turned out to be the entrance to a long round corridor. As Rue's name for it implied, the corridor was strung with hundreds of rubbery straps, each as wide as Michael's waist. They crisscrossed the space at various angles, making it impossible to see down the length of the cylinder.

"This is bizarre," said Katz unnecessarily. "What the hell are these things?"

Herat said, "I'd say the logical equivalent of handholds or steps, for something that uses its whole body for locomotion. Bequith?"

His scalp crawled looking at the things. "Maybe." Rue was hauling herself from strap to strap, closely followed by the two marines. The lights cast weird tongues of shadow across everything.

"This is like nothing I've ever seen," said Katz.

"But we can infer a lot from it," said Herat. "They were less than two meters in diameter, probably not more than three long; look, if you were a fish or an eel, you'd be able to bounce your way along this corridor pretty quickly. If it were completely open, you'd be whacking the walls or adrift—there'd be nothing for your body to undulate against."

"You think they're *fish*?"

"Why not? After all, everything below here seems to be full of some kind of liquid."

The corridor ended in a large long space Michael recognized from photographs as the shore of Lake Flaccid. It was spookier in real life: a long cylinder, like a cave or tunnel, lit only by darting flashlight beams, with darkness at its far end. Rue had overshot her landing and now hung in the very center of the space. She was fiddling with her wrist rockets, trying to jet back. In freefall, up and down were arbitrary choices; Michael could choose to think he was looking down a wide deep well, but it was more comforting to choose one side of that well and decide that it was "down" and that the side opposite it was "up." Indeed, in unspoken agreement everyone drifted over to one wall and oriented their feet down to it. Michael did the same and now he could imagine the cylinder was lying on its side and he and the others were standing inside it.

"Strange. What are these?" Katz's voice made no echoes here. He was shining his lamp at some translucent circles set in the floor. "Lights?"

"That's what we thought," said Corinna. She took a tiptoe step and sailed over to one. "But they're gelatinous and have things embedded in them. Like a jelly salad."

Katz joined her. "It's dark stuff, different shapes and sizes. Looks like . . . peas . . . and something cylindrical . . . and a square block. Can't be a light."

Herat dismissed the circles with a wave of his hand. "Signs. Actually," he said, looking around, "this place is festooned with writing. It's just that it's for beings who see with sonar."

Everybody turned to stare at Herat. Michael hid a smile; the professor was showing off, but he had to admit it was impressive. Herat's ability to look at an alien artifact and determine its purpose was legendary. These scientists were seeing that ability in action for the first time.

"Let's see what this lake is made of, shall we?" Dr.

Herat folded himself cross-legged and gradually drifted down to rest on the lip above the gray substance Rue had called a lake. Michael wouldn't have known that the gray stuff wasn't solid if he hadn't been briefed. It simply looked like the ends of the cylinder were metal and the slightly wider middle part was this gray material. It was hard for the planet-born to imagine a *cylindrical* pool, after all; the lake was below him, but it also curved up to each side and was overhead. Reason told him that because the habitat rotated, the liquid would move outward because of centrifugal force. It was much easier just to ignore the liquid above him and see only what was below.

One of the scientists, Dr. Salas, was a materials specialist. He hunkered down with Dr. Herat and they dipped things in the lake for a while, talking in low murmurs, sometimes laughing. One of the marines had unpacked some fish-shaped mesobots and now held one over the lake; its sonar was able to penetrate the strange surface with ease. Michael opened an inscape view of the sonar signal and got his first view of the bottom of the lake.

Evan Laurel saw the inscape window and drifted over. "Stuff conducts sound really well." He pointed out a feature in their shared window. "Hey, that looks like an armchair. . . . Except it's a good four meters across."

"There are openings in the walls," said the marine.

"Yeah. We figured we'd make some of those our first target. Gravity gets pretty steep as you go down. At the bottom it's twice Earth-standard."

The other marine had drifted out across the lake and was inspecting the far end.

Dr. Herat began to laugh. "Of course! It's a perfect solution!"

They all clustered around him. He grinned, holding up a jar full of grayish stuff. "It's not a liquid at all! It's actually made of fine little beads, a bit bigger than sand grains. It's a granulated aerogel!"

The marines exchanged an uncomprehending glance.

"Aerogels are ninety-nine percent air," said Herat. "We use them as insulation. They weigh almost nothing, but they're pretty strong. Our hosts, here," he waved around at the tunnel, "found they could make a kind of substitute for water, at a thousandth the weight. The grains don't crush easily, but they'll deform and move past each other. They behave mechanically almost exactly like a liquid."

Katz nodded vigorously. "Cheaper to accelerate," he said.

"I kind of thought that was what it was," said Evan. "But I didn't want to say so in case I was wrong."

"So now what?" asked Rue. "Can we go in it?"

"Oh, sure! It's not going to have any effect on our suits. And the sonar penetrates it. Perfect."

"In that case, we'd better set up camp. Corinna?"

She and Evan began unpacking and pasting down a pressure tent. "Just like old times, huh?" said Evan with a grin.

Herat shot a significant glance at Michael; that was his cue to butt in and make sure the halo-worlders followed proper quarantine procedure. He went over and politely asked to help. Meanwhile Herat, Rue, and the others crouched at the edge of the lake and ran their hands through it, discussing how best to proceed.

They erected two pressure tents and stuck them to the floor using a degradable glue. After several more hours spent surveying the axis, they retreated to the tents. Michael was in the larger tent, with Herat, Salas, Katz—and Rue Cassels. They stripped out of their suits, but left the black skintight underlayer on, as per regulations. In the event of a depressurization, the underlayer would protect them for several minutes.

There was almost no gravity here, so they pitched their sleeping bags standing up. That left plenty of floor space, where Salas and Herat hunkered down to play with samples of the aerogel. Katz fussed with the air mix for a while, then put on blinkers and earplugs and climbed into his sleeping bag. "See you in the morning, if that concept still has value around here," he said.

Michael sat down next to Herat. His employer had an uncharacteristically dreamy expression on his face. "Look at this place," said Herat, peering out of the tent's small window.

Michael called over his shoulder. "We've seen alien technology before."

"Yes . . . but this is different."

Michael nodded.

"How?"

They both turned their heads. Rue Cassels stood behind them. "How is this different?" she asked.

Herat scratched his ear. "Hmm . . . pretty fundamental question." Herat and Michael turned, offering a place in their circle. Rue drifted down to sit with them.

"Well," said Herat, "you know the R.E.'s been expanding through what used to be the cycler civilization for sixty years now. We actually had the FTL drive twenty years before that, but Earth hushed it up and started slowly, with exploratory vehicles that deliberately avoided the suns colonized by the cyclers. Even then the plan was to arrive at the cycler worlds with overwhelming force and complete knowledge about the stellar neighborhood.

"We sent exploration ships out to search for Earthlike worlds. The program concentrated almost exclusively on single, G-class stars like the sun. We did find life, everywhere, in fact. The universe is overflowing with it, it appears in unthinkable environments. It thrives brainless and without senses on nearly every world that could sustain liquid water. But intelligent life? That's another story. We didn't find any during that period—not currently existing intelligence, that is. But everywhere we went, we found the ruins of great ancient civilizations . . . cities and shattered fleets; burnt-off continents still radioactive after a million years . . . and everywhere, we found Earthlike planets that had been bombarded by meteors all at the same time, sixty-five million years ago.

"I spent a summer on the Yucatan peninsula, in Mexico,

studying the Chicxulub crater. It's sixty-five million years old; the meteor that made it caused the extinction of the dinosaurs. I'm partly responsible for naming the particular aliens who made that crater and thousands like it throughout the galaxy. The Chicxulub, you see, were the last pangalactic civilization. They wiped out every other sentient species in the galaxy by sending out self-reproducing planet killers—*von Neumann* machines—that bombarded every world that had animal life bigger than a fly. Then they died out in turn.

"The Chicxulub left the galaxy empty of technological species. Our studies showed that it took at least thirty million years for new toolmaking species to develop from the Chicxulub extinction event.

"The Chicxulub partly explain why the galaxy is so empty of intelligent life—but not completely. In the early years of the exploration the Panspermia Institute was formed and I was one of the first graduates. They filled our heads with idiotic notions; I was starry-eyed and intent on uncovering a galactic pyramid of consciousness, with microbes at the bottom, ancient wise species at the top, and us somewhere in the middle—A vision inherited from the mystical writings of Teilhard de Chardin, though I had never even heard his name at that point. But the stupid ideas we got from him resulted in the fiasco the Institute's in now.

"Our goal was to find our counterparts—conscious, toolmaking aliens whose civilizations might help us understand our own. We would find or help establish a galactic government, integrate our culture with those alien ones and follow the path to species-maturity. It was a fine vision and heavily funded by the R.E. We even built a giant orbital station, called Olympus, which was to be the home for our ambassadorial counterparts."

Rue nodded. "And you sponged our wealth off relentlessly to pay for it, until places like Chandaka can no longer survive on their own."

"Yes, but we thought it was for a good cause! We genuinely believed that the outcome would be a galactic civilization with a future history of millions, maybe billions of years, with humanity as the founders and chief patrons. Think of it! What greater dream could there be?"

Rue shook her head. "But the halo worlds could never be a part of it. We can't travel at faster than light. We could never visit Olympus."

"Well." Herat looked uncomfortable. "Nobody on Earth ever really believed anyone would live in the halo by choice. How could people live their whole lives without seeing the light of a sun? No—anybody born on a lit world would wither and die in the halos and we thought—they thought—that over time, the halo worlds would be abandoned. That's still the prevailing opinion in the R.E.

"So the Rights Economy went from being a completely local, Earthbound incestuous loop into a kind of panhuman taxation empire. It expanded like a swarm of locusts, devouring the inhabited lit worlds of the cycler civilization, bypassing the halo worlds and leaving them stranded and alone." Herat sighed. "I know it's a tragedy. I saw it happen. But at the time . . . it made so much sense. The R.E. was the only way to maintain control over the far-flung colonies, to prevent them from developing into political rivals, or from going transhuman on us.

"Anyway, thousands of ships were fanning out across the galaxy, searching for intelligent species. There was life everywhere, after all—why not life like ourselves?"

"Hang on," said Rue. "It sounds like you're saying you never found aliens. But I've heard about them—they do exist."

"Ah, well." Herat smiled sadly. "For political reasons, we have found it necessary to label certain species and . . . things . . . as aliens. Don't get me wrong—there are starfaring species out there, like the hinge foxes, or the autotrophs. We have found intelligent entities. Just . . . not what we expected. Not what we were looking for.

"Take the autotrophs. Because their planet had a more active carbon cycle than Earth, oxygen from photosynthesis took a billion years longer to concentrate in their atmosphere. Animals never developed, because autotrophic life—life that produces its own nutrients from ambient energy and minerals—had a billion extra years to evolve.

"The autotrophs developed in a kind of Eden, where predation didn't exist. They developed technology more as an outgrowth of their own bodies than as a cultural phenomenon. Imagine their shock when they began to visit other worlds and discovered that creatures who actually *ate* one another were dominant nearly everywhere.

"We've met the autotrophs. But they won't speak to us. To them, we are the worst possible moral abomination, right down to the cellular level.

"Then there's the solitaires. They're individual creatures, we know that. Each one has built a starship around itself and they travel all over the galaxy. But they don't have the concept of language at all; they're solopsists. Since we haven't even met one, we can only theorize about how they developed technology; I think they reproduce by budding and the new bud takes away the knowledge of its elder. But who knows?

"And there's the sylphs, who are incredibly dangerous. We set up colonies on six sylph worlds before we even knew they existed. A biologist on one of the colonies made the discovery that every form of life on her planet had identical DNA—from the giant fern forests to sea slugs at the bottom of the ocean, it was one species, just expressing different genes to become different life-forms. And even the plants had nervous systems. What's more, the colonists had all reported various levels of radio and electronic interference on these worlds. It turns out the sylphs communicate constantly—it's a global network that passes experiential information back and forth. By the time we realized this, a good ten percent of the colonists themselves were sylphs—changelings, replaced in the womb by mimics.

"After an initial panic we realized the sylphs weren't attacking, they were just doing what they do—adapting to a new feature of the environment, in this case us. The changelings didn't even know they were sylphs—their human consciousness was completely separate from the underlying sylph mind.

"Discovering this, we made the fatal mistake: We tried to communicate with them.

"The result," said Herat sadly, "was the extermination of a colony of twenty-five thousand people and the subsequent cauterization of the continent they'd lived on by our navy. It turns out that to the sylphs, the highest ideal is adaptation. To them, the notion of adapting your environment to suit *you* is horrifying.

"They happily cohabited with us as long as they saw us as just another feature of the local environment. When they realized we were conscious beings like themselves, they were so outraged that they moved to destroy us. We had to wipe out one entire sylph culture in order to prevent the information spreading to the others. The sylphs have FTL and they're incredibly powerful. We're now in the midst of pulling our colonies off their worlds—slowly and carefully."

Rue took off her sunglasses and rubbed her eyes. "That's awful."

"Well, the R.E. became a lot more cautious after that. About eight years ago, I was assigned to explore the various ruins we'd found and try to come up with a general pattern for the rise and fall of galactic civilizations."

"Really?" She seemed fascinated by that idea. "Is that when you hired Mike?" She turned her dark eyes in his direction.

"Shortly after," said Herat. "We visited hundreds of worlds and we did find a pattern. But we resisted accepting it, until we visited a place called Dis and were hit over the head with it." He smiled ironically.

"Go on," said Salas. "I've heard of Dis—what's it like?"

"Dis is a rectangular piece of woven fullerene, ten meters thick, four hundred kilometers wide, and five hundred long. Three billion years ago, it was part of a ring-shaped orbital structure almost two thousand kilometers in diameter. It had two-hundred kilometer high walls on the edges of the ring to keep atmosphere in and it rotated to provide gravity. At some time after its abandonment it must have been hit by an asteroid, which tore it apart. The part we found is in a highly elliptical orbit around a white dwarf star that was once a G-class sun. This sun long ago swelled up, swallowed its planets, and shrank again. Dis is the only legacy of a magnificent species three billion years old.

"Most of the soil and structures that were on the inside surface of the Dis ring were knocked off it in the catastrophe, but we found one nearly intact city and thousands of kilometers of subsurface tunnels. They left records and we were able to piece together a little of their history.

"They wanted their civilization to last forever—that's the one thing we do know about them. They built for the ages in everything they did. The evidence is that they did last a very long time—maybe eighty million years. But early on, they discovered a disquieting truth we are only just learning ourselves. It is this: Sentience and toolmaking abilities are powerful ways for a species to move into a new ecological niche. But in the long run, sentient, toolmaking beings are never the fittest species for a given niche. What I mean is, if you need tools to survive, you're not well fitted to your environment. And if you no longer need to use tools, you'll eventually lose the capacity to create them. It doesn't matter how smart you are, or how well you plan: Over the longest of the long term, millions of years, species that have evolved to be comfortable in a particular environment will always win out. And by definition, a species that's well fitted to a given environment is one that doesn't need tools to survive in it.

"Look at crocodiles. Humans might move into their environment—underwater in swamps. We might devise all

kinds of sophisticated devices to help us live there, or artificially keep the swamp drained. But do you really think
that, over thousands or millions of years, there won't be
political uprisings? System failures? Religious wars? Mad
bombers? The instant something perturbs the social system
that's needed to support the technology, the crocodiles will
take over again, because all they have to do to survive is
swim and eat.

"It's the same with consciousness. We know now that it
evolves to enable a species to deal with unforeseen situations. By definition, anything we've mastered becomes in-
stinctive. Walking is not something we have to consciously
think about, right? Well, what about physics, chemistry,
social engineering? If we have to think about them, we
haven't mastered them—they are still troublesome to us. A
species that succeeds in really mastering something like
physics has no more need to be conscious of it. Quantum
mechanics becomes an instinct, the way ballistics already
is for us. Originally, we must have had to put a lot of
thought into throwing things like rocks or spears. We eventually evolved to be able to throw without thinking—and
that is a sign of things to come. Some day, we'll become
like the people of Dis, able to maintain a technological in-
frastructure without needing to *think* about it. Without
needing to think, at all . . .

"The builders of Dis faced a dilemma: The best way to
survive in the long run on any world they colonized was to
adapt yourself to the environment. The best survivors
would be those who no longer needed technology to get
by. They tried to outlaw such alterations, but how do you
do such a thing for the long term without suppressing the
scientific knowledge that makes it possible? Over tens or
thousands of millennia, you can only do this by suppressing all technological development, because technologies
intertwine. This tactic results in the same spiral into non-
technological life. So inevitably, subspecies appeared that

were better survivors in a given locale, because they didn't need technology in that locale. This happened *every* time, on *all* their worlds.

"The inhabitants of Dis had studied previous starfaring species. The records are hard to decipher, but I found evidence that all previous galactic civilizations had succumbed to the same internal contradictions. The Dis-builders tried to avoid their fate, but over the ages they were replaced on all their worlds by fitter offspring. These descendents had no need for tools, for culture, for historical records. They and their environment were one. The conscious, spacefaring species could always come back and take over easily from them. But given enough time . . . and time always passes . . . the same end result would occur. They would be replaced again. And so they saw that their very strength, the highest attainments they as a species had achieved, contained the seeds of their downfall.

"This discovery finally explained to us why toolmaking species are rare to begin with. It takes an unusual combination of factors to create a species that is fit enough to survive, but at the same time is so *unfit* in its native environment that it must turn to its weakest organ, its brain, for help. Reliance on tools is a tremendous handicap for any species; only a few manage to turn it into an asset.

"The builders of Dis knew they were doomed. We all are: technological civilization represents a species' desperate attempt to build a bubble to keep hostile environments at bay. Sentient species also never cooperate with one another over the long term, because the environments they need in order to live are incompatible. Some, like the Chicxulub, accept this easily and try to exterminate everyone else. Even they can't stop their own evolution and so eventually they cease to be starfaring species. Destruction or devolution are the only choices.

"It's hard to see how we can cohabit with the autotrophs and the sylphs, if humanity is bent on expansion and so are they. Something catastrophic is bound to happen; and if not, well, we'll just evolve away from what we are, sooner or later."

"That's about as bleak a story as you can get," said Rue. She scowled off into space for a while. "But you still haven't answered my question: how is *Jentry's Envy* different?"

Herat nodded. "Two things. One is something we found on Dis, something that scares me even to think about. But I'll start with the other, obvious one: *Jentry's Envy* appears to have been built for more than one kind of species to use—not just more than one species, more than one *kind*. It implies the one thing we've never seen: multispecies cooperation. If it's not a fluke, a one-time happening in the history of the galaxy, then it suggests there may be a way to break the cycle of competition and destruction that's ruled since the first stars were born.

"But the other thing, the thing that scares me right now, is that while we were on Dis we found evidence that a number of other races had visited Dis in the past—searchers, like ourselves. In two places, we even found Lasa graffiti."

"Graffiti?"

"Well . . . artifacts and writings, like the ones on the habitat here. We haven't fully translated it, but the point is that one of those pieces of writing dates to the Lasa period, two billion years ago. We know it's Lasa because it illuminates the meaning of other samples we have—it's either Lasa or somebody who could think in the language. But the other . . .

"The other thing was a piece of Lasa technology that also appears genuine, because its integrated data storage has the unforgeable mathematical signature of the Lasa," said Herat. "But when we dated it, we found it to be only twenty thousand years old."

Salas whistled and sat back. "Two billion years . . ."

Herat shook his head. "It's impossible. But every time I

see the pictures of that habitat out there, with the Lasa writing on it, I wonder . . . Were the poor inhabitants of Dis right—is a permanent civilization possible? If so, how? What's frightening is the thought of how you might have to live—how you'd have to understand the world—in order to maintain a civilization for two billion years."

1 2

"YOU'RE SET TO go, people," said Rue Cassels. She waved down at Michael. "All signs looking good."

They were not wasting time. Michael had only just had breakfast and now he found himself clutching the lip of Lake Flaccid's shore, preparing to dive into who knew what. It was probably better to do it this way. Otherwise he might have to think about where he was about to go and that would be bad.

Michael heard Herat sigh. "Okay, let's do it." Michael let go of the shore of Lake Flaccid and let himself sink.

Real vision was impossible here. As the surface of the lake closed over the top of his helmet, Michael had a startling moment of déjà vu: He remembered as a child standing on the edge of a cliff in wintertime. He was all bundled up in a parka with the hood up and had been gazing out at some mountain sheep on a far slope, when a snow squall came up. In seconds everything went blank and he couldn't see more than a meter beyond his feet. Terrified, he had stood there for half an hour, englobed in white, until the storm abated and he could once again see the sheer drop at his feet. He had never gone to stand on that particular spot again.

The evac suit felt much like a parka and as soon as he entered the lake he was embedded in milky whiteness. For a while he just stared at it, able to see swirls and layers in it as he descended. He waved his arms experimentally. It certainly felt like he was underwater.

Then Dr. Herat's voice broke him out of the reverie: "Look at it! It's magnificent!"

Michael switched to the inscape view provided by the mesobot "fish." The sonar mappings of all three fish were combined into one 3-D model and Michael's POV was adjusted to match his actual position in that model. He could look around and it was almost as if it were his own eyes that saw, in false color, the interior of the alien habitat.

The first thing he noticed was that the wall he was following down did not extend all the way to the bottom of the habitat. There were windows just below him, then under that great arches opened up. The material of the walls swept down to become pillars that grounded in a blurry maze at the bottom; of course, since the habitat was a rotating sphere, the arches looked more like the arms of a star radiating out from the cylinder at the axis.

There were numerous round "signs" like those they'd found above, set in vertical rows in the wall. When the sonar hit them just right, they turned into complex three-dimensional swirls that seemed to move. *Beautiful.*

"It's all open down here." Herat was enjoying this altogether too much. In some ways, the man had no imagination, Michael had decided; he couldn't picture the nightmares that most people glimpsed in shadows. To him, this was just another place. True, Herat knew the utility of imagination; that was why he had hired Michael.

Their lines could snap (though they were fullerene, strong enough to suspend a whole building) and they might fall into jagged wreckage or even traps down in that blurred substrate. Or the weird aerogel beads could penetrate the suit somehow.

Or there might just be live things in here after all . . .

"How are you guys doing?" asked Rue. The marine answered, "Great, thanks," with more than a tinge of relief in his voice. "I'm good, Rue," said Michael.

Experimentally, he switched off the inscape view. It was

dark down here now—an unremitting slate gray, not at all like water. He held up his hand and couldn't see it until he plastered his palm against the faceplate.

"Tell me again what you're looking for?" asked the marine.

"Evidence of habitation," said Herat. "That means organic materials, ad-hoc structures—bodies would be ideal. We want to know whether this cycler was launched with a crew who later abandoned it or died here. Why is it empty? That's what I want to know right now."

"Yes, sir. My instructions are not to allow you to enter any small spaces, sir."

Michael flipped back to inscape. Dr. Herat's fuzzy outline was floating near one of the "window" openings. It wasn't dark in there—sonar shadows in this view were like solid extensions of the objects casting the shadow. Every now and then the triangulation of the three mesobots failed and one of the space-suited figures would grow a long spike-shaped tail for a few seconds.

"Bring one of the bots down here," commanded Herat. Something small and sleek slid up through the water to him, and the archway below Michael's feet vanished. He saw his own feet grow long pillars that grew down into indeterminacy.

This was the perfect place to try to capture a kami—but not right now. Michael's mouth was dry and his heart was thudding painfully in his chest.

As the mesobot approached the window, the opening took on more definition, despite being farther away from Michael than his own indistinct, overlapping hands. Since vision in his neighborhood was deteriorating, he swam in that direction.

"It opens up just past the entrance," said Herat. "I see . . . looks like a swimming pool."

"Maybe you should go topside, sir," said the marine.

"I'm not hallucinating, man—I'm looking at a wide,

long chamber with a low roof—maybe a meter high. The sonar hits a kind of boundary layer at the bottom and under that it's like another chamber. I'm going in."

"No! Sir—" Herat disappeared into the opening. The marine followed.

There was some scuffling and a sharp exchange of words. Then Herat and the marine emerged.

"It's water!" Herat had forgotten his anger immediately in the light of a new discovery. "There's long tanks of water in there. We're at about the one gee level here; you could swim in there and just sort of glide into the water. Maybe that's where they slept—the equivalent of living quarters. We have to do a thorough investigation—"

"Not before we've secured the approach, sir." The marine waved at the vaults below them. "I suggest we see what's down there before we proceed. And then, only with Admiral Crisler's permission."

"We don't need Crisler's permission," scoffed Herat. "Only Ms. Cassels's."

"He's right," said Rue. "It's my ship."

"You are correct," said the marine. "The ship is your responsibility. However, your safety aboard said ship is our responsibility. We are not threatening your ownership, merely doing our duty to protect you."

"We'll see about that," said Rue.

"Meanwhile," said Dr. Herat, "let's take this young man's suggestion and explore under the arches. Shall we?"

They backed the fish out of the opening and began to lower it and the others. Michael let out his line and drifted down after, with Herat behind him and the marine above.

The pools of water had sparked his imagination. This environment was alien, but something Herat had said last night came back to him: *What we will share most fundamentally with aliens will not be mathematics, or reason, or language, but basic bodily functions. If we're going to commune with them, it will be on that basis first and the others later or not at all.*

Indeed, the slope of these arches told him nothing—they were geometrically minimal structures and any cellular automata program could have evolved their design. No, what made this place make sense was the image of someone coming home after a hard day's work in an uncomfortable medium and slipping gratefully into real water for a rest.

He knew he was half-consciously building the empathic basis for a NeoShinto revelation. A few months ago that would have pleased him; now he saw it as making himself vulnerable to a frightening truth he didn't want to see; he angrily shrugged off the feeling.

They dropped past the top of one of the arches and for the first time the rest of the spherical habitat became visible.

"It's a town!" Herat laughed. "An underwater town!"

"Beware the metaphor, Professor," muttered Michael.

It did look kind of like a mountain village back home, though. Farthest away was a smoothly curved latticelike structure suggesting boxes or buildings that rose up from the valley at the equator of the sphere toward its rotational pole. The boxes had openings on all sides, even the roofs. Inside, the sonar presented various complex shapes as multicolored blurs.

The middle distance was cluttered by a number of closed spherical structures atop tall pillars. Some of these had closed tubes or ducts that angled up and away to merge into the distant walls.

Michael looked up. The arches made a vaulted ceiling just above his head. Above that, he knew, were the tanks of water Herat had spotted, then the axis where Rue and the others waited. If those tanks were the living quarters, then what they were now seeing was where the creators of this habitat spent their days.

Something about the tanks seemed out of place. After a moment, he had it: "Professor, if the bottom of this place is at two gees of gravity, why did they put the water tanks at one gee if two was their natural gravity level?"

"Hell, I don't know. Comfort? Low-gee for sleeping? Hmm—urmm."

"By rights then we should find some more water at the very bottom, for a normal homeworld environment." He looked down; the sonar didn't show the sort of boundary layer there that Herat had described—only a jumbled blur.

"Why don't you swim down and take a look?"

"Yeah. Give me one of the fish." A shimmering, shape-shifting form drifted in his direction: the metal mesobot fish, viewed with sonar.

He switched from the inscape view for a moment: It was completely dark here now. The sensation of being flipped over slowly—an artifact of the habitat's rotation—was all he could feel. Best not to think about that; he returned to the inscape view.

Michael dropped a few meters and began to notice a change in the feel of the aerogel liquid. It was thicker, more viscous. Probably the little spheres were more tightly packed down here—something that didn't happen with water, which was essentially incompressible. He was just wondering whether it might harden into a solid mass at a certain level, when something caught his eye. He felt a flood of adrenaline hit him even as he realized what he was seeing.

"Shit! There's a fan down here. It's a big-bladed thing, on its back. It's turning at a few RPM; I don't know if it's pulling or blowing."

He had his answer a second later, as the mesobot fish passed him on the left and began arcing slowly down in the direction of the fan.

"Professor! The combination of the fan and higher gravity's pulling us down! Grab my line."

The fish turned around and began undulating, trying to escape the pull of the fan. For a few seconds it stayed suspended above the blades, which in sonar-light looked more like pyramids or blocks, their undersides shadowed solid.

"Bequith, your line's played out and fallen down behind you. We're getting them to reel it in from above."

He looked around. The line, visible as a kind of wing behind him, was indeed draped down into the blur below. He could see the vague other end of it lifting up past the arches, but too slowly. He was directly over the fan now.

He looked down and saw a Dalíesque fan blade swinging out to touch his line, just as the mesobot fish lost its fight to climb and fell among the blades.

Instantly everything blurred; he heard a loud *clang* through the aerogel. Then something had hold of his line and was pulling him down.

Yelling, he clawed at the safety clip on his belt. Precious seconds were lost as he fumbled at it; all he could see were vague looming shapes surging by under his feet.

He found the quick-release and pushed it. The line jerked away and then Michael was sucked down by turbulence. Something struck him hard in the stomach. He fell, landed hard and rolled, hammering his head against the inside of the helmet.

MICHAEL KNEW EXACTLY where he was and what had just happened, but he wasn't sure whether he had been lying here on his back for a few seconds or an hour. It was completely dark and silent. The darkness made sense; the silence didn't.

"Dr. Herat?" There was no answer. He called up inscape; a flood of diagnostic windows opened like flowers all around him. Since they were artifacts painted on his sensorium by nerve implants, their light didn't make him wince, nor did it illuminate the darkness beyond his helmet visor.

The diagnostics were clear, though: He had been here about ten minutes and still had almost a day's worth of air left in the suit's recycler. The suit's comm unit was damaged, however.

He tried to sit up; his head spun and it felt like a great hand was trying to push him down again. He stood, slowly, and though movement was like pushing through a strong wind, he had no difficulty staying up. The worst part was the continuous spinning sensation, which he knew was real: It came from the habitat's rotational gravity.

From somewhere nearby a steady *chop-chop* sounded. That would be the fan. He could feel its effect, in regular pushes that almost made him stagger.

He was supposed to weigh twice his normal weight down here, but it didn't feel like it. Except for the thickness of the medium, it felt more like a standard gee. He could walk, or at least stagger under the strong coriolis effect and his feet touched down as fast as if he were standing in air on board the *Banshee*.

Of course. He bet that the creatures that built this place were more buoyant than a space-suited human. They probably couldn't sink in this aerogel and there would be a lower limit below which they couldn't swim—they'd just pop up again. What to him was a floor, would to them be as inaccessible as a distant ceiling.

By that logic, he would be standing in their machine attic. He might stumble into another fan in this blackness, or something worse.

But he couldn't just stand here. Or could he? They should be lowering the other mesobots more carefully even now and casting sonar illumination all through this area.

Wait a second—ten minutes? That was plenty of time for them to have illuminated the whole area and even brought down another diver and some safety line. Where was everybody?

Maybe he wasn't visible lying down. He tried waving his arms, after cautiously reaching out to make sure he wouldn't hit something. That should do the trick.

Michael stood there for a few minutes, waiting, while his head throbbed and he imagined all sorts of threats converging on him in the blackness. He waved his arms again and shouted, which was absurd since he just hurt his own ears.

Nobody answered. Nobody came.

After a while he decided he must have fallen in the sonar shadow of something big. He would have to walk. Arms out like a blind man, he shuffled forward. Almost immediately his fingers touched a solid wall.

He groped his way along it. It turned out to be a big metal box, just taller than he was. There was open space beyond it, but he only went a few meters before he encountered a low box with a grill; aerogel was surging up out of this, though not strongly enough to lift him. He skirted it and tripped over some cables. The weird combination of rotational gravity and viscous aerogel made him land on his face again.

Where were they? Michael ran through his entire repertoire of curses. His voice in his own ears sounded weak, boyish. He didn't want to die down here. Once he had believed death was merely a remerging with the universe. Now he saw that universe as vastly indifferent and himself as trivially small within it. To die was not to merge; it was simply to cease.

He forced himself to crawl, waving one hand ahead of him. And after a while, he began to see light ahead—at least, a change from total black to graphite gray.

They must be searching in the wrong place and they'd brought in floodlights to help . . . ? No, that didn't make sense, this stuff wasn't transparent at any wavelength.

The light brightened and it became evident that it wasn't coming from above but from something on the deck ahead of him. Michael stood up cautiously and walked forward. His faceplate became gray, then white, then bright and milky. He put up his hand and saw it as a shadow. Following the shadow brought him to another collection of shadows, a sort of crosshatch pattern. Some bars with a bright light behind them? He reached out.

His hand fell on a pipe of some kind. Running his fingers along it, he discovered it ended in a vertical junction about half a meter to the right—and another, on the left. And above. . . .

It was a ladder. They'd let down a ladder for him.

Michael laughed in huge relief and began to climb. This would be a story and a half, that was for sure. It was strange, though, how had they gotten a ladder in here in ten or fifteen minutes? He kept climbing, idly wondering at this, as the light fell away below him. No light emerged above.

He slowed his climb, then stopped. The ladder was a bit too steady under him to be something that had just been lowered from above. His people hadn't put this ladder here. It was part of the ship.

For a while he clung there in indecision, feeling his inner ear flip over and over from the habitat's rotation. He *had* to be visible on this thing. Nobody came, nothing happened, so he resumed his climb.

After a while he bumped his head and reaching up felt a smooth surface above him. A dead end? He felt about and his hand fell on an indentation, which had several knob-shaped things in it. He twisted one at random, then another, then reached up again.

His hand felt the surface again, but this time it was soft. He put his hand through it—this was an airlock like the one on the outside of the habitat. Eagerly, he pushed up through it—and into light.

"Gods and kami." He'd thought he must be back at the axis, but this was not the case. Instead, Michael found himself in a small round room with virulently green walls. Most of the floor space was taken up by the bulging round magnetic lock. The place was illuminated by, of all things, a sort of mirror-ball that hung in the center of the space. Four small spotlights spaced about the edges of the ceiling were aimed at it.

The room was a little more than a meter and a half tall. He had to crouch to stand.

A corridor led off from one side of the room. He hulked his way over to this; he seemed to weigh more than usual here, but not unduly much. The corridor sloped up steeply. It too was lit by little spots and mirrored pyramids set into the ceiling.

Michael checked his suit's readings. External air pressure: five bars, very high by human standards. Temperature: twenty-eight degrees Celsius. Humidity: forty percent. Atmospheric composition: ninety percent nitrogen, eight percent oxygen, two percent carbon dioxide. This might be breathable if you used CO_2 scrubbers; he didn't know enough about partial pressures to be able to say for sure.

Well, there was only one way to go. Michael started climbing.

The corridor ran a long way. Somewhere around halfway up he realized that the round room must have been in one of those spheres they'd seen balanced halfway up the cathedral space of the habitat. This corridor would be in one of the ducts that had angled up from them to join with the habitat's outer skin.

The habitat was designed for two entirely different species to use together. Herat, were he here, would doubtless be chattering on about all that. For once, Michael was glad his boss wasn't around; it felt much better to be panicking by himself and not having to do it for two. Herat wouldn't even know he was in danger in a place like this.

Michael's weight fell rapidly as he climbed. Finally the low corridor ended at a T-intersection. He estimated he was at about the level of those tanks Herat had seen. He would have to get higher than this; if two species inhabited this place, there should be another entrance at the rotational axis. There wasn't one on the shore of Lake Flaccid, but hadn't Corinna said something about there being airlocks at both ends of the sphere? Maybe there was one for each species.

The corridor he was in now curved off in both directions. It might well circumnavigate the sphere. There were square doorways at regular intervals. He picked a direction at random and walked, glancing with some apprehension through the first several doorways before passing them.

The doorways led to rooms of various sizes. These were filled with . . . sheets. Each room held dozens of vertical rods, always in pairs, and between these were tautly strung thick sheets of some clothlike substance. They were usually about three meters wide and six to eight long and were fairly tightly packed in the vertical; he counted up to fifteen stacked above one another. They filled the rooms right up to the door; the only way to get in would be by burrowing through these layers and maybe that was the idea: He pictured some sort of social animal, molelike, used to burrowing and being surrounded by friends and family. Among the taut sheets he glimpsed folded frames of some kind, as well as stacks of complex metal items and what looked like plain old ordinary boxes.

Tempting as it was to try to reach those, he had already had one close brush with disaster and who knew what traps awaited him in these strange chambers? Over and above that, he just shouldn't touch anything. This location was pristine and should be studied with care.

Before he was a quarter of a turn around the circle, he found another ramp going up—as well as one going down that he had no desire to investigate. He ran up the ascending way; it curved, indicating that it was following the outer skin of the habitat and not diving into the interior. By the time he reached the top he was weightless.

This was no longer a room, but something like the space between the walls of two cylinders, laid on their sides. He had no doubt that the inner surface was the floor that verged on the lake. He bounced around the space until he found a gray oval with an indentation next to it, set into the inner wall. He couldn't recall seeing anything like this from the lakeside, but if the aquatic residents of the habitat were blind then they wouldn't have signified the door with color anyway. He pushed the indentation and when the door had deliquesced, he borrowed Corinna's maneuver and flipped himself through it.

The light here was different—yellow and multishadowed. It came from floodlights that poised in the microgravity like cobras on their cables. He was inside the axis cylinder . . . and there were his people.

Rue Cassels perched on one hand on the edge of the lake. Beside her Evan Laurel was playing out line. Their eyes were intent on the surface below them, as if they could drill through it by eyesight alone.

The temptation was too great. Michael eased off his helmet and drifted over as silently as he could, careful not to cast a shadow over the two watchers. When he was right behind them, he said in his most innocent voice, "What's up?"

"Listen, we're going after him no matter what you say," said Rue without looking up. Evan did look, did a double take and shouted, "Hey!"

Rue looked up too. Then, "He's back, he's back," "We've got him, come back!" they were shouting. Both grabbed the lines that led into the aerogel and began hauling on them.

Michael watched them pull for a few seconds; then he said, "Aren't you going to ask me how I got here?"

"Sorry," gasped Rue. "We gotta get out of here."

"What . . . ?" A gloved hand gripped the side of the lake and a second later Dr. Herat was flying through the air, scattering sparkling aerogel beads. He was mouthing something inside his suit—grinning, of course.

"There's been an explosion on the *Banshee*," said Evan. "We've got to get back there with the sleds right away."

"The bastard wanted us to leave you," said Rue. She pulled and Corinna Chandra's faceplate broke the surface. "We told him to get stuffed."

Herat had his helmet off now. "Bequith, good to see you! Nothing broken, not too shaken, I hope?"

"A bit shaken," he admitted with a grin of his own. "But nothing serious. Professor, I've found it! Proof of the multispecies theory."

Herat gave a whoop and threw his helmet. It flew up past the axis and splashed into the aerogel. "Oh, I guess I need that. Excuse me." He dove after it.

The marines emerged from the gray soup and immediately started gesturing in the direction of the strap palace.

Michael watched Dr. Herat retrieve his helmet. "What about this explosion?"

Rue sighed heavily. "I don't know. Crisler said it was in the main life-support stacks. Dr. Katz flew back right away to help save them. Crisler wanted us all to come back and the marines pulled everybody out of the lake. We told them to go yank themselves and went back in."

So that was why nobody had come to his aid. He didn't feel any better about having been abandoned, but still the news was chilling. Had the explosion been deliberate? If so, was somebody willing to risk suicide in order to stop the expedition? Because destroying their life support this far from home was just that: suicide.

"Was anybody hurt?" he said after an awkward pause.

She shook her head. "But if the stacks are blown . . . we won't be able to stay. We'll have to go back into cold sleep and try to make it back to Chandaka." He could hear the deep disappointment in her voice, though her face showed nothing.

He frowned. "Maybe not. I don't know about food, but we might be able to get our air from here." He told her about the passages he had gone through. Rue listened in silence, then pushed her hair back with a gloved hand and puffed out her cheeks.

"Okay," she said. "That's the first good news I've heard in a long time. Thanks, Mike."

"Move out!" commanded the lead marine. They secured

their helmets, grabbed their instruments and data packs and one by one flew up to the strap palace.

They had no idea what awaited them back on the ship, but Michael found himself absurdly happy anyway. He had made a discovery, survived an adventure, and he had brought news that had made Rue Cassels happy. Maybe he had been right to come after all.

13

HALFWAY BACK TO the *Banshee*, Rue's radio crackled into life.

"Rue, they're locking us up! We haven't done anything, but the bastards are blaming us for the explosion!" It was Max's voice; he sounded outraged. "Hey, give me that, you—" The radio went dead.

Rue felt fury wash over her. "Crisler," she said. She'd been right not to trust him—he was a control freak just like Jentry.

The two sleds seemed motionless, while in the distance the two-lobed white shape of the *Banshee* approached. She could see a black smear on one of the lobes now: a torn section of hull, right where the life-support stacks had been. So Crisler wasn't lying about that, anyway.

"What do we do, Rue?" asked Evan. He was on the other sled.

"Just wait a sec," she said. Rue had to keep reminding herself that Jentry was not the model for all men. She was probably overreacting. She put a call directly through to Crisler.

He appeared in a little inscape window down near where her hands gripped the sled. "Ms. Cassels, I'm sorry for this inconvenience," he said immediately. "But we've got a situation here."

"When I spoke to you ten minutes ago you said you had everything under control," she said.

"Yes, well . . . the important thing right now is to ensure that no further damage is done. Since I don't know who caused this explosion, everyone's a suspect. I'm confining everyone to quarters and that includes your people. It's just until we can investigate properly and make sure the *Banshee*'s safe."

"And what about me?"

He hesitated, for just a second. "Naturally, you'll be free to move about as you wish."

She didn't believe him. That little hesitation said it all.

"All right then. Cassels out." She closed the window and leaned back. Her marine was at the front of the sled, his helmet turned toward the *Banshee*. Behind him was Salas, then Corinna. Rue had boarded the sled last.

They were still several minutes from the decel burn. She eased her feet out of the straps that connected her to the sled. Her heart was pounding. "I'm going to count on you guys to cooperate," she said on a public channel. "Do what you're told and answer any questions they might have. We'll get through this quicker that way. I mean, none of us did it, so we've nothing to worry about."

She spread her arms wide and cocked her hands down. Lifting her legs from the sled slowly, she gently fired her wrist jets. For a second it felt like she was hanging onto something with both hands. Then she cut the jets and watched the sled glide away.

"But what about Max?" blurted Evan.

"Max throws a fit over anything that keeps him from his hammock," she said. Her mouth felt dry as she watched the two sleds converge on the habitats of the *Banshee*. It wasn't that she was afraid of being out here in space—this was her home. She was frightened of facing Crisler's anger.

Well, hell, he was pushing her buttons and besides, she didn't have to justify herself to him. Really.

Now she was getting mad at herself. Cursing, Rue

flipped over and oriented herself to face Lake Flaccid. With a couple more squirts of the jets, she was headed straight for it.

"Cassels, what are you doing?" She wasn't sure whose voice that was, but whoever it was, they were pissed.

"I'm looking to my ship," she said. "How do we know they won't bomb that, too?" Then she switched off the radio.

This ought to start 'em guessing.

It was with a feeling of déjà vu that she found herself grabbing the cable outside the lake's airlock and hauling herself in. Last time it had been her brother chasing her. This time it would be marines—they'd be sure to have turned the sleds around, or launched more by now.

Wryly, she thought, *who's it going to be next time? The Lasa?*

Rue flipped her way through the airlock and dove for the strap gallery. They'd shut off the lights here, so she used her helmet spot to navigate. This was dangerously fun, actually—nothing better than thumbing your nose at authority. The only thing that made her feel guilty was the fact that she had a crew to look after. They'd be feeling pretty bewildered right about now.

But, as Jentry often said, "always negotiate from a position of strength." If she was locked up aboard the *Banshee*, she'd have no way to influence the outcome of Crisler's investigation. Especially if he, say, rigged the explosion himself as a pretext for taking control of the whole cycler.

Not that she believed this, she thought as she launched herself across the length of the axis cylinder. She was just a paranoid yokel from the Stations. Well, maybe. But she would still negotiate from strength.

They'd catch up to her pretty fast. Even now they might be at the airlock. Rue reached the far shore of Lake Flaccid and found the corresponding strap palace there. As they'd discovered, the axis of the lake was indeed symmetrical, with two shores, two strap palaces, and two airlocks.

A minute later, she was outside again, perched on the hull of the lake and out of sight of the *Banshee*.

There was no handhold here and no light except from the stars. That was plenty of light for Rue, who spotted what she was looking for almost immediately. She sailed over to the cluster of rings and little robot arms that held onto one end of a thin white cord. This cord rose slackly into the night, spiralling away to infinity.

Rue had seen the radar maps of the cycler habitats. They were all still connected to the plow sail by cables and not much slack had entered the system since the last turn.

She clipped herself to the cord and kicked off from the Lake. As she rose she gave herself a few tugs on the line to speed herself up, then used a third of her remaining jet pressure to accelerate some more.

The jets had accelerated her to about 150 kilometers per hour. She concentrated on trying to keep the cord from touching the ring of the clip; it rattled when it did so and would reduce her speed. Too much of that would be bad: She had a thousand kilometers more to go today. So she unclipped it, played out a little of her own grappling cable, made a much bigger loop and put that around the cord. As long as she wasn't going to drift away, she'd be all right.

It would take at least six hours for her to get to the plow sail. She had almost a day's worth of air and power in the suit, so that wasn't a worry. But she fretted, wondering what was going on back at the *Banshee*, while the gray line of the tether stretching out ahead of her wavered and swung as it passed through her loop.

RUE FELL ASLEEP despite her best efforts. She had an inscape window open next to the wavering cord and had reviewed her suit's recording of the trip to the lake. Then she put on some music she'd downloaded into the suit months ago and sang along with it. She ran through all that too and ended up staring at the long line as it zipped by her, until she was hypnotized and finally, dozing.

She came to with the impression that something was wrong and had no idea where she was for a few seconds. She saw only stars, heard herself breathing in the suit and reached out reflexively.

Her glove found the cord and clutched it before she realized what she was doing. She let go immediately, but not before she realized what was wrong: She had stopped moving.

Rue looked behind herself. The cord seemed to coil up back there; she must have hit a really slack part or a long curve, which had pulled on the loop of belt line until it braked her to a stop.

Great. She checked the time: She'd been asleep for three hours. Rue knew she had passed the halfway point before falling asleep, but beyond that, who knew? There was no way to tell where she was; the plow sail might be two hundred kilometers away or only five.

For a few seconds she just hung there, discouraged and cursing herself for a fool. What was she doing out here, anyway?

She would have to boost up to speed again. That meant losing more propellant. She'd be dangerously low when she finally got to the sail. But it was too late to turn around and go home.

The alternative was to pull herself along, which would be slower, but wouldn't waste any fuel.

Rue compromised, by hauling herself along the cord until she was going as fast as she could, then giving herself a little boost with the jets. Once she was going again, she checked her instruments.

Hmm. The magnetometer was going crazy and the Geiger counter readings were rising fast . . .

Something black had blocked out the stars ahead of her. It expanded quickly until it filled her vision.

"Crap!" She grabbed the cord with both hands; it scraped her gloves, yanking her to a stop just meters from the terminus of the cord. Rue found herself perched on the end of a long, insectile arm that curved away toward a gigantic black object. She hung on for a few minutes while she stopped cursing and her heart rate slowed. When her faceplate had unfogged, she took a careful look around.

The plow sail was like a huge black spider, cylindrical of body, with at least a dozen long legs fanning out from its open end. Each arm ended in a spinnerette that held a delicate thread. The threads trailed away to infinity behind or below, depending on how she wanted to look at it.

Everything was perfectly still against the stars. The monstrous shape made Rue decidedly uneasy—it looked like it was frozen in midconvulsion and might at any second thrash those giant legs and draw her into its mouth.

The eeriness of it made her remember Dr. Herat's story about Dis. For a moment she could vividly picture the place—the dead roads and buildings black under the stars, a weightless cityscape where bodies frozen for three billion years still drifted through the rooms like ghosts, or embodiments of despair.

She tore her gaze away from the plow sail and opened an inscape window. In it, she issued the call to awaken the cache.

When they came to *Jentry's Envy* the first time, they had not done so in just one shuttle. Max had insisted that they fit two for the journey, the second being redundant and packed with extra supplies. It was horrendously expensive and nothing had gone wrong to warrant using it, but every day that they spent out here Rue had been thankful for its presence. When they rode the beam in to Chandaka they had left it behind, to further guarantee their safety upon their return. And Rue had instructed that no one should mention its existence on Chandaka.

She found it after a minute's searching; it had lit up as per her instructions and now appeared like a dim pearl in the night. Rue unclipped herself from the cord that connected her to the plow sail and Lake Flaccid and jetted out to meet it.

Ten minutes later she floated before a console in the cache, orienting an inscape camera so that it showed the wealth of netted food bags and equipment behind her. The picture was lined up perfectly, but she still hesitated a long moment before pinging Crisler. Her head hurt and she had to talk to herself for a few minutes to get her voice to stop shaking.

When she called he responded instantly. "So," he said. "Where are you?"

"I know how it looks," she said, "and that can't be helped. But I'm not your bomber. In fact, I think I can help."

He arched an eyebrow disdainfully. "My life support blows out, you disappear and the next morning there you are in what looks like . . ." he peered past her, "a treasure trove. What *should* I think about it?"

"This is our local cache of supplies."

"Supplies? You never told us about any cache," he said.

"Why should I have?" she said, her face hot. "The *Envy* is my ship; it's under the jurisdiction of the halo worlds. You are visitors."

"And now that you no longer need us, you're sending us packing back to the R.E." He said with an angry nod. "I see."

"No, you don't," she said. "Why would we blow up your life support? We need it, too."

"Do you? Not according to what I see behind you. Plus which, how many other caches have you got stashed around the *Envy*?"

"Oh yeah," she said with a laugh. "We could have lifted thousands of tonnes of stuff out of Erythrion, right? Infinite amounts. Get real, admiral. We came out here the first time with two balloons full of stuff and we flew into Chandaka with one of them. Do the calculations yourself—it was the best we could do with the energy budget we had. Would you have brought all your material back down from near-c if you were me? And would you have told people that you'd left stuff there? Think about it."

"I've been thinking about it," he said darkly.

"Then you know it doesn't add up," she said. "Why would we blow up the *Banshee*'s life support while most of us were aboard it, if we wanted to scuttle you and send you home? If that were the plan, all my crew would be aboard the cache with me."

"Bad timing?" he said.

"We'd have to be idiots to be even getting ready to do something like that right now—we just got here! If we were going to do it, we would have waited a week or two until we were thoroughly camped out somewhere, say in those rooms Mike found in the lake. And you know perfectly well that all I'm after here is proof that the *Envy* is going to return to Erythrion at the end of her cycle. We don't have that proof and I don't know how to get it—so we still need you and your scientific team."

"So why did you cut and run, then?"

"You were going to lock me up, weren't you?"

He met her eyes. "No, Rue. I gave you my word and I would have kept it. Do you distrust me that much?"

"I . . . I had to imagine the worst," she said. "If the saboteur's smart, he'd make it look like we did it. And while we were cooling our heels in your brig, you guys might have found the cache on your own and that would just clinch it then, wouldn't it?"

"So? You're still out there with it. But I have your crew."

Rue made a face and waved a hand at Crisler. "Oh, stop it. Like I said, you wouldn't have my crew if it really had been us who did this. Look, Admiral, nobody wants this mission to succeed more than me. My future depends on it. For that reason, I'm bringing the cache back. We can try to rebuild the life-support stacks with my supplies."

Crisler scowled. "In exchange for . . . ?"

"Nothing! Don't you get it yet? This isn't a negotiation, Crisler. I'm *giving* you the cache. As a gesture of good faith and to prove that I'm not your bomber."

The admiral's scowl gradually subsided into a frown.

"Okay," he said finally. "We might be able to get back on-line with the material you've got there. Then what? I still have a saboteur to deal with."

"It's somebody who doesn't want the expedition to succeed," she said. "Or somebody who desperately wants to get back to Chandaka with news about what we've found here. Which is more likely."

He nodded. "I'd been thinking along those lines myself. Your disappearance threw me—because you're right, it doesn't make sense that it was you. But . . ."

"What?"

He was scowling again. "We're still in danger. Look, Rue, I'll let your people out and meet you in the boardroom when you arrive. We've got to work out a strategy to deal with this—either find the saboteur or neutralize his effectiveness."

"I'd rather talk about everything in the open—everybody present, no secrets," she said.

He shrugged. "If you want."

"Okay. The cache is pretty unwieldy. I'll be a day or two in getting there."

"We'll send some sleds on ahead to get the critical gear," he said. "Otherwise, we're going to run out of air before you get here."

"All right. Are we done?"

"Yes. And Rue . . . I'm sorry for my presumption of guilt on your part. Thanks."

"You're welcome." She cut the connection, and felt herself slump in relief. She hadn't been crazy to act this way; that was something to remember.

So was the fact that Crisler could be dealt with. Humming, Rue turned to the task of reviving the rest of the cache's systems.

MICHAEL HAD WATCHED as Crisler talked to someone through inscape, but he couldn't hear the dialogue or see the other person. That damnable military inscape was clouding his senses again. Finally Crisler's lips finished moving, he turned, and Michael found he could hear again.

"I suppose you know why you are here?" said Crisler. He had an expression of distaste on his face, as though Michael's mere presence offended him.

"Yes, I've written up a full report about my discovery in Lake Flaccid—"

"That's not what I mean." Crisler smiled grimly, and Michael felt his confidence evaporate. He had just spent the last few hours locked up with Rue's crew—with no explanations or apologies from the marines who guarded them. He had assumed some kind of overall quarantine was in effect.

There were other reasons why Crisler might take an interest in him, though.

The admiral was waiting. Michael cleared his throat. "Are you presuming some . . . involvement on my part in this explosion?"

"Bombing," said Crisler. "It was a bombing. We found traces of a chemical explosive."

"But why assume one of our people? I hate to say it, but the halo-worlders have the best reason for wanting us gone—"

Crisler shook his head. "The explosive was tagged."

"Tagged? What do you mean?"

"Everything's tagged," said Crisler. "From tables to starships. The tags are molecular-scale. It's impossible to get them out of a manufactured object without destroying that object. This bomb had tags, ergo it came from the R.E. and not the halo."

"The rebels."

"A rebel." Crisler leaned over his desk. "Maybe this rebel."

Michael's past was far behind him, but he still shifted uncomfortably under Crisler's gaze. "I had a brief flirtation with the rebels when I was a kid," he said. "So did a lot of people."

"Maybe. But you have also maintained illegal religious

activities ever since." Michael must have reacted, because Crisler laughed. "Yes, we knew about your NeoShinto activities all along. Tolerated them, because you were useful. But you must admit it looks bad for you: a known connection with the rebels; current membership in a secret order that seeks to undermine the R.E. through religious proselytizing."

Michael's defensiveness gave way to anger. "I'm just continuing an old tradition, a tradition of my homeworld. A tradition your people destroyed."

"My people? Interesting turn of phrase." Crisler sat back, steepling his hands. "Of course, I don't have any proof it was you. Just supposition. But one slip-up this far into deep space, and we're all dead. So I can't afford to take any chances."

"What are you going to do? Put me into cold sleep for the remainder of the trip?"

"I actually thought of doing that. But Professor Herat has told me that he'll go on strike if you're put down. Anyway, I don't need to lock you up. Not if you wear this." Crisler tossed something small across the table. Michael picked it up.

It was a little earclip, with a beadlike lens on it. "Wear that at all times," said Crisler. "We'll be monitoring you through it. Take it off, and we'll find you and shoot you. That is all."

Michael's face burned with fury and shame. He fumbled to clip the damnable monitor to his ear, then stood.

He had just put his hand on the door switch when Crisler said, "Oh, I nearly forgot!" Michael turned.

The admiral waved a hand and an inscape window appeared above the desk. "Have you ever seen this man before?"

Michael glanced at the picture, then looked again. He put his hands behind him to hide a sudden tremble. With difficulty, he kept his voice steady as he said, "No."

"Hmm. Too bad. And quite surprising, given that this

man Jason Errend was the rebel leader who headed the failed insurrection on Kimpurusha. We thought he'd changed his allegiance, and we trusted him for a while. Now he's disappeared again. Think about it, Bequith. If some memory comes to you of this man, please don't hesitate to come see me. My door's always open." Crisler smiled pleasantly, as though they'd been making lunch plans.

Michael lurched out the door, thoughts and emotions whirling in confusion. He couldn't help but feel the weight of the little traitor on his earlobe; it made him want to avoid meeting the gazes of the people he passed.

It was all too much to take in—particularly the shock of seeing Errend's face again, after all these years. Michael had always believed Errend had betrayed the resistance— had turned in his fellows on Kimpurusha. Michael included. Yet Crisler said he was still an active rebel leader.

Michael had trusted Errend, and the trauma of betrayal had driven him into the arms of the NeoShinto brothers.

Had he been wrong?

He went directly to his stateroom, but when he entered he saw that someone had been here. His Mark 820 datapack, in which he had stored illicit kami during his travels with Herat, lay on the bed. It was an open invitation for him to pick it up and access it. He knew that if he did, someone would be watching through the clip on his ear. They would see if he discovered the pack had been wiped clean of its illegal contents. They would see the kami if he accessed the pack to see if the files were still there.

He sat and stared at the black case—unable to pick it up, unable to ignore it.

He did not leave his stateroom for the remainder of the day.

RUE ARRIVED BACK at the *Banshee* the next morning, and Crisler immediately called a general assembly in the ship's round gymnasium. The science team was there, and Rue brought her people—all except for Max, who couldn't be bothered to move today, damn him. The small space barely held everyone; Rue ended up perched atop a piece of exercise equipment.

"The news is pretty grim," the admiral said as soon as the last stragglers arrived. "We have enough oxygen and food to maybe keep everybody going for a few days. If Dr. Bequith's discovery pans out, we may have resources we can use on the *Envy*." Rue smiled at Bequith, but he stood with his head down, eyes fixed resolutely on the floor. Odd.

Dr. Katz nodded vigorously. "We could put excess personnel in cold sleep after we find out how well we're supplied."

"Then what?" asked Crisler. "We can't complete the surveys here if we're understaffed."

Rue stood up on her bench. "But we're in the halo now. If we can get enough food stacks going to keep at least a skeleton crew alive for a few months, we can drop a rendezvous ship on the Colossus beam. We buy some new stacks from Colossus and we're back in business."

Crisler scratched his chin. "Can we do that? We'll be passing Colossus at near lightspeed. If we stopped there, the *Envy* would be . . . maybe years away before we got back to it."

"There are ways," she said. "It takes a dangerously high-g arrival and departure. You only get a few days of stopover before you have to leave. Then you have to accelerate to a higher velocity than the cycler just to catch up, then slam on a braking magsail and match speeds. It's punishing and expensive, but my people have being doing it for centuries."

"It might just work. The alternative is to return to Chandaka for supplies and that'll cost us a good year—though if your skeleton crew turns out to be too small, R—Captain Cassels, then we don't gain anything, do we? If we can't explore the rest of the *Envy* in the meantime . . ."

"Well, let's work out our minimums," she said. She

knew they were surrounded by uncertainties, but it wasn't the first time for her. They had to stay focused on the critical issues or let the whole expedition collapse.

"This scheme of visiting Colossus seems highly risky," said Katz. "What have we got to buy new stacks with at Colossus? These things don't come cheap."

Rue had thought of that. "We can sell our preliminary findings, or passage on the *Envy* to its next stop, if the passengers bring their own stacks."

"Unacceptable," said Crisler. "I don't want information about the *Envy* getting out."

"Oh, come on! Colossus is two light-years from the nearest lit world. Even if your precious rebels heard about what we've got, it would take them years to find out about it!"

"Nevertheless," said Crisler. "And two years isn't that long."

"All right," she said. Her hand strayed to her throat. "I do have a . . . negotiable item independent of the *Envy* that I can sell. I'm sure we can get the stacks and more with it." She carefully ignored the looks of surprise that passed over her crew's faces at this revelation.

"So are we going to fly the *Banshee* into the Colossus system?" asked Katz.

Rue shook her head. "No, that would take too much energy and time. We send a small group, and they ride the beam in—just like we did at Chandaka."

"That sounds suicidal," sputtered Katz. "Admiral, are we really going to rely on this—sorry, Rue—primitive cycler technology?" She glared at him.

"Rue's right," said Professor Herat. "Why interrupt our investigation of the *Envy* by shipping out in the *Banshee*? For that matter, if Rue's negotiable item is information, we could sell it and order the stacks without having to leave the *Envy* at all. Isn't that right, Rue?"

She nodded. "Dr. Katz, the Cycler Compact has functioned for centuries. It's far from primitive. They would have to honor an agreement like that. Unfortunately, my item can't be radioed on ahead. I'll have to sell it in person."

"All right," said Crisler, "so we have the beginnings of a plan. Now, assuming we use the supplies that Captain Cassels has graciously donated, we can survive until we reach Colossus if we put . . . how many people?"

"Forty," said Katz, rather quietly.

". . . Forty people into cold sleep."

This news did not go over well. Rue watched the scientists eye one another, and tighten into small groups, muttering. "I know," said Crisler, one hand raised, "forty of sixty-eight people is a huge hit. We have our unknown saboteur to thank for the situation and we'll just have to make the best of it. If Rue is right that we can pick up supplies at Colossus according to time-honored cycler tradition, then we revive everyone afterward. This means that we are committed to the full year-and-a-half exploratory mission, but considering what we've discovered in just scratching the surface here, I don't think that'll be a problem. We'll disembark at Maenad and return to the R.E. with our results. Comments, anyone?"

"Well, yeah," said a young chemist named Hutcheons. "Who's going into the tanks?"

"We want to maximize the science presence, obviously, but we can't completely eliminate the support team," said the admiral. "We can't ask Captain Cassels to spare any of her people, so a reasonable cut would be twenty of my people, mostly on the military side, except for a squad that will guard the tanks and other essential equipment from further sabotage. Twelve of the support staff leaves eight to be cut from the science team. Dr. Herat will have to decide on who he needs the most."

Hutcheons shook his head vigorously. "That's not fair. We all know Herat will keep the priest awake no matter what. Somebody's going to get put down in his place."

There was more muttering. *The priest?* Rue looked

around at the crowd. Then she noticed Michael Bequith standing to one side, eyes still fixed on the ground. Other members of the science team were looking at him too.

"Oh, stop whining," Herat said. "You're only going to miss the initial exploratory phase—something Bequith has years of experience with. The real work comes later anyway, you know that."

Herat walked to the front and turned to fix his team with a determined look. "You all know I seriously object to tampering with alien archaeological treasures, but as Admiral Crisler keeps pointing out, this is a survival issue. We're going to have to search the *Envy* for usable supplies. One thing we can say is that oxygen is oxygen and we're not going to learn anything from the gas stored in the tanks we've seen attached to some of the *Envy*'s habitats. We can harvest that gas if it's not being used by the habitats themselves. Now, we will learn from the tanks, damn it, so I don't want them busted, drilled, reamed out or painted! We need isotopic and engineering studies of them.

"Doubtless we could find a lot more supplies if we ransacked the place, but if we do that then we make a joke of the scientific expedition. So we will proceed slowly and systematically. Is everyone clear on that?"

There was no more grumbling. After a moment, Herat nodded sharply and said, "It's important to know what progress we've made in the little time we've been here. Dr. Katz, could you present our findings from the habitat Rue's people so colorfully call 'Lake Flaccid'?"

Katz was taken a bit by surprise. To cover himself, he began summoning inscape windows, until they surrounded his head like a cloud of playing cards. He glanced at these and cleared his throat.

"Well, the main finding is, of course, that *Jentry's Envy* really is a multispecies starship. This has profound implications; it could revive the project at Olympus and the political impact is going to be huge.

"Even so, this raises more questions than it answers. If

there really are at least two species involved in creating *Jentry's Envy*, where are they? All the stars within twenty light-years are either inhabited by humans, or empty of useful planets.

"Secondly, we've completed isotopic analysis of Lake Flaccid and, by laser, on two other structures. The isotopic distribution matches several stars in the local stellar group. Most important, the hull of Lake Flaccid contains a record of its age: There's a steady rain of cosmic rays on the *Envy* and from the number of tracks in the hull metal you can directly calculate how long the ship's been travelling at this velocity.

"The answer is exactly forty-seven years." Katz waited while the now excited buzz of conversation died down. "If there is no FTL drive on this ship, then it's impossible for the *Envy* to have come from more than about forty light-years away. If it's a true cycler it's travelling in a rough circle and will eventually return to its starting point. We think that starting point is less than twelve light-years from here.

"If that truly is the case, then we have a paradox, since this whole volume of space is well known. At this point . . . I'd welcome any ideas," he ended weakly.

The scientists proceeded to get into a roaring debate. Crisler stood back, arms folded, and watched with satisfaction. Rue took the opportunity to edge in the direction of Mike Bequith, who was standing aloof; apparently no one would talk to him. Some kind of revelation had occurred concerning him, and Rue had to know what it was.

After letting the argument go on for a while, Katz raised a hand and said, "People, please! We can talk till we exhaust the stacks, but it won't get us anywhere. The evidence is there to be collected, if we just go look. I suggest that our next stop be the habitat that has the Lasa writing on it."

This touched off even more debate, but Rue had reached Mike now. "I wanted to thank you again for your discovery yesterday," she said. "I thought we'd lost you, and I apologize for getting you into that situation to begin with."

Mike appeared surprised. "It's . . . my job," he said, his voice a bit husky. "But thanks."

"I wanted you to know that you've served my ship and crew well," she said. "Now tell me, what was all that about?" She nodded in the direction of the arguing scientists.

Mike squinted at the wall for a few seconds. "I'm a suspect in the bombing," he said. "The only suspect, it seems."

"What? Why?" Then she remembered her first impression of Mike: He had been eavesdropping on her conversation with Evan in the gardens at Chandaka. She'd thought that impolite at the time, but not sinister. Now, though . . .

He grimaced. "I was briefly involved with the resistance, years ago. It was the kind of foolish thing you do when you're young. But it seems there's no outliving your mistakes."

"Hmm." She decided not to judge that, now—it might pay to be more cautious around Michael Bequith in the future; on the other hand, he had been nothing but charming and helpful during the expedition, so far. "Why are they calling you 'the priest'?"

"Because Crisler's told everyone that I practice a banned religion," he said.

Well, that at least was not a total surprise. "NeoShinto. You told me about it, so I looked it up. It's banned in the Rights Economy, but not in the halo. If you can't practice your religion in peace and quiet on the *Banshee,* all you need do is visit the *Envy.* Remember that."

He stammered his thanks. The meeting was breaking up, so Rue took her leave of Mike.

He might be the threat Crisler was searching for, or he might be innocent. Either way, by offering him a haven

Rue had hopefully made him less of a threat to her own people.

Besides, he was kind of cute.

14

"STERLING ACCOMMODATIONS," SAID Dr. Katz. "But I'm sure we'll get used to them."

"Thanks for the support, Henry," said Laurent Herat. They were watching some of Crisler's marines unload boxes into one of the more capacious chambers of the Lake Flaccid warren. They had figured out how to unclip the sheets that were wadded into the rooms and here had packed them into a corner, leaving uprights standing like too-thin pillars everywhere. Two members of the scientific team sat in the corner, suits off, reading about partial pressures and trying to program their scrubber implants to handle the local air. There were public inscape windows everywhere, full of equations, photos, and journal articles and one or two hovering models of life-support equipment that the techs were using as schematics. You walked through them like clouds.

Michael Bequith was depressed. He had been struggling against admitting it to himself, but the strain of Crisler's accusations and the revelations about his past that had followed the explosion had mired him down. It didn't help, today, that Katz was in such a good mood.

"It'll be fun," said the habitat specialist. "We've gotten way too soft, let our machines do all the work for us. You know, when I was young I used to design habitats from scratch with big constraints on them—not enough air, or no free water supply. The more these halo-worlders tell me about their lives, the more I think I should have been born out here."

Herat laughed. "You're one of a kind, Henry."

It continually astonished Michael how men like Katz and Herat could completely fail to notice their environment. They crouched now in a long, rectangular chamber, a meter and a half high, its perimeter stacked with boxes. Fine: But every time Michael really looked at his surroundings, his breath caught. This was what Rue Cassels called "the creeps" and over years spent with Dr. Herat, Michael had learned what caused it. It was the sensation you got when the wind took an inanimate object, say, a shirt and for a moment made it flap its arms and reach for you. It was the sensation he'd had on their one visit to Earth, when he had stood at Stonehenge and found that the stones looked simultaneously natural and artificial; his mind couldn't reconcile the two.

This place was deliberately designed and yet no human person had ever stood here. Human instinct reacted just as though these walls had fitted themselves and the lights assembled from nothing and lit on their own. In a sense they had; an independent inhuman part of the universe had created *Jentry's Envy* and perceiving this, the part of the human mind that once saw spirits in stones awoke.

"No, don't put that there, we're going to partition that corner for the toilet," Katz shouted. "These jarheads," he muttered. "We're well rid of them. Told one to put up some numbers on the doorways and he just slapped numbers and letters up randomly. Just not thinking."

Two marines shuffled the boxes over to where Michael was standing. "Excuse me, Father," said one; they both laughed and one or two of the scientists hid smiles.

Everybody knew about Michael's NeoShinto activities. Apparently, he was a joke now.

"Ah," said Katz. "Here, look at this. Team B is inside the Hive."

He waved to a large inscape window; several members of the science team were clustered around it, including Dr. Herat, who would obviously have preferred to have been at the Hive than here. The image showed a gray oval blob;

Michael couldn't make head or tail of it until a space-suited figure crawled into view, providing scale. The image shook and moved and the blob took on dimension: It was a sort of oblong chamber. The chamber was a little more than a meter high and twice that long, more like the inside of a large cocoon than a room.

"Captain Cassels told us that they'd visited only one other habitat before reaching Chandaka," Katz said. "That was the Hive. They didn't take any photos because, as she so eloquently put it, they 'freaked.' I can see why."

The camera moved through a narrow slit in the papery end of the cocoon and emerged into another identical space.

"That's the fifteenth of these in a row," somebody said. Michael could hear a faint chatter of voices coming from the window, including Rue Cassels's.

"No, left, left!" said Herat. "Ach, idiot, wait, I'm coming over."

"We're not waiting for you," said Rue. "You have to give us some autonomy, Professor."

She and Herat proceeded to descend into an argument over procedure. Rather than get drawn into that, Michael left the room through its wide door (labeled with a big sticky "I") and looked for the steep ramp he had first come up when he'd found these chambers. Maybe the feelings this place awoke in him had always been illusions, creations of his own that he used to fill a void in his life. Maybe this really was just a thing, magnesium alloy and aerogel filling, no more or less significant than any rock. It had been created by blind evolutionary fate, as had he; he wasn't going anywhere but where his genes led him; nor was the human race going anywhere. Herat had proven that—they were at the top of the evolutionary arc, with nowhere to go now but down. So all this investigation was futile. You could already see the seeds of decay in the inequities of the R.E. itself.

He found the ramp (labeled N) and headed down. He

found he had to crab walk because of the steepness of the descent. Michael wasn't sure why he was coming this way, but maybe it was because the chambers above were no longer his—Katz and his troupe were taking the heart-pounding excitement of Michael's discovery and transforming it into a hotel.

Not that Herat wasn't excited. Proof that somewhere, somewhen, alien life had banded together in the same spirit of oneness that humanity took as its own essence . . . well, that had always been Herat's dream. And now it had come true.

Michael reached the bottom of the ramp. Here was the little round room he had climbed to—exactly as it had been, save for the letter taped by the entrance: P.

Whoever put down these letters must have been more than half asleep, Michael thought idly as he walked around the magnetic airlock. The randomness of the lettering seemed apt somehow—it was like this whole place, a purposeless jumble.

He sat down by the airlock and rested his gloved hand on it. Soon enough they would get the air balance right and then he could take this suit off and feel these walls himself. He wasn't completely here yet, insulated as he was by the suit.

After an empty moment Michael snatched his hand back. He knew what he was feeling: The kami of the place were calling to him—or, at least, that was how he'd been trained to describe the feeling. As a child he'd thought this feeling to be simple loneliness and maybe he had been more right then than now. But if he was going to escape the feeling, whatever its name, he no longer felt that the kami were the way.

Which left him back where he'd started.

The monks of Kimpurusha had their psychology; Dr. Herat had his. If Herat ever felt down he would just do something—anything, from reorganizing his files to taking a walk. Dr. Herat was rarely unhappy for long and maybe there was a lesson in that.

Thinking of the professor reminded Michael of the explosion and before that, the murder of Dr. Ophir. And there, of course, was something he could do.

He glanced around the chamber. If he sat down here and started to meditate, would Crisler see and send someone after him? Probably not; although the sensor clip was still on Michael's ear, there was no evidence that anyone was actually watching what he did through it. Maybe no one was; maybe the clip was inactive, just a cruel joke by Crisler—like the fact that Michael's offline datapack had not been tampered with.

Crisler could probably monitor anything Michael did in the public inscape network through that clip. But there was no way he could monitor the private loop-back network made possible by Michael's NeoShinto implants.

He sat down in full lotus facing the corridor and called up his private inscape foyer.

Instantly he was surrounded by dozens of iconic objects, slowly rotating photos and control surfaces. These would not normally be visible to anyone else, but his suspicion of inscape ran all the way back to his childhood and Michael had spent a long time adding various semilegal privacy devices to the foyer. They were stored, with the rest of his private data, in the data chip in his skull. He had novels in there, hundreds of hours of music, movies, and all the reference material he might ever need in his work. All that storage was too cramped to accommodate even a single NeoShinto kami, of course.

With luck, Crisler's sensors would not be able to tell his connection to this data from ordinary meditation. If they could . . . well, he would find out when they came to arrest him.

He sat for a while, wondering where to start. If Linda Ophir's murder had not been a crime of opportunity committed by someone still on Chandaka, then it was safe to assume that the perpetrator was also *Banshee*'s saboteur. In that case, there were two likely motives for her murder: She'd found him out, or she knew something else that he couldn't allow anyone to learn. Michael had wondered all along what she had been about to tell him, when she asked to see him that day.

Before the sabotage incident, Michael had uploaded all the research data and preprints done so far on the expedition. He also had a crew roster and some background on everyone.

He would start with learning a little more about who Linda Ophir had been.

RUE WAS RELIEVED to see stars again. She faced away from the long oval habitat she'd dubbed 'the Hive,' listening with half an ear as the others exited its rotating airlock. The scientists were all agog at what they had found, which puzzled her since what they had found was absolutely nothing: chamber after paper-wrapped chamber full of nothing. The Hive was just that: a giant, empty wasp's nest awaiting its wasps.

"If the others pan out, then we'll have proven the Hypothesis," gushed Hutcheons. The Hypothesis, Rue knew, had something to do with whether *Jentry's Envy* had been abandoned or whether it had never been used at all. That didn't really interest her—she knew the answers would present themselves eventually. No, she had entered the Hive again to try to find more supplies of raw materials, like water and oxygen. They had discovered none—just a cloying methane atmosphere, dry as a bone.

She had an inscape spreadsheet open above and to the right in her sensorium at all times; on this spreadsheet, she juggled numbers trying to guarantee their survival until they should reach Colossus. It was a familiar exercise, one she had engaged in over a year ago, the first time they reached the *Envy*. Max called it obsessive—but then, Max didn't take responsibility for the crew of the *Envy* or anything else for that matter.

A ghostly circle blotted out some stars in the opposite direction. Evan was repositioning the cache by the lake, now that most of its cargo had been off-loaded at the *Banshee*. She had begun using it as her crew's primary living quarters, while the scientists had largely moved into the warrens Mike had discovered. Its carrying capacity was written in glaring reds and greens across her spreadsheet—good, but not enough. Whoever had blown up the life-support stacks had better be found by Crisler's boys, because if she got to him first, he would be out the airlock.

"All right, gentlemen, where next?" she asked cheerily as she swung around. The science team were clambering aboard their sled; five helmets swung to face her simultaneously.

"What do you mean?" asked one. "We've been out here for eight hours. We're going home, aren't we?"

"The suits are good for another twelve to fifteen hours and as long as we're out here in them we're not putting a direct drain on the *Banshee* or the *Envy*," she said. "We need as much information as we can get as quick as possible. There's a whole bunch of places we could visit before we go back."

There were groans from the team and she sympathized; they must have found it as nerve-wracking as she to spend all day crawling through those chambers, picturing huge dry insect bodies scraping through them, possibly waiting beyond the next door-slit. She no longer believed they would find living aliens on board the *Envy*, but that didn't prevent the imagination from putting them around every corner.

"How about the Lasa sphere?" Hutcheons suggested hopefully.

"Nope. You remember what Herat said: It's potentially the most fragile find here, so we leave it for him to open. That is, unless we don't find any more water, in which case we'll have to break in tomorrow and clean it out if it's got any.

"Okay, here." She called up an exaggerated inscape view of the other habitats, which seemed to hang like moons at random across the sky. "Somebody pick a direction and let's go! We're wasting air."

"Oh, all right . . . that one." Hutcheons reached out and in their public inscape, one of the habitats flashed. This one was a big rusty cube, fifty kilometers away.

"Right. Hang on, everybody . . . away we go."

INSCAPE NORMALLY SHUT down when you closed your eyes. That had puzzled Michael when he was young; his father refused to discuss the subject, so he had asked a teacher at the seminary school. "If I closed my eyes I'd be able to see all the colors and shapes so much clearer! But every time I shut my eyes it goes away."

"They did that because of bad things that happened to people back in the beginning," his teacher told him. "Men and women tried to use inscape to hide from the real world. They spun themselves fantasy worlds and then shut themselves away in little airless rooms, slowly starving to death while they built a false paradise for themselves in the Net.

"After some people died they made it so that you could only take your senses away from reality in special circumstances. Rather than build something that appeared to be a separate reality—but isn't—they decided that everything should appear to be here, in this reality, with us. So the public and private inscapes were developed. Private inscape is made up of those things that only you can see, public ones are the windows and shows that you share with other people. They all reach you by the same means, through the implants in your sensory nerves.

"Now, we believe that this trend has gone too far in the opposite direction; the Rights Economy has layered its version of reality on top of what everyone sees and hears—strictly in the name of economics, they claim, and the alternatives could be far worse. True—they could completely control the appearance of reality if they chose. But as it is, though they think they are being moral, they are godless people, because they have made it appear that the essence of things is money—that a thing only really exists if it can be bought or sold. When you look at a rose, you no longer see the immanence of the thing itself; all you see is a price."

Michael contemplatively turned over the offline data-pack he used to store kami. Crisler had neither taken it from him nor wiped the kami already stored in it. He was sure that was deliberate: Crisler was saying more clearly than words could express that he could take the pack away any time he chose.

The kami of Ember and the terrifying kami of Dis were still in there. He knew he should erase the kami of Dis, but even with those huge files in the system there was plenty of extra storage space left. Enough for him to try something he had not done since his final days at the seminary.

One of the reasons Dr. Herat encouraged Michael's religious activities was that the kami often revealed insights into alien places and things that Herat himself missed. The professor had a brilliant mind, but not everything could be seen with the rational faculty. On more than one occasion he had called upon Michael to scry an object using the NeoShinto AI—calling up a history half imagined, half inferred. Herat knew that the deepest engines of human thought are unconscious and he respected Michael's ability to tap those powers directly. Michael himself always found the experience disquieting.

He had gotten nowhere with his search of the databases he'd archived from the *Banshee*. Terabytes of data were arrayed about him in diffuse clouds and he was certain that the right kind of analysis would show a clue as to why Linda Ophir had been killed. If there was no such clue, that was also proof of something—namely that her murder had been one of opportunity.

His analytic powers and even those of the semilegal search tools he'd brought from Kimpurusha, weren't up to the task of finding that clue, or its absence. So he was faced with a choice.

Years ago, when he was testing the limits of his ability to touch the kami, Michael had tried to find the kami of inscape. He had no doubt that they were there; everything that came to human consciousness as a presence held kami. So one night he had sat down in the middle of a marble floor under the wan light of Kimpurusha's faint ring and summoned the kami of Data.

He activated the data storage unit now and held it up to eye level. He could feel a connection being made between the AI in his skull and the unit; he lowered it, closed his eyes and overrode the safety defaults of the inscape interface.

With a wrenching twist, all his sense of place and position vanished. He seemed to be hanging in a vast ethereal space, high above the misty galaxy of data he had been exploring. The illusion was total—vision crisp, murmurs of musical pattern thrumming all around him. This place was seductive, as always, in its perfection. And already he could sense the kami here.

When he was younger, the kami of Data had almost killed him. They were infinitely powerful and mercurial. They defied identity while greedily sucking it from everything in their domain. They embodied the spaces in between the blocks of information that were known to people using the Net. So they had come at Michael as answers to questions he'd never thought to ask; they had promised unifications of senses, like the texture of green or the sound of height. As soon as he entered their influence they fell upon him and he was trapped in their realm until his brothers found him in the morning and pulled him free.

The Michael of today was far more disciplined and his attention more focused than that younger man. As he felt the kami beginning to swirl around him like the precincts of a hurricane, he pulled them deliberately, one at a time. He examined the towering half-minds each in its turn and discarded it. The kami of this data resembled those who had stored information here; after months or years of being constantly half-connected to inscape, everyone left tracks. The papers written by the science team were here, each hyperlinked a thousand ways to notes, observations, citations, and personal logs of the authors. Many links trailed off into private inscapes whose data were not replicated in Michael's archive; but most were public. They made a collective music that came to him as ghosts of the authors' personalities.

He was looking for one ghost in particular and it didn't take long for him to find it. Linda Ophir lived on in her writings and in the thousands of small personal touches she had left in her public inscape galleries. The NeoShinto AI took hints of connection and spun them into personality. In seconds Michael found himself standing in front of Linda—or a composite of her whose age was indeterminate, sometimes childlike, sometimes wise and of dizzying depth. It stared back at him quizzically and opened its mouth to speak. He heard a thousand recordings of her voice—notes, voice messages, recorded lectures—blur together into a single yearning for meaning and in that yearning he understood completely why she had chosen science as her religion.

The ghost's eyes were mesmerizing; Michael was falling into them, disoriented, overwhelmed by her voice and the force of her character. He clutched for something else to hold onto and found, strangely, the hollow emptiness of Dis. Remembering it, he was able to look away from Linda's eyes.

"What are you hiding?" he asked her. He sensed turmoil and looked back.

Unlike most of the scientists in the expedition, Linda had kept almost nothing private. Her whole life was open in her writings and recordings. So the single, tiny block of files that were conspicuously missing from the continuum of her work were as instantly visible to Michael as a crack in a pane of glass.

He reached down, grabbed the absence that should have

been several hours of Linda's work and pulled. As he did he shut down the NeoShinto AI. The ghosts fled and he was left holding a set of files.

He blinked, returning to the strange little airlock and now finding it homey. For a minute he just sat there, breathing, trying to forget the ghosts and the electric power of the kami of Data. Eventually he looked up from the floor between his knees. Several files were rotating in the air in front of him—photographs, by their icons. They had been stored in a public photo archive called "Waste Disposal Systems: Schematics."

Hidden in the open.

This guile was suggestive—was Ophir trying to hide her data from her own people?

When he felt ready, Michael opened the first, then, in puzzlement, another and finally all of them. This was not what he had expected—not that he knew what it was he'd expected, really.

The images were all of the Lasa habitat, the final one being a holo globe mapped with the pictures to create a miniature model. The black sphere with its red cuneiform lettering was instantly recognizable. These images were all tagged B. G., which hyperlinked to Blair Genereaux—but they had been annotated and the annotation layer was initialed L. O.: Linda Ophir.

He opened all the annotations. He rotated the globe; it looked like the one in the public archive all the scientists were using. Nothing odd there.

But in the annotated version, several of the photos had some of the background stars and certain Lasa words circled. With those highlighted, it was easy to see that four of the photos were in fact duplicates. He looked closer: The coordinates on the photos were different, suggesting that they had been taken at different points in an orbit around the habitat. But no, the photos were the same.

He looked at the globe again. The lettering formed discrete units—paragraphs—that were separated from one another by large areas of black hull. There were twelve of these paragraphs and it had already been noted by the science team that not all of them were written in Lasa. But they were all unique—except for one duplication.

He sat back, startled. One of the Lasa paragraphs was repeated, on opposite sides of the sphere. No other text was duplicated. And that duplicated text was the text from the duplicate photos.

So somebody had removed one or more of Rue Cassels's original photos of the habitat and reordered them to hide the fact. There were precious few reference points from which to tell what you were looking at: Every picture was identical to the others except for different letters splashed across the dark circle of the habitat. But if you looked closely enough, you could see the deception—and Linda Ophir had obviously looked close enough.

He should be getting back; his keepers would be wondering what he was up to. He felt a surge of anger at the thought of the spy camera on his ear, and decided to defy it. He turned his attention back to the photos.

For a while at least, Michael's attention was not on the dark ancient whisperings of the kami of Dis, but on the faint traces of another kind of more tangible spirit; those of a deadly human who hid somewhere aboard the *Banshee*.

"DON'T YOU HAVE anything to say to me?"

Max had tried gamely to lose her in the *Banshee*'s corridors, so Rue had simply stood in the doorway to the cold sleep chamber until he arrived. She had waited, biting her lip and fuming, and now here he was, skulking up guiltily, but trying to look casual. He planted his feet a few meters away, dropped his satchel and squinted at her.

"What?" he said.

"Come on, Max. Weren't you even going to say good-bye?"

"Good-bye?" He scratched his head, eyes looking everywhere but at her. "I'm just taking a nap."

Rebecca had called Rue an hour ago; all she'd said was, "You'd better get over to the *Banshee* right away."

"Why? What's happened?"

Rebecca had sighed heavily. "It's Max."

She hadn't had to say more. Rue had never thought Max would duck out on her like this—but it was obvious in that moment, and she had simply said, "Yes," to Rebecca, and flown over.

"Six months is not a nap, Max," she said now. "Why are you doing this to me? I need you!"

He finally looked at her. "No, Rue, you don't. You never did. If I hadn't fronted this expedition, you'd be happily surveying a mountain on Treya somewhere. You'd be living modestly, but you'd have a stable relationship and a social set. And now?" He shrugged. "You're more of a natural leader than you know. You don't need me as a crutch, that's for sure."

It drove her to distraction when he talked like this. "But *why*?"

He rubbed his hands on his pants, shrugging again. "There's nothing for me to do here. You're perfectly happy living in a can like this. I grew up under sunlight, such as it was. Anyway, I'm no scientist and I'm certainly not starship crew." He sighed heavily. "What do you want from me?"

"A straight answer."

"If you don't want me to go, say the word. You're the captain, after all." She heard the resentment in his voice and that just made her feel worse.

"Max, you know I love you. I'd never hold you back from doing what you want to do. But this isn't healthy. You're running away from something. What?"

He laughed. "You only just noticed? Oh, couz, sometimes you're so naive."

Max picked up his satchel and moved to pass her. She stood her ground.

"Look," he said, "some of us find life easy. I have no

idea how. You're one, I knew it the instant I saw you. You've got courage, Rue. But me . . . all my life, I felt like I've been running on water. The instant I pause, down I go." He gently put a hand on her shoulder and moved her aside. "I'm okay if I've got something to fight against. Something to do. But if I have to sit down and face myself . . . the pit opens. You don't understand and I'm sorry that you want to. Not all of us can be heroes, Rue. Not all of us can even face the day. There's no *why* to it. It just is that way."

He walked into the cold sleep chamber without looking back.

Rue watched him go. She was astonished, not at what he'd said about himself, but at what he thought of her. Courage? Courage? She had never had that. What others took for courage in her was just another kind of fear: fear of not measuring up, of failing her people.

She wanted to call him back, force him to understand that she needed his support now more than ever. But she couldn't bring herself to step across the threshold. She couldn't ruin his dignity that much.

It wouldn't do for any of her people to see her cry. Rue went to one of the *Banshee*'s washrooms, locked herself in a stall and put her face in her hands.

1 5

THAT EVENING, RUE undertook yet another pointless inventory of the remaining supplies. She was in the "attic" of the cache, feeling bad about herself, missing Max. Funny how she'd turned into the sort of person who worked compulsively; she remembered how she'd had contempt for that sort of laborer at Allemagne. Well, maybe they'd known things about life that she hadn't, at that point. Once upon a time, her only task had been keeping out of Jentry's way.

Max had picked a rotten time to bail on her. He'd said that for him, life was like running on water. She understood that, more than he seemed to know. Rue had been running too, she felt, ever since Allemagne. Not running to keep herself up, maybe, but running away from Jentry, and everything that she had been raised to be, there in that little station in the middle of the void.

What Max didn't get—the idiot!—was that without him she'd have faltered and fallen long ago. Rue kept going forward, true, but she understood how less and less. Responsibility, doubt and insecurities beaten into her in her childhood all pulled at her, all the time. Max had been a rock to cling to. He seemed so certain of what to do, there at the beginning. Now he'd taken that certainty away.

Now she was arguing with him in her own mind, the sort of satisfying internal dialogue that one always wins. She had just scored a major point when she heard the airlock cycling; expecting it to be Corinna returning from the *Banshee*, she returned to her checklist. Across the attic space from her, Evan was running simulations on their approach to Colossus. Good for him.

Rebecca's voice floated up from downstairs. "Dr. Bequith! How nice to see you!"

Damn that woman. Rue and Rebecca had discussed the possible romantic prospects among the *Banshee*'s crew the previous day. Rebecca had shied away from mentioning any men she found attractive, but had suggested a few prospects for Rue. It had been frivolous banter—but Rue had mentioned that she found Mike attractive. Had Rebecca invited him over?

"Please, call me Michael." It was Mike's low, soft voice. "Is your captain here?"

"Rue! Visitor!"

Rue paused, looked at her checklist, bit her thumbnail.

"Would you like a drink?" continued Rebecca. "Apparently Max hid some whisky nanospores here and Blair's been growing them in an aeration tube. We were just about to sample his first batch." Rue heard them moving into the kitchen area.

"Hardly a batch," said Blair. Rue moved to the open hatchway and peeked down at the kitchen area. Blair was holding out a small closed jar. A single large drop of amber liquid floated in its center. "I think there's enough for four people to get a taste."

Mike waved it away politely. "Please, go ahead. I was never a fan of whiskey."

Blair held out the jar to Rebecca, who also shook her head. "Your loss," he said with a shrug. He uncapped the jar and tossed the little ball into his mouth.

For a moment he floated there with an odd look on his face. Then, carefully but very quickly, he bounded in the direction of the cache's small bathroom.

Rebecca hung in midair with her hands on her hips, watching. "I guess it's not mature yet," she said.

Rue stifled a laugh and flipped herself down through the hatch. "Hi." She realized she should say something more and added, "Have you had dinner?"

"I ate before I came," he said. "I'm not good at eating in freefall, I'm afraid. Despite having done it a thousand times."

"Coffee?"

"Sure."

Rebecca shot Rue one of her annoyingly smug looks and went to make it, leaving her alone with Mike at the cache's standup table.

"What can we do for you, Mike?"

He grimaced. "I'm not sure I should be here at all. Admiral Crisler suspects me of being the saboteur, so he's made me wear this . . ." He pointed to his ear. Rue had noticed the little adornment there earlier, and had thought it odd that the austerely dressed Michael Bequith should wear jewelry.

"You're bugged?" She let go of the table in astonishment, then caught herself before drifting away.

"Yes, I thought you should know if I was to come aboard your ship." He looked Rue straight in the eye, and his expression held eloquent pleading.

"Give me that!" Rue reached out quickly and rolled the little bead off Mike's ear. She held it up to eye level. "Admiral, I should have been informed of this. Since I wasn't, I'll take it you were willing to let Dr. Bequith be your spy in my terrain. But the *Envy* is *my* ship, and I will not permit such devices to remain aboard. Rebecca!" She tossed the bead to her doctor. "Put that out the lock, will you?"

They watched as Rebecca cycled the lock. When that was done, Mike turned back to Rue, grinning apologetically. "Thanks. I—"

"I do not like being manipulated, Dr. Bequith," she said as icily as she could. "You came here to get me to do that, didn't you?"

He frowned, apparently tamping down on some anger of his own. "I can't go back to the *Banshee* now," he sat at last. "They'll arrest me. I came here to ask you for asylum."

"Oh, I like this less and less," she said. "You'd better have a good explanation for this. Otherwise I see no reason why I shouldn't let them arrest you. How do I know you aren't the saboteur, after all?"

He looked her in the eye again, quite confidently now. "I discovered something," he said. He didn't elaborate, just let the words hang there.

Rue hesitated. Behind Mike, Rebecca started to open her mouth; Rue waved her silent. "Tell me," she said.

Mike brought out a large black datapack and clipped it to the edge of the table. "It's about Blair's photos of the Lasa habitat," he said.

Blair had been watching from the door to the bathroom. Now he jumped over. "What's wrong?" he said, a bit indignantly. "I did a complete photomosaic last time we were here. I was very thorough." He hooked his feet into the floor loops under the table.

"Yes, I know. But I have reason to think your photos have been tampered with."

Rue was surprised, but not as much as she might have expected. As Mike's words sank in, she realized she had been waiting ever since the sabotage for something to happen—for some sign that the uneasiness about this expedition she felt was well-founded. Well, here it was.

"Ah, do you have a holo card?" asked Mike. "I can show you."

"Just a sec." Blair raced away to get one. When he returned, Mike put his hand on the card and downloaded something through its galvanic interface.

Some pictures appeared in ghostly transparency above the table. Blair squinted at them. "Yeah, those are mine."

"Do you have original copies of this data?"

Blair made a sour face. "I didn't have enough storage units to leave backups here when we went to Chandaka. The originals of all our data ended up in Crisler's hands—as partial payment for our rescue."

Mike brought up an annotation layer and pointed at the circled stars. "What does this mean?"

Blair examined the photos for a few seconds, then blinked in surprise. "Holy tholin, you're right. Somebody's screwed with my data."

Mike showed the extent of the changes and showed that they were connected somehow to Linda Ophir. Blair, the reporter, was visibly impressed by his detective work. Rue was pretty impressed herself.

It didn't add up, though. "But why . . ." she began.

"Because there's something written on the missing part that we're not supposed to know."

"We can just look at it through the telescope," said Evan, who had come up behind them silently.

"I thought of that," said Mike. "The problem is that the Lasa habitat's north pole is pointing at us. The missing stuff is on the south pole. But, we're going out to explore the habitat tomorrow. I came here to ask you to bring some cameras that aren't connected into the expedition's inscape system. We should insist on doing a new photomosaic then."

Rue nodded. "But what are we looking for?"

"Not sure. More Lasa writing, maybe."

"But we can't read Lasa, can we? And anyway, if this stuff has been deliberately hidden, won't we give away that we know about it? That could be dangerous, depending on who did the hiding . . ." She didn't mention Crisler's name, but then, she didn't have to. "Remember, Dr. Bequith, the *Envy* may be my ship, but it could be taken away from me at any time."

"Maybe we can find a more subtle way of taking the pictures," said Blair. "We could throw a little mirror past the habitat, and aim the camera at that."

"Anyway," said Mike, "You're right that we can't read Lasa writing—not with the resources we have here, anyway. So until we get back to civilization, whatever's written on the hidden part of the habitat will remain obscure. Whoever hid it in the first place will know that."

"Why can't we read it?" asked Rebecca.

"Our AIs aren't smart enough," he said. "We could figure out the writing in denotative terms, but that wouldn't get us anywhere."

Rue raised an eyebrow. "What do you mean, denotative?"

"Surface meaning—dictionary meaning. The problem is, most meaning is carried through context and implication; it's connotative. In the case of the Lasa, the context is so alien that even when we translate the words and know what they mean, we, well, don't know what they *mean*." That was a pretty thick description and it must have shown on her face, because he immediately said, "Imagine an alien trying to figure out what a Haiku poem means.

"If we had a context-switching AI we might be able to

do it, but the nearest one's on Mars as far as I know. So, no, we don't really know what the writing means. Even so, somebody's gone to great lengths to hide a piece of it. Since you did such a good job with your photomosaic," he said to Blair, "nobody planned to do another. There didn't seem to be a need."

Rue leaned back, examining the ceiling. She was relieved that her worries had finally taken on a tangible form. "You suspect Crisler, don't you?" she asked.

He shrugged. "Not necessarily. However much I detest the man . . ."

"It's more than that," she said. "I don't know why he's *here*. Do you?"

Mike looked puzzled. "Surely, if there's a multispecies civilization nearby . . ."

"Isn't the fastest way to find it through FTL?" She watched him intently through the diaphanous panes of holo light. "Don't you think he'd have a dozen ships scouring the nearby lit stars? What if one of them found the alien homeworld while he was stuck out here? It doesn't make sense. I'll bet he'd already completed a search of those stars before he even hired you guys."

"Meaning . . ."

"Meaning he already knows where the *Envy* came from, or he knows that it's not from any nearby sun; either way there's no threat of the rebels finding the homeworld first, is there?"

"That's right," said Evan. "Unless Linda Ophir told the rebels about the *Envy*."

"And they planted a spy on board," finished Rebecca.

Rue shrugged. "I bet she did and I bet there is one," she said. "But how does that connect with the faked photos? And it still doesn't explain to me why Crisler is here and not waiting in High Space for us to send him information about the homeworld by message laser."

Rebecca passed some bulbs of coffee around. "Thanks,"

said Mike. "I . . . Rue, you think the missing writing tells where the *Envy* came from?"

She nodded. "It might. In which case, Crisler already knows . . . but then why not go straight there?"

"Unless it was Linda who faked the photos? Or the rebel?"

"This is getting us nowhere," laughed Rebecca. "No, I don't think the missing writing is about the homeworld. But you guys are going to bust a blood vessel trying to figure what it is. Why not wait until tomorrow?"

"So true," Rue agreed with a laugh. "We're just getting ourselves worked up."

They drank their coffee and the discussion drifted from topic to topic, though it always returned to Crisler and the sabotage. Rue liked having someone outside her tiny crew to talk to—Michael Bequith wasn't so stuck up as the rest of the scientific team. She supposed he wasn't on the career treadmill like so many of his colleagues on the *Banshee*. At least, not on the same one.

That reminded her of something. "Oh!"

They looked at her.

"You told me to ask you about NeoShintoism sometime," she said to him. "So . . . I'm asking."

Mike didn't look happy at the question for some reason. Maybe he'd been getting a lot of the same inquiries lately. "NeoShinto is simply a system for summoning and contemplating kami," he said.

Well, that sure explained it. "Kami?" she pressed. "Who're they?"

"Spirits of a place," said Evan. "Right?"

Mike nodded.

"Oh." It sounded a bit cultish.

"There's nothing metaphysical about it," Mike said quickly. He described a truly frightening set of neural implants he'd gotten when younger; having some bizarre AI altering your consciousness went way beyond any of the control mods Jentry had tried. Rebecca listened with particular (doubtless clinical) interest.

". . . So I can record the stimulation pattern for this vision and literally e-mail it into the galactic inscape network. You see, it's a technology, not a mythology. NeoShinto is a branch of Permanence, which is a nonmetaphysical religion, like Buddhism would be if it stayed purely methodological and didn't keep holding onto ideas like karma and reincarnation. Permanence is a scientifically developed meditation program that is tailored to the individual; if you follow it properly you're very likely to reach a state of mind that used to be called 'enlightenment.' We try not to label that state because everyone has different interpretations of it until they experience it and after they experience it they generally laugh at the idea of describing it in words." Mike sounded positively stuffy when he talked about this; the thought made her smile.

"NeoShinto is all about creating and capturing an artificially generated mystical experience, similar to our target state, so that people can 'visit' the state and decide whether they want to pursue the program."

"Hm." She understood, but played dumb because now that he was rolling, he obviously did enjoy talking about it. "It's like a oneness with the universe sort of thing?"

He nodded. "My particular task was to collect the kami of alien places. I undertook this task because we recognized that humans are spreading into some pretty inhuman environments and living in these makes it harder to commune with the Absolute. My kami give people a starting point, at least."

Rue sat back, thinking about the idea. She'd never heard of this sect, or these kami things. The idea of merging your identity with your surroundings was very seductive, though. It made her realize just how separate from the world she usually felt.

After all, she had been raised to disbelieve cults and religions. There was no transcendence to be found; this had been drilled into Rue from an early age, as if she needed any more proof than the limits of Allemagne and her own puny body.

The kami sounded wonderful; but they couldn't be real. "My mother always told us," said Rue, " 'believe what you want, but always put it to the test.' "

"What test is that?" asked Blair.

"She called it 'the Supreme Meme,' " said Rue. Now that she'd started talking about this, she was a bit embarrassed. Jentry's crowd scoffed at any metaphysical talk.

She pressed on. "It's what you call a thought experiment, a way to test whether something you believe is good for you or not. You know what memes are?"

"Memes are the genes of culture," said Evan promptly. "They are ideas and behaviors that use humans and our culture to propagate themselves. Religions are usually full of memes—ideas that don't mean anything, or serve any useful purpose, but are just so compelling that they get passed on generation after generation."

"Right. Well, the Supreme Meme is like a way of exploding all other memes—other ideas about life, you know? It has the power to destroy beliefs that are bad for you."

"And what is it?"

"Simple," she said. "We know the multiverse is infinitely old and spawns new universes in infinite amounts all the time. That means that infinitely far in the past and infinitely far in the future, there's a universe just like this one, where everything happened just the same way, with the same people; and you and I and this place and this conversation, all happened before and will happen again, not once, but an infinite number of times." Now she was sounding stuffy; she had recited this description from memory.

"Yeah, I've heard that idea," said Evan dismissively.

"Oh, that's not the idea," she said with a grin. "The idea

is this: Say you had just died and the angels or kami or whatever asked you where you would like to go now—anywhere in the multiverse, any kind of rebirth or heaven you want. Here's the Supreme Meme: How would you have to feel about the life you've led and your universe, to say to that angel, 'let me come back to where I started and live *this* life over, exactly as it was, no detail spared.'"

"Well, that's, just—" sputtered Evan.

"How would you have to *feel*? And could this or that religion or ideology that I believe give me that feeling—even in theory? That's the question and you apply it to the religions people try to sell you on. Because if a religion can't, well . . . sanctify . . . everything, even the crappy parts of your life, then it doesn't measure up."

Evan looked horrified.

Mike sat back, a bemused look on his face. After a moment he half-smiled. "And has anything ever measured up for you?" he asked.

"No," she said. There was an awkward silence. "Anyway, that's what my mother taught us," Rue said.

"I'll have to think about that," Mike said with apparent sincerity. "But for now . . . you never did answer my original question."

"What question?"

"Can I call upon you for asylum?"

"Oh! Of course."

"We've got a spare bunk if you'd like," said Rebecca, with a sidelong glance at Rue.

"Ah, well, I . . . Isn't Lake Flaccid part of your territory? That's where the science team is setting up, anyway."

"Of course," Rue said firmly. "I'll tell Crisler to keep his hands off you as long as you're anywhere in the *Envy*. I'll tell him I'm keeping an eye on you myself." Of course, Rue knew she had no power to enforce her orders. She had to assume that Crisler wouldn't feel too threatened by this. If he did . . . well, she had to try.

They left the table and Mike shook hands with each of them at the airlock.

After he was gone Rue scowled at Rebecca. "You're shameless. Haven't you got anything better to do than try to set people up?"

"Hey, matchmaking's an old and respectable tradition," she replied with a grin.

"Not on my ship it isn't." But they were all laughing at her and after a moment she joined in.

RUE COULDN'T SLEEP, so she drifted out into the common area. Rebecca was sitting up, talking through a holo window to one of the women from Crisler's security team. She noticed Rue and said, "Call you later," then closed the connection. Then she frowned at Rue. "Back whence ye came."

"I can't." Rue settled down at the table next to Rebecca. She clasped her hands in front of her and stared through the holos. "I'm glad Mike came over tonight," she said. It wasn't what she wanted to say, but she didn't know how to approach that.

Rebecca arched an eyebrow. "You like him, don't you?"

"Yes, but . . . It's just . . . I was starting to go seriously crazy worrying, when he showed up. He proved I was right about not trusting Crisler. But he also took my mind off things."

"What things?"

She shrugged angrily. "You know what's at stake tomorrow."

Rebecca sighed. "I know what you think is at stake."

"Rebecca, we haven't found anything like a control system anywhere else in the *Envy*. If it's not in the Lasa habitat, then maybe there isn't one. Not one we'd understand, anyway." All during their search for supplies to repair the stacks, Rue had kept an eye out for anything that might be a control surface. They hadn't opened all the habitats yet, but they'd certainly visited the biggest ones. For days a sense of helplessness had been growing in her and she'd confided in no one, until tonight she felt like bursting. "We've got to think about what happens if we can't control the *Envy*," she said.

Rebecca put a hand on hers, "Yes, Rue, we do need to do that. But we don't need to do it tonight. There's months to go before we reach our rendezvous with Colossus. Anything could happen in that time.

"Hmm." Rebecca looked at her appraisingly. "I remember when you showed up at Treya, all jittery and determined. You didn't seem to know *what* you were determined about, but you were determined." They both laughed. "But that's just it, Rue; have you asked yourself what you're going to do if we *do* find out how to control the *Envy*?"

Rue stared at her. The question was infuriating somehow, though she couldn't have said why. "I have no idea what you're talking about."

"Ah, I think you do." When she saw that Rue wasn't going to answer, Rebecca continued. "You know, Rue, you're one of the most driven people I know. But you don't think of yourself that way."

"I'm just trying to survive."

"By doing this?" Rebecca waved around at the habitat. "This is more than just survival. We could have settled down on Chandaka; I could have finished my education there, you'd have found something—"

"We'd have been poor! Worse than poor—indentured. Same as I was at Treya."

"Rue, you were perfectly happy working in the mountains and living hand-to-mouth. I remember it very well."

Rue shrugged angrily. "But I wasn't responsible for all you guys then."

"We can look after ourselves, you know." The words stung. "I'm not saying you're not a wonderful captain—

you are—it's just that you've got to learn that your responsibility ends where our ability to think for ourselves begins. You're upset about Max putting himself in cold storage, aren't you?"

"Of course I am! I should have taken better care of him."

Rebecca shook her head. "You did all you could for him. After a certain point, how he takes the help you give him is up to him. Max's problems run too deep for you or I to help him. We can be supportive; and ultimately you were, when you allowed him to put himself on ice."

Rue sat back, absorbing the words. They were silent for a long time; then Rue said, almost against her will, "Then I don't know what it means to be captain. Rebecca, I don't get it."

"You will. Just . . . not tonight." Rebecca pointed imperiously in the direction of the staterooms. "Now go to sleep. I want to see you fresh in the morning."

"Yes, doctor," said Rue unhappily. "Beck, I . . . I'm glad you're here."

Rebecca hugged her and Rue sailed back to her room, feeling a little lighter, though no less confused.

Rebecca was right, though; Rue had no picture in her mind of what her life would be like after this expedition. No picture at all. Success or failure seemed the same to her—a blank.

She resented Rebecca's insight, so when she strapped herself into bed, Rue fought down all thought—since to think would be to think about the question Rebecca had raised—and soon fell fast asleep.

16

THEY APPROACHED THE Lasa habitat in three sleds. This was the largest party to visit any of the *Envy*'s strange, self-entombed vessels; even Crisler was along this time. That was unfortunate, because the admiral had made it plain that he considered Michael a renegade now, and the marines were watching every move he made. That would make it difficult for him to execute his little plan. He remained stubbornly determined, however. Crisler had made him angry.

The slowly spinning habitat glowed beautifully in the floodlights—a finely iridescent black, like velvet, with crimson lettering set in it in discrete islands. By Michael's reckoning, they were approaching from the side opposite to the side whose photos had been faked. On the face of it, this made sense: They were simply approaching the pole of the spinning ball that faced the *Banshee*.

When they were a hundred meters away, Michael said, "Let's take a quick orbit of the place. That way we can get a higher quality photomosaic."

"I don't think that'll be necessary, Bequith." Interesting—that was Crisler's voice.

"The more detail we have the better analysis we can make," he retorted. A couple of the scientists murmured in agreement.

"All right, then," said Crisler. That was a bit surprising.

He reached down into a thigh pouch and drew out the camera Rue had lent him. The mirror he left in the pouch. If for some reason they were not allowed to make this orbit, he had been planning to toss the mirror and try to photograph the far side of the habitat in its reflection. He was almost disappointed at not getting the chance to be so devious.

Maybe it was someone on Chandaka who had faked the Lasa photos, in which case all his caution was unnecessary. Maybe it was the saboteur . . . He should know in a few seconds.

The far side of the habitat rotated into view and the floodlights played over it. Michael had an inscape window open with the existing photomosaic in it and he looked at this, then at the habitat, then back at the mosaic.

"Gods and kami," he murmured. The full paragraph

came into view and it was exactly the same as the one in the photos.

Was this somebody's idea of a joke?—take a photomosaic and doctor it to look like something had been faked when nothing had? Or had Blair just copied four pictures to complete an incomplete photomosaic? That was so sloppy as to be ridiculous—and Blair himself had insisted his photo documentary was complete. He had not missed this side of the sphere.

Michael looked over at sled two, which was briefly silhouetted against the red script. The third figure back was Rue Cassels. She was turned his way, a human shaped erasure of the lettering. He made an exaggerated shrug. She turned away.

It didn't make any sense. Frustrated, he aimed the camera and took a few shots of the paragraph anyway.

They returned to the "north" pole of the habitat—the one facing the *Banshee*. There was an airlock here, but not at the "south" pole, which only had a ring tying down the cord to the plow sail.

This airlock was of the same design as the one at Lake Flaccid. The iridescent black material of the hull gave way to a burnished metal ring—beryllium, Salas had declared—with the familiar black disk inside it like the pupil of a giant eye.

"Hold up here," said Crisler. The three sleds braked to a stop a meter from the lock. Michael took a flashlight and shone it on the black surface of the sphere. He was astonished to see that the surface was not smooth. "It's fur," he said. "The thing is covered in fur."

He reached out to touch it, even as Katz was saying something about fur being a better insulator in vacuum than air. The fine black pelt didn't seem to give at all under his touch. He pushed harder and felt a sudden sting in his fingertips.

"Damn!" He pulled his hand back. A red diagnostic window popped open, telling him he'd suffered a minor breach of suit integrity.

"What happened?" asked Crisler.

"It's hard as diamond—it poked me right through the glove."

"Well, nobody touch it, then."

The red writing was apparently bald hull. Very weird. While the others focused on finding the latch for the airlock, he swept his light along a long swath of hull. Now he could see texture to the fur, as if it had been mussed by the hand of a passing giant. It was like the back of some enormous, sleeping creature.

"Here it is," said one of the marines.

"Good work, Barendts." Crisler and Herat drifted over to the man. Without hesitation Herat reached out and put his hand in the switch hollow. The black disk roiled in a now-familiar manner.

Crisler put his arm out to block Herat's way. "We should send in a mesobot first."

"I suppose you're right." Herat gestured to Michael, who fetched a fist-sized explorer from the sled. Herat pushed it into the liquid material of the lock, letting go only when he was up to his elbow. "That's got it."

Michael made a public inscape window of the mesobot's camera readout and put it next to the lock. Everyone gathered around to watch. For the first few moments there was nothing to see but blackness.

"Registering magnetic field—very strong," said Herat. "And the walls are vibrating. Temperature rising rapidly . . . this place is alive, whatever it is." The little mesobot's lights came on, illuminating a metal wall several centimeters away; it swiveled around at Michael's command.

There was a collective intake of breath among the watchers. In the window, a large curving space appeared, cluttered with drifting debris. "Look at that crap," said the marine Barendts. "Something must have blew up."

"No." Michael skewed the camera around again. Now it was clear what the curving space was. The outer hull of the Lasa habitat was separated by a space of at least five meters from an inner sphere which was made of white metal. This inner sphere had no writing on it; instead, it was covered with hundreds of outward-dimpling airlock doors, one every four meters across the whole visible surface.

The space between the hulls contained various freely drifting objects. They were mostly spherical, but some were torus or bolo-shaped. Michael stared at one for a few seconds, trying to puzzle out what it was.

"Models!" shouted Dr. Herat. "Those are models of habitats!"

Crisler cursed under his breath; it was an exclamation of wonder. Michael shook his head. Once again, Herat had beaten him to an essential realization. He was indeed looking at a model habitat. In fact, the little sphere, which must be about a meter in diameter, was a dead ringer for Lake Flaccid.

"What are we waiting for?" said Rue. She sounded tense. "Let's get in there already."

Just then the inscape window flashed so quickly that Michael almost missed it. "What was that?"

"Not sure. Wait—there's some kind of light source coming on in there."

"It knows we're here?"

A slow pulse of light welled up from several small points on the inner hull. It started out deep red, then rainbowed all the way to blue before fading away completely. The mesobot reported that it had started out in the deep infrared and went up to ultraviolet before fading. It happened again and began repeating at nine second intervals.

"What's it mean?" asked Crisler.

"Damned if I know," said Herat. "It doesn't seem dangerous, anyway. We'll wait and see if there's any change. If it's still doing this in five minutes, I'm going in."

As they waited, Rue drifted over to Michael's side.

"Hey." She made a sign for him to go on private channel. "Did you get your photos?" she asked when he had.

"Yeah—but none of it makes any sense." He was beginning to feel like he was being had, somehow.

"Well, I'm glad I'm not the only one who thinks so," she said. "What about this place? *Models?* What does that mean?"

"I can't even begin to speculate. And Dr. Herat's stymied too, for once." He said it with some relish.

"The pattern's not changing," said Herat. "I'm going in, unless one of you burly gentlemen has some objection?"

Crisler waved a gloved hand indifferently. Herat reached into the edge of the airlock disk and pulled himself through.

"No resistance," he said as his feet vanished into the black surface. "There's no atmosphere at all in here."

"Any ice?" asked Rue. "We need to find more oxygen."

Michael groped inside the lock and found the familiar bar, then flipped himself through. Pride demanded that he be second inside after Dr. Herat and he was, but only by seconds as the rest of the team followed, leaving three marines with rescue training outside. They snaked some umbilicals through the airlock; these stood up out of the disk like surreal reeds in the light of Michael's helmet lamp.

He called the mesobot and it obediently returned to him. Just then, a sweep of prisming light swept over it, causing Michael to miss his first grab for the bot.

"This is wild," said Rue. "Beautiful—but weird."

For someone raised on planets like Michael, it was a hard environment to get used to. It was natural to choose an up and a down to orient yourself, but here the choice was arbitrary and none of the options was comfortable. If he decided that down was in the direction of the airlock on the outer hull, that meant he was floating at the bottom of a giant bowl, with a huge metal sphere hanging over his head. If he put down in some direction tangent to the airlock, then he was in midair beside a sphere, with a long drop beneath him that curved out of sight. And if he pictured himself at the very top, then he had nothing to hold onto and could imagine sliding down that inner sphere and falling into the space between them.

"The light's brightening," said Crisler.

Michael turned his head and at that moment the small circles that were flashing went out. In their place, a series of red expanding rings appeared on the outer hull. One of these swept over Michael before he had time to even look away. His eye was momentarily dazzled by crimson laserlight. The marines started shouting.

"It's all right!" said Dr. Herat. "We're being scanned, is all. We can't see the beams because we're in vacuum—only the reflections off the outer hull. I think whatever it is that's in here is trying to decide what we are."

"We should leave," said Crisler.

"That might be prudent." They swarmed the airlock disk. Michael let go of the mesobot and popped out into familiar starlight last. The others were all talking at once; he counted to make sure they were all there, then connected to the mesobot again.

The little lamps had come on again, this time steadily. They illuminated the space between the hulls with a bright, steady, yellow-white light. "Look!"

There was another change happening too. The mesobot reported the presence of a faint gas pressure, rapidly rising. The gas was warm—in fact it was a mix of nitrogen and oxygen at the same temperature as the inside of Michael's suit.

It was Michael's turn to swear, very quietly.

"I think we've just been invited in," he said.

RUE WATCHED THE others slide through the black circle of the airlock. It was frightening to think that something inside the Lasa habitat knew they were here and was opening the way for them. On the other hand, Rue had always known she was just the finder of the *Envy*, not its real owner. The scattered habitats that made up the cycler had kept their secrets for almost two years now; without knowing where it came from or why it was here, she was forced to be humble. So her anxiety was mixed with relief at the thought that if the *Envy*'s true masters appeared now, they could at least take the burden of doubt away from her.

Her turn came and she flipped through the airlock with ease. She nearly ran into somebody's back and climbed over them to get a better view.

The place was transformed. "Humidity, temp, pressure, oxy mix, they're all identical to our suit standard," Mike was saying. The interhull was lit up now too, in brilliant white light like the false sunlight the R.E. people favored. Rue dimmed her faceplate so she wouldn't have to squint.

"Eerie," somebody said. Rue nodded; this cavity between the spheres was strangely like a place on Allemagne known as the Gallery. The Gallery was the last insulating space between the outer shells of the colony and the inner part, where the centrifuge and power plant resided. It was much bigger than this space, but perspective was tricky here due to the smooth reflective metal everywhere. If she just glanced around casually, though, the place had a weird familiarity to it. Almost like home.

"I suggest we designate the airlock as bottom," said Herat. "We can string some lines up the sides so we can orient ourselves." The other men grunted agreement and soon were unreeling lines and jetting off around the sphere in pairs.

Slowly, like a shy animal, one of the little habitat models was drifting in Rue's direction. She held onto the lip of the airlock and studied it. It was an elongated doughnut shape about sixty centimeters wide and a hundred long, made of some burnished white metal. It didn't match any of the *Envy*'s habitats, so it was hard to get a sense of how big the object it modeled would be. But there was an obvious airlock etched in one end and a whole slew of tiny machines, intricately shaped, stuffed into the tubular doughnut hole.

It glimmered like some fantastical toy; for a moment she fantasized about some day being able to hang this bauble over her son or daughter's crib. Of course, it might be solid and weigh five hundred kilos.

For some almost superstitious reason, nobody had touched one of these models yet. Rue wasn't about to be the first. As it reached her she drew back, letting it parade slowly past.

"The readings are pretty clear," said Michael. "No organics of any kind, just the perfect breathing mix for us."

That got her attention. "Can we export it? Tank it and take it back to the *Banshee*?"

"Please!" Uh oh, she'd set Herat off again. His suited figure jetted over to her. "If this is a first contact situation I hardly think we'd make a good impression by stealing their air."

Chagrined, Rue fell back to the airlock. But Herat didn't know how dire their life-support situation was. Rue's inventory last night had revealed some cracked stack tubes, which was going to reduce the carrying capacity of the *Banshee* even further. She'd told Crisler about it, but so far the news hadn't percolated down. There was a good chance, though, that this would be their last EVA for a while.

It was pointless to argue with Herat. If this air became crucial to their survival, she would requisition it; he would have no say in the matter. Better just to avoid the confrontation, since it would do no good.

"If the air is breathable, we should at least conserve our suit supplies," she said. It was a small defiance, but saying it made her feel better.

"Good point," said the professor. "Bequith? Can we take off these damnable head-clamps?"

"Yes. We could even renew our suit supplies here; I doubt the Lasa would object to that."

She threw Mike a grateful look, which he probably

didn't see as he was in the process of taking off his helmet. She quickly did the same. Her first sniff of this alien air revealed a metallic tang and the faint sharpness she associated with cold and ice. But the air was warm.

"Where's the heat coming from?"

Mike clipped his helmet to a shoulder loop. "In there." He jerked a thumb at the inner sphere.

Crisler and one of the marines had flown over to one of the black circles on the inner sphere. "What do you make of those?" asked Crisler. "Looks like airlocks covering the whole surface. Makes no sense."

"Not human sense, maybe," said Herat. "I'm more interested in why the air is perfect for us. I know *how*; The lasers must have taken a spectroscopic reading through our faceplates. But why?"

"Like Bequith said," said Crisler. "We were invited in."

Herat was scowling. "That makes a lot less sense than you might think. And what sense it makes isn't good. You might think they want to talk—but Bequith and I have found ample evidence that symbolic communication is only really useful within a species; different intelligent species are usually *so* different that communication between them is useless at any level above threat/reward signals. We never have anything in common above basic bodily functions, so what's to talk about?"

"What are you saying?"

"Well, Admiral, ask yourself this: Under what circumstances does one organism invite a member of another species into a place?"

Crisler looked alarmed. "When it's trapping the other for a meal."

Herat nodded. "This place has already extracted quite a bit of information about us without asking."

What Herat was saying was unsettling—but Mike shook his head.

"They are asking," he said. "These open doors are an invitation more clear than a symbolic communication. So was the air. They're gestures of friendliness."

"So is the scent on a Venus's flytrap," said Herat.

One of the marines shouted. Rue looked over in time to see him leaping away from the inner sphere. The airlock disk next to him had irised open.

"I just reached out to touch the thing and it opened!" he said. He had his sidearm out and ready.

Silently, all across the surface of the inner sphere, other airlocks opened.

No one moved. All conversation had ceased and they waited to see what would emerge.

Rue was in a position to look directly into the first airlock that had opened. Unlike the outer lock, this and the others had collapsed from disks into rings around the lip of a round opening. The magnetic liquid spiked up in cones and fantastical arcs that must follow the reshaped magnetic field. They were perfectly still, though the surface of the liquid roiled like oil.

The airlock opened into a can-shaped chamber about four meters long and half that wide. At its far end was another, closed, airlock disk. Floating in the center of the space was a large, perfect ball of water.

"The trap opens," muttered the marine.

"Quiet, Barendts," said Crisler.

"Only some of them opened," said Mike quietly. He and Herat had drifted together. Rue jetted over to them; she felt safer next to these experienced alien-hunters.

"I wonder why that is," said Herat, also quietly. "We need to get around the other side and see what's happening there." Rue felt a thrill of fear when he said that; something might be emerging opposite them while they hung here gaping.

Crisler had heard and motioned two marines to move. They reluctantly jetted off around the small horizon of the sphere, appearing a minute later from the other direction.

The one Crisler had called Barendts shook his blond head. "Some open doors; funny things inside, but nothing moving."

"What kind of things?" asked Herat.

"Balls of water with various amounts of mud in it. Dirt in a couple. Sand. That kind of thing."

"This is insane," said Crisler.

Mike and Herat were grinning at one another. "Actually, it makes perfect sense," said Herat. "This is an attempt to communicate, though there's no way to know whether the ultimate aim is hostile or not. In any other situation I'd say it was a trap—but we have evidence of multispecies cooperation outside. Maybe . . ."

"This? Communication?" Crisler shook his head.

"Not symbolic communication," said Herat. "Physical communication—the kind most species use between one another. It's more universal and reliable than language. Of course the Lasa would use it for first contact! The only reason we never have is because we're . . ."

"Stupid?" said Mike with a small grin.

"I was going to say, 'infected with a number of academic prejudices,'" said Herat. "But 'stupid' will do."

They were acting like such boys now. It was infuriating, considering everything that was at stake. "Speaking of stupid," said Rue, "are we going to investigate or float here gabbing? Let's check these things out."

"Not so fast," said Herat in his most condescending tone. "We don't know which questions to ask yet."

"What questions? Just send the bot into one of these doorways!"

Herat looked indignant, but Mike had that subtle little smile going again. "I can do that," he said. He concentrated for a moment and the glittering little mesobot scooted over to the nearest open door.

Rue accessed the inscape feed from the bot. It roved around the surface of the meter-sized ball of pure water that was the only contents of the chamber. There was no piece of scrip with a message written on it, no readout screens, no arrows pointing anywhere—but there was a latch next to the inner door, similar to the one on the outside airlock.

They retrieved the bot and sent it into several more open doors. Rue watched the proceedings with growing impatience. Michael and Herat had turned into plodding researchers like the rest of the science team—taking no chances, noting down pointless details, like small differences in lighting and temperature in the various cells. Each cylindrical chamber held a different sample of material: salt water in one, epsom-salted water in another, a cloud of dry silicate sand in a third. None of it even hinted at a way to control the vast cycler scattered through thousands of kilometers of space around her. It was all beside the point, but the scientists didn't seem to care.

Finally, after Rue had descended to nagging, Herat shrugged and said, "Let's try one of the inner doors. The question is, which one?"

"What do we need most?" she shot back. "That should be our prime consideration."

"That's shortsighted, Rue. We need to know what kind of question this place is asking us before we can answer."

"It's asking us what we like. Salt water or pure water, or no water," she said. "Isn't that right?"

"Well . . . probably . . ."

"So what do we like? Pure water, right?"

"Well . . ."

"As captain of the *Envy* I am ordering you to pick a chamber for us to investigate further."

The professor glowered, but after a minute said, "The pure-water one, then. We really don't know enough to—"

She held up a hand, conscious of Crisler's eyes on her. "We are not going to know the right answer, Professor, because we've been given a *choice*. This isn't about what the

Lasa want us to do—it's about what we want. Let's try the water room."

"All right. Let's trip the switch."

Crisler held up a hand. "Not you, Professor. We don't know whether it's safe."

"I'll do it," said Barendts. Crisler nodded and the marine entered the small cylindrical room. He contorted his way around the water sphere and, without preamble, tripped the switch next to the inside airlock.

A splashing sound echoed through the interhull, like many glasses of water being tipped on the floor simultaneously. Rue had been watching Barendts, so she'd missed it: All the other other open doors had collapsed closed.

"Getting power readings from inside," said Michael.

"It's not opening," said Barendts.

"Weird," said another of the marines. "This is just weird."

"Hey! There's more doors opening!"

Rue looked away from the chamber containing Barendts. All across the sphere, other round airlocks had opened. These were different ones from those that had been open a moment ago. She smelled metallic odors, ozone, and sulphur. All the new doors contained floating balls of mud.

"Question. Response," muttered Herat. "New question."

"But what was the question?" asked Crisler. "And what was our response?"

Herat shook his head. "I . . . have no idea."

"WE ARE ONE step ahead of the souvenir-collectors," the professor said some hours later, as they were settling in to the little camp of balloon-tents they'd tethered next to the airlock. Nothing new had happened since Barendts opened the inner door; the Lasa machinery seemed quiescent, so Michael had gone with two of the marines and brought back the rest of the science team and some supplies. Between this place and Lake Flaccid, he mused, they could have years of investigation ahead of them.

Except, of course, that they would only be here a few more months.

"Look at this place," Herat went on, gesturing through the mesh of the tent foyer at the smooth metal walls. "Are you really going to make this into a habitat of your cycler, Rue?"

She sighed. "You've got me all wrong. What would be the point of reworking this place? It would take more equipment to scour out and refit these habitats than it would to ship up new quarters."

Herat grunted. "It's just a shame that this place is so inaccessible."

Rue stretched and yawned. "Inaccessible? Only to your people, Dr. Herat."

"Uh oh, there they go," Michael said to Barendts as Herat worked up a response. The marine grinned; of all Crisler's men, he was the only one who hadn't become frosty in his relations with Michael since the sabotage.

Michael climbed out of the tent and did a hand-walk up one of the ropes next to the inner sphere. He felt they were safe here, at least as long as they didn't flip any switches. This place seemed purely reactive; their act of entering through the airlock had stimulated a response, as had other actions they'd taken. As long as they touched nothing, nothing would happen.

It wasn't a frightening environment, anyway. Not like Dis had been. Dis was a place of death, so old that objects that had come together in the ancient past had become fused. He remembered finding the mummified corpse of some kind of animal, cemented to a floor in the tunnels.

It had been stupid of him to call the kami of that place. Of course it would scar him.

Having reached the horizon of the inner sphere, Michael let himself drift out into the center of the interhull space. One of the little models floated nearby; they'd spent an hour photographing those from every angle, but still no one had touched one. To do so, he suspected, would be to awaken some new Lasa response.

He felt an old itch at the base of his brain. The NeoShinto AI was awake, preparing to skew his neural pathways in the direction of a mystical experience. All he had to do was give it a subject to focus on.

Michael hesitated. This was what he had come here to do. Ever since Dis, Michael had felt uncomfortable in his own skin; he was adrift, because the kami of Dis dominated his consciousness. He had wracked his brains, but could think of no other way to get that feeling back than to find and contact stronger kami.

He looked back at the camp. Herat was looking at him; the professor nodded slightly. Herat knew what he was going to try. Michael felt a surge of affection for the older man and grinned. It would annoy the hell out of Crisler if he realized what Michael was doing—but they were on the *Envy* now, and Michael was under Rue's protection. Remembering this decided him.

Jetting over the horizon so that the camp was out of sight, he found a spot where the cables the marines had strung weren't visible. All he saw was the curving Lasa space itself. One of the marines followed him, looking suspicious, but Michael turned his back on the man. He opened his eyes wide, let go of verbal thought and tried to become pure awareness.

The AI took over smoothly; Michael felt his consciousness expand to fill the cool geometric perfection of the habitat. He thought he heard a sighing laughter echoing off the chamber's walls—the sound of something ancient shrugging awake for a moment.

For a few seconds he felt a swelling sense of wonder; that wasn't hard, considering where he was. He waited for it to translate into something more, but it didn't happen. All he got was a sense of something watching—a mind vast and cool and ultimately indifferent.

Michael blinked, staring at the metal walls. *No.* He

couldn't leave things as they were. He had to find the kami again. He shut his eyes and consciously awoke the implants. *Show me!*

Nothing happened.

Michael squeezed his hands into fists. He felt trapped. But it was not the implants that were at fault, he knew. How could he find the kami anymore, now that he no longer believed in the doctrines of Permanence?

For a long time he hung there, bent over, hearing faint sounds of conversation echoing over the horizon, but uncaring to listen. Then, gradually, shame overtook him. Here he was in one of the most incredible alien artifacts of all time and he wasn't even looking at it. He was hardly here at all, in fact, so preoccupied was he with his own problems. No wonder he couldn't sense any kami; he hadn't formed any connection with this place.

Maybe. But if I did, would the kami help me?

He stared upward for several minutes, deliberately taking note of the fine details of the metal walls, the drifting models. Then he shook his head, shrugged at the marine who had watched this performance, and jetted back to the campsite.

"Did you get it?" asked the professor.

"No," he said. He tried to say more, but the words wouldn't come. Finally he just shook his head. "No, I failed."

"Failed at what?" asked Rue.

"It doesn't matter." He drifted down slightly apart from the others. Rue cast him a puzzled look, but didn't say anything more.

Herat also looked over. "Let's turn in," he suggested. "Tomorrow will probably be a long day."

They retreated to the interior of the tent; Barendts hung by the door, obviously not intending to sleep. Michael curled up and tried to dispel the sensation of falling. He could hear Rue breathing a few centimeters away.

For some reason, he thought about Rue's tale of the Supreme Meme. What would happen if he applied that little test to his beliefs? Would they come up short? Probably. Probably.

How would you have to feel? The words seemed to bounce around inside his skull, like a catchy advertising jingle. *How would you have to feel, to want it all again?*

17

THEY ENTERED ONE of the newly opened chambers after breakfast and then to Rue's intense frustration, Herat called a halt to proceedings.

The scientists had analyzed the composition of the "mudballs" that had appeared in the second set of chambers. Most were toxic in one way or another: saturated with cadmium, sulphur or PAHs. Rue had wanted them to flip the door switch in the chamber full of PAH and tholin mud; it was the nearest thing to the material that made up Allemagne's trapped comet. Herat had refused and so they had gone into a cylinder whose mudball was full of complex hydrocarbons, hydro-cyanides and other nasty volatile chemicals that Herat thought most closely resembled the constituents of the early Earth environment.

"It's asking about us, starting with the most elementary questions, literally," he said. "This is what we're made of. We say yes here."

Once again the stoic marine Barendts had gone into the chamber and tripped the switch inside. Again the other open doors had closed and a new configuration gaped seconds later.

The problem was, what was behind these doors was so unnerving that even the normally adventurous Herat was stopped dead by it.

"Looks like . . . meat," observed Crisler as they clustered around one of the doorways. A large red quivering sphere hung several meters below them. It was joined to the walls of its chamber by veinlike threads. Worst, Rue could *smell* it, a reek like an open wound.

"We need specimens," muttered Herat. "Is this their kind of life or . . ."

"Or what?" asked Rue. "What else would it be?"

He just shook his head. The other open chambers contained even more bizarre things; one of them looked like a kind of leafless bush that seemed to hum with electricity. Another was an immense solid sphere, apparently of cuticle.

"You know what really annoys me?" Herat asked no one in particular. "It's that." He pointed at the innermost wall of one of the new chambers. Where there had been a single switch next to the inner airlock of the previous chambers, in this and the other new chambers, there were two switches.

"Before we just had 'yes,' " he said. "Now what do we have? Yes or no?"

"Let's find out," she said.

He shook his head. "Not until we know more."

"How are we going to know more if we don't try something?"

The professor looked down his nose at her. "We analyze the data we've collected so far, of course."

"Data?" She laughed. "What data?"

He ignored her. She appealed to Mike, who was wrinkling his nose at the smell of the chamber. "We have to continue. We have to know how this place works!"

"In time," he said.

"We don't have time!" Finally she had their attention. "Crisler, tell them about the cracked stacks."

The admiral winced. "Our life-support situation's a bit more dire than we thought," he admitted. "Nothing to panic about. But we're going to go critical in just a few days unless we cut down the awake personnel again."

"Cut down?" Mike cable-walked his way over to the admiral. "To what?"

"Well, a full complement of ten seems likely," said Crisler. The marines received this news with no reaction, but the scientists were visibly dismayed.

"We can't work under these—" and "Why didn't you tell us?" were two of the themes she extracted from the babble of scholarly voices. Crisler crossed his arms and waited; she realized with an uneasy start that she was doing the same thing.

"This could be our only chance," Rue said when the talk had died down a bit. "If we don't figure this place out in the next day or two, we're all going to have to go back in storage and it'll be too late."

Herat glowered into the middle distance. "A bad break," he admitted. "The problem remains that this . . . interface . . . with the Lasa system only seems to work in one direction. If we go down the wrong alley, we can't turn around and start over. Like it or not, this place expects us to know what we're doing. And we don't."

"So we do nothing?"

"No," he said with exaggerated patience. "We analyze our data. Like I said."

"Damnit!" She jumped off the inner sphere and bounced herself off the outer hull, then over the horizon—just like she used to do in the Gallery back home.

She heard them all talking again, somebody laughed, doubtless at her antics. Rue didn't care. She found a doorway on the opposite side of the interhull and perched on its lip, looking inward. Slowly rotating inside was something like a big ball of bark. It wasn't at all attractive, but certainly wasn't threatening.

Eventually they were going to have to choose a switch next to one of these live things. It might take Herat days to analyze this stuff; the problem was nobody could tell how many more close/open sequences like this there might be before the habitat got to where ever it was going. Or had answers to whatever questions it was asking.

It didn't help that she couldn't decide which one was best either. The most tantalizing was a green thing like a giant cabbage; it smelled lovely. But were the Lasa asking if this was what she liked to eat, or were they asking if this was what she was made of? There seemed no way to know.

After a time, solitude and reflection calmed her down. She still had nothing to say to anyone, though, so she hung out by the chambers on this side of the sphere, speculating. About an hour after she'd left the main party the little mesobot scooted around the horizon and began nosing around the open airlocks.

She watched as it glided up to her and stopped, a meter away. "Hi. How are you?" it asked in Mike Bequith's voice.

She laughed. "I'm fine. Sorry about the display back there. Your boss just knows how to push my buttons, that's all."

"It's not just that, is it?" asked Mike. Somehow he made the mesobot tilt itself in a quizzical gesture. "The success of your own mission is riding on what we find here."

"Well, there is that." She crossed her arms. "The professor doesn't see that."

"He sees more than you might think."

"Whatever. Have you found out anything more about these things?" She gestured at the open hatch next to her.

"Yeah. They really are alive—and the DNA is derived from human DNA. Somehow we got sampled after arriving here and this place," the mesobot tilted toward the inner sphere, "has been making variations on the theme of human biology ever since. All these life-forms share the basic organic composition of humans, but put together in different ways. The one you're sitting next to is probably the one we'd consider most edible; a couple of the others are really off-putting, like that bone thing four hatches over from you."

"So what next?"

"Herat thinks these things are a gold mine. He wants to study them all."

"Damn him! Can't you make him see reason?"

"He thinks if we select one of these chambers, the others will close and he'll lose his chance to examine them."

"Yeah? So?"

"Rue, you have to face the possibility that this whole process isn't going to lead us to the information you need."

Rue reached out and grabbed the mesobot. It let out a surprised beep. She whirled her arm and flung it away in the general direction of the horizon.

"Hey . . ." Mike's voice faded away as the bot receded. She watched it stop itself just short of the outer sphere's skin, then jet away indignantly.

Rue caught herself on the edge of the hatch and settled again. Mike might well be right that exploring these hatches wouldn't get her anywhere; but that was no excuse for not trying.

IT WAS OBVIOUSLY prudent to leave Rue alone when she was in this kind of mood. Michael returned the mesobot to its inspection duty, opening more and more inscape windows around himself until he was almost boxed in by them. The other scientists crowded around, starting their own analyses and soon the whole space near the main airlock was full of windows.

It was good to lose himself in work. Michael had awoken from their rest period feeling the accustomed lightness of freefall and another lightness he hadn't felt in years. He knew a part of his life was over, had ended yesterday when he failed to summon the kami of the Lasa. For months, he had agonized over this coming loss, which he could foresee but not divert. Now that it had happened, he felt . . . nothing. At least, no despair. Just a kind of expectancy. As he worked now, he turned that feeling over in the back of his mind, trying to figure out what it meant.

The kami had been his anchor to a meaning in life. He'd

thought he would be lost without them—and he was; it was just that being lost didn't seem to mean so much all of a sudden.

There was more to it . . . but understanding eluded him, for now.

Crisler drifted into the constellation, eyeing the microscopic views and spectral analyses with some irony. "In your element, I see, Dr. Bequith."

"Yes, Admiral." Michael kept his tone neutral.

"I've been watching you," said Crisler. "I'm aware that you've been doing a good job with this investigation. I just wanted you to know that this information is going into my report. If it should turn out that you are not the saboteur, you'll be receiving the highest commendation for your work here."

Michael appraised the admiral; for once Crisler wasn't showing his usual hail-fellow-well-met face. He looked serious and sincere. Michael had to restrain himself from punching the man in the face.

"Thank you, Admiral," said Michael as cooly as he could. "I hope you realize that I took asylum on Rue Cassels's ship so that I would be able to continue my work unhampered by . . . politics."

"I reserve my judgment on that. Carry on." Crisler glided through some windows and vanished behind them.

Well, I wonder what that was all about? Michael returned to work, but his halfhearted concentration was quite broken now.

What an unbelievably clumsy attempt to be chummy! Crisler's little pep-talk had doubtless been meant to be reassuring, but to Michael it just seemed forced. How could he think that Michael would ever trust him? Which reminded him of how Rue mistrusted Crisler; that, in turn, brought his mind back to Rue and her present dilemma. Would she end up at this man's mercy, if she was unable to find a way to control the *Envy*?

He needed a bathroom break. Michael left the open windows where they were and headed for the cylindrical, man-sized portapot they'd set up last night. He hated performing bodily functions in freefall, so tended to wait until the last minute. As usual his need was fairly urgent by the time he got to the can.

As he was buckling up his jumpsuit again, something tumbled out of one of the pockets. It was the little camera he'd borrowed from Blair and used to photograph the outside of this habitat. The pictures were still in the camera—presumably useless since they appeared to show nothing new.

The camera had its own little preview screen. On a whim, he turned it on and brought up the first photo.

There was the black of the Lasa sphere and the writing . . .

The writing was different.

Michael gaped at the image in astonishment. His mind was a complete blank. He was jerked rudely out of that state when somebody knocked on the door to the can. "Hey, what are you, dying in there?" It was one of the marines.

"Hold on." He hid the camera again, finished zipping up and left the portapot.

A few meters away, the science team was poring over the results from the mesobot. They were all quite absorbed in their work, especially Herat. Even the marines were interested, since some of the inscape pictures showed the squishier parts of the life-forms under analysis.

Michael drifted off to the horizon and settled down with his back to the camp. Then he brought out the camera again and looked at the pictures.

Somehow, the camera had seen something completely different from what he—and the others—had seen as they approached the habitat. Where Michael had seen spidery Lasa writing, the camera had recorded something different, right at the spot where Linda Ophir's annotations suggested a deception in Blair's originals.

There was writing there, all right, but only one of the large paragraphs was Lasa. The other paragraph, Michael recognized as the dense, multilayered and multicolored lines of Chicxulub script.

And now he remembered how, on board the *Spirit of Luna*, he had been literally unable to see any part of the ship that he was not authorized to visit. Doors had been invisible; stairs had looked like walls, all due to an override on his inscape. What if . . . Michael called up an inscape search interface and tried to connect to the camera through it. He got no reply. Like most simple mechanisms manufactured in the halo worlds, this camera was not connected to the inscape network.

The only way that he and the others could have had the complete sensory experience of seeing Lasa writing instead of what was really there was if inscape had overridden their senses whenever they looked at the outside of the habitat.

The thought was disturbing. How could he know what was real about this place and what fake? No—everything couldn't be faked, that would place too great a burden on the inscape system. Even on the *Spirit of Luna*, only key items had been disguised. Nothing so magnificent as this space he was now in could be completely constructed for everyone's senses without some signs that it was unreal. But strategic information could be hidden, essentially in the open, if everything else was left alone.

Nobody could mess with inscape without massive computing power and direct control of the inscape system. Only Crisler had that control. So Crisler knew about the Chicxulub writing. Crisler—and how many of his people?

Michael quickly replaced the camera in his pocket and turned toward the camp.

As he did there was a great splashing sound and the steady light that had been ever-present in the habitat since yesterday, went out.

People started shouting. He could see the luminous inscape windows where the scientists had been working, but of course they cast no real light since they existed only in his visual cortex. After a few seconds the marines had their spotlights operating and began shining them around, casting columns of light that were multiply reflected back from the metal walls.

"Bequith!" Herat flew up just as Michael made it back to the constellation of windows. "The doors. They've all closed!"

He turned. It was true: The dozens of open portals had reverted to being solid black disks.

Something about those disks looked strange, but it must be a trick of the wobbling lights. Michael blinked and looked again.

"Professor . . ."

"What triggered it? Where's that damned mesobot."

Michael grabbed Herat's arm. "I think you'd better look at this, sir."

Herat looked where he pointed. "What, I . . . oh. Oh!"

The black airlock disks on the inner sphere were *growing*. Where before each had been separated from its neighbors by a good four meters, now the distance had shrunk to three. And the disks were continuing to grow, in liquid tendrils like a stain spreading through fabric—or the arms of an amoeba absorbing a meal.

"The magnetic liquid's overflowing—or being redirected," said Herat. "It's going to cover the whole surface . . ."

As they watched, the white metal of the inner sphere slowly vanished under an advancing tide of black. After several minutes they were left in a space with the same dimensions as before, but the beams from their lights were now absorbed by what had come to look like a vast drop of black oil. The outer hull of the habitat was still there, still mirror-bright, but what it mirrored was as dark as a starless sky.

"Is it growing? I think it's growing," somebody said.

"Everyone fall back to the main lock," ordered Crisler. "Now!"

With a sinking feeling, Michael realized what must have happened. He counted heads, then checked the view from the mesobot just to be sure.

Then he said, with some hesitation, "has anybody seen Rue?"

THE BIG QUESTION had been, was she acting from impulsive anger like she had when she ran away to the plow sail—or was Rue right when she thought that they should open the next chamber now? She perched outside the entrance to the green ball for a long time, tugging back and forth at the issue.

She was still a bit ashamed of how she'd acted after the sabotage. Rue couldn't decide whether she'd been right about Crisler; logic and, well, everybody else said she had overreacted. He hadn't been about to lock her up with her crew, that was just a paranoid fantasy.

But it wasn't paranoia now that made her think they were at the limit of what they could do. The *Banshee*'s life support was continuing to degrade and in a day or so it would all be over. Rue would have to go into that terrible half-sleep stupor along with Max and the others and when she awoke they would be decelerating into the empty Maenad system, from there to return to Chandaka. And Rue would be poor again and there would never be another chance to return to *Jentry's Envy*, or in all likelihood the halo either.

So Herat's caution be damned. *I'm right*, she thought as she swung herself into the narrow cylindrical chamber that held the chlorophyll-green cabbage thing.

Edging around the tangle of leaves/vanes, which looked ready to pounce, she found herself at the black disk of the chamber's inner airlock.

There were two switches here. In the earlier chambers there had only been one; logic suggested that they should open the inner airlock door, but when tripped they had made the other outside chambers open and close. Here were two switches—but one of them was right next to the door itself, the other several hand-spans distant. This time, she was sure, she could open the inner door if she wanted.

But why would she want to? Rue looked back at the giant cabbage, wondering what question she was supposed to be answering by tripping the switches here. These living things were obviously not attempts to re-create humans from their DNA; unless the Lasa mind behind this place was an idiot, it could see that its productions didn't resemble people. Its previous questions seemed to have been about human preferences in environment—what kind of water they liked and what kind of soil. By that logic, this time the question was 'what kind of food do you like'?

Tentatively, she broke a small piece of leaf off the cabbage and nibbled it. Herat would kill her if he saw her doing this—but the mesobot had investigated this thing and said it wasn't poisonous.

It had no real taste, which was reassuring, actually. She chewed and swallowed.

"Okay." Of all the weird life-forms in these chambers, this one seemed most benign. That made her answer clear, at least on a gut level. It was increasingly clear to her that it was the gut-level answer that the Lasa were looking for.

She reached out, hesitated, and pressed the switch next to the inner airlock door.

With a splash the door irised open, really before she could register the fact that she had made an irreversible and maybe critical, decision. Rue found herself staring into a new chamber, one level further into the inner sphere of the habitat.

"Well, well, what have we here?" She pulled herself in.

This chamber was spherical, about four meters across. It

had eight airlock doors in its walls. Floating in front of each airlock was a model, like the ones in the interhull. These models, however, were made of something transparent and each one held a tiny ball of leaves and earth, lit by tiny pinprick lamps inside it.

"Oh boy." This was major. She glanced back up the cylinders, wondering whether she should get the others in here now. Like as not Herat would want her locked up for what she'd just done—but damn it, this was her ship . . .

The outermost airlock door was closed.

"Hey!" Rue flew back to the door and pressed her hand against it. Her fist deformed the liquid slightly, then slid about frictionlessly on it. She couldn't push through it and there was no switch on this side.

"Oh, Meadow-Rue, you've done it this time." She almost laughed, it was so pathetic. She was on her own now.

Rue returned to the round chamber. Her heart was pounding, but she was more excited than scared now. The Lasa had locked her in, but she didn't think arms were going to come out of the wall to dissect her. If that had been the Lasa's intention, they would have done it a year ago, when she first arrived here.

No, this room was another question and she needed to answer it. Summoning her determination, she hand-walked over to the nearest model and examined it gingerly. This was a half-meter wide sphere, a little crystal ball, really, with a miniature version of the cabbage growing from a wet ball of earth in its center. There were little openings in the crystal; she put her nose to one and sniffed. It smelled like a terrarium, of wet soil.

The little plant was lit by eight tiny lights that were mounted in the outer crystal. It was beautiful, but what was most intriguing was the tiny black disks near the lights.

If Rue was right, then she knew exactly what the Lasa were asking her this time. Excitement mounting, she went to another model—this one a less beautiful can-shaped thing. She could only see through the transparent end caps of this model. Its soil and water were distributed around the inside walls, with tiny grasslike plants innermost, basking under the light of a string of lamps strung down the can's center.

She checked the other models quickly. There was a cube, a doughnut shape, a flattened sphere. She came back to the can, though it was really the ugliest of the lot.

"This is perfect," she said aloud and pressed the switch for the door next to the can.

THEY WERE ALL outside now. The black airlock liquid had expanded in arcs and curving spikes, until it filled the entire interhull; the last marine was literally squeezed out through the lock. Michael now hung in space with the others, their jittery spotlights flitting across the placid face of the habitat as they talked excitedly about this development.

He felt sick. Rue was in there, devoured by the black liquid. There was no doubt in Michael's mind that she had tripped a switch and been caught like a mouse in a trap. He shouldn't have left her to brood.

Crisler's voice came loudly through his earphones. "Okay, people, we're falling back to one kilometer. The *Banshee*'s weapons are on-line and trained on this place. If it looks like it's going to open fire on us, we'll have to hit it first with everything we've got."

"That's insane," said Herat. "We haven't found any evidence of hostile intent in this place."

"Except that your precious Lasa have just eaten Rue Cassels."

"Beware of using loaded terms, Admiral. We don't know what just happened. We certainly don't know it was a hostile act."

"You were the one urging caution before."

"I was saying we shouldn't act without certain knowledge and I still am."

"Sirs," said one of the marines. "The airlock's overflowing."

"Everybody back! Now!"

Reluctantly, Michael turned on his maneuvering thrusters and jetted back with the rest. When he was in place at Crisler's one-kilometer line, he turned and looked back at the habitat.

It was hard to see unless you knew what to look for, but the smooth black of the habitat's hull was being replaced by the oily shimmer of the magnetic liquid. It was being pumped out through the airlock and was slicking rapidly over the furred hull. Frightening as it was to look at, Michael had to admire the genius behind it: Using ferrofluids, the Lasa could make their airlock grow big enough to bring the entire habitat inside it. Its spiky outthrusts showed that this liquid had to follow the lines of the magnetic fields—it couldn't be filling all the space under its surface. He pictured a large and growing chamber inside; anything could be happening there.

"It's swallowing itself," he said. Herat grunted in response.

"Explain, Bequith."

"This looks more defensive than aggressive, Admiral. Of course, we can't see what's going on underneath, but we were in that situation before."

He watched as the oily blackness ate away the letters of the Lasa writing. Soon the entire paragraph was gone and the black marched on to meet itself on the opposite side of the sphere.

A new voice cut in—one of Crisler's staff, calling from the *Banshee*. "Sir, the surface you see is actually moving five centimeters above the actual hull. It's a very thin layer of ferrofluid, supported from below by some pretty impressive magnetic gymnastics. But a picosecond blast from the main laser will open a three-meter hole in that stuff. We can do it at any time."

"Ready to go in, sir," said Barendts.

"Hang on there," snapped Herat. "If it's all that thin, it's obviously no threat."

"Maybe," said Crisler. "At the same time, it has one of our people. I for one am not inclined to leave her in there."

Michael looked at the habitat. It was completely covered in the black oil now; there were no telltale words to signify that it was a physical object that could be written on— there was only a complete absence of stars in a starburst shape to show that anything was there at all.

The staffer's voice cut in. "Sir! Registering a change. Heat levels are rising in a number of spots. No change on the surface, but the ferrofluid's radiating, probably from sources underneath. We might be able to image the sources."

"If anything breaks through the surface, shoot it off," said Crisler. "Marines, prepare to enter the thing."

"Sir, wait," said the staffer.

"What the hell is it?"

"Sir . . . it's changing shape."

SIX CHAMBERS IN, Rue found the control panel.

The previous rooms had been more and more specific; when it came, this one wasn't a surprise.

Rue moved in a daze, a kind of ecstasy. She knew exactly what was happening and it was the fulfillment of every possibility that *Jentry's Envy* had ever hinted at. The outside world, the past, her worries, even hunger and thirst, had all dissolved in the wonder of the present.

This chamber glittered with light and hummed with sound. It had eight doors, as had the others. The auroral glows and sparkling-edged images projected all around her were beautiful and alien, but she knew their purpose. They were the question that followed her last answer.

She moved slowly into the chamber and entered a region of focused sound. The tones were ordered, a kind of wonderful chorus, and when she moved they shifted and modulated. It was like the air itself held little clouds of sound and she could poke her head into one or another and hear its particular song.

Sadly, it was not practical. Herat would have spent a whole career in this little space, writing dissertations on the use of holographic sound to convey metric information. Mike would have heard endless kami in it. She was with Mike on this one.

Hulking near the next door was a large metal frame, surrounded with interpenetrating rings like one of those medieval globes of the heavens. At its center the whole contraption held a set of straps and manacles in places where they could be clamped around arms, legs, neck, torso. It looked very disturbing, like a high-tech torture device, but when she figured out what it was, Rue was actually tempted to try it. Herat would be even more fascinated by this thing: a display and input device that used physical pressure, orientation and position to convey and read information. A full-body joystick.

There were two places whose models she couldn't figure out at all; two which were strictly visual and beautiful, but whose input component eluded her. At the seventh door, she found the one she needed.

From outside, this area of the chamber had a kind of polarized sheen to it. When she glided into the space it defined, though, she found herself surrounded by stars. The holography was beautiful and precise; she could faintly see the rest of the chamber through it.

Also in this space were several little pens, more like chopsticks. She didn't know whether they were real or projected until she picked one up. It was cool metal, smooth and comfortable to hold. She took another, held them like chopsticks and reached out to pluck a star from the air.

To her amazement, the whole display zoomed in the blink of an eye. Before her was a blazing star, its tiny retinue of planets twinkling next to it. Dozens of tiny crosshairs floated in the display; they could represent asteroids, ships, or colonies. She felt that she was seeing a processed telescopic view and not something completely made up.

She waved the chopsticks and the star retreated to its original position.

Hmm . . . Rue looked around until she found another set of tiny crosshairs. It was down by her feet, very faint. She reached down and plucked it.

Jentry's Envy soared into view around her. She recognized Lake Flaccid, the red cube and there was the *Banshee*, balloon-sides glowing with internal light.

Rue wiped her eyes and looked about for the Lasa sphere.

There it was, superimposed over something cylindrical and familiar from the previous chambers she'd navigated. Yes. She was right about what was happening. She selected the sphere and it expanded around her.

Instead of an inner sphere made of metal and with airlock doors in it, though, she found herself floating above a giant sphere of light, with meridianal lines dividing it into many sections. Within each translucent section, small models glowed.

It's a menu. Laughing, she selected an element and it zoomed out around her—leaving a new sphere, its elements composed of variations on the item she had chosen.

She zoomed out, took one chopstick and waved it. It left a glowing line in space. She signed her name in thin air and laughed again.

Then she navigated down the menus until she found a little image of herself and she picked it up and deposited it outside the whole sphere.

The airlock below her blew outward in a big bubble, which opened, swallowed her and her display and closed again. From outside it she suddenly heard a tremendous *crunching* sound, like a giant's molars consuming a building. And she was moving.

That was okay; she knew where she was going. Rue was in charge of her ship at last.

"IT'S LENGTHENING OUT," said the staffer. "Becoming more cylindrical." Michael could see that with his own eyes now. The black surface was bulking up in places, then the bulges subsided again. It looked for all the world like a man dressing in a too-small survival bag.

"Sir?" asked Barendts.

"Hang on," said Crisler. "I need to know what it's doing."

"The heat signatures are intense," said the staffer. "We're getting radar showing all kinds of turmoil in there, sir. Very large masses in rapid motion."

"What kind? I need more information, damn it."

"Um . . . I think it would be unwise to send anyone in there at this time, sir. They'd be minced."

A space-suited figure jetted over to Michael. "What do you think?" asked Herat over a private channel.

"She triggered some kind of transformation, that's for sure," said Michael. "But it doesn't make any sense, based on where we were on the sequence. The Lasa were asking us something about how our life is organized, but why would the answer lead to this?"

"Maybe they're like the autotrophs," said Herat. "If we replied that we ate life like them, they might go ballistic. After all, wouldn't that be a major part of their assessment? Seeing what kind of risk we are?"

"I prefer not to believe that they're paranoid, sir."

"You prefer to think she's still alive," said Herat quietly. "So do I, Michael."

"We need to do something!"

"I know. But I don't know what."

The habitat had finished reshaping itself. It was much bigger now and shaped like a shaggy can. Now something started to bud away from one end. A large sphere, black as everything else, but . . .

Michael spotted a little dot of red on that sphere. The dot grew to become a letter of Lasa writing. Then a whole word emerged.

"The habitat's reappearing!" he shouted.

"I'll be damned," whispered Herat. "It's squirting itself out."

Over the next several minutes, the original Lasa habitat emerged from the end of the black cylinder. The black liquid was draining off it in an orderly way. The habitat seemed unchanged by the strange transformation that had taken place.

"It's given birth," said Herat. He began to laugh. "And what a bunch of nervous fathers we were!"

"Keep the lasers ready," said Crisler. "Marines, check out the Lasa sphere."

"Sir." The squad jetted away, the mesobot following them. Michael watched them approach the red-lettered sphere from its perspective. His head was spinning. Just what had happened here?

The marines found the airlock, now reverted back to its original condition. They stuck some periscopes through it, then one pushed the mesobot in. Michael's view suddenly went black, then came back as the little bot entered the interhull.

Except it was an interhull no longer. The interior of the black Lasa sphere was almost empty—just a smooth collection of arcing reflections from the metal walls. There were only two objects in here now.

One was a large black sphere of roiling ferrofluid, maybe eight meters across. It drifted near the far end of the sphere.

The other object was harder to figure out. It glowed with faery light, even seeming to have wings, or fans of auroral light around it. It too was a sphere, only this sphere was made of crystal or glass.

Inside it Rue Cassels moved in a slow but purposeful dance. Her space suit's helmet was off and he could clearly see the huge grin on her face.

"She's alive," he said.

"Sir, look! The black, it's peeling off the cylinder now!"

Michael brought his view back from the mesobot. Spotlights had the new cylinder outlined and in their glow he could clearly see the black liquid draining away from a bright metal hull. As it crept away from the end caps of the cylinder it revealed glass and the spotlights refracted into some kind of open interior.

"It's a habitat," murmured Herat. "It's built us a habitat."

"*Yes, Professor.*"

It was Rue. Her voice sounded dreamy, jubilant. "It built us a new home, according to my specs. And it's showed me the origin of *Jentry's Envy* and its course. This habitat is for humans, Professor. It's ours, as part of the Lasa's crew. *Jentry's Envy* was a gift all along, you see. All we had to do was unwrap it."

Michael turned on his jets and headed for the Lasa habitat. Out of the corner of his eye he saw Herat jetting toward the new one—curiosity getting the better of him, as always. Crisler was shouting for them to remain where they were, but Michael just wanted to make sure Rue was all right and tell her how happy he was that she had succeeded at finding her dream and desperate necessity.

"Decant Max," shouted Rue. "Bring 'em all out! We're going to have a damned big party! And then *Jentry's Envy* is open for business!"

Behind Michael, Crisler and his men didn't move. For once, the admiral gave no orders.

PART FOUR

Dinner with the Autotroph

18

Rue awoke to the sound of birdsong.

It was something she had heard in recordings, or synthesized, many times. The first time she'd heard live birds was on Treya; the second time, on Chandaka.

Then this must be the planet Oculus, at Colossus. She opened her eyes.

A billowing canopy of pale blue silk hung over her bed, extravagant as something from history. The bed was a four-poster, strictly for use under gravity. Her head was embraced by a luxuriously soft pillow.

She stretched and yawned. Other than the birds, there was no sound; no fans, or pumps, or footsteps overhead. No wonder she had slept so well, despite the heat in this room.

Sitting up, Rue spotted her clothes neatly folded on a nearby chair. This was her first awakening at Colossus and yet she was not surrounded by doctors, nor was she shivering in a cold-sleep vat waiting to be tended to. She didn't feel a million years old like she had every other time she emerged from cold sleep—in fact, she felt great.

Her feet touched down in deep warm pile carpet. This room was at least seven meters on a side and almost that tall. One entire wall was taken up with high, leaded-glass windows; there were French doors there as well. Rue dressed without looking at her clothes; her eyes were fixed on the vista outside.

She needed to go to the bathroom, but there was no way she was doing that before she got past those windows. She turned the handle on the doors and they opened to let in a beautifully cool breeze. The air smelled of ice and bare rock, like the penumbral mountains at Treya. Eagerly Rue stepped out onto a wide balcony.

A quick glance told her she was halfway up the side of a

gigantic building perched on an equally huge cliff. Then she turned her attention to what lay beyond.

The sky at Treya had been alive with clouds. This sky was alive in a completely different way. The whole firmament glowed with sunset mauve and peach, but these colors didn't radiate from the horizon the way sunset had on Chandaka. Rather, at the zenith hung a round golden disk, its edges perfectly sharp. She could look straight at it without difficulty. Near this disk the sky was a lovely peach color, becoming rose, purple, dark blue and finally black at the horizon.

A brilliant aurora danced throughout this beautiful sky. Wavering curtains of light at the horizon, the auroral bands became coiling serpents when directly overhead. The combination of firmament and aurora laid fairy light over a seascape that stretched away to incredible distance before her.

That golden disk must be the brown dwarf Colossus, she knew, but it was nothing at all like Erythrion. Neither was this place like Treya, or Chandaka, or any world she had seen in movies or sims.

A city brimmed over the cliff her building stood upon. Its walls and minarets gleamed like an hallucination in the sinuous light. The cliff itself was pearly white and was backed by ramparts of equally white mountains. It stretched off past the horizons to either side.

Rue had never seen a real ocean, but she knew that the one before her must be unique. Mountains reared out of it, white with emerald and turquoise highlights: icebergs. Smaller chunks of ice floated in the dark water, their sides licked by white foam. The air that blew back her hair was well below freezing—a perfect temperature, in fact. She leaned against the balustrade and closed her eyes, just breathing it in for a while.

Someone cleared their throat.

Rue turned, to find a tall man in the severe black uniform of the Cycler Compact standing at the French doors. "Captain Cassels," he said. "Welcome to Lux and the planet Oculus. I am glad to find you awake. I am Griffin, the abbot of this monastery."

"How long have we been here?" she asked. "Are the others awake?"

"You are the first, since you are the captain of the *Jentry's Envy*," he said with a bow. "You must tell us the order in which to awake the others."

"How long?" she asked again.

"A week since we recovered your shuttle," he said. "There was no indication of urgency in your messages, so we took the liberty of awaking you in a traditional way, more civilized than one finds in cycler travel lately, I'd wager."

Rue was at a loss as to what to say. She just nodded. "We've taken the liberty," Griffin said, "of tailoring you a uniform as befits your station." He gestured at a side table by the windows. Through the leaded glass, she saw folded black cloth.

"Oh. Well . . . thank you." She went to the doorway; he retreated and she went to the table.

"If you and your companions are willing, we would be pleased to give a banquet in your honor at second shift-over," he said. "In the Great Hall of the monastery, of course."

"Banquet?" Her head was spinning. "Sure." She unfolded part of the uniform. It was an absolute black, with silver epaulets and piping. Her heart flipped as she saw on the breast something she'd seen before only in movies and sims: the silver infinity symbol inside laurel leafs that signified the rank of cycler captain.

Rue dropped the uniform back on the table. A roaring filled her head and the world faded in and out for a moment.

"Are you all right?" Griffin was at her side, one hand just touching her elbow.

"No—I mean yes, I, I'll be all right." She turned away from him, so that he wouldn't see the tears starting in her eyes.

"I'd hoped to give you a tour of Lux this afternoon," said the abbot. "But I see you've not fully recovered from your flight."

"No, it's all right." She wiped her eyes and turned to smile at him. "Abbot Griffin, I would love a tour. Maybe, if you gave me an hour to freshen up? Please, I wouldn't miss it for the world."

He smiled graciously and bowed again. "Of course. One of the sisters will be waiting outside the door if you require anything. An hour then?"

She nodded. After he left Rue turned back to stare at the folded uniform. It seemed to draw light to itself, as if it were the magnetic focus of the room. Her hand hovered over the smooth cloth for long seconds before she summoned the courage to turn a fold aside and gaze again on the infinity symbol. That symbol was no doubt chiseled into the stones above this monastery's gate. It was the symbol of her civilization.

TWO HOURS LATER, Rue was high above the city in an air-car, staring down at the domed towers of Lux. Many of the buildings had atria or open shafts penetrating them; from above, the shafts made patterns of dots across the rooftops. The Abbot had explained that since Oculus was tidally locked, Colossus never moved from its position near the zenith. The builders of the city could put skylights and light-pipes in permanent place, confident that Colossus would throw its amber light deep into the heart of any building without pause.

For all its medieval appearance, Lux was built of plastics and ceramics, all based on minerals and chemicals mined from the ocean. The ocean was global, for Oculus was a Europan world, covered in continents of ice with a twenty-kilometer deep ocean beneath them. Only here at the point closest to Colossus was the water exposed, in a circular ocean two thousand kilometers across. Lux clung to the edge of this ocean, but most of Oculus's cities were dug deep under the ice, at its interface with the unfathomable depths of water.

"See down there," said the abbot. Rue followed his pointing finger to the base of the ice cliffs. There, dark archways opened into the white walls. As she watched, a large ship exited one archway. It cast wings of water up and behind it from small feet of some kind that it ran upon.

"Hydrofoils," said the abbot. Rue smiled politely, though she didn't understand. Now she saw there were many ships on the water, from very small sailing vessels to huge square things loaded with shipping containers.

"I hope you are with us long enough to go sailing," said the abbot. "The bergs are beautiful and home to many birds."

She nodded again. The view was spectacular, but by now Rue was so overwhelmed she was barely registering it. She was still trying to get over the experience of walking the halls of the monastery wearing a cycler captain's uniform.

Everyone who had seen her dressed this way had stopped. The men had bowed; the women curtsied. There was no irony to it. They were sincere in their respect. Rue kept wanting to say, "hang on, I'm not what you think I am"—but she *was* what they thought she was. The implications had just never registered with her until now.

Before they had entered cold sleep for the trip down here, Crisler had summoned everyone to a meeting and said, "Here are the things we can't talk about while we're at Colossus." He had spoken of the necessity of not revealing details about the nature of *Jentry's Envy*. "We have to claim ignorance of its origins and course for now," he had said with grim authority. At the time Rue had nodded with the others, but she knew that Crisler's priorities only made sense to those of her passengers who were from High

Space. He couldn't be trusted anyway: Mike's discovery of the hidden photos proved that.

She felt she had managed to convince Crisler that she would adhere to his wishes. As soon as he awoke, though, he would realize that this was her world and she could and would say whatever she wanted to these people. There was no reason for her to keep the secrets of the *Envy* for his sake and no way he could enforce his wishes here. She was tempted to rub his nose in that fact.

Earlier, when the abbot had asked if she had a preference as to who to revive next, Rue had been strongly tempted to say, "Leave Crisler and his men in cold sleep." It would have been so easy. But she didn't know whether she had the authority to do that, now that they were all under the care of the monks. And also, the level of cold sleep they were under was light; it wouldn't be healthy to leave them in that state for much longer.

She no longer needed Crisler and he must know it. That was probably why he had come along personally on this expedition, but what could he do about it?

"Ma'am?" She blinked in surprise. The abbot had asked her something.

"I said, would you like to return? Your people should be awake now and you'll want to orient them before the banquet."

"Of course, Abbot. Forgive my inattention." *I said that the way Grandma would have wanted*, she thought to herself.

"You have much on your mind, no doubt," said the abbot neutrally. He steered the car back toward the massive monastery tower.

Rue sat back in the deep upholstery, no longer seeing the cliffs with their wheeling birds and overhanging towers. She was thinking that she could completely isolate herself from Crisler while they were here and there was nothing he could do about it. If she was truly a cycler captain, it was time for her to adopt the responsibilities to her own people that went with the title—far away from the grasping hands of the Rights Economy.

RUE AND MAX stared down at the Great Hall from behind an ornate carved screen. The place was packed with extremely rich looking people. "Oh, shit," said Rue. "What are we going to do?"

"Don't look at me, this was your idea," he said. Max was still annoyed that she'd had him decanted. The taste for adventure he'd had on Treya seemed entirely gone. Even the exotic wonders of Lux seemed to hold no fascination for him.

The monks had dressed him up in a gray cycler crew uniform and so far Max hadn't been able to muss up this suit. She knew he would before the evening was out, but at least he'd get through the reception line with his reputation intact. And he looked great just now.

She told him that and he shrugged. "I clean up well. Shall we do it?"

They walked down a long curving hallway that finally opened up on a gallery above the cavernous space of the hall. A sweeping limestone staircase dominated this end of the chamber and they were forced to walk down this, arm in arm, while everyone in the place watched. This was the idea, apparently; everybody else had done it.

They were met at the foot of the stairs by the abbot, who proceeded to introduce Rue to the mayor of Lux, several iron-haired industrialists with predatory eyes, the entire city council, some artists and musicians whose names or reputations she pretended to know, a famously charitable philanthropist, and a deep-diving adventurer invited to the party to add zest. This was before they'd gotten ten meters into the hall, which was forested with suits and gowns.

"Ah, yes, I'd forgotten why I became a recluse," said Max during a brief break. He smiled and nodded at someone in passing, then said, "Two rules: one, stay near the drinks table. Two: never agree to do anything with anybody, even if it sounds like fun. Hey, in fact, tell them I'm in charge of your schedule and they should come to me to arrange things."

"What are you talking about?" Nobody had done anything except say hello to her.

"You'll see."

They met Rebecca near the center of the scrum. Rue's doctor looked stunning in a long silver ball gown, her hair done up with amber pins. She hugged Rue and Max. "This place is wonderful! I'm so glad I came; I just wish we'd been able to bring Mina."

It had been something of a shock when Rebecca had taken up with one of the female officers on the *Banshee*. In retrospect, it had explained much to Rue—to her embarrassment she realized she should have known early on in her acquaintance with the doctor. "We'll have to take pictures to show her," said Rue to Rebecca now. "Where're the others?"

"Laurent and Mike are over there," she pointed.

"You see? The drinks table," said Max with a nudge.

". . . And Crisler and his people are there."

The admiral was all decked out in full uniform and looked completely comfortable among the generals and flight jockeys who had surrounded his men. He seemed to be having a good time.

A succession of charming middle-aged men drifted past, all making invitations for Rue to join them for dinner, or golf (whatever that was), or a tour of the city. Max stood off to one side, imperceptibly shaking his head. She thanked them for their invitations and said she was booked up. She supposed they saw a business opportunity in her cycler.

Enthusiastic couples stopped her to ask about the *Envy*. She told them superficial things about the cycler, but by now her natural caution had asserted itself and she let out only the smallest bits of information she could get away with.

In truth, the new habitat was amazing and she was bursting to talk about it to somebody. A kind of cylindrical crystal palace lit from its axis, the habitat rotated to produce about one g, a rather dizzying spin considering its small size. Its interior was one open space, which over the first few days after its creation had sprouted a kind of grassy plant that could (Katz had discovered) be eaten.

The grass had more in common with human DNA than any Earthly plant. It was also an efficient recycler of gases, liquids, and solid waste. Katz estimated that it could support a population of well over a hundred humans, maybe indefinitely.

Orchestral music started up somewhere and Rue saw that couples were starting to waltz in a cleared area of floor. No sooner had she noticed this than a young man stepped up boldly and asked her to dance.

"Oh! Uh, no, thank you. But thank you, I mean . . ."

She fended off several more offers over the next minute. Dr. Herat and Mike were drifting over, occasionally pausing to talk to various bald, distracted looking men who were minimally well dressed and thus must be scientists.

"This place is amazing!" Herat was saying. "They say there's some kind of ruins in the ocean, but they're so far down nobody's been able to do more than map them by radar. I'd love to come back here when we're done with the *Envy*."

"Mr. Bequith," Rue said as they strolled over. "Do you know how to waltz?"

"Yes, I do," he said.

"Then perhaps you can teach me."

Rebecca grinned and tipped her glass to Max.

"I realize you're the captain, but I think you should let me lead," he said.

"Whatever you say."

He showed her the basic footwork. It was easy enough; they moved to the edge of the dance floor and Rue took a deep breath and let him pull her into the swaying throng. Michael Bequith put his hand on the small of Rue's back and she forgot everything else.

She stumbled a lot and laughed at herself, but Mike's strength literally pulled her through her missteps. It was thrilling and her only regret was that she wasn't decked out in one of those fantastic confections the other women were wearing. It must look odd, two uniformed figures dancing out here.

But no, there went two men, who were obviously into each other. To hell with it, it was time she just cut loose and enjoyed herself. Rue laughed again and let Mike twirl her around so that she almost lost her sunglasses.

The song ended and they danced another, then another. Just when she was getting giddy and tired, a strong voice behind her said, "May I have this dance?"

She turned. This man was unknown to her; he was probably in his forties and had strong, severe features and close-cropped gray hair. A gaudy ring through one ear spoiled the military effect.

He was dressed in a well-worn counterpart to the uniform she had on.

Mike bowed and let go of her hand. He had that mysterious smile on his face that he sometimes got—he seemed to be scoring some point in a game only he understood.

"R-Rue Cassels," she said as the cycler captain took her hand. "Captain of *Jentry's Envy*."

"Travis Li, captain of the *Dauntless*."

Somehow, they were dancing. She looked around for Mike, but he had vanished among the bodies. Rue tried to think of something clever to say to this captain Li. Her mind was a blank.

"I hear you've just returned from Chandaka," he said. "What's the situation there?"

She frowned. ". . . Situation?"

"You rode a beam into Chandaka. That must mean they're still maintaining their ties with the halo."

"Ah, I see." She was dancing with a dashing cycler captain and he wanted her opinion on something political! Where was Jentry when you needed to rub his nose in something?

"We were not welcomed with the same . . . enthusiasm as here, I'm afraid," she admitted. "The Compact maintains the monastery there, but I got the feeling . . . well, that they were going through the motions. They wouldn't have let us ride the beam in if it hadn't been a humanitarian situation."

"The *Envy* isn't ready to support full-time occupation, then?"

"It wasn't at that time." Was he grilling her about her ship, now?

"If you need appropriations for supplies, I know who to talk to locally," said Li. "This is my homeworld; that's why I'm visiting."

"Appropriations? Tell me more." The little Ediacaran still huddled against Rue's breast; she had been planning to see about selling it tomorrow. But of course, the monasteries of the Cycler Compact existed to maintain the fleet. Now that her cycler was officially part of that fleet, she must have access to all kinds of resources.

They danced and Captain Li told her what was possible for her now.

MUCH LATER, AN exhausted Rue made her way to the drinks tables. Sure enough, there was Max, holding forth to a small crowd of matrons. Herat and Mike stood nearby, discussing something intensely with a bearded man and his wife.

She ran up and grabbed Mike's arm. "I'm so sorry!" she said. "I got caught up talking cycler talk with Captain Li. I didn't mean to abandon you."

Mike looked surprised, then pleased. "You look worn out."

"Well, I've never danced before, have I? But I had a

good teacher." She smiled at him. "I promise I'm yours for the rest of the evening."

Herat looked over, raised an eyebrow, and turned back to his conversation.

"Am I to understand," said Mike as she steered them toward the drinks, "that this is a date?"

She stopped them and looked up at him, mock-serious. "Mr. Bequith, would you like to go to the ball with me?"

He grinned and offered her his arm.

Rue drank two tall glasses of something icy, then they went back to the others. They arrived in time to see Dr. Herat smack his forehead and say, "I don't believe it!"

Max glanced over. "Careful, Professor, you'll break your meal ticket."

"The autotrophs have a delegation here!" said Herat. "Bequith, this is Professor Waldt; he's met them. Can you believe it? We've been trying to talk to them for twenty years and here they are sneaking off to the halo to study us in secret."

"It's hardly a secret to us," said the bearded man.

"So they actually talk to you?" asked Michael.

"Well, not directly." Waldt sipped his drink. "They use intermediaries. There's a group of radical Buddhists who've had themselves genetically engineered to be phototrophs—they're green, if you can imagine that. Lost their stomachs, sealed up their anuses and adopted the autotroph way. They're ice-blind crazy, but the autotrophs do seem to accept them. They've got this little encampment on the edge of the 'troph cavern and they seem to come and go as they please."

"Bequith, this is too great an opportunity to pass up," said Herat.

"I thought you were on vacation," said Mike.

"What better place to spend it than on the shores of an autotroph oasis?"

Max sidled over to Rue as Mike and Herat were bickering. "Something about this doesn't add up," he said.

Rue knew Max's various tones of voice by now; he had

been thinking (a quality of Good Max). This was to be encouraged. "What is it?"

"Well, only three of Crisler's guys are here. I see Barendts and Wallace and Manduba. Where are the other two?"

"In the washroom?"

"No, they never showed up. And Crisler's being awfully friendly with some of those industrialists."

"Why, Max, are you jealous of his charisma?"

"No, I just don't understand what he's up to. And this whole party . . . it's out of whack. I mean, Colossus is important, true, it's one of the biggest halo worlds—but am I just being a provincial bumpkin or is there ten times as much wealth and power sloshing about this room than we'd ever see on Treya?"

She looked through the crush of people. There were a lot of military people and many influential supporters of the Cycler Compact. "They're celebrating the discovery of the *Envy.*"

"I'm not asking why they're here," said Max. "I'm asking why are they *here.* On Oculus."

She had no idea what he was talking about and said so.

"All right, I'll try one more time," he said. "Did you know that there's no less than *three* cycler captains here tonight, not counting you?"

"Three? That's impossible!" Most worlds couldn't expect more than ten cyclers to pass by in a single year. And their crews could never visit for more than a few weeks at a time.

"It's true. See?" He pointed out two black uniforms she hadn't seen before. Even now, Captain Li was walking in that direction.

"Maybe you should introduce yourself," said Max.

"I don't think so." Li had been quite enough for one evening.

"Well, there's something goin' on," said Max.

"All right. You tell Mike about it; between the two of you I'm sure you can figure it out."

. . .

THE BANQUETING FLOWED ON, in long stretches of conversation, moments of laughter and delirious spells of dancing. Many hours later, things began to wind down. Couples strolled up the stone steps and disappeared. Crisler's people left in a knot, several men in suits in tow. As Rue and her crew were drifting in the direction of the exit, Travis Li approached.

"Captain Cassels, we'd be honored if you'd attend a meeting of the Compact in two shifts' time, at one after shift-change," he said. "We'd like to talk to you about *Jentry's Envy* and about what it might mean to the local worlds to have a new cycler ring operating."

"I'd be delighted," she said. "Where?"

"Council Room Fifteen," he said. "The monks can give you directions. One after in two, then?"

"Ah, yes. Sure."

He walked away. Rue admired his military bearing; she wondered if she would ever walk that way.

They went up the stairs and to the elevators. "I'm not tired yet," she said impulsively to Mike. "Want to take a walk?"

"Sure. But where?"

"This place has a roof. Let's find it."

Despite the fact that they had lived in close proximity for some months now, this was the first time Rue had actually been alone with Mike Bequith. The only truly private spaces on *Jentry's Envy* were hostile to life. The halls of the great monastery seemed deserted, so she and Mike walked and talked, completely forgetting their surroundings or the various cares that had oppressed them.

Eventually, after wandering a labyrinth of carpeted hallways for a quarter hour, they found an exit onto a broad balcony that looked like it might wrap around the whole building. The roof sloped up steeply above them; it was festooned with gargoyles which, in true halo tradition, looked hand-carved.

The light was exactly the same here as when Rue had awoken. It was only night for one shift of workers; there were shutters over a third of the light wells of the city. She took off her sunglasses. "I suppose it looks dark here to you," she said.

Mike leaned on the balustrade. "Twilight," he said. "Very strange."

"Strange? Not beautiful?"

"Oh, very beautiful," he said, smiling at her. "I must confess I felt very underdressed when I saw you in that uniform earlier."

"I wanted a ball gown."

"Maybe next time."

There was an awkward pause. They stood very near to each other at the railing. Rue wanted to feel his hand on her back again, but what to say? He was always so polite, even distant, that she didn't know where to start with him.

"You've got a meeting tomorrow," he said.

"Yeah. Big time cycler captain stuff." She grinned.

"Dr. Herat wants to visit the autotrophs tomorrow. He will expect me to go."

"Oh . . . Well, I'm sure I'll be wrapped up all afternoon."

"You know, I've hardly ever seen your eyes."

Rue's heart started pounding. She looked up at him and bit her lip.

"You have beautiful eyes," he said, "but I can never tell what you're thinking, because they're always hidden."

"I'll have to make sure you see them more often," she said.

"Well," he said with an ironic smile, "I can only think of one way for that to happen—for us to be together with the lights off."

Why, the sly boy! She laughed. "I do believe you've just propositioned me, Mr. Bequith."

"Maybe." He took her hand and raised it to his lips. "I guess it was the eyes. What do you say?"

"I suppose the view will still be there tomorrow," she said and let him lead her back inside.

19

ICE RUSHED OVERHEAD. There were a million varieties of it—smooth and blue, white and decayed, soot-streaked, all whipping past just a few meters away. Michael stood on the top deck of the boat that Professor Waldt had provided and breathed deeply the scent of the ice.

Oculus had three levels of habitation: surface cities, like Lux; 'coastal' communities, which were really just caverns melted out of the glacial ice at its interface with the ocean; and 'deep' communities, which were similar but situated elsewhere on the planet where the bottom of the glacial continents lay kilometers below northern sea level. Luckily the autotroph settlement was not a deep community, because it would have taken them days of pressurization and acclimatization to be able to visit and days to depressurize, even with the help of their mesobots. The autotroph town was located just a few hours inland.

The network of tunnels they were skimming through was vast and mazelike; it helped that there were signs everywhere, saying things like KOROLEV 15 KM. or DRY-DOCK SIDING, NEXT STARBOARD. There was a lot of traffic, which was one of the reasons Michael was up top: Arcs of fizzing water from passing hydrofoils regularly drenched the lower decks. Herat didn't mind, of course; he and Professor Waldt were bundled in bright yellow rain-slickers. Herat kept leaning over the rail to stare into the quickly passing water.

The cold air was wonderful on Michael's face. More wonderful was to grip a rail that wasn't overlaid with the ghostly indicators of its ownership. Inscape was used in the halo, but sparingly. The manufactured objects here—buildings, cars, clothing—all seemed as feral and natural as the stone and ice to Michael, simply because he could see them without seeing ownership and ideology branded on them through inscape.

Rationally he knew he was more attuned to this reality today because of his new feelings for Rue. On the other hand, his depression since Dis seemed more and more like the result of his having cut himself off from the real world. It took an extraordinary person to be able to travel to the universe's most lonely spots and remain content. Dr. Herat might be able to do it, but it had never really been the life for Michael.

No. It wasn't that simple. The shadow of Dis was still on him and one night with Rue wasn't going to change the fact.

For now, though, just being with Rue was enough. She had a tendency to knock his mind off its tracks, which seemed to be a good thing. That 'supreme meme' idea of hers, for instance, kept coming back to him, like a rumor: *How would you have to feel . . .* He found he was half-thinking about that a lot of the time now.

A side-tunnel had appeared up ahead. Michael heard the engines throttle back and they began a turn toward the entrance. This tunnel was low and wide, recently rough-hewn into the turquoise wall of the main highway. Small white bergs bounced in the choppy water there and it was dark, unlike the highway which was lit by regular ceiling lamps.

For a few seconds it looked like they were going to scrape the ceiling; Michael actually had to duck as they slid into the opening. He found himself crouched within a boundary layer of freezing air that seemed to insulate the ice. It was tempting to try to reach up and catch a piece of that ice, which must be millions of years old; but they were moving too fast. He crab-walked back to the stairs and went down.

"Not long now," said Herat. "This was a good idea. It means we can expense this trip."

Michael had to laugh. Herat was so completely the academic. "Well, you're in a good mood this morning," said Herat.

He shrugged. "It's the fresh air."

"I see. No immediate plans to leave my employ, then?—say, to take up piloting a cycler?"

"No," said Michael curtly. He and Rue had talked for a long time after the banquet. She didn't know what she was going to do now that she had confirmed her ownership of the *Envy*. It was incredibly flattering to be considered a cycler captain and she felt very protective of her starship. At the same time, she longed to go home. She was in the grip of some internal conflict that she herself didn't completely understand; discussing the future simply made her unhappy right now. Since Michael didn't know himself what he was going to do after this expedition, he hadn't pressed the matter.

Herat turned back to ask Waldt something. Searchlights at the prow of the ship lit long fans of glittering ice on the tunnel walls, but the water was black and the glacial breath of the air had penetrated down here, too, so that both men shivered.

Michael moved nearer to the other two. "So it's not really the autotrophs we're dealing with?" Herat was asking.

Waldt shook his head, grinning. "No. It's the garbage-pickers. But they seem to have access to autotroph technology."

"Garbage-pickers?" asked Michael.

"You'll see."

"Do you really think they'll be able to translate the inscription?"

Waldt shrugged. "Even if they don't it's hardly a wasted trip."

Herat eyed Michael. "Linda Ophir?" he said.

Michael shrugged. Yes, he was still trying to find out who had killed her. Herat smiled, nodding in approval.

"Well, let's hope we get real answers from these garbage-pickers," said Herat. "The nearest human AI with a Chicxulub context is light-years away."

Far in the distance the tunnel seemed to end in daylight.

As they approached, Michael could see that the waterway ended in a collection of docks. They were lit with solar-intensity lamps and he could see several human figures waiting on the platform.

"Ah well," said Waldt. "You'll know soon enough, it seems." He pointed.

Michael looked over, then did a double take. Three of the men standing there were ordinary enough in appearance, though they were stocky and grim, like professional security types. The other man, though . . .

He stood completely naked in the vaporous cold. His eyes seemed strange—wide and completely black—but that wasn't the strangest thing. For from toes to crown, his entire body was colored deep green.

The green man turned his face up and seemed to match Michael's gaze. He bared his teeth, in a way that didn't even begin to suggest a smile.

So here Rue was, sitting in a room that was higher than it was wide, at a table that looked to have been made from real trees, with three cycler captains, a minister of foreign affairs, the abbot and several ministers visiting from different halo worlds. Rue felt like she was in court, about to be judged by a jury of strangers.

She missed her family. Just knowing Grandma or Mother were alive might have given her the courage she needed. But none of them would ever know how far she'd come, with the exception of Jentry whose opinions didn't count. Rue wanted desperately to be able to jump up and said, 'Hey, look what a Cassels woman did!' But her grandmother was dead; so was Mother. There was no one to send excited messages home to.

"We've got a lot on the agenda today," said the minister, "so I'm not going to waste any time. You've all met Captain Cassels?" There were murmurs and nods around the table. "She's arrived after a tremendous adventure," said the minister. "We've only heard bits and pieces of the story. I hope you'll tell us more before the day's out," he said to her with a smoothly political smile. "But in the meantime, we need to focus on the future of *Jentry's Envy* as a functioning cycler in the Compact."

Rue nodded. She had anticipated this meeting. Li had filled her in on some of the obligations and powers of a cycler captain (including the ability to marry people) and he had shown her some surprising and exciting details about the worlds the *Envy* was to visit on its ring. The *Envy*'s ring was priceless—but she knew from her own reading that cyclers had often been political and economic prizes and though the captain had final say on a cycler's course, the worlds of competing rings could tug it to and fro. The more cyclers you had passing your world, the greater your trade options, after all.

"It's no secret that the Compact is in trouble," said the abbot. "A lot of radical schemes have been bandied about to try to solve the problem of our ever-dwindling cycler supply. Before we get started I just want to make sure that everyone at this table is clear on one thing: Permanence was established to ensure the indefinite existence of the Compact. Our people will not cooperate with any plan that dissolves the current cycler system."

Rue saw a couple of shaking heads around the table. What possible alternative to cyclers could there be? she wondered. The abbot sat back. "Proceed," he said.

The minister addressed Rue. "How much do we know about *Jentry's Envy*? Do you have her complete ring mapped?"

"We think so," she said cautiously. She tapped out a command on the desk and a holo projection of the ring she'd seen at the Lasa habitat appeared.

"What we're really interested in, is her origin point," said the minister. "Which I believe you've determined."

"Yes. It's an uninhabited halo world that's next on the *Envy*'s course after Maenad." She pointed to a small jewel of light in the display. "Osiris and Apophis."

There was a murmur around the table. "That's my point," said one of the visiting ministers, a short, heavy-set man named Mallory. "That's just a pair of brown dwarfs in close orbit—they have no planets. It's a well surveyed system. Your information must be wrong."

"It may well be," said Rue quietly. "But can we afford to ignore the possibility?"

"That's the crux of the matter," said the local minister with a nod. "You see, Captain Cassels, Mr. Mallory is from New Armstrong, which as you can see from the projection, is . . . here." He pointed.

Cycler rings were not exact circles. They had to take into account the random three-dimensional distribution of stars, brown dwarfs, and drifting superplanets; *Jentry's Envy* followed a twisting, jagged crown-shaped course that tried to maximize the number and proximity of worlds visited while still bending back on itself to form a rough circle. Drawing a line like this in three-dimensional space made for some tough choices of which worlds to visit; sometimes two or three equally good choices existed that would all permit the cycler to complete its course.

If all the cycler rings in this part of space were shown, Rue knew there would be dozens, with some overlaying one another and some tangential, meeting at key worlds like Colossus. Anywhere that more than a couple of rings met, commerce thrived.

New Armstrong, Mr. Mallory's home world, lay nearly the same distance from Maenad as Osiris and Apophis—but on a course sixty degrees divergent from the existing ring.

Mallory stood. "I submit that Apophis and Osiris can't be the origin of your cycler, because it's a planetless system—as are three of the others on your existing ring. It's true that the *Envy*'s ring cuts through the halo in a unique way and could unite several worlds that until now have been at least two rings distant from one another. This might be desirable, but the cost is too high; there's too many useless worlds on this ring. Your cycler would spend up to ten years at a time between habitable worlds. I propose that we alter its course at Maenad and establish a new ring—like this." He overlapped Rue's holo with his own. It was at a different angle, so it took some rotation and zooming to match the two images.

Mallory's proposed ring included both Colossus and New Armstrong—but it missed Erythrion. Rue sat back, arms crossed, and tried to cultivate a neutral expression.

Pleased expressions appeared up and down the table as Mallory waxed poetic about the new trade possibilities. But as he spoke, Captain Li caught Rue's eye and, almost imperceptibly, shook his head.

When Mallory was finished, Captain Li cleared his throat and said, "And what if Osiris and Apophis *is* the origin of *Jentry's Envy*?"

Mallory waved a hand negligently. "Well, clearly we need to determine that . . . but do we need to sacrifice an entire cycler to do it? Look at the chart. Once the *Envy* passes Osiris and Apophis it can't return to another viable ring without doing one hundred twenty degree turn—impossible for any massive cycler at that velocity. It'll be committed to visiting a series of empty worlds before it reaches port again. I suggest we outfit a scientific expedition to ride a small habitat on that course and survey the Twins on the way by."

Li shook his head. "They'll pass the system at nearly lightspeed. There's no way they can do a proper survey without decelerating in. With no beam to ride, how are you going to get in and out?"

"We could do it with a self-powered ship like the *Banshee*," said Rue. "That's Admiral Crisler's ship," she explained. "It's a ramjet. It could take us in and out, but firstly, it's an R.E. ship and secondly, Crisler's already planning his own visit to Osiris and Apophis. Once he gets to Maenad he'll return to the R.E. and round up some supply ships. He'll take these and *Banshee* to the Twins. The

Banshee will be used to ship them all out again when they're done exploring the place."

"How far is Maenad from the *Envy*'s position?"

"About six light-months. Longer, granted that they have to decelerate in."

The captains glanced at one another. "We have time," said another of the captains, an old man named Serle. "But we'll be tipping our hand."

"It may not matter," said the minister. "I think it's a risk we have to take."

Mallory leaned forward. "What do you mean? Are you saying we can get there first?"

"Of course not," said the abbot—a little too adamantly, Rue thought. And the minister had an odd look on his face, as if he'd said something he shouldn't have said. Mallory obviously saw these things; he frowned and sat back.

Well, that was interesting! Too bad Max wasn't here. He was good at reading subtext.

"Let's restrict this discussion to the possible," said the minister. "We have to sacrifice a pawn by letting Crisler's supply ships get to the Twins first. Once there, they're trapped until the *Banshee* arrives."

"Any chance we can take the *Banshee* over?" asked Mallory.

Rue stared at him; he really seemed serious. "Uh . . . I don't think so," she said. "It's an antimatter-drive ship. Doesn't that mean it's got enough power to burn off a moon if it needs to?"

"Erm, yes," said Mallory. "But we could disable or destroy it fairly easily."

"I will not allow murderers on my ship!"

The abbot raised a hand. "That's not in the plan, Captain Cassels. Mr. Mallory, you're out of line. There'll be no military action against the *Banshee*. All we need to do is ship up a smaller, lighter ramjet of our own. The only problem is it will take almost all our beam power to do it."

"Well that is a problem," said Mallory. "My people and I are eager to return to New Armstrong. There's considerable cargo we need to take with us. The *Envy* would literally shave years off our schedule."

"*Your* schedule," said Rue coldly. "Is that what all this is about?" She looked around the table. "I appreciate the economic advantage that Colossus and New Armstrong stand to gain by altering my cycler's course. The ring you're proposing would pass a number of core systems and obviously it would make me unbelievably rich. But you've only told half the story, Mr. Mallory."

She tuned up the holo so that her ring glowed more brightly than Mallory's. "What you didn't say is that four of the 'empty' worlds on my ring were surveyed a hundred years ago and found to be prime locations for new colonies. Abbot Griffin began this meeting by telling us that the Compact is in trouble. That's because we're losing all the lit worlds that were once a part of it. Cyclers that once picked up and deposited cargoes at the lit worlds are passing them by—there are holes in our rings now. Distances between stops have increased for nearly all the cyclers because of this.

"I know we've been redrawing the rings to compensate, but more cyclers for fewer worlds is a false economy—and it means increasing isolation for the most distant halo worlds. Mr. Mallory's plan would be profitable in the short run, but have we completely lost sight of the long run here?" *What about Erythrion?* she wanted to shout. Captain Li had shown her plans for the new, smaller rings. There were no cyclers for Erythrion in that plan.

"I will not alter the course of the *Envy*," she said. As Mallory opened his mouth to speak she continued. "I have very good reasons not to. First, there may well be an alien cycler-building industry at Osiris and Apophis; we need to get to it before the R.E. does. The *Envy* is going there anyway. We need only tag along with the small ramjet the abbot mentioned. With the *Envy* as backup, the ship can do a quick insertion and return flight. Otherwise, you're contemplating a starship that has to carry as much resources as a cycler, because it'll have to be autonomous for years. It's not going to be a 'light' ramjet if it has to survive on its own all the way back here from the Twins.

"But the second reason's much more important. Is the Cycler Compact dead? Are we just marking time? Are we so demoralized by the loss of the lit worlds that we're going to withdraw from exploration and just get by with what we've got? Or are we going to seed the worlds along the *Envy*'s existing route with beam-builder robots? In twenty years when we pass by again, the beams will be ready and we can begin dropping colonists on those worlds. Just think! Four new systems! How many new worlds among them? Ten? Twenty?"

Mallory and the Oculus minister were both glowering at her. Li was smiling and the abbot's face was neutral. Rue spread her hands and said, "It's the only reasonable course of action. My cycler is open to any legal cargo, naturally, but I'm keeping her on her present course and that means our best bet will be to ship up some beam-builders and a light ramjet or pion drive cutter to visit the Twins. I'm not qualified to figure out those details, but as to the course itself . . . that's set."

No one objected. In fact, to her surprise she saw they were nodding, all except Mallory. For Rue, something had crested and passed at this moment. She was no longer nervous; she no longer feared the men at this table.

The world was full of Jentries and Crislers and Mallories. But they could be opposed and beaten. This, she promised herself, she would remember.

"And what about your own course?" asked the abbot.

"What do you mean?" she asked.

"You're in an unusual position," continued the abbot. "You're both a cycler captain and the cycler's owner. Most cyclers are commissioned by consortia or governments, then run by a captain chosen by the Compact. Since your salvage claim on the *Envy* has been upheld, you no longer need to reside on the vessel itself. You could choose to settle somewhere. Will you be returning to the *Envy*? Or returning to Erythrion—which will take years?"

"I . . . I don't know," she said, off balance again.

"I just wanted to say that you have a third choice," said the abbot. The others were smiling and nodding now.

"What choice?"

"You could settle here, with your crew. Colossus would be honored to accommodate a cycler owner of your stature. And we're wealthy as halo worlds go, Captain Cassels. You could live in luxury here—your whole crew could."

Rue's mind was a blank. Somehow she had never contemplated this possibility. She had been so focused on staking her claim on the *Envy*, for so long, that what came after had remained a blur in her imagination.

"Uh," she said after an awkward silence.

The abbot laughed. "Please, don't think you need to answer right now! Think about it. I just wanted to make sure you knew the offer was there."

The meeting continued, but Rue seemed to be floating above it somehow, watching herself debate and listen with the others.

Could it be that her long flight from Jentry's anger would end here?

MICHAEL KEPT SNEAKING glances at the green man as they walked. It wasn't as if someone had applied green paint to his body. The color had a depth to it, so that the contours of his body shone a deeper shade than the planes. Even his long tangled hair was green. He stalked rather than walked, balancing on the balls of his feet, nostrils flared, eyes wide. He looked ready to fight, or flee.

The strange man had not spoken at first, merely staring at Michael, Herat, and Waldt. Finally one of the other humans had introduced himself, as a Mr. Arless. "These are the ones you asked for," Arless had said to the green man.

"Phages in the house of God," said the green man. His voice was thin, as if he had to force the words past some obstruction. "This is a catastrophe."

"We were informed that the autotrophs will see us," said Herat.

"They see no phages," hissed the green man. Then he looked down at his feet. "But you may see them."

Arless hovered at Michael's shoulder. "We gave the monks of the Autotroph Way a hand when they were starting out," he whispered. "The 'trophs accept them and in turn they owe us big time. So trade happens."

"Who is 'we'?" asked Michael.

Arless shrugged. "Business people."

"Of course." Michael knew the R.E. would never tolerate such an arrangement. Genetic alteration of humans was illegal—as were the personal neural implants of NeoShintoism, he thought sourly. The R.E. was terrified that humanity would radiate into a thousand subspecies, as had happened to so many spacefaring civilizations in the past. That fear was one of the reasons they used to justify the tyranny of the Rights Owners.

"I can't believe the 'trophs have agreed to see you," said Arless. "You must really have something they want." He glanced at his men.

"It's nothing you could use," said Michael quickly. "You might say it's a shared hobby."

"Come," said the green man. He had turned and marched into the green mouth of a tunnel. For almost half an hour now Michael had let himself be drawn though a seemingly endless maze of corridors hacked out of crustal ice. The walls and ceiling of the tunnel were of deep blue, emerald where lights shone in nearby, hollowed-out chambers. Cables ran along the ceiling and the footing underneath was loose plastic plates.

Finally the green man stopped at a dead end. A ladder was set into the wall of the tunnel here. It led upward.

"We'll wait for you here," said Arless as Michael and the

professors moved to the ladder. "Say hi to the 'trophs when you see 'em."

They followed their guide up the stairs, which rang loudly under their feet. Michael shaded his eyes and looked ahead to try to make out their destination. He could see a triangular network of girders, mist, and, somewhere in the distance, a rich red surface like a theater curtain. The light was too bright to make out more.

The steps passed through the girders and let onto a large concrete surface. To Michael's left, the geodesics of girderwork swept up and into obscurity, at least half a kilometer overhead. Blue and green ice brooded outside the triangles. Where sight foundered in dim mist overhead, the eye met glowing crimson, which swept down inside the geodesics to become a second wall to Michael's right. This space—outside a wall of girders and inside a wall of billowed crimson—curved away to either side. The girders must form a geodesic sphere and inside that sphere was another, this one of the red material. Michael and the others stood at the bottom, in between the two walls.

There were more green humans here, striding back and forth or riding small carts, carrying supplies and tools. A few stared in their direction. The concrete floor was a maze of stacked boxes and pillowed tarpaulins. It was damp in here, the air heavy, but no longer cold.

"Phages are not allowed beyond this point," said the guide. He scowled at Michael and the professor. "They must not know that you are here. Walk only where I say."

"Are the autotrophs afraid of us?" asked Herat casually. Michael stared at him—how could he be so tactless? But the guide simply shook his head.

"Fear is an emotion. Emotions are a pollution of phages, not autotrophs."

"That doesn't sound very attractive," said Herat. "Why do you admire them so much if they have no concept, say, of love?"

"There are . . . affects . . . that autotrophs have, but

phages cannot." The guide was proving to be positively chatty. Michael was once again surprised at Herat's ability to ferret out information from seemingly impossible sources.

"But do these affects correspond to states like fear or attraction?"

"This way." The guide started walking again. In the distance, Michael could see a slit of bright light in the crimson wall.

They rounded a stack of huge crates and came to the slit in the curtain. The red material was at least two meters thick, Michael now saw, and rubbery. As they approached he put his hand out to touch it. It felt like a leaf—alive and delicate. He snatched his hand back.

The slit rose a good ten meters above them, narrowing gradually.

The green man gestured to a rack of pressure suits. "Dress." He picked one off its hangar and began suiting up. Michael grabbed another; it was an unfamiliar design, with markings in a language he had never seen before on its metal cuffs and wrist pad. He tried to imitate the green man's actions. Getting a suit properly sealed was a matter of life and death; because he couldn't read the suit's HUD display, he wasn't sure if he'd done it right. Did green lights mean safe or danger to these people?

Waldt had reached for a suit, but the green man stopped him. "Only three may safely enter at a time," he said. Waldt started to protest, then shook his head in obvious disappointment and stepped back.

The now-suited green man walked over and checked Michael's suit, then Herat's. Michael's earphones crackled and he heard the voice of the green man say, "Good. Come." Their guide walked over to the glowing slit in the wall and pressed himself into it. The material gave slightly. The suited man pushed and wriggled his way deeper into it.

"You don't suppose the whole place is like that?" asked Waldt. "Solid, I mean?"

"You don't know?"

Waldt shook his head. "I've never been allowed beyond this point," he said.

Michael went up to the slit and tentatively pressed his hand into it. It gave like rubber. He pressed forward into crimson glowing material; this was much less pleasant than the Lasa airlocks had been. Like being born, in reverse, he thought. He got about a meter in without difficulty; then he began to encounter a strong pressure. The light was changing, becoming brighter and what he could see of the arm extended ahead of him was beaded with moisture.

Abruptly his hand was free of the material and with relief he pushed himself out, into a realm of dazzling light and noise.

As his eyes adjusted he made out a vast space, at least a kilometer across, carved out of the ice and draped with the folds of this red stuff. No—not draped, he realized as he began to see more. The red material rose up in petals, like a cyclopean rose, with the glassed-over shaft leading down to icewater at its base. At its crown, banks of arc lights lit everything in shadowless, blue-white. The color of this light darkened the red of the huge flower to a bruised purple. The radiance was hot on Michael's skin even through the faceplate.

Narrow catwalks crossed the open space in a profusion of bright lines and rising up from around the circular water shaft were numerous scaffolds, upon which bright machines twirled and roared. The whole space echoed with noise, in fact—an industrial bedlam completely at odds with the strange and opulent flower that cradled the machinery.

Michael now stood on a nexus of scaffolds; five radiated away from this spot and ladders and odd spiral poles rose up from the railing. In the nearby air tiny black flecks—insects?—danced distractingly.

"One thing we do know," said Herat. "The autotrophs

like a temperature of about a hundred Celsius, at high pressure. Their atmosphere is mostly compressed steam with a bit of nitrogen in it. Look—you can see the air ripple with the heat."

Michael looked about for some sign of the autotrophs. He saw things moving—strange, looping tetrahedrons that rolled to and fro, sometimes stopping to balance on two legs while the other two grabbed some piece of machinery or piping and passed it off to the spidery metal robots that swarmed over the scaffolds. At least he assumed they were robots.

"Are those the autotrophs?" he asked, pointing to the distant tripod shapes.

The guide simply gestured for them to follow. He headed out along one of the narrower catwalks, which passed over the dark pit of the water shaft.

Looking out, Michael could now see a few glassed-in platforms suspended over the shaft. One of them was a broad dome joined to the catwalk by an ordinary looking airlock. There were what looked like beds inside this dome and green forms on many of them. He did a double take and realized he was looking at almost a hundred green men and women, apparently asleep in the blazing light.

"We have provided an interface to the autotroph information net," said the green man. "You will use that to ask your questions." He pointed and Michael, following his gaze, at first could not see what he was pointing at. There was a thing like an inscape terminal, but it was covered with a dense crawling carpet of bugs.

Then he got it. The autotroph AI was a cloud of black metal beads, each about the size of a bee. They had wings and were distributed throughout the vast space of the enclave. Here, though, the green people had built a device to attract them. So were they going to speak to the autotrophs through this device—or only to it?

"Visitors," said a voice in Michael's earphone. It seemed

human, male, nondescript. Reluctantly, he admitted to himself that this was probably the voice of an AI, not that of an autotroph.

"Hello," continued the voice. "We are with you now."

"Who are you?" asked Herat. "Who speaks? The autotrophs? Or their agent?"

"I am the interface with God," said the voice.

Herat sent Michael one of his patented long-suffering glances.

"Why did you ask us to come here in person?" asked Herat. "We know we could have just transmitted you the text we wish you to translate."

"Our outside interface is untrustworthy," said the voice.

"Outside interface . . . you mean Arless and his people?"

"Yes. This information is not for them."

"Why not?" asked Herat.

The AI did not answer.

BY THE TIME Herat's investigations took them to Dis, Michael had come to believe he was an old hand when it came to aliens. True, he'd never met a live one, but for years he and the professor had rooted through the debris left by civilizations that had preceded humanity into space. So when he heard they were going to Dis, he was interested—but not apprehensive.

On the morning of their arrival he and Herat had ridden an elevator up from the spin-section of the opulent research ship they had brought and Michael suited up in freefall. He had seen photos of Dis during the trip out, but these were muddy and dark and he really didn't know what to expect. As the airlock opened, he found himself staring at a landscape—complete with hills, forests, and buildings—floodlit by their ship and hanging perpendicular to him like a wall. Everything was magically clear, as if this were a model suspended a meter away. He resisted the urge to reach out; he knew what he was seeing was kilometers away.

They jetted over and as they flew Michael began to feel

a presentiment—an inkling that he should have prepared himself better for this place. The ruined landscape—large patches of which had drifted off into space leaving a mesh of girders behind—stretched off into darkness in every direction. He struggled to retain his impression that it was across from him, not down, but failed. In an instant he found himself descending, like some kind of hesitant angel, onto what appeared to be a frozen circle of Hell.

After that experience he was more judicious in his preparations for encountering the alien. He thought he'd done pretty well at *Jentry's Envy*. But since he had not expected to meet autotrophs here at a human world, he had not prepared himself for coming out here. The autotroph compound was nothing like Dis; it was, if anything, too inhabited. But as they stood next to the buzzing cloud that was the autotroph's artificial intelligence, he found himself struggling to keep his attention focused on the matter at hand.

The green people's AI was silent. They had shown it the Chicxulub writing and now it was querying the autotroph database. Apparently, there were several levels of connotation to Chicxulub writing. It wasn't simply a matter of surface meaning and implication; each word in effect punned off its neighbors and contained multiple allusions. Also, the primary physical metaphors of Chicxulub were inhuman: a metaphor using a galvanic proximity sense as its basis couldn't be simply converted into a visual or tactile equivalent. The AI might be laboriously changing its own mind into something like a Chicxulub/human hybrid. For a few minutes, it would become alien not only to Michael and Herat, but to its own creators.

Michael's attention kept drifting away from it to the chaos all around them. He had no doubt this was the equivalent of a bustling human town and he supposed such a place would look just as incomprehensible to the autotrophs. But he couldn't even tell which things *were* the aliens and which were machines or helper species.

There were things like big birds here. They circled up near the intense lights, above the flower. Were those the autotrophs? He'd noticed hundreds of odd oval pods, which hung from the inside folds of the red material. Most were still, but one or two thrashed like flies caught in a spider's web. The motion was unsettling; though he knew the autotrophs did not devour one another, or indeed anything living, he had to look away from those twitching bodies.

One of the tripod things wheeled by. It was really just four legs joined at a central pod; each leg was as loose as a tentacle and it tended to roll along on three while holding the fourth up like an attentive head. The tripod that passed stood a good three meters high. It didn't turn its leg/head as it went by and Michael didn't turn to watch it go; he knew it was still moving away because the catwalk bounced slightly with its movements.

"I have several translations," said the AI abruptly. Michael looked at the Herat, who grinned.

"Are they all true, or is one better than the others?" Herat asked the cloud. To one side, their guide had crossed his arms and was looking the other way.

"You must decide," said the bug-covered terminal. "I do not have the context to know.

"These are some translations into terms you may understand. Chicxulub language is self-modifying, so the best translation is one that uses what you call puns to convey the meaning:

"Self-containered: to evert, encome-pass farship's pre-creative behestination. Your orgasmasher's detournement is presended."

Michael and Herat exchanged glances.

"The Chicxulub were funny guys," said Herat after a moment.

"There is another translation that shows the allusive layer of the message," said the AI. "It could be translated into any number of human mythologies. This one is Greco-Roman:

"Daughter of Saturn, you may escape your devouring father's belly by wielding the bright sword that we have forged for you."

The words hit Michael like a shock of cold water—or the sudden presence of powerful kami. He didn't understand what he had just heard, but he felt there was a vast and authoritative mind behind the words.

"The most literal translation," continued the AI, "would be:

"To the Chicxulub or those like them: The Other you fought has become your Self. To resolve that crisis, follow this starship to its birthplace. There you will find a new use has been made of your ancient weapon."

Herat frowned. "This is a Lasa speaking."

Michael felt a sinking feeling. He knew what ancient weapon the Lasa referred to. There had been only one Chicxulub weapon that mattered: the self-reproducing starships that had fanned out across the galaxy sixty-five million years ago. They had visited millions of planets and obliterated any world that threatened to develop sentient life. They had visited Earth; it was their weapon that had caused the extinction of the dinosaurs.

The Chicxulub had wanted the galaxy to themselves. They got it—and were the galaxy's sole inhabitants for millions of years, until they died out.

Michael leaned against the catwalk's railing. He stared out over the busy autotroph amphitheater, not seeing it.

Herat was scowling. "But *Jentry's Envy* was not intended just for the Chicxulub," he muttered. "It's a gift for everyone or anyone who comes along."

"There's still something we're missing," admitted Michael. The translation that rang most loudly in his mind was the one that began, *Daughter of Saturn . . .*

"Saturn is Chronos—god of time," said Herat. "Saturn devoured his children. Like the Chicxulub destroyed all their potential successors?"

After studying the deep, misty well below them for a

while, Michael said, "I think we're focusing on the wrong thing here."

"What do you mean?"

"It'll be great if we can figure out exactly what this means," Michael said reluctantly. "But more important right now, is to ask what this message has to do with the murder of Linda Ophir? And who concealed it from us and why?"

"Who?" Herat shrugged. "Only Crisler had the authority to spoof the inscape system. So he did it. That means he probably had the message translated before we arrived on the scene . . ."

Michael nodded. "And that he probably had Linda killed as well." They had discussed this possibility a number of times since they learned of the inscape spoofing. But the speculation had never led anywhere before.

He hesitated to say where his thoughts were going now. "If this message is a reference to a weapon—or even if Crisler only thinks it is," Michael said, "then maybe we have our motive. Crisler is after the Chicxulub weapon."

The Chixculub had built self-reproducing starships that fanned out across the galaxy, destroying any world that hinted at having or developing sentient life. Humanity had hitherto outlawed self-reproducing machines; there was no human research to which Crisler could turn to develop such a horrible weapon. And that was as it should be.

Herat cursed. "He wants to wipe out the rebels by creating weapons that can reproduce? Michael, that's crazy. How are his machines to distinguish between rebel and loyalist?"

There were hints in the archaeological record that the Chicxulub had been wiped out by their own machines, after inevitable genetic drift and social pressures had rendered them unrecognizable to those machines. The final era of the Chicxulub must have been a nightmare time: All innovation was outlawed, all social and genetic innovation crushed, and everything that could be done had been done. Everything that could be thought had been thought. Everything else was illegal, and lurking in deep space were the soulless executioners who would wipe away any group who tried to change things.

Herat was shaking his head. "Michael, I don't think this message really says that there's a weapon at the Twins. It's something else."

"It doesn't say that the Lasa made a weapon. But the technology behind it might be turned into one. I bet that's what Crisler's thinking."

Herat nodded sharply. "We'd best get this news to the local authorities. We need to have Crisler questioned. Think Rue's people would be up to it?"

"I don't know. Certainly the R.E.'s arm doesn't reach this far—"

"Leave now!"

They both turned. Their guide was walking back along the catwalk.

"Thank you," Michael said in the general direction of the AI as they clattered away after the green man. The swarming dots of the AI made no reply.

Herat told Professor Waldt what the message said, but Michael noticed he didn't mention Linda Ophir or anything else about the *Envy*. He had odd notions about discretion. Michael was thinking hard about the murder; he barely noticed their surroundings until they were back at the base of the ladder, where Arless waited.

Before the guide could escape back up the ladder, Michael turned to thank him for his help. "One more thing," he said as the green man turned indifferently away. "I know I'm unfamiliar with the autotrophs, but . . . we saw a lot of creatures and machines in the compound. Which ones were the autotrophs themselves? The tripod things?"

The guide shook his head.

"The bird things?"

The green man shook his head and this time he laughed, a harsh and contemptuous sound.

"They were all around you, but you did not know how to see them," he said.

"I don't understand."

The guide shrugged and began to climb. "You wouldn't," he said. "An autotroph is not a *thing*. An autotroph is a *system*."

Michael watched the green form recede up the shaft. He didn't understand—not even remotely. After a few moments Herat put a hand on his shoulder and returned his attention to the world of humanity and politics.

20

THEY HAD ONLY a few more days at Oculus. *Jentry's Envy* was still travelling at speed and in order to catch her Rue would need to gather her crew and passengers together in a new cargo magsail and ride the beam to rendezvous. If they missed this window, there would not be another one for years; no other cycler followed the *Envy*'s route and without her Erythrion was inaccessible.

Though tired after her meeting, Rue was determined to make the most of her time here. Still, she dawdled as she made her way through the huge and bustling market of Lux. She wore her captain's uniform and felt eyes upon her wherever she went. She hadn't enjoyed the sensation on Treya, where she was more of a curiosity than a celebrity; here she reveled in it.

Most amazing was that she simply didn't need money. Some shopkeepers vied to give her wares for free, simply for the honor of being able to say that she had chosen goods from their establishment. They would have followed her, Max, and Rebecca out of the stores and down the street, were it not that the crew of the *Envy* was accompanied by a glowering security man from the monastery.

"I just can't believe we're really here," said Rebecca for the third time. Directly overhead, Colossus glowed placidly. All the towers of the city were built to twine like vines upward toward its fixed light. The palette of colors used in the street was complementary to that serene amber radiance; the street was thronged with colorful people, who in the distance faded into a kind of silken dream-landscape of pastels.

Rebecca held up a transparent bag that held a folded, shimmering gown. She was loaded down with such bags, but seemed to be enjoying the extra weight. "Corinna will never wear this!" she said with a grin.

"Because you were hoping she'd let you have it," laughed Rue. They had gifts for everyone: some recently imported R.E. movies for Evan and, in addition to the gown, some new Oculan symphonies for Corinna. There was much more to buy of course and everything they bought here would be worth a hundred times its price back on Erythrion. The most valuable trade items within the halo were, after all, hand-crafted works of art.

The better shops advertised their class with intricately carved and painted facades. Rue stopped indecisively between a jewelry store whose front was one gigantic jaguar's-head (door in the mouth) and an antiquities dealer whose storefront looked like the entrance of an Earth-Egyptian temple. "Ooh, where next?"

"Jewelry is light," Rebecca pointed out. "You can carry more of it on the trip." She strolled toward the jewelry store.

Max watched until she was inside the shop. "Remember how I said last night that there were too many politicos and ship captains around? I started nosing around. It seems there's a movement afoot to break up the Cycler Compact."

Although this didn't come as a complete surprise, Rue was still shocked. She had been about to follow Rebecca into the shop, but hesitated. "How?" she asked.

Max grimaced. "The line is that faster-than-light travel makes the cyclers obsolete. Too expensive. Instead, they want to ship cargoes directly to the lit worlds. From there they can go by FTL to any other halo world, after all."

"Or to any R.E. world," she pointed out, "and more cheaply."

"Exactly. If we dismantle the Compact, the halo worlds are at the mercy of the R.E. The idea's being sold as a way of bringing the far-flung parts of the Compact together through FTL, but in the long run it's still more expensive than travel between the lit worlds."

"We'll just wither and die," she said. "Like Erythrion is."

He nodded grimly. "The chief proponents of this new deal are a bunch of idiots from—"

She held up a hand. "Let me guess. New Armstrong? And their head man is named Mallory?"

"How'd you know that?"

"Just a guess."

"We'll completely lose our autonomy," Max went on. "The only way to get to another halo world will be through the R.E."

"I wonder how long this has been going on?" mused Rue. "Do you think New Armstrong's been siphoning off the remaining cyclers somehow? . . . That's not supposed to be possible, but maybe they got to one or two of the captains. That could explain why Erythrion hasn't seen a cycler in years." The very thought outraged her; could the decline of Erythrion and the coup at Treya and the lawlessness of the Stations that had led to her running away, have all had a common source?

"No place is free of politics," said Max in a tired voice. He had been enjoying the shopping, Rue knew, but he looked sad again now.

She bit her lip, wondering whether to tell him what she had been thinking. "Max . . . do you like it here?"

He shrugged. "It's way better than Treya."

"If you could settle down here . . . would you?"

He appeared surprised. "What are you saying?"

"Just that we've been offered a chance to do that. We could ship a new captain and crew up to the Envy. Buy houses here, live well . . . not worry about this political stuff anymore."

He shook his head. "But Evan and Corinna—"

"Could join us. We'd get them to disembark at Maenad and fly back here by FTL—or buy them tickets back to Erythrion. I think we're rich enough to do that."

Max scratched at his head. Clearly he hadn't thought of this possibility. Slowly, a smile spread across his face. "You know . . . I, yes. I think it would be good for me, being here. A place to rest, finally, away from Leda and Erythrion's silly excuse for society."

Rue was happy and simultaneously felt a flutter of anxiety. Had Max decided at this moment? And would that decision draw the rest of them along, just as his decision to go after the *Envy* had drawn her here?

She looked around at the market, speculating seriously for the first time about being able to return here—maybe as often as she wanted. Now that she was noticing details, a small, nondescript door caught her attention. It was sandwiched between the ostentatious facades and she wouldn't have given it a second glance were it not that a small neatly carved sign over it said, "NeoShintoist Chapter of Oculus."

"Don't tell Rebecca about this idea yet," she said to Max. "It's just an idea, so far." She eyed the door again. "Why don't you join her? I've got something to do; I'll be back in a minute."

"Hmm? Uh, okay," said Max, puzzled. "Suit yourself. But Rebecca's a good shopper. Don't be surprised if all the good stuff is gone when you get back!"

Her bodyguard followed as Rue gently knocked on the door, then, when there was no answer, eased it open. A set of stairs led up from the street. Apparently the NeoShintoists weren't wealthy or important enough to afford a storefront.

Rue felt slightly nervous as she mounted the stairs. She was invading Mike's territory, in a way, by coming in here. But as always, her curiosity was stronger than her caution.

The stairs let into a surprisingly sumptuous lounge that overlooked the street. An elderly man sat in a deep armchair by the window. As Rue entered the room he rose and bowed to her.

He was dressed in typical Oculus fashion, in a brocaded jacket over a tuned-down chameleon cloth shirt and loose leggings reminiscent of the practical cold weather gear the first settlers had made. He looked comfortable and a bit rumpled, like an older version of Max.

"Can I help you?"

"Yes, I . . ." She wasn't sure where to begin.

"Captain Cassels, isn't it?" he said before she could decide.

"Yes." Rue felt herself blushing. "Everybody seems to know me. I—I've come to ask you about NeoShintoism."

He showed no surprise. "What would you like to know?"

"Well, I have a friend. He's a NeoShinto monk. He's told me a little bit about it, but I . . . just want to know more."

The old man nodded. "You're Michael Bequith's captain."

"You know him?"

"In a way." The old man smiled enigmatically. "We've never met. Oh—where are my manners. My name is Vogel." He held out his hand to shake.

"Come with me," said Vogel. "I'll show you what we're all about." He led Rue and her guard through a side door into another lounge, this one windowless. The walls were covered in shelves, like an old-style library. Instead of books, the shelves held black data storage units. They looked familiar.

She walked over to the shelves and drew out one of the units. "Mike totes one of these around."

Vogel nodded. "These are containers for kami. Most of them are kami from our own world—primarily the kami of the glaciers and deep ocean. Very prosaic, from our point of view. But some! Some of these units hold kami from other worlds and the best, the very best of those, are the ones captured for us by Michael Bequith."

He went to the back of the room. There, a broad set of shelves sat nearly empty, except for a line of about a dozen data units. "These are his," said Vogel, running his finger along the units' spines. "I've entered their presence many times, Captain Cassels. They have brought more hope and inspiration to our order than the whole of this library."

"Why?" She came to stand by him. Her Mike a religious celebrity? It was hard to picture. "What's so special about Mike?"

"Brother Bequith has had opportunities the rest of us only dream of," said Vogel. "He has been able to capture the kami of the most exotic places in the galaxy. We have learned more about the limits of human reverence from his recordings than from any one else's."

Rue frowned at the data units, then said, "I guess I just don't understand what it is about these things that's so precious."

Vogel chuckled quietly. "You're seeing only their shells. You have to experience the kami directly to understand. That's the whole point."

"How can I do that?"

"With these." Vogel pointed to the armchairs scattered about the lounge. On each rested a fine, filigree cap, attached by data ribbons to a dock just the right size to hold one of the data units. "Michael would have no use for these, any more than I do," said Vogel. "Our implants allow us to meet the kami directly. These headsets are for people who don't have the implants. You can use one of these to experience what he's experienced."

"And that is what, exactly?"

"Transcendence of life, death . . . time itself," said Vogel without irony. "Truth."

Rue smiled, a little sadly. Her mother had warned her

about movements like this. *Transcendence,* mother had said, *is another word for escape. But escape to where? This life is all we have. To desire escape from life is to desire death.*

"It sounds wonderful," she said wistfully. "I wish I could believe in it."

Vogel laughed. "Belief is entirely unnecessary," he said. "None of us believe anything. NeoShinto is a method, not an ideology."

"Huh?"

"NeoShinto is part of the philosophy of Permanence," said Vogel. "Permanence is the attempt to create a human culture that can survive indefinitely here in deep interstellar colonies. NeoShinto is a Permanence program that explores the limits of human neurological programming.

"Humans think metaphorically. Most of our thoughts are built up of more primitive metaphors. Our most atomic metaphors are hard-wired in as a result of where we evolved. One of those hard-wired metaphors is something we commonly call 'I.' It's the metaphor of *self-as-object*.

"Religions throughout history have tried to replace this primary metaphor with *self-as-world*, but it's very difficult unaided. Takes years of effort by specialists, because you're operating on basic neurological programming. By the twentieth century they had drugs that could explode the 'I' metaphor, but they didn't have the conceptual framework to understand what they were doing. We have it.

"NeoShinto is just a technology for replacing your 'I' with a perceived Other—what we call the kami. We attach no mythology or dogma to the experience. You're free to interpret it however you'd like." There was irony in his smile now.

"I don't understand," she confessed.

"Of course not," said Vogel. "You can't until you've met the kami. Would you like to try?" He gestured to the armchairs.

She didn't like the idea of undergoing some procedure here, under this man's power. But . . . "Can I take one of these headsets with me? And . . . a kami to try?"

"Of course. You can take a headset now. I'll have some kami copied for you—including the best of Brother Bequith's. That will take some hours; I'll have them delivered to your suite."

"Thank you."

"But tell me," said Vogel. "Why has Brother Bequith not come to visit us yet? We've received no communication from him since he arrived."

"I . . . I don't know," she said sincerely. "But I will ask him."

Vogel's question stayed with her as she rejoined Rebecca in the street and it distracted her from the rest of the day's shopping.

"RUE, WHERE ARE you?" asked Michael.

She smiled to hear his voice. Through inscape, it seemed to thrum inside her head, nice and intimate. "I'm in the city," she said, looking around for a landmark. There were too many of them—minarets, domes, faery bridges between glittering towers. "How did your meeting go?"

"That's what I'd like to talk about. Listen, we're still in the ice caves, we should be back in the city in half an hour. Can you meet us at Pier 47?"

"Well, if it's urgent . . ."

"It's very urgent. I think we've found evidence of what Crisler is up to. We translated the Chicxulub message and, well—I'll tell you when we meet."

"Um, all right."

Michael disconnected. *Well, that was odd*, she thought. Rue was suddenly aware of her guard, who scanned the crowd unceasingly. The bustling streets didn't look so peaceful as they had moments ago.

"Rebecca, could you head back to the keep? Max and I are going to meet the boys at the docks."

The doctor was visibly tired from hiking around all day. "Sure," she said. "Want me to take this stuff?"

"If you could."

They went their separate ways, Rebecca toward the distant monastery and Rue and Max through narrow streets in the direction of the docks.

At the center of Lux, roads and maglev tracks entered into a whirlpool-like spiral that led down. They walked through underpasses and over bridges as traffic zipped by and finally reached the edge of an immense, round shaft that punctured the ice. The roads spiraled down its outer walls, then disappeared as the shaft opened out into a gigantic domelike cavern half a kilometer below. As their elevator fell past the roof of this dome, the roads reappeared, hugging the curve of the roof as they continued their way down to the dark ocean water below.

Dozens of warehouses and docks clung to the base of the cavern walls. Trucks and maglev cars were loading and unloading cargo within clusters of freighters at the docks. Dark cave entrances opened off the cavern at intervals and ships came and went through these.

It was a long walk from the elevators to Pier 47. Rue was tired and the crowds and growling machinery that raced back and forth here began to give her a headache. She sat down gratefully on a bench and rummaged through the one bag she hadn't given to Rebecca. This held some jewelry and the NeoShinto headset Vogel had given her. She toyed with this as she waited.

"Think that's them?" asked Max. He had become positively jovial in the past few minutes. As if new possibilities had opened for him, she thought. Where he pointed, a rust-streaked freighter was edging its way toward their pier. The only other vessel here was a battered looking lozenge-shaped thing that she thought might be a submarine.

Rue was not so happy. She found herself dwelling on the idea that the man Mallory could himself be responsible for the abuses of her past. And the idea that this place might become her home was equally disquieting, though she couldn't have said why. She didn't snap back to attention until she heard a gangplank thump down, and Mike ran up to her. Herat was sauntering down the gangplank behind him.

"Oh!" She leaped to her feet and hugged Mike. "How did it go?" she asked.

The freighter pulled away from the docks. Professor Waldt was still aboard; he waved from the deck, then turned to go inside.

Michael waved back and laughed. "We had as much fun as alien-hunters are likely to have. But listen, we know what the message on the Lasa habitat says. We've got to inform the abbot as soon as possible; can you get us in to see him as soon as we get back?"

"Sure, but what—?"

Rue stumbled over the words and stopped. Something weird had just happened; she shook her head, thinking for a second that her ears had popped.

The sounds of the crowds and machinery had stopped, as though cut off by a switch.

She started to say something about it to Mike, but he was staring past her open-mouthed. Rue turned.

The docks were empty. Not just their pier, but all the other piers as well. And the freighters, roadways, the maglev tracks, and the distant elevators. In a split-second and with no warning, the thousand or more people sharing the docks with them had vanished.

So had their bodyguard. The only people in this gigantic cavern, it seemed, were Rue, Mike, Max, and Herat.

"Oh shit," said Mike, "they've messed with the ins—"

"*Get down!*"

The figure appeared out of nowhere in the middle of the

pier: a running man, his arms cradling a large laser gun. *"Get down!"* he shouted again. *"Ambush!"*

Now Rue heard the vicious hissing that accompanied laser fire. She threw herself to the ground and Mike landed on top of her.

"It figures." It was Max's voice. Rue looked up.

He stood there with a vaguely disappointed expression on his face. He was looking at the black-edged hole that had appeared magically in the center of his chest. He started to say something else, but blood suddenly gouted from his mouth and he crumpled to the ground. His head hit the bench on the way down, but he didn't make another sound.

The man who had shouted wavered and disappeared, reappeared a few meters away. He was aiming his laser somewhere down the pier. "Get moving!" he yelled.

His words made no real impression on Rue; she was staring at Max. Her cousin lay on his side, his face turned toward her. His eyes were open, but she knew he couldn't see her. Still, she started to crawl toward him. He couldn't be comfortable in that position, she needed to help him lie more comfortably . . .

Hands clamped around her wrists and Rue was dragged away from Max. She screamed and fought to get away. He needed her, she wasn't going to abandon him.

Words fluttered around her: "Can't keep the system frozen for long. You've got to get out before they get it—"

"Professor! Are you okay?"

"It's just a singe. Where are we going to—"

"Down there!"

Rue was thrown over somebody's shoulder. Dimly, she realized it was Michael who was carrying her. She didn't care. Every step he took put her farther away from her cousin.

Why was Mike jumping off the pier? Rue went flying and landed on her back. Her head bounced off something really hard and she tasted blood in her mouth.

The pain made her mad and she rolled to her feet, narrowly missing a tumble into dark waters. She found herself standing on a long, rounded gray thing barely above the level of the waves. Mike was a few meters away, trying to open some kind of hatch. Herat sat next to him, his left hand clutching his right arm.

The man who had yelled at them was still crouched on the pier. He was shooting at something. Flames burst out of the concrete next to him and he rolled out of the way, then fired again. "Is it open?" he yelled over his shoulders.

"No . . . Yes!" Mike raised the metal hatch and gestured to Herat. The professor needed no urging, but almost fell into the opening.

"Come on, Rue!"

She staggered over to Mike. Before she reached him, the man with the gun cursed and rolled backward off the pier. Rue smelled burning cloth and then he'd hit the icy water and splashed her.

She knelt down and put out her hand, even as Mike did the same. The man floundered for a moment, abandoned his gun to the water and reached out.

She found herself staring into the face of Barendts, one of Crisler's marines.

"Come on!" urged Mike. They hauled Barendts out of the water and all three threw themselves at the hatchway. Rue went down first, lost her footing and banged her chin against a rung of the ladder before hitting the deck below.

Barendts was the last in. He stayed on the ladder to close the door. "Can you lock it?" asked Mike.

"Don't know. Have to override the ship's system." The marine reached into his sleeve, bringing out a tangle of wires. He pressed these against the door control and they writhed into life, twining themselves into the cracks around the door mechanism.

Footsteps thudded through the ceiling. "They're here," muttered Barendts. "Think I've got it, though." He withdrew the wires and stepped down off the ladder.

"Can we call for help?" asked Herat. He was slumped against one wall of the narrow space they were in.

"No, the whole area's jammed. It'll take them a while to burn through that, though," said the marine.

Herat laughed. "They won't burn through it at all, young man. If this is a deep-dive sub, then its walls are made of diamond."

Barendts brightened. "Good."

"Of course, they can always put explosives against the hull and kill us with the shockwave," pointed out Herat.

Rue turned away from the discussion. This place was more cramped than any shuttle she'd ever been in. Its ceiling was low and pipes ran everywhere. She stalked past the men to the nose, where big windows showed a view of rich blue water flecked with drifting motes. Several comfortable-looking couches faced these windows. She dropped into one of them and just sat there.

"Got to get command of this thing . . ."

"They won't answer? You're sure?"

Max was dead.

"—They can't keep the system hacked for long. The local police will be down here any minute."

He had been all she had of family and home. If he was gone, so were they, forever.

"What's that!"

A smell of burning wafted up from behind Rue. She craned her head around the side of the seat.

A roving patch of fire was moving in loops and arcs across the ceiling. Behind it, charred paint dropped to the floor and what was left behind glowed with outside light, like foggy glass.

"Or they could do that," said Herat. "Shine the lasers right through the hull. It's transparent, after all."

"We have to get out of here!" shouted Mike. "Take control of this sub, now!"

"I'm trying," snapped the marine. The smoke was everywhere.

Rue leaned back and shut her eyes. Maybe it didn't matter anymore. They were all about to die.

Something exploded with a *bang!*; she jerked in surprise and pain spiked her ears from sudden overpressure. Now she heard sizzling sparks and a cracking sound.

"I've got partial control," said Barendts. "Taking us down." The decking lurched under Rue. She kept her eyes closed, her fists balled at her ears. One last *bang* sounded and Barendts cursed lividly.

The seconds dragged and no new sounds issued from the back. After a while she opened her eyes, found thick, smarting smoke in them and turned to look behind her.

The three men were all alive. They were sitting on the deck looking at one another grimly. Herat coughed once or twice and shut his eyes. "Gotta rest," he said.

Rue cleared her throat. "What's happening?" she asked.

Barendts glanced at Mike, then gestured to a blackened, half-melted box against the wall. "That's the ship's computer," he said and coughed. "I told it to dive just before the boys upstairs got a lucky shot and took it out. We're still diving and we're out of touch with anybody."

Rue looked around herself. "Aren't there manual controls?" she asked.

"Maybe. Yeah, there must be," said the marine without much optimism. He came forward and eased himself into the seat next to hers. "These look like they might be . . ." He pulled on a joystick that jutted up next to the seat. Nothing happened. "Well, that's great."

The blue light outside was rapidly fading to black. Barendts fiddled with some switches and succeeded in turning on some internal lights and external floodlights. These showed an irregular wall of ice some meters away, rising steadily out of darkness below and into darkness above.

Darkness . . . Rue shut her eyes and let herself cry.

21

RUE AND PROFESSOR Herat were resting on cots at the back of the sub. Michael sat next to Barendts, watching the wall of ice slide inexorably upward.

They'd been dropping for nearly an hour. Every now and then the sub creaked from the pressure; every time it did Michael tensed, waiting for the walls to collapse around them. The walls of the sub were icy cold now; little heaters under the seats were working overtime, but without much success, to keep the cold at bay.

Michael and Barendts had been trying to slow their descent, with even less success. They'd gone over every instrument and switch in the narrow space, finding nothing that might help. They had control of a set of manipulator arms outside the craft, but there was nothing for them to grab onto. It seemed as if the sub's cruising controls were centralized through the computer. With it gone, they were helpless.

They weren't falling very fast, luckily. They'd only dropped four or five kilometers and so far, the sub shrugged the pressure off. If they were five kilometers down, there were still fifteen kilometers of empty water to fall through before they hit bottom. Michael had no illusions that the sub would survive those depths. Thousands of atmospheres of pressure awaited them at the bottom of the abyss.

After yet one more run-through of their checklist of possible fixes, Barendts sat back with a frustrated sigh. "I should have acted earlier," he said.

Michael looked at him appraisingly. "You're the saboteur," he said. He didn't mean it as an accusation, just a statement of fact.

The marine shrugged. "Card-carrying member of the rebels, that's me."

Michael seized on the distraction. "Tell me about that."

"I had been ordered into deep cover two years ago. Told to get close to Crisler, which I did." Barendts seemed relieved to be talking. "When the *Envy* showed up, it seemed like a pointless distraction. I didn't pay much attention until Crisler moved us all to Chandaka and hired Linda Ophir. He needed some Chicxulub inscriptions translated. She agreed to that and then the whole matter was dropped. That's the way it looked, anyway.

"One night my contact at Chandaka called me. Ophir had been trying to get out, he said. She had some kind of information about the *Envy*—something that had scared the hell out of her. That was two days before you and Herat showed up.

"I didn't get a chance to find out what she'd discovered. She was murdered—well, you know about that. Crisler went into overdrive. I guess he looked calm in public, but boy he was on the edge the last day or so. Wanted us to get the hell off Chandaka in a hurry."

"And that's why the rebels attacked the city," said Michael. "But not the Redoubt. Why?"

Barendts grinned mirthlessly. "They did. You didn't see that attack, and you weren't told, on Crisler's orders. The attack failed. Crisler put a lockdown on all news about the war after we left. Well, he got those orders from higher up, I guess. The fact is, the R.E.'s losing."

Michael put his head back and stared out at the dark water. "Unbelievable," he muttered. He was remembering the riot he'd been caught in during the attack. Years ago, he had helped instigate such chaos. Was Kimpurusha still part of the R.E.? Or had it been liberated while he was away? The thought filled him with a pang of something—regret, loss, he wasn't sure. He scowled at the dumb metal of the sub's controls. Maybe if he'd stayed there, he might have been able to help . . .

"What do you think that is?" Barendts was pointing through the window.

Something long and threadlike rose past the sub. It couldn't have been more than a few millimeters thick and when the floodlights hit it, it shone pale white. But outside the lights, it glowed pale green against the darkness.

"Is there supposed to be indigenous life here?" asked Barendts.

"I have no idea. We never got to that part of the tour." They watched as more of the threadlike things passed. They seemed benign enough.

"Anyway," said Barendts, "The R.E.'s taking a beating. They can't exempt their own ships from the economy, after all: even the *Banshee* has to keep up her micropayments for all the shipboard systems. They're living on credit right now, but if the ship stays here in slow space too long, they'll run out of credit . . . and the whole ship'll just shut down."

Michael stared at him. "You're joking."

"If a ship can operate without oversight from the Economy, it can be used to set up an independent colony," said Barendts with a shrug. "Lots of military ships would join us in a second, if they weren't utterly dependent on the Economy."

Michael laughed without humor. It made sense, in a sick sort of way. "They used to say, back home, that the R.E. only survives by continuing to expand. The core worlds are utterly dependent on revenue from the colonies to function."

"Yeah. An ecologically sustainable economy can't require surpluses. The R.E. does. So it has to keep growing to exist. If places like Chandaka join us, the core worlds stop dead just like the *Banshee* would. The Rights Owners would either have to give up their franchises, which they won't do, or else . . . no money, no transactions, no operating machinery."

"Billions would die," said Michael.

"If we don't get to them in time, yes." Barendts didn't

look too concerned. "They made their bed, they'll have to lie in it. But you see, that's what Crisler's trying to prevent. If we win, everything unravels. The R.E. will collapse more completely than Rome.

"But Crisler seems to think he's discovered a secret weapon to beat us with."

"He has," said Michael. "Or he may have, anyway." He told Barendts about the von Neumann machines of the Chicxulub. The marine's eyes widened as the implications sank in.

"But how are the things supposed to recognize rebel worlds? We all use alien technology, we have to until we set up our own industries . . ."

Michael nodded. This was the conclusion he had come to on the way back to the city; it had fuelled his urgent need to collect Rue and the others and go straight to the authorities. "It all depends on how the Chicxulub systems identify ships and worlds. Herat thinks they would have to be sneaky, nosing around the outskirts of a system and sniffing out enemy action. Because they can't get in close, they have to rely on fairly crude detection methods to tell who's who. Basically, anything that's not broadcasting R.E. integration codes would be suspect. Presumably the rebels encrypt all their transmissions, so the von Neumann's couldn't even tell if those were of human origin or not.

"So because you use alien technology, the von Neumann machines would have to treat all alien worlds as possible rebel worlds. The only worlds that would pass muster would be those using nanotags and Rights payments—those inside the Economy. Everyone else—everyone—would be suspicious."

"So," said Barendts, "in order to guarantee wiping out the rebels, Crisler's machines would have to wipe out every alien world."

Michael nodded. "We just found this out. We were on our way to tell the Compact when the ambush happened."

For once, Barendts looked abashed. "I'm really sorry I didn't get to you guys sooner. I wasn't sure whether you were sympathizers or what. I was basically on my own when we were at the *Envy*," he said disconsolately. "I wanted to force the *Banshee* to turn around, so I blew the life-support stacks. Of course, Captain Cassels turned out to be a lot more resourceful than I'd counted on." He grimaced.

"When we got here to Oculus, it took us totally by surprise when it turned out there were autotrophs here. And then you and the professor lit out for autotroph territory . . . Crisler went ballistic. I gather you went to get the Chicxulub stuff translated?"

Michael nodded.

"We got our orders an hour ago," Barendts went on. "It was all I could do to set up a hack on the inscape spoofers, so that the other guys' aim would be off for a few minutes. That's why you're still alive: I ghosted you, threw their aim off."

"Except for Max."

"Yeah . . . a lucky shot, I guess."

They were silent for a while.

Michael frowned out at the dark water. "We seem to be slowing down." The giant wall of ice was passing at a slower rate now. It was also sloping away from them, an uneven inverted landscape.

"You're not telling me everything," said Michael. "There's something else going on: Crisler didn't just come along on this trip to chaperone Rue, did he? He had people to meet at Colossus. For instance, why weren't all of you at the ball the other night?"

"Oh, that. There's a local politician, Mallory, who wants to bring the halo worlds into the R.E. It'll never work, but that's why Crisler had us ride the beam down here; some big political maneuvering's going on here between his supporters and the Compact. Mallory wanted the *Envy*'s ring changed to pass by his home world . . ." Barendts glanced over his shoulder. "You think she refused? And Mallory got Crisler to order the hit?"

Michael nodded. "Crisler might be taking us out of the picture so he can control the *Envy* directly and throw Mallory a bone," Michael said. "But it hardly matters at this point."

"There's some consolation," said Barendts. "For you guys, anyway."

Michael laughed humorlessly. "Oh, yeah? What's that?"

"The *Envy* was designed for slower-than-light travel. The original Chicxulub ships must have been designed for FTL and Crisler's going to want the new ones to be built that way too. His enemies are all in High Space; he doesn't care about the halo worlds, so odds are his von Neumann machines won't be visiting the halo."

Small consolation. Still, as Michael sat back and listened to the creaking of the sub, he found himself wondering whether the Chicxulub had held the same attitude sixty-five million years ago. Had they exempted the halo worlds from their genocide?

The idea seemed important somehow, but he was too exhausted to think about it. He leaned forward and stared at the spare instrumentation that dotted the nose of the sub. "Why don't we run through this stuff one more time," he suggested. "Maybe we missed something last time."

"And the time before that?" Barendts sighed, but nodded. "Okay. Starting with this panel . . ."

IT WAS RUE'S turn to sit in the command chair and stare out at the ice, which was now passing overhead in a slow procession of bizarre forms. Mike and the marine had gone to the back to snatch some sleep; Herat was under the influence of some healing nano from the sub's first-aid kit and slept soundly in the chair beside hers. Rue was alone with her thoughts.

It was unbelievable that Max was dead. She made herself face the fact, though doing so brought all kinds of really bad conclusions home.

She shouldn't have taken Max up on his mad plan to chase the *Envy*. He'd given her a chance to play cycler captain and she'd taken it up eagerly, not realizing what it meant. Max obviously hadn't realized either; he was dead now and it was all her fault.

Rue knew she had willfully ignored the danger when they'd set out to catch the *Envy*. Even at the time, she hadn't been able to explain why to herself or anyone else. All her explanations had been excuses, really. Why had she knowingly embarked on a suicidal quest?

The ice passing overhead reminded Rue of stories she'd heard of the boatman who transported the dead to the underworld. Here they were. She hugged herself and looked down.

The bag she'd brought with her from the marketplace lay crumpled at her feet. Absently she picked it up and rummaged through it. Jewelry—how pathetic, she thought.

She was about to drop it when her fingers touched the NeoShinto headset. She'd forgotten all about it. Now Rue drew it out, turning it over in her hands.

Religion had never interested her. She had accepted the simple message of the Supreme Meme: no matter how infinite the universe, time circles back around to here and now, to this very second. No matter where you went after you died, you'd end up back in this life again. Paradise was no more permanent than this very second. So your responsibility was to this life, not any afterlife.

But where did that leave Max? Was he fixed like a bug in amber, forever living out a life of depression and disappointment, dying again and again in the same pointless way? The thought filled her with horror.

And for herself? Rue had always felt herself swept through life by currents of incident way out of her control. When had she ever owned her own life? Certainly not when she'd been growing up on Allemagne.

Her eyes blurred with tears as Rue realized that it had been that control she had been fleeing when she agreed to go after the *Envy*. She wasn't used to running her own affairs; when she walked the hills of Penumbra North, sowing seeds, she had been a completely independent woman. And the experience was foreign to her, strange and threatening. She had leaped at the chance to throw away her options.

By committing to chasing the *Envy*, she'd deliberately thrown away her freedom. From the moment they embarked, she had been swept up again by forces beyond her control. That was what she was used to and she was happy in it.

She put her hands over her mouth, afraid she was going to throw up. Shame burned so deeply in her that she doubted she could ever face Michael Bequith, or even Dr. Herat again. And her willingness to throw away her own freedom had doomed Max and probably all of them.

The minutes dragged on. Nothing was happening except that the ice continued to pass overhead: the visible underside of the world-spanning glacial continent of Oculus. Occasionally, long tendrils of something organic-looking drifted by.

She had to do something—anything, to escape her own thoughts. A faint notion at the back of Rue's mind was growing in volume, steadily more and more loudly: This botched life was hers, infinitely. She would live the same mistakes over and over and there was no escape and nothing she could do to prevent the repetition. Even if over the aeons, a billion versions of Rue lived and died—some triumphant, some wise—given enough time this one would always return. She would always be here, in this crippled vessel, drifting slowly into the darkness.

Rue stood up and stared around at the interior of the sub. Maybe she could raid the rations in the meager galley—fix breakfast for the men. Anything to keep her hands and mind busy.

Her gaze fell on Mike's sleeping form and Rue felt a pang of regret and guilt. He shouldn't be here, he was an innocent in so many ways. Then she noticed his beltpack, which lay on the deck below the cot.

Jutting from the pack was one corner of a datapack. Of course; he always carried that thing with him. She hadn't really understood its significance until her visit to Vogel.

Rue wiped at her eyes and knelt next to the cot. She wanted to throw herself onto Mike and cry, but his sleep was precious. She took out the datapack and crept back to her seat in the front.

This was completely stupid, she thought as she connected the leads from the headset to the datapack. Then she slipped the headset over her ears.

A simple inscape menu blossomed into being in front of her. It listed several titles:

> Kimpurusha Dawn
> Dis
> Spirits of Ember
> Voice of the Cataract

Only the name Kimpurusha was familiar. Rue hesitated, then reached out and tapped the half-real words *Kimpurusha Dawn*.

The sub disappeared. Disoriented, she felt weightless for a second and relaxed into it. Then Rue was standing on a high mountain slope.

This place was not like the Penumbral mountains of Treya. These peaks reared thousands of meters into the predawn sky and were clothed in virginal snow along their flanks. Strong black rock patched the night-blue of the snow. The simulation was so complete that Rue felt the thin cold air in her lungs and shivered at the icy breeze that flowed down to her from the peaks. She stood on a spur of rock jutting out from a cliff. How had Michael gotten to this place?

The silence and height were awe-inspiring, but Rue was disappointed. Was this all that the famed kami were: postcards of particularly beautiful places? How could Mike have devoted his life to simple virtual realities like this?

Then she heard a distant rumble. Rue turned and saw that a jagged line of peaks in the distance were glowing with a gorgeous rose light. The rising sun had touched them and the echoing thunder that rolled up and down between the peaks came from six or seven avalanches that the hot light had touched off.

She watched the tumbling snow, enrapt, and the sound seemed to swirl around her and pick her up and then with a jolt Rue was gone. There was only the peaks and the avalanche and where she had been there was a great clap of sound that raced from peak to peak.

The sound stood up over the mountains and felt their shapes, their ancient solidity, in the standing waves of echo that crashed between them. Each peak proclaimed its millennial sovereignty to the others.

She rose, trembling, to touch the lower clouds. The reality of this place, this moment, was so overwhelming it erased any doubt. A million years these peaks had stood and in a million more they would still be here. Years nor light-years could erase them.

And way down there, all the parts of the mountains were as real: the tumbled rocks, the straggling trees, the lichen, and, on a jut of stone halfway up one peak, a standing woman—a woman as real as the mountains and as much a part of them as the stone and ice. They, as much a part of her.

The sound broke and fell back to sleep in the stones and snow. Rue blinked, felt herself spinning and then she was sitting in the sub again.

The echoes went on and on in her head. She reached out a trembling hand and touched the cold wall of the sub. It was hard to say what was her and what was outside her. For a few seconds, Rue had the hallucinatory sense that she was both herself and the ocean around her. The distinction between the two had been shattered.

The sensation faded gradually, but Rue sat still, in shock, for a long time. Then, half in fear and half in eagerness, she summoned up the menu again.

None of the other names on the menu were familiar, so she chose one at random.

She tapped the word *Dis* and blackness and stars bloomed around her.

MICHAEL AWOKE FEELING groggy. Somewhere nearby, he heard Herat talking. He opened his eyes; metal pipes formed a bizarre ceiling above his head.

Rolling over, he found there was no more bed under him suddenly and he crashed to the floor—to the deck, rather, for he was still in the submarine. Remembering that brought everything else back to him.

"Rue?" He stood up, rubbing his shoulder. She sat facing away from him in one of the two chairs at the front of the sub. The marine, Barendts, sat next to her and Herat was leaning over his seat and pointing out into the dark water.

Michael went to crouch next to Rue's chair. She looked up and smiled wanly. Putting her hand on his, she turned away again. She was turning her little medallion over and over in her fingers, touching it and examining it as though it held some secret.

Keeping hold of her hand, Michael turned to the others. "But why would they grow so long?" Barendts was asking.

Herat shrugged. "A very long organism might be able to trap the electrical current that Colossus pumps through this planet. Maybe that's their alternative to photosynthesis."

"What's happening?" asked Michael. There was nothing visible below them except darkness. Above, ice moved past at what looked like a walking pace. Some of the long threadlike things he'd seen earlier were passing by; they seemed to be undulating under their own power.

"We're caught in a current," said Herat. "It's probably one of the thermals that circulates between the exposed ocean and the far side of the planet. The sub's working fine and has plenty of power and life support left. We just don't have control."

"So we're headed for the coldest spot on Oculus," said Michael.

"It's not as bad as it seems," said Herat. The laser burn on his arm seemed to be healing; he was alert and in no apparent pain. "Remember, there are cities down here. At places where the glacial ice is thinner—higher above us— there's giant caverns, much bigger than the autotroph compound. With luck we'll drift past one of those."

"And then what?"

Barendts laughed. "Professor Herat spotted something we'd overlooked." He pointed through the diamond window.

Michael could dimly make out some of the sub's manipulator arms. They were mostly out of sight below his feet and were silhouetted by the floodlamps in front of them. One arm appeared to be holding something.

"See it?" asked Herat. "No? Well, it took us a while to figure it out ourselves, but one of those arms snagged the strap of Barendts's laser rifle after he dropped it jumping onto the sub. See it now?"

Now that he knew what he was looking for, Michael could plainly see the shape of the weapon, dangling from one of the larger arms. "What good does that do us?" he asked.

"I'm not sure, but no doubt an opportunity will present itself."

He was too tired to indulge Herat's usual optimism, so he turned back to Rue. "How are you doing?" he asked her gently.

She looked down at him again; she seemed very far away. "I'm good," she said, almost inaudibly.

"You don't look good," he said. She seemed stunned. "Did you take something from the medkit?"

Rue smiled sadly. "No." She stood up, a bit stiffly. Michael had to stand and back up to give her space. "Professor, do sit down," she said.

"Thanks." He plonked himself into the seat she'd vacated and Rue stretched, then went to sit on the edge of one of the cots. Michael sat opposite her.

"I've been thinking," she said listlessly. "I've been very stupid."

"What do you mean? You can't blame yourself for Max's death," he said, reaching out to take her hand.

"It's not that—I mean, I was, I was blaming myself. It's so awful, what happened." She wiped tears away from her eyes with a fist, then opened her fingers to reveal the pendant. "And I was blaming myself. Until . . . Mike, I met your kami. They told me to stop blaming myself."

Met the kami? The statement was so totally unexpected that for a moment Michael couldn't make sense of it. "How . . . how did you . . ."

Rue looked down, seemingly embarrassed. "I went to the local NeoShinto . . . temple, or whatever, before we met at the docks. They gave me a headset and, uh, while you were sleeping, I borrowed your datapack."

She shrugged awkwardly. "I needed to do something, to take my mind off Max. And I was hurting so much. But I met the kami and I feel . . . different, now."

He held her hand tightly and fixed his eyes on hers. "Which kami?" he demanded.

"All of them," she said, "but especially the ones from Dis."

Michael felt like someone had punched him in the stomach. He sagged back against the cold wall of the sub. He should have erased that kami long ago. Just thinking about it brought back the sense of hollow emptiness to him. "Oh, Rue," he said. "I'm so sorry."

She chewed on her lip, absently brushing her hair back from her eyes. "Yes, well, I know you would never have pushed me to meet them. You were good that way."

To have lost her cousin and then to have faced the soul-destroying kami of Dis . . . He was amazed Rue could still function. "I'm sorry," he croaked again.

Now she looked puzzled. "What? Why? I was falling apart, Mike. I miss Max so much and I was blaming myself for his death. Everything looked so dark and pointless, I could have died. Your kami saved me."

"What?"

She nodded. "I saw Dis. It's such a cold and lonely place. But when the kami appeared, I—I disappeared! I became the universe itself, staring down at this one little place in the cosmos. I turned away and Dis disappeared, Rue was gone, and there was only the stars. And, at that moment, I was ancient, so ancient, Mike! Older than humanity, or even this little fellow." She smiled fondly at the galaxy-shaped ediacaran. "All the cares and responsibilities of Rue Cassels seemed infinitely small. And Max . . . well, he was a part of me then. Max was a part of the universe, a part I loved. I'll mourn and always miss him, but it would just be so self-absorbed of me to blame myself."

Michael started to speak, stopped and finally said, "The kami of Dis showed you that?"

"I've been going like crazy since I left Allemagne," she said quietly. "I couldn't explain why before. Now I know I was running away, all that time. Even going after the *Envy*, I was running away from having to face myself. I was eager to panic about Crisler, you know to go from crisis to crisis because that meant I could make other people, or just the situation, responsible for what I was doing. Now that I see it, I'm not going to let myself get away with it anymore."

"Rue, you're being unfair to yourself," he said. "You've been a voice of reason all through this expedition. You found out how to control the Envy! You've taken good care of your crew. I think you've acted responsibly all along."

She grimaced. "I did okay. But it was all reacting. Max was the one who planned things. I just went along for the ride. Not anymore, though. Crisler's killed Max. He and that bastard Mallory have a lot to answer for. I'm going to stop them, Mike." Her gaze was level and serious now; the pendant was forgotten in her hand. "We're going to bring them down."

Michael stared at her. This Rue was a person he had never seen before. She had always shown hints of iron strength, in her determination and unwavering focus on her goals. She had been charismatic, before. Now, she seemed unstoppably sure of herself.

She hung the pendant around her neck. "We need to plan what we'll do when we get back," she said. "You're good at politics. Who do you see as the most influential people in the Compact now?"

He started to protest—she must need his comfort, he was sure of it. No one could have faced the kami of Dis and come out intact. And yet it seemed she had.

Seeing her calm alertness, all sense of shock and fear gone, the words died on his lips. He had thought he knew the mind behind her face; now he had to admit he didn't understand her at all. Even if she was wearing a mask over her emotions, it was seamless. She had work to do, it seemed, and nothing was going to dissuade her from it— not even the kami of Dis.

He knew of no way to respond other than to accept the mask for what it appeared to be.

Michael took a deep breath. "First of all," he said, "you need to tell me how your meeting went yesterday afternoon . . ."

22

ALL THE BAD feelings remained: guilt, grief, a sense of horror at how senselessly life could end. Rue would not let them prevent her from acting, now or ever again.

The others were not so easily entertained. Rue knew her responsibilities, so she convened strategy sessions with Mike and Barendts. At the first one she started off by saying, "How was Crisler going to explain our deaths? Or were we to disappear?"

"Disappear," said Barendts. "I don't know how he was going to explain it."

"*He* wouldn't," said Mike. "If none of you were seen and if the inscape spoofing worked, there would be no evidence to point at him."

"Rebecca would finger him," Rue pointed out.

"Maybe, but would she be heard? And what proof would she have? I think Crisler's working with some of the pro-R.E. factions here. They would lend support," said Mike. "What they would do is put a spin on the whole event—blame it on some rival faction, produce a patsy even."

"So we'll nail him as soon as we get back," said Rue. "After all, we have the proof." She nodded at Barendts.

Michael sat back, shaking his head. "Except that the assassination didn't go off as he'd planned. He knows Barendts botched the inscape spoofing. If that was detected, suspicion will point straight at Crisler, because the R.E. military has the most sophisticated inscape technology. Hell, he might have been arrested already. Even if he hasn't been, he can't be sure we're dead, unless the other marines lied about what they saw when the sub sank."

Barendts shook his head. "They wouldn't lie. It's their necks on the line too."

"So he's on the hotseat," said Mike. "What's the best thing he could do now?"

"Retreat to the *Envy*," said Rue bitterly.

"Yes. He'll probably take your man Mallory with him. The deal would be Mallory helps Crisler out here on Oculus and in return Crisler publicly pledges the R.E.'s support for the plan to integrate the halo with the R.E. In your absence, Mallory takes command of the *Envy* and when they get there Crisler lets Mallory take the *Envy* away to form the new cycler ring he's been wanting. Meanwhile Crisler himself takes the *Banshee* and heads for the Twins."

Rue cursed. It made an awful kind of sense. The worst part was, trapped as they were, there was nothing she could do about it.

Well, that might be true. But she'd be damned if she would let herself be bullied anymore.

"We need to plan our response," she said. "How are we going to head Crisler off, assuming we get out of here?"

Mike and Barendts glanced at one another; she saw a faint smile hover around the marine's lips for an instant. Then they leaned forward and started scheming.

TWO MORE DAYS passed before they got the opportunity they were looking for. By that time the air in the submarine was growing stale, the recyclers pushed to their limits. There were signs that the ship's power was fading. Herat said it had a typical muon-catalyzed fusion reactor, little more than a tank of hot hydrogen gas surrounded by muon-generators. Not much could go wrong with the generator itself; power must be bleeding off into the water around them. The oxygen recycling system also worked well; its pedigree was hundreds of years of closed system spaceship design.

More immediate was the fact that they were out of food. The sub continued to drift under the vast ice-sheets of Oculus. Rue watched that strange ceiling pass overhead for hours at a time, feeling frustrated and angry beyond any means of description. She felt now like anger was all she would ever feel. Mike's presence was comforting, but until all of this was over, she couldn't let herself give over to grief. She held his hand and drew on his silent strength, but that was as much as she would allow for now.

In turn, he seemed to be keeping her at a distance. He seemed guarded, as though she had offended him somehow. Once she saw him holding his offline datapack, contemplating it as though debating what to do with it. When he saw her looking, he quickly put it down with a hurried smile.

Strangely, it was Herat whose conversation helped pass the time best during the long hours of waiting. It was now clear that a whole ecology flourished down here and he was studying it as best he could in the illumination of their dimming floodlights. At its base were kilometers-long filaments, rich in metals, that drew electricity from the global currents that the magnetic field of Colossus sent through Oculus's oceans. The filaments used electricity the way plants elsewhere used light, so they formed a robust basis for the flourishing of thousands of species of plant and animal. Herat could sit rapt for hours, staring at the clouds of krill and the iciclelike holdfasts that hung from the glacial ceiling.

Naturally, then, it was he who first saw the lights in the deep.

"I knew there'd be something," he said, after calling them all to the front of the vessel. Where he pointed, Rue could see a deep, diffuse blue, radiating up from the depths. They had switched off the external floodlights to conserve power, so the light could not be reflecting back from some submerged mountain.

"Why is it below us and not above?" asked Barendts. Herat shrugged.

"Mining, maybe? The only way to get many minerals and metals on this planet is to dredge the bottom."

The lights slowly resolved, like waking ghosts, into spotlights that illuminated giant gantries. Taut cables hung from the gantries, disappearing into the gloom below. The gantries were mounted into the glacial ceiling, but they could see no sign of control stations or submarine docks there. What exactly these cables did remained a mystery.

"Should we try it?" asked Barendts, gesturing to the laser rifle still held in the sub's metal arms.

Rue pictured them bickering while their only chance drifted away behind them. "Let's do it."

Barendts sat down in the copilot's chair, rubbing his hands. "Action at last," he muttered, setting his hands on the controls for the manipulator arms. He had been practicing over the past days, learning how the limbs amplified his own movements. Once he'd gained confidence, he and Herat had gingerly transferred the laser rifle from the large arm it was hanging off to a small set more suited to fine work. Then they'd fired a test shot with the laser, just to make sure it would work.

Herat's plan was brutally simple. The front part of the sub was an egg made of transparent diamond-matrix. Behind that was more ordinary machinery, made of metallic hydrogen impervious to almost any pressure. The lasers of Barendts's former friends had wreaked havoc amid this machinery. It was dead weight now: ballast. Herat proposed to cut it away.

Rue kept watching the gantries slide by while they maneuvered the arms around to aim the rifle at the back of the sub. Suddenly she saw a glimmer of bright light ahead and above—a line on the ice ceiling that rapidly grew into an oval of glowing green. "Look!"

It might have been a natural formation—a weaker and softer core of ice that had melted upward, forming a natural dome in the ceiling kilometers across. One or two nukes could have carved it out in seconds. As the highest point for many kilometers around, such a dome would naturally pool any gases that bubbled up from the ocean depths. Humans could as easily have pumped nitrogen and oxygen into it, until now there was a round cathedral of ice, hundreds of meters of airspace above the ocean, lit with floodlamps and with many buildings bolted to the ice around its periphery. Rue stared, fascinated, at spindle-shapes bobbing in the water that must be the hulls of boats or subs like the one they were in now.

The whole cavern was only a few kilometers across. "Hurry, or we'll miss it!" Rue said. Barendts was frowning, obviously trying to decide what structural members of the sub to cut first.

"Fuck it," he said. A line of bright blue light suddenly joined the laser to the back of the sub. Bubbles shot up in a row from a centimeter or so above this line and bright flares of light splashed out from the back. Barendts waggled his hands and the bright line zipped back and forth, impossibly fast.

The sub lurched. Rue watched a large piece of machinery plummet into darkness. "Good," she said. "I think we're rising."

"Just to be sure," said Barendts and waved the beam again. Bright sparks flew and abruptly the cabin lights went out and the noise of fans that had been omnipresent for days, ceased.

"Oops," said the marine. "I guess we're committed now." Rue could barely see his shrug in the blue glow from the approaching cavern.

They were rising, but not fast enough. Rue watched in frustration as bright water began to scroll past overhead. She saw catwalks, boats tied up just meters above them.

"Maybe we should swim for it," she suggested hesitatingly. Herat shook his head.

"We'd freeze to death or drown—or both," he pointed out. "Listen, Barendts, does that laser have a flashlight setting? Maybe we can get someone's attention."

"Good thought." The marine pointed the laser upward and fired it. The bright blue light jutted up, throwing wild shadows across the wavering image of the cavern's ceiling.

"No flashlight setting, by the way," said Barendts, just before a huge chunk of ice slammed into the water meters away. "But that ought to get their attention."

They were barely a meter below the surface now, but the current had taken them almost all the way across the cavern. She saw the ice ceiling coming up again ahead of them.

Suddenly light flooded the cabin. Underwater spotlights

had come on around the periphery of the cavern. Now the sleek shapes of divers appeared in the water, wrapped in bubbles like spiraling wings. Six or seven of them swam after the sub.

"Here we go," said Barendts. The lines of blue light shot out from the vicinity of the divers and sparks flew right below where Rue was standing. She jumped in surprise.

The sub's manipulator arms, including the laser rifle, sank quickly out of sight. One of the divers approached them, his own rifle held out prominently.

Barendts grinned. "This is the part where we put our hands up," he said, demonstrating.

Three of the other divers were towing lines. They attached these to the sub and soon they were on the surface, being towed toward a set of docks where a number of other subs lay at berth.

"Let's get out of here," said Rue. She headed for the hatch. Herat laughed and shook his head.

"We never equalized pressure, at least not as far as I can tell from our busted instruments," he said. "The air out there will crush you like a grape if you open that hatch."

"Oh." She pointed at the divers now squatting atop their hull. "Do they know that?"

"Let's hope so." The divers hopped off, into the water, and their sub was hoisted out of the water. As it slowly turned, water rolling down the sides, Rue got a good look at the cavern they had come to.

Halfway up the blue wall of the cavern, a huge opening gave onto an even larger space, this one well above the waterline. The cavern they were in was just a lower dock area for what looked like an entire city carved out of the ice.

"What are those?" Tall shapes like smooth stalagmites stood in bright glimmering ranks under the lights of that other cavern. Rue pressed her nose against the diamond hull and peered at them. As the water stopped running past her eyes, she got a good look, but still couldn't figure out what she was seeing.

"They look big, but what are they?"

"Autotroph technology?" asked Mike. Barendts shook his head, pointing down at the docks below. Men in uniform were running about there; none were the conspicuous green of the fanatical humans who had seemed to worship the autotrophs.

"Hey, what are they doing?" protested Rue. The sub was being lowered into what looked like a giant trash compactor. It was a heavy cube with airlock hatches on the sides and top. It was attached to a larger, windowless cube. Their view of the cavern beyond was cut off as the cube's walls rose around them; then they were grounded with a thud. Fit-looking young men with buzzcut hair hopped into the cube and proceeded to roll the sub on its side. Stuff fell about the cabin and Rue found herself skidding over to sit on the wall.

Now their airlock was right next to a door that led into the larger cube. The fit young men clambered out of the cube and its walls started closing in, accompanied by a deep throbbing of motors somewhere. *This is it,* thought Rue incredulously, *they're going to squash us.*

The sides of the door to the large cube flattened and deformed around the sub's hatch, as though it were made of rubber. The sub settled a bit, creaked and then someone was undogging their hatch from the other side.

A little puff of air came in. A man-sized robot stood there, little laser lenses aiming at them from its hips. It stepped back with a clank and gestured in a very manlike way. "Come in," it said.

Rue and the others climbed out of the sub, finding themselves in a large cube-shaped room with bunks along the walls and a small partition behind which there was a toilet. There were no windows.

"Pressure equalization will commence now," said the robot. It slammed the inside door of the cube and stood in front of it, arms crossed.

Herat went over to it. "Please don't equalize the pressure," he said. "We need to get back to the surface as soon as possible!"

The robot said nothing. It seemed to have shut itself off.

HOURS PASSED. RUE'S sinuses hurt and her ears kept popping painfully. Her private inscape told her she was being subjected to mounting air pressure that her circulatory nano were having a tough time compensating for. They kept popping up windows in the corner of her vision, asking whether she could please eat some silicon and iron so that they could start building more units. They anticipated a need to protect her from the bends at a later time. There was nothing to eat in the cube, so she ignored them.

She and Herat continued to plead with the robot to let them talk to someone in authority, but it continued to ignore them. Mike sat on the sidelines, looking despondent; he was polite but not warm when she spoke to him. It was frustrating to face walls of silence on two sides.

Just when Rue was eyeing one of the cots in resigned exhaustion, the robot jerked and stepped forward. "Apologies," it said. "Our apologies."

Rue's ears popped and simultaneously an inscape window appeared. Her nano were telling her that the air pressure was dropping again.

"What the *hell* is going on here?" demanded Herat.

A new inscape window opened in the center of the room—a public one, obviously, from the way the others looked at it.

The abbot of the monastery of Permanence, Griffin, stood there. He held out his hands in a supplicatory gesture. "We are so sorry, gentlemen, captain. We just found out about your rescue. It seems the military police who fished you out of the ocean had some trouble ascertaining your identity, because the I.D. tags of your sub had been lasered off."

Barendts grinned sheepishly and shrugged.

"We've been talking ourselves hoarse for hours," said Herat. "Wasn't anybody listening?"

Griffin looked, if possible, even more embarrassed. "There's a local human rights policy that forbade the police from taking a deposition from you without a human physically present. It comes from an old case of long-distance interrogation, the ugly details of which I won't go into. And there were . . . further complications . . . due to where you chose to be rescued."

"What complications?" asked Rue. She was rapidly tiring of Oculus and all its political mazes.

"It appears you've stumbled on a military secret that no one, least of all citizens of the Rights Economy, is supposed to know about."

"What secret?" But even as she said this, Rue remembered the strange spikelike things they had seen in the cavern above.

"Please, this is a very sensitive matter. We're reversing your pressure equalization and will have you shipped topside immediately. These are matters that we cannot discuss through inscape, due to," the abbot coughed politely, "certain parties' uncomfortable skills with inscape hacking." His image looked directly at Barendts.

"Hey, don't look at me," said Barendts. "I'm just here for the food."

TWELVE HOURS LATER Rue stood in the lavish council chamber of the Permanence monastery. Once again she faced an array of faces around the oak table that dominated the room. The faces were different this time and Rue suspected that these men and women were the real powers of the Cycler Compact.

The politician Mallory was conspicuously missing.

Rue had been separated from the others early on their journey up here. She was assured that Mike, Herat, and Barendts were safe and were being taken care of. They were citizens of a foreign power, however, and it was time to discuss matters that they should not know about.

She resented the implication; as soon as Rue saw Mike and Herat again, she was going to fill them in on the situation, no matter what was said in this council chamber. She trusted them. Of course, there was no way she was going to tell that to the military police who had escorted her here.

Captain Li was present. He stood up as she entered; the others followed suit. "Captain Cassels," he began gravely, "let me express my deepest condolences on the loss of your cousin."

Rue had been all business, but this simple gesture stopped her. She felt her eyes filling with tears and wiped them angrily away.

"Yes, well," she said, as she dropped herself into an empty chair. "Thank you. But let's get on with things, shall we?"

Li nodded and sat, as did the others. Rue tried to still the quivering of her lip by biting it.

"You've been briefed on the overall situation," said a woman Rue did not recognize. "After the murder of your cousin and your disappearance, Admiral Crisler exercised diplomatic immunity and retreated to your magsail with his people. You had already secured beam time from the monastery and with the help of Mallory's people, Crisler got the schedule moved up. They left two days ago and are now nearing the outskirts of the Colossus system."

"Rebecca went with them?" asked Rue for the tenth time. She couldn't understand why her doctor and friend had deserted her.

"She did," said Travis Li. "We spoke before she left; she genuinely believed you were dead. She told me that she wanted to defend the *Envy* from Mallory's people—first of all by making sure crew members Laurel and Chandra learned, as she put it, 'what really happened on Oculus.'"

"I see. Thank you, Captain." This time, she held her expression completely neutral.

Captain Li continued. "We know now that Crisler has committed high crimes, but it is absolutely forbidden to withdraw beam power from a cycler cargo once it's on its way," he said. "You understand the sanctity of the Compact's laws? We have to honor our commitments regardless of local consequences." She nodded.

"We'll be questioning your companions about Crisler and the rebellion against the Rights Economy," said Griffin. "Don't worry, it won't be an interrogation. But we want to get your impressions most of all, as a citizen of the halo. We know Mallory's people have cut a deal with the R.E.; they want to abolish the Compact and make us dependent on the R.E." The abbot scowled, shaking his head. "They paint it as an opportunity, but it's really a power grab; we think Mallory and his cabal have been promised rights to all commercial travel between the lit worlds and the halo. As Rights Owners, they'd become fabulously wealthy . . ."

"And we'd be paying them to communicate with our own people," finished Rue. The prospect was appalling, but had its own sick logic.

She told the assembly the scenario she had worked out with Mike and Barendts, wherein Mallory got the *Envy* and Crisler whatever treasure lay at Apophis and Osiris. "Crisler is looking for some ultimate weapon he can use against the rebels and he thinks it's to be found at the Twins. We have to head him off."

"Why?" asked an elderly woman. "What does it matter to us if the R.E. tears itself apart? In fact, why shouldn't we just sit back and let them do it?"

Rue told them about the probability that Crisler's von Neumann machines would have to target alien worlds as well as human in order to guarantee wiping out the rebels. "This would amount to humanity declaring war against all other sentient life," she said. "I don't believe we could be neutral and I don't believe we could let it happen without being party to genocide beyond anything we've ever witnessed before. Do you really want that on your hands?"

They shifted uncomfortably; she could see they did not relish the prospect.

"But if you need a reason that's more ... self-interested ..." she said slowly, "think about this: If we're right and Crisler certainly believes as we do ... if we're right, then what is waiting for us at Apophis and Osiris is some kind of technology that would make it easier for us to produce cyclers. Maybe they would produce themselves, we don't know. If Crisler gets his hands on it, we lose ..." She shrugged. "Well, we lose everything. I think it's fair to say we lose the Compact. After all, who's building new cyclers these days?" She looked around the table.

"That's why we have to stop Crisler. We need to signal the *Envy*, get Evan and Corinna to break her free of the *Banshee* at any cost and head straight for the Twins. Think of what it would mean to the halo if we found, not just one new cycler, but a whole line of them!"

Even as she said this, Rue knew it was useless. They might agree with her, but Crisler held all the cards. Even if they sent a message to the *Envy*, Evan and Corinna had no way to stop the *Banshee* from going to the Twins. It, on the other hand, could blast the *Envy* to smithereens without a second thought. More to the point, Evan and Corinna could be rounded up at any time by the marines aboard the *Banshee*.

Even now, messages to that effect must be winging ahead of Crisler's magsail. By the time he rendezvoused with the ships, the *Envy* would be his. And no other ship from the halo could hope to get to the Twins first.

One of the people at the table was a government minister whom Rue remembered from her first meeting, lo those distant several days ago. He leaned forward now and called up a holographic starmap above the tabletop.

"Don't worry," he said, "this image is isolated from the inscape system. I just want us to be clear on the logistics before we make the next decision."

He pointed at the center of the display. "Apophis and

Osiris. And here is Maenad, the *Envy*'s next destination after Colossus. Crisler will arrive there, return to the R.E. and round up some extra ships. Then he'll fly to Apophis and Osiris. Captain Cassels, what do you think the likelihood is that Admiral Crisler will forego the extra ships and simply jump straight to the Twins from Maenad?"

She thought about it. Crisler was a control freak, but he was also cautious and thorough. He already had a complete scientific team aboard the *Banshee*, but he had no idea what he might find at the Twins. He might need more ships and if he discovered that too late, it would take years for him to return to High Space and gather them. She shook her head. "No. He'd want to have everything he needs before going in."

Nods up and down the table. "Right," said the minister. "Maenad is a light-year from us. Crisler will reach it in about fourteen months. Then he has to round up his new team—which may involve politics and we all know how slow that can be. When he's got the ships, he can fly out to the Twins in essentially no time at all. Call it . . . sixteen months."

"Sixteen months." It was the older captain, Serle. He was shaking his head in disbelief. "There's no way we can be ready in that time."

"We're going to have to be," countered Captain Li.

"Ready?" Rue put her hand up, looking ironically meek. "Ready for what?"

The minister glanced around the table, nodded. "Rue, what we're about to tell you cannot be spoken about outside this room. After our experience with Crisler's men hacking into our inscape system, we no longer trust public communications systems for this kind of thing. We know we were not compromised before his arrival, but now that the R.E.'s ties to Mallory's people are exposed, security is more vital than ever.

"You are now a captain of the Cycler Compact. You have certain rights and powers, including a security clearance high enough for you to hear what we're about to tell you. First, however, we need your solemn assurance that you will not tell your travelling companions, the professor and this NeoShintoist, Bequith, anything that we reveal to you now."

Rue chewed her lip, thinking. It was astonishing; from being a rejected kid on a cometary station, she had arisen to cycler captain. One small step remained to be taken and she would be in the central circle of power for the Compact itself, so far above where her ambitions had lain that she had no idea what it would mean for her.

"No," she said curtly. "I trust those men with my life, sir. They have my confidence."

Travis Li leaned forward. "They are citizens of the Rights Economy," he said. "We can't permit the R.E. to know—"

"They're my crew," she interrupted.

Li sat back, obviously startled. "Crew? But they were hired by Admiral Crisler to do research for him."

"Ask them," she said, though her heart was pounding. "One of the rights of a cycler captain, as you explained to me so kindly at the ball the other night, is to confer citizenship. I hereby say that Laurent Herat and Michael Bequith are citizens of the Compact, in my eyes, if they choose to be. Ask them. But I won't swear to you that I won't tell them whatever secrets you're offering me."

The powers of the Compact muttered among themselves and Rue sat with her face hot, feeling like she'd blown it for good this time. And what was this secret, anyway?

Travis Li was frowning. "You realize that as captain, you will be responsible for their conduct and if they betray the Compact, you will bear the consequences?" She nodded.

Then the abbot clapped his hands sharply and everyone turned to him. "This is Compact Law," he said. "She has the right to what she proposes. And since Apophis and Osiris lie along her ring, Captain Cassels must be informed of any actions the Compact takes toward any worlds on that ring. It seems, gentlemen and ladies, that we are at an impasse."

He stood and bowed to Rue. "We will ask your friends if they will forego their citizenship in the Rights Economy to become sons of the Compact. If they do, they may continue to fraternize with you and may be party to our plans. If not, we must ask you to end your association with them, at least for now—lest they should leave Colossus by cycler and communicate what they know to the R.E."

And the meeting broke up, simple as that.

I'VE DONE IT this time, Rue told herself for the tenth time. She was being escorted down a corridor hacked into the ice deep beneath the city. Eight hours had passed since the strange meeting and she'd had just enough time to ponder things and get very depressed. It was late in the shift now, she was tired, and way out in space, Crisler must be laughing himself sick as he and Mallory winged their way toward the *Envy.*

Two military policemen were escorting Rue to the cells (they called them apartments) where Mike and Herat were being held. Apparently they had been asked the question Rue, in her stupidity, had maneuvered them all into. Give up the R.E.? A world where they could traverse the galaxy in weeks? When both men's lives revolved around the hunt for alien intelligence? No. Why would they voluntarily remain in the halo, when they had that to return to?

This whole fiasco threw her relationship with Michael Bequith into sharp relief. It had been ridiculous for her to hope he might stay with her, she saw now. She hadn't even dared to fantasize that he might—but the hope had been there, underlying all her thoughts and actions these past few weeks.

She was a girl from the stations, after all, her eyes too weak to stand the sunlight of Mike's world. The dark was her home and the cold of the orphan worlds between the stars. He lived in the light and he would be returning to it as soon as he could.

She bit back tears as the MPs barged through one last set of metal doors and into some sort of waiting room. There were benches on the floor and a podium at one end, behind which the infinity symbol of the Compact was etched on the wall. Travis Li was here, seated on one of the benches. To her surprise, so was the abbot. He smiled at her kindly and handed her a thick book.

She stared at it. The abbot coughed politely, so Rue made to sit on one of the back benches. The abbot took her arm, shaking his head and gestured forward. She walked to a front bench and started to sit. He shook his head again; both he and Li were smiling now, damn them. The abbot gestured forward again.

But there was nothing up there except . . . Oh, the podium. Rue walked up to it hesitantly and laid the heavy book down on it. There was a ribbon bookmark in the center of it, so she opened the book out to that page and made to return to the benches. But the title on the page of the book caught her eye.

Ceremony of Citizenship in the Cycler Compact

"All rise!" shouted one of the marines suddenly. Travis and the abbot stood, grinning, and the doors at the back opened. In stepped Laurent Herat—alone.

Rue felt nauseated. She was sure she would faint at any second, and barely registered Herat's presence as the man came to stand at the front of the room, right before the podium. When she finally did look into his face, she saw the apologetic expression there, and that just made her feel worse.

"Why?" she croaked, almost inaudibly.

Herat shrugged. "My career was in its twilight anyway—the whole Panspermia Institute is on its way out. My wife is dead, my children grown. And my people . . . you know, years of investigating the ruins of alien civilizations have taught me a lot about what makes a healthy one, and which ones are doomed to fail.

"It's all about time, Rue—a species' attitude to time, I mean. The problem with faster-than-light travel is that it promises instant escape from any problem. The Rights Economy is proof of that: We expand and expand, with no thought to limits or tomorrow. Meanwhile, we rot from within.

"The *Envy*, and you, and this place have convinced me that there's another way. Maybe that's the secret of the Lasa—maybe they turned their back on FTL and conducted their civilization at a slower rhythm. . . . Anyway, if you'd asked me twenty years ago which of our cultures had more potential, yours or mine, I'd have said the R.E. But I don't believe that any longer.

"You've allowed me to see what it was we nearly destroyed when we took the lit worlds away from the halo. For that, I'll be eternally grateful to you."

His expression became more sober. "I have the benefit of my years. Bequith . . . Michael gave me a message for you," he said. "He told me to tell you that he cannot abandon his people—those on Kimpurusha or elsewhere in the Rights Economy. He said that while he is a citizen of the R.E. by conquest, still he can't abandon his world while it's under the kind of threat that Crisler represents. He wishes to find a way to go home as soon as possible, to warn people about Crisler's plans."

You fool! Rue wasn't sure if she was angry at herself or at Mike. She should not have created this dilemma for him. Mike didn't know why she had asked him to take citizenship; as far as he knew, Crisler had cleanly escaped, and even now Rue herself didn't know how the powers of the Compact might catch him. For Mike, this ceremony must seem like an admission of defeat—an attempt by her to get him to abandon the chase, and settle down on Colossus.

She blinked until she could see the words on the page before her, and began speaking past a dry and tight throat:

"Whereas it is in the nature of human beings to grow and accept new conditions; and whereas it is in the nature of our great society to welcome into its bosom those who have embraced our principles and customs . . ."

PART FIVE

Treasure World

23

THE CALL CAME, as regular as clockwork, one month after the last one. This time, Michael was too busy to even politely decline to speak.

Slow bubbles trailed up from behind his breather. The way they popped up to the ceiling of these flooded tunnels, then skated along the translucent blue ice like quicksilver never ceased to fascinate him. He had swum on many different planets in the years of his service to Herat; swimming through the flooded tunnels of these abandoned Oculus settlements was an experience unlike any other. The ice that made up the walls, ceilings, and floors of the chambers ranged through thousands of shades from emerald green to deep azure. The quality of color changed as the lights on Michael's helmet and helper bots moved. It only took one person to turn their head and his surroundings could change from dark tunnel to jewel-lined hall.

The caller remained on the line for a few moments, her presence visible as a flashing triangle to Michael's upper left. He had instructed his answering service not to take messages from her, so after a minute the triangle faded out. He found himself sighing in relief, though he knew there was no way he would have answered. When the triangle vanished, though, it left a hollow feeling which was all too familiar lately.

"What's up?" Barendts had been forging ahead, as usual, and now he returned, kicking strongly through the icy water. His entourage of jet-driven bots spiraled around him, little lamps darting to and fro like the flashlights of inquisitive fairies.

"They've been here, I'm sure of it!" Barendts waved at the tunnel behind him. "Just a bit further."

"I'm with you." Michael couldn't read the marine's expression through his facemask. He knew Barendts was ea-

ger to prove that this abandoned sub-ice town held autotroph trash. He was as unhappy as Michael to be
stranded on this halo world, so far from the action. He
wanted to have something to show for their time here, if
and when they succeeded in getting back to High Space.

The tunnel he was pointing to looked unstable, however.
Large slabs of its wall bulged inward, become as malleable
as wax from the pressure of all the ice above it. Long
cracks ran up those swollen walls.

The bots seemed calm, though; Michael sighed again
and swam after Barendts. "Just this last one," he said.
"Then we go back, empty handed or no."

The autotrophs didn't exactly trade with their fanatical
green-skinned worshippers. They disposed of garbage by
either dropping it into the deep ocean, or hiding it in any of
thousands of abandoned tunnels that riddled the coast of
the Northern Ocean. Humans had lived here for centuries,
and boom towns had sprung up and vanished many times,
some on the surface, some in the depths. The green men
explored the caverns, and occasionally came out with
treasures they could trade to the university for hard cur-
rency. Michael and Barendts had spied on them long
enough to pick up their search habits, and then had begun
looking themselves. Several times now, they had discovered lodes of autotroph technology, hidden deep in the col-
lapsing grottoes where no sane human would normally
venture.

A chain of madly swimming bots lit the ice tunnels
ahead of Michael, so that even when Barendts went behind
a wall, he could see the marine's moving green trail
through the ice. He followed the bots around the corner,
and found himself at the bottom of a shaft braced with cor-
roded rails: the familiar shape of an old elevator shaft. This
was a lucky find, it might give them access to levels of the
settlement unreachable by other means.

Barendts's shout confirmed his hope. "It's the frickin'

town hall!" His helmet lamp whipped back and forth at the top of the shaft, casting shadows and highlights down the walls. In moments Michael was beside him, gasping despite himself at the place they had come to.

Sometime in the distant past, settlers had carved out a large cavern here, maybe with a clean nuke. Michael's headlamps couldn't reach the end of it. Maybe it was a hundred meters across—maybe a thousand. All was darkness beyond the feeble fan of his light, but that glow was strong enough to pick out drowned buildings: He saw walls and the black maws of open doorways, windows.

"Supremely creepy," said Barendts. The marine sounded happy—as he always was when he had something to do.

They had been sharing an apartment now for four months. Ever since Rue Cassels stranded Michael here on Oculus, he had been trying to get back to the Rights Economy. (Well, she hadn't really stranded him, he knew; she was stuck here, too, at least for now.) Michael had been adrift for too long, and was almost grateful to her for forcing a decision upon him. He was no longer permitted to speak to her, or to Laurent Herat, and so he'd had to make some long-deferred decisions. He had decided to become a rebel again.

It was just a shame that there was no way he could act on that decision, trapped as he was in the halo worlds.

"Come on!" Barendts shot away into the submerged streets of the cavern settlement. Michael followed, trying to ignore the way this place reminded him of Dis.

Those dire kami seldom visited him these days. He felt he was, if not getting over that experience, at least slowly reaching an accommodation with it. Unfortunate, then, to have to swim past these empty facades and hear the kami whisper in the back of his mind, so strong, so sad.

"Heads up!" That was Barendts, his voice suddenly urgent. Suddenly, all the bots went dark, leaving Michael staring into the narrowed cone of light from his own headlamp—light that showed only grainy water, and the corner of a long-abandoned building.

Prudently, he tuned that light down to a vague glow, and switched on his goggles' light amplifiers. "What is it?" he radioed.

"Visitors," said Barendts curtly. It took Michael a few minutes to find the marine in the speckly gray shadowland of the now-dark town. Barendts was hovering behind a half-fallen wall that might once have defined someone's garden, back when the invisibly distant ceiling held sun-lamps and there was air here instead of water. Barendts pointed over the wall as Michael slid next to him.

Lights wavered in the distance. Michael counted seven sources, about half a kilometer away. This cavern was indeed huge. From here, all he could see was diffuse greenish lozenges slowly moving around the abandoned buildings.

"I'll send a bot," said Barendts.

"No." Michael put a hand on the marine's shoulder. "I want to see this myself."

Barendts started to protest, but Michael ignored him, kicking strongly into the darkness beyond the wall. It made sense to send the bots ahead, but Michael had never been one to hide behind remotes—a trait he'd picked up from Herat, most likely. Better to do fieldwork yourself.

Anyway, he had not ceased to be a scientist by choice. Michael was still welcome at the university, but he couldn't work with Laurent Herat, because the professor had signed some kind of secrecy deal along with Rue Cassels. Whatever the secret was, it was paid for by turning their backs on the struggles of the people in the Rights Economy. Michael was surprised and hurt that Herat of all people should be willing to do that—the Cycler Compact might be a declining power, but its decline was slow and graceful. It didn't involve the deaths of millions.

Michael had petitioned the Compact to allow Barendts

and himself to return to the R.E. It was absolutely critical that the rebels learn about the weapon Crisler hoped to find at Osiris and Apophis. Rue knew that, and she had the ear of the highest officials in the government.

The petition had been turned down, without explanation.

Every day that passed, Crisler drew closer to the Twins, and to escaping with the Chicxulub weapon. Frustration had drawn Michael back to the autotrophs as much as curiosity. Frustration drove him now as he closed in on the distant lights, for the university had refused to allow him to visit the green men again. Herat could; Michael was only partially mollified by the knowledge that even Herat had not been allowed to visit the autotrophs themselves.

He took a roundabout route, hiding behind the softening outlines of buildings, confident in his destination because the glow was constantly visible. Finally only one building separated him from whoever it was; he took a chance, and swam into the crumbling structure itself.

The walls were peeling, the floor covered in a layer of hazy mud. The feeling of desolation here was overwhelming, and he could feel his NeoShinto implant stirring, finding echoes of the kami of lost lives here. Michael ignored it, and made his way to a room at the front of the building.

The wall here had numerous holes in it. Light shone strongly through them, and he could hear a thrumming sound through the water now. Michael swam slowly over and put his goggles against one of the lower holes.

Not three meters away, a thing like a giant silver scarab was lowering boxes and canisters off its back, and arranging them carefully in the silt. There was no recognizable head to the thing, nor any sense organs he could see. But drifting around and above it were hundreds of tiny bright beads.

Michael recognized them: They were like the ones that had swarmed around him and Herat during their visit to the autotrophs four months ago. The swarm had spoken to them; it was an integral part of the autotrophs' artificial intelligence.

Michael had recovered some dead beads from other autotroph trash sites. He'd taken one apart, and figured he knew how they were powered. And the aliens didn't seem to keep good track of the things—which sparked an idea.

Some of the beads were hovering very close to the wall. Michael rose up on his haunches and peered through another crack. One hovered not twenty centimeters away. Its little black head was pointing down and away—watching the silver thing deposit its cargo, no doubt.

Months of anger at his betrayal by his companions made Michael unwilling to hesitate: He simply reached out and grabbed the bead, popping it into the metal mesh bag he carried at his waist. Then he put his eye to the crack and watched to see what would happen next.

Nothing happened. He heard a faint *bzzt* come over his radio, but the beads outside didn't move and the silver thing went on arranging its trash. The metal mesh probably blocked the thing's signal. And there were more of the beads hovering within reach.

In seconds he had a dozen of them in his sack. They circled lazily inside it, as if made lethargic by the cold water and high pressure. Maybe that was true. Michael eased back from the cracked wall and made his way to another building some distance away. There he found an interior room and turned up his headlight.

He opened the sack while tuning his radio across frequencies. The beads swirled lazily inside the mesh; after a minute he hit on the right frequency. A complex, sonorous hum came from the little things.

"Hello?" he said through the radio. "Do you guys speak Anglic?"

"Ph-ph-ph-phage," said a pipsqueek voice in his ears. "You eat us now."

"No," he said. "I just want to talk."

"No talk," said the tiny AIs. "We leave now."

"I'll let you go after we talk. How's that?"

"No. We leave planet. Ancient weapon in hands of phages. Must warn others of the Real."

"You're leaving Oculus? Leaving this planet?"

"Here to make preparations. Leave caches where phages not find."

Michael chewed his lip, thinking hard. "You know there's humans going after the Chicxulub weapon. You're going to pull up roots here—warn the autotroph empire?"

"We warn. Destroy phages before weapon built."

Michael raced back to where he'd left Barendts. The marine was startled when he ducked back over the wall; Michael had come from an unexpected direction.

"What the hell are you doing?"

"We're done here, at least for now," said Michael. "We've got to get these things back to Lux."

"But there's a veritable trove of stuff there—"

"Which we can come back for later."

"Are you crazy? The green guys might find it."

Michael swam determinedly toward the black maw of the elevator shaft. "Forget about the trash. Something more important's come up."

As he swam, he heard faint flashes of radio from the mesh bag. The little beads were clamoring to be let out.

Soon, he thought. *When we have the right audience.*

A CONSTANT WIND soared through the towers of Lux. It flooded in across the mountains and wound sinuously around the hills, coming from the dark hemisphere of Oculus. Sometimes, when Rue stepped out onto the balcony of her apartment high above the city, she had a momentary panic reaction: hull breach! This reaction was never more than a flash, but it always left her jammed with adrenaline. Lux held no outlet for the jagged energy of fear; not now that Crisler and Mallory were gone.

She didn't miss the bastards, of course; it was Max she longed for. And (though she tried not to admit this to herself) Mike.

So, at times like this she walked. Walking was a luxury she'd never known on Allemagne, but on Treya she had learned to associate walking with freedom. On this occasion, as commonly happened, her steps had taken her into the Night City.

Since Colossus never moved in the sky, day and night were conventions on Oculus. The day was defined by three eight-hour shifts, and social networks arose chiefly among people who shared shifts. Soon after their rescue from the ocean depths, Rue had taken care to move her "day" shift to correspond with Michael Bequith's "night." That way, she could minimize the chances of their meeting.

Sometimes, as she walked here, Rue would think about Dis. She had only visited Michael Bequith's nightmare one time, on board the submarine; but it had been enough. In its loneliness and isolation that frozen scrap of world had been akin to Allemagne and the *Envy*. Yet, of all Mike's kami, those of Dis were not spirits of a place, but echoes of an ancient species. Rue had felt them—present, yet fading, like a dying ember. They were merging back into the all-encompassing sky of stars—yet Rue had not felt that they were vanishing. Rather, they were expanding, like the sphere of light from a star, gradually becoming one with the vast and eternal stillness of space itself.

All her life Rue had thought of herself as small and singular, like a mote of dust battered to and fro by fate. In one moment of understanding the kami of Dis had shown her fragile individuality to be an illusion. The reality of who she—or anyone—was, was infinitely greater.

The Night City was a vast sprawling complex of arcades and sub-ice warrens, all windowless. There were huge caverns here, their ceilings studded with lights to simulate stars. The city held markets, restaurants, theaters, and the inevitable prostitute's quarter. The constant murmur of crowds was seductive, the press of bodies allowing a reassuring anonymity—but Rue often walked the darkest streets, because what was pitch-black to others was perfectly visible to her. She could easily avoid those who lurked in what they thought were shadows.

After two years of struggling to better herself and her people, Rue found herself alone again. The remnants of her crew were scattered, Rebecca, Blair, Evan, and Corinna back aboard the *Envy*, but as prisoners; Max forever dead; and Michael Bequith exiled into the streets of Lux. The only soul who knew even the slightest thing about Rue or her dreams was the academic Herat, and though she saw him during their regular sessions of militia training, she didn't feel close to him.

Few recognized the slim young woman who paced through the crowds, head down, hands jammed in the pockets of her tough workers' slacks. Anyone who thought they recognized the famous cycler captain from Erythrion probably decided they were mistaken. What would someone so wealthy and powerful be doing passing like a shabbily dressed ghost alone through the back alleys of the Night City?

She understood now that there were two states of being in the interstellar halo: in transit and stranded.

Rue was standing hipshot outside a dance club she sometimes came to, when she received a call. She hesitated before answering; it might be better tonight to lose herself in the crush of moving bodies and the pulse of the music inside. Sighing, she said, "Yes?"

"Rue, it's Laurent Herat. I know it's late, but I need to talk to you."

"Why? What's happened?" She stepped to one side of the club's door, allowing several other young people to enter. They were laughing carelessly and she watched them with envy.

"I received an extraordinary visitor earlier tonight," Herat went on. "One with an equally extraordinary message."

"Who?" Her thoughts flew to their various mutual acquaintances, but there was really only one person it could be. "Michael?"

"Apparently he's been making his own attempts to communicate with the autotrophs. Amazing! We've been unsuccessful, as you know, the green men won't let us visit them again, but . . . well, I believed Bequith when he said he had information about them. He says they know about what Crisler's intending, and they're leaving Colossus to warn their own people."

"Gods and kami." But it made sense—if Michael wasn't lying. Lying didn't seem to be in his nature.

"He brought some proof—several of the little remote AI bees that we spoke with once before. They're not very intelligent or knowledgeable, but they say the autotrophs are scared of the Chicxulub weapon, that they're pulling up their roots here."

Rue felt a terrible sense of helplessness. "That could mean war between humanity and the autotrophs."

"Yes," said Herat, his voice sounding old. "But Michael proposed a solution." He laughed humorlessly. "He's always been a good negotiator."

"What solution?"

"He's determined to warn the rebels about what Crisler's intending. He thinks he may have a way to communicate with the autotrophs, and he's willing to give it to us in return for passage to the nearest lit world for both him and Barendts."

"He's blackmailing us!" She was appalled, then infuriated. This was not the man she thought she knew.

As soon as she felt this, though, Rue reminded herself that Michael was, as far as he knew, abandoned in place here. What had she just been thinking about the halo herself?—that here, you were either in transit or stranded?

"He's desperate, and in no small part because of what we did to him," said Herat, as though reading her mind. "Anyway, I have no authority to give him what he wants."

"But I do," she said, her heart sinking. Yes, she could requisition two berths on the next cycler that came by. But if she did that, Rue would be letting Mike go without his ever finding out the reasons why she and Herat had become separated from him. The secret they were now party to was huge, as important in its own way as the existence of *Jentry's Envy* had become. She couldn't betray that secret, but was the price of her silence to be letting go of any chance of reconciling or explaining herself to Mike?

"In a way, I think this might be for the best," said Herat gently. "Bequith needs a calling, and maybe that calling was to be a rebel all along. Maybe his time with me was just a distraction."

Rue winced. Had she been a distraction as well? "If that's his price, we have to pay it," she heard herself say. "There's too much at stake. It would be . . . a shame to lose him, though. There's nowhere he'd be more useful than at the Twins, and I'm sure if he knew what we were planning, he'd drop this rebel foolishness in a second."

"If he knew, Rue. But there's no way to tell him. The law is very clear. Even if you and I know he would join us the instant he knew . . . we'd have committed treason to tell him."

"Treason . . ." Rue had a sudden idea. It wasn't pleasant, but she smiled grimly as she realized how perfect it was. "I think I know what to do, Professor. Let me handle it from here."

MICHAEL WAS TRYING to meditate when his door announced a visitor. Concentration broken, he glared past the little telltale in his periphery, then remembered his visit with Herat yesterday. Maybe this was some messenger with a reply.

He unfolded himself from full lotus and stood. Barendts was out, probably at the gym exercising, as he did obsessively. The little flat was stark and bare, more a cell than an apartment, but Michael kept it neat. Just now as his mind had quieted toward a meditative state, he had been feeling, if not happy, at least as though he were doing something worthwhile for the first time in months.

Musing about this, he opened the door.

"Hello, Michael," said the woman on the other side.

He almost closed it on her, but after a moment's hesitation, Michael waved her in. Irina Case, NeoShintoist and general pain in the neck, stepped into his little room.

"I've been trying to contact you for months!" she said.

"And I've been avoiding you," he said. "Or hadn't you noticed?" But he waved her to a seat and said, "Would you like something to drink?"

She shook her head. Irina Case was about Michael's age, but blond and with pale, almost white eyes. She came from New Armstrong—had arrived, in fact, with that traitor Mallory. But she claimed not to have any involvement with the New Armstrong plotters.

"I know the Order sent you to try to bring me back into the fold," he said as he brought Case a cup of coffee. "I've dodged calls from the brothers here as well. But why they think you would be able to succeed where they failed is beyond me."

Irina quickly put down the cup. "Oh! I think there's been a misunderstanding." He stared at her; she looked uncomfortable. "I didn't come here to try to bring you back into the Order, Dr. Bequith, although we'd obviously prefer that."

He was puzzled. "Then why are you here?—to apologize for your countrymen?"

She took a sip of the coffee, unsuccessfully trying to disguise annoyance. "New Armstrong is a *world*, Dr. Bequith. Not a conspiracy. And not an evil empire.

"I suppose you haven't bothered to learn about us. Well. Our world orbits a gas giant only a little bigger than Jupiter. It's a halo world; if it didn't have a huge magnetic field for power, we wouldn't be able to live there at all. Our cities are built on the ice mares; I come from Mare Labrynthus."

Michael translated the name to himself: *Sea of Mazes*.

"New Armstrong is thriving," she said, "from an economic point of view. But in other ways. . . . For a long time we were staunch supporters of Permanence and the Compact. The Compact gives people direction, you know— many of our young people took the vows and became members of the Order. But since the fall of the lit worlds . . . well, people's faith has been shaken. A lot of the younger ones feel abandoned and alone and New A is such a hard place to live that . . . there's been violence. And suicide. People walking out onto the ice without a suit . . . and talk of joining the R.E."

He nodded. "And that talk reached the highest levels."

Case grimaced and nodded. "Of course. We would incur all the costs of such an association, and it would cripple us. Nonetheless, there's a powerful group aiming for just that. Mallory and his people are not the disease—just a symptom."

She took a deep breath and went on. "There must be an alternative. Recently, some of us have started a new church. We want to reverse the damage, give the people of New A their pride and sense of destiny back."

Michael suddenly realized where this was going. "Wait a second—"

"You can't have any idea how profoundly your kami affect people from New A," Case rushed on. "Particularly the *Euler Night*. I've seen a man who was in a deep depression visit those kami and come back laughing. Laughing!"

"I won't be your guru," said Michael. "I merely found the kami, I don't possess their . . . power."

"Oh, we know that. We just want your blessing to use the *Euler Night* in our initiatory ceremony. The religion's a mystery cult, adhering to the principles of *Permanence Study 19-A*. We're not exploitative economically or socially. People can come and participate in the mysteries and if they choose they can volunteer to run centers or learn to conduct initiations. There's no metaphysics or myth system, we're purely methodological. All clean," she said, holding her hands up.

Michael looked around at his tiny apartment. This was the last thing he'd expected. All his life people had asked him to serve, in one way or another. This woman Case was asking for something he didn't even believe he could give: a blessing. "But why?" he asked, trying to sort out how this made him feel. "Why do you need my blessing?"

"People respect you—your accomplishments," she said. "With your stamp of approval on the ceremonies, we'll be able to bring in more people."

"And I should do this because . . . ? Anybody can visit a NeoShinto chapter or buy the equipment to visit the kami privately. They hardly need us, do they?"

Irina Case shook her head. "It's Leary's principles of Set and Setting. We provide a social context for the experience. The ceremonies help visitors to the kami to bring their experiences back to their daily life." She drew herself up and said in a more formal voice, "I would be honored if you would attend one of our initiations here in Lux. If you approve of what we've done, I'd like you to endorse our statement of intent. That's all."

Mike's mind was a blank. He opened his mouth, thinking he would just reject her request out of hand. To his own astonishment, he just said, "Call me tomorrow," he said. "We'll set something up."

MICHAEL CLOSED THE door behind himself and let out a *whoosh* of breath. For some reason he felt good—very good. He knew he would never rejoin the NeoShintoist Order. But he hadn't known how deeply he'd needed to believe that the years he'd spent in their service had not been wasted.

Yes, he could bless this new mystery cult. Caught between a spiritual awakening and political adventurism, the people of New Armstrong needed to decide a new course for themselves. His kami could help with that, he was sure. And if New Armstrong could rebuild its soul, then he might have won without a shot a war that his people had long ago lost on Kimpurusha.

He had just stepped away from the door when a knock came on it. Irina must have forgotten something, he thought, swinging it open and saying, "What now?"

Three uniformed men stood there. "Michael Bequith," said the one in front. "I hereby place you under arrest for violating the terms of the injunction forbidding you from contacting your former companion, Laurent Herat."

TWO DAYS LATER, Michael was pacing the confines of his cell when an officer appeared outside. "Where's my council?" Michael demanded. He had tried the soft approach with these stone-faced men, and got nowhere.

They seemed to be military police, not like the ones he saw regularly in the streets of Lux. And this was no local police station: He had been flown for hours out over the ice, to finally land at a simple station in the middle of nowhere, and then to drop in an elevator until his ears hurt from the pressure change.

His guard merely grimaced at his question, and said, "You've got a visitor."

He stepped aside, revealing a diminutive woman in a cycler captain's uniform. It was Rue Cassels.

Michael backed away and sat down on the cell's bunk as she stepped in. Rue looked around herself appraisingly, then said, "I'm sorry I had to do this, Mike."

"Do what?" He clutched the edge of the bunk in sudden realization. "You! You had me arrested!"

"Yes," she admitted, looking of all things a bit embarrassed. "It was the only way to get you here."

"What did I do to you? First you strand me here, cut off all communication, steal the professor away, now you have me thrown in jail for trying to get out of this hole? What next? Am I going to be executed?"

She reddened, but her voice was calm as she said, "I

only want what I've wanted ever since . . . since we came here. I want you to join my crew."

This answer was so unexpected that Michael laughed. "You let me stew in this place because you wanted me to join your crew? Are you crazy? And what crew are you talking about here, Rue? You lost the *Envy*, remember?"

He'd meant the words to sting, but she appeared unruffled. "Not for long," she said.

Her calm reminded him of how she'd been when he last saw her—shortly after she had inflicted the kami of Dis upon herself. The words he had been about to add died on Michael's lips.

Maybe, he thought, she was crazy. Maybe it wasn't the Rue he'd begun to fall for looking through those dark eyes—maybe it was the spirits of Dis.

Whatever. Either way, she couldn't get away with what she was doing. "Not for long? You and I both know that your ship is beyond reach." Maybe she had trumped up some reason for the local authorities to arrest him, he thought, but if so she couldn't have told them she intended to go chasing after her lost cycler. They would know she was mad, they would never agree to that. Michael sat back, crossing his arms. He would wait for her to leave, then he would tell them.

"I'd like you to listen to something," said Rue. She came and sat on the bunk next to him. He caught her scent, and it filled him with regret and anger. He leaned away from her, but she merely gestured, opening an inscape window in front of them.

The picture was hazy and runneled with lines of static. Even through the distortion, Michael instantly recognized the face of Rue's friend, Rebecca.

"This message is for the authorities at Colossus," she was saying. "My name is Rebecca France. I am the doctor on board the interstellar cycler *Jentry's Envy*. I have to report that the *Envy* has been boarded by hostile forces. Admiral Crisler of the Rights Economy, to be exact. I . . . huh, where do I start? After the assassination of Captain Cassels at Lux, I discovered that the admiral and some traitors from the halo were going back to the *Envy*. In the absence of Rue—my captain—the Compact was legally obligated to restore visiting passengers to their cycler. So they were going. I went with them, because I felt an obligation to the crew who are under my care.

"A man named Mallory has assumed command of the *Envy*. It is he who had Rue Cassels assassinated. He's not aware of this transmission, I'm sending it on the Compact's emergency frequency from the supply shuttle. Corinna Chandra instructed me in how to do this. She and Evan Laurel are under constant guard; apparently Crisler doesn't think Blair Genereaux or I are threats, 'cause we're not technical. So Mallory's ensconced himself with two of my people and some of Crisler's boys in the new habitat that Captain Cassels made.

"It is vital that the authorities know that Admiral Crisler and Mallory have plotted together. Crisler intends to take the *Banshee* and appropriate the Lasa's cycler technology at Apophis and Osiris. Mallory provided some special technology to speed up that operation. It seems Mallory's people on New Armstrong have been building a new kind of plow sail. They had built one at Colossus to try to convince the Compact to back their plan to merge with the R.E. It was small enough that they were able to bring it along with them.

"Mallory's given the plow sail to Crisler. Crisler's going to use this new plow sail with the *Banshee*. He's not going to decelerate to a normal stop at the star Maenad, like he'd planned. With the new plow sail, he's going to pull some high-g slam into the corona of Maenad itself. He'll go FTL there, coast to the Twins and then emerge from FTL and decelerate in. He estimates it'll cut three months off his schedule.

"In return, Mallory gets the *Envy*. He's trying to turn it, he's going to take it onto a ring to serve his own world. This means it will never return to Erythrion—my home.

"Crisler wants to take us—I mean, myself, Blair Genereux, Corinna Chandra, and Evan Laurel to Apophis and Osiris. It's because we have experience with the Lasa cyclers. Mallory had argued that he needed us as crew, but the new habitat Rue made runs itself and . . . well, Crisler pointed out that Mallory can't trust us. We might try to mutiny—or rather, take back our ship. He's right, of course.

"So they're going to stick us in the *Banshee*'s brig and use us as expendable explorers when we get to the Twins. Mallory will report us accidentally killed aboard the *Envy* and he'll arrive at New Armstrong a hero.

"It is vital that this information reach the leaders of the Compact, both at Colossus and at New Armstrong," Rebecca said. "Mallory is a traitor and must be punished. Crisler is engaged in an attack on our fundamental right to exist. If he escapes with the technology behind *Jentry's Envy*, the halo may have lost its last chance at survival. Please, if you get this message, forward it to the proper authorities at once." The window closed.

"This message arrived three weeks ago," said Rue. "As a result of it, we've had to push our timetable back. We need your help, Michael. We're going to beat Crisler to the Twins."

He stared at her. She seemed completely serious, and that self-assurance saddened her. "Rue," he said softly, "there is no way we can get to Apophis and Osiris before Crisler. He's got a head start, and we have no way to catch up. . . . If we had an FTL ship, maybe, but Colossus is too small to start an FTL drive near it."

Rue nodded. "You're right. We can't start an FTL drive anywhere near Colossus." She stood and briskly walked to the door of the cell. "Come with me." She gestured imperiously. Apprehensive, but curious, he stood to follow.

They walked, escorted by two soldiers, down long corridors empty of people and down stairway after stairway. He had the feeling they were somewhere deep in the ice. Finally Rue stopped before a great metal door that had warning signs, cameras, and autoguns around it. She turned to Michael. "Up until this moment, it's been possible for me to let you go. Once you step through that door, Mike, you're one of us—whether you want to be or not."

Now he was afraid. "What are you doing?"

"What I have to," she said. The door slowly ground open and Michael, prodded by his guards, stepped through.

He stood on a balcony high above a gigantic cavern hewn out of the ice. And on the floor of that cavern . . .

Bright lamps lit the blue ceiling and walls of the place and the cool light reflected from the gleaming hulls of dozens of sleek starships. Each stood twenty meters tall. They were built for gravity, judging by their strong, diamondite and fullerene construction. Michael had glimpsed shapes like these once before in the distance, the day they had been rescued from the deep ocean. Now, as he stared at them, a hitherto unsuspected possibility came to him.

He turned, and saw that Rue was grinning that mischievous grin he'd only seen once or twice before. "You were right that no FTL ship can start its drive close to a brown dwarf this size. Its mass is so small that a ship would have to be inside the dwarf's atmosphere to do it."

"These . . ." He turned to Rue. "They're built like reentry vehicles. You're not . . . you don't expect to—"

She nodded, still grinning. "We'll get to Apophis and Osiris first. And now that you've seen these ships, you can't be set free again. I'm afraid, Mike, you're coming with us."

24

MICHAEL WATCHED HIS interceptor's approach to Colossus through a nice safe inscape window; no real window was permitted in the design of these craft. The narrow cockpit he lay in was filled with cushioning liquid and crisscrossed with girders of diamond. Michael's body was strapped and enfolded by a variety of devices designed to soften the impact of a fall into the demonic gravity of a brown dwarf.

He still couldn't believe where he was, and what was about to happen. All these months, he'd believed Rue wanted him to abandon the chase, settle down on Oculus as she appeared to be doing. He'd thought she must not be the person he'd thought she was, since she had seemed to ask him to follow her, forgetting his obligations to his own people. Michael had been angry at her, and hurt that she never called after their rescue from the depths of Oculus's ocean.

And then to find out that she had been unable to call, prevented by her own obligations! To discover what secret she had been sworn to protect: a secret that dovetailed perfectly with Michael's own needs, had he only known. Every time he thought about the months of time he'd wasted in anger and solitary work on Oculus, he felt sick. He still blamed Rue for all of that, however he might know intellectually that it wasn't her fault.

He reached out to touch the solid hull of the interceptor. But he was really here! And, miraculously, they were on their way to the Twins to preempt Crisler. No matter how confused Michael's feelings, he couldn't suppress the excitement he felt at what was to come.

Rue was in another ship, which was something of a relief. Each of these interceptors could hold six people, no more. Michael and Dr. Herat were together again, ironically. It had not been by his or Rue's choice; Rue rode with Barendts as well as a master tactician from the Compact's military academy, a man whose weapons and systems were at her command. Michael and Professor Herat had to play escort to a member of the expedition that was Michael's proud addition: a thing from the autotrophs.

Michael's plan to communicate with the autotrophs had been simple: He talked with the bees he'd stolen from the abandoned settlement, repeating over and over the message he wanted them to take back. Then he'd returned to the subsurface caves, located some of the autotroph garbage-dropping things, and simply let his bees go. They had joined the existing swarm seamlessly, and after that all they had to do was wait.

The answer—delivered with reluctance by the green men—was too alien to communicate with directly, but Michael nonetheless thought of it as an ally.

Every now and then he turned to check the high-heat bubble at the back of the cabin. Inside, visible through a small square window, was a strange coiling thing and a swarm of autotroph bees. This little swarm, though dull in most respects, seemed able to translate Lasa and Chicxulub, and that was all he really cared about right now. It had come with a message, of sorts, from the autotrophs: Humanity threatened to unleash the Chicxulub weapon. Humanity must stop that weapon from being unleashed.

He couldn't see Herat through the cabin's liquid and impeding buttresses, but he could hear him in inscape, humming. The professor was delighted to be traveling again—and delighted to have Michael along as well. Although Herat had also kept silent about the secret of the interceptors all these months, Michael found it impossible to feel anger at his former employer. He wasn't sure why that was; but his loyalty to Herat had survived through everything that happened over the years.

"You're strangely silent, Bequith," the professor said.

"Can't you hear my teeth gritting?" he shot back. He had no illusions about the sanity of what they were about to do.

"These things are well tested, man," said the professor. "Besides, you know what they say, it's not the fall that kills you, it's the landing."

"Very funny." Brown dwarfs had no solid surface, Dr. Herat had reminded him earlier. Michael had not made the obvious reply then, but he thought it now: In twenty gravities, anything you hit was like a solid surface, even air.

They were plummeting like darts at the dwarf's atmosphere: sixteen sleek, aerodynamic interceptors. They couldn't hope to simply fall into the dense, incandescent atmosphere of Colossus and this fact had stymied earlier attempts to get faster-than-light ships deep enough into a dwarf's gravity well to activate. The first ships that tried had splatted like bugs against the dwarf's upper atmosphere.

The Compact's eventual solution was brutally simple, but they had proven it to work, at least most of the time. Each of the interceptors would begin firing a powerful antiproton beam ahead of itself as it fell into the atmosphere. The explosive shock would open a rarefied channel, through which the ship would fall. There would still be enough atmosphere to slow the ship, but not so quickly as to reduce its passengers to jelly.

"Relax, Bequith," continued Herat. "We've been in some pretty exotic places before. This one's just a bit more . . . extreme, than most."

He barked a laugh. "And are we going to get out and take a walk when we get down there?"

Herat sighed. "If I could, I would."

The curve of Colossus's horizon was becoming a flat line. Beyond that horizon, a giant plasma flare made an arch like a gateway to heaven. Herat was still speaking, but Michael was too mesmerized by the sight to listen.

Colossus was young, by the standards of brown dwarfs. Its heat was generated by its slow gravitational contraction, just like the planet Jupiter. But at eighty times Jupiter's mass and only twice its radius, Colossus was still flaming hot after a billion years of existence; and it would continue to glow like a fading ember for another billion. Its surface was banded, like a gas giant's, but under its gravity the clouds were flat, more like oil slicks or impurities in liquid metal. They glowed various shades of orange and red and gigantic lightning flashes shot through them randomly.

As the horizon flattened, Michael saw the world's edge fade slowly purple, then blue; the distant arch of fire lost its dimensionality, becoming like something painted onto the sky rather than in it. His interceptor was in free fall, but he felt no movement. Rather it seemed like the brown dwarf was uncoiling somehow, from a giant ball into a flat net spread to catch him. It began to seem as if the horizon were curving above, like a closing mouth: orange flame below, a crimson ocean of fire to all sides and in the unimaginable distance, where the incandescent thunderheads became small as specks, that royal purple began and climbed the sky and ate away the stars.

"Engaging beam," said the pilot crisply. Michael saw and felt nothing of that—but an instant later they struck the atmosphere.

The first jolt knocked the wind out of him. It felt like a giant mallet had struck the interceptor and was impelling it back into space. Michael struggled to breathe through his mask; his limbs were forced to his sides and he heard his neck crick. Something had gone wrong. Surely they were being shot upward at some ferocious acceleration. He blinked away spots and focused on the inscape window.

The blue was still rising and the clouds below were getting bigger. The window showed the interceptor to be standing on a pillar of solar fire that stretched down to puncture the cloud banks. That must be the particle beam, he thought in terrified amazement.

"Systems normal," said the calm voice of the ship's computer.

Normal? This was normal?

The pilot's voice came over. He was using a subvocal through inscape and so his voice sounded normal, though

Michael had no doubt he was having as hard a time breathing. "We're trying to maintain as close to free fall as we
can," said the pilot. "We're currently experiencing only
eleven gees, which means we're still gaining speed as we
fall. Well within tolerances."

An object dropped here would pass the speed of sound
in the first second of its fall. *This is insane,* Michael
thought again.

And that cloudscape . . . never, even on Dis, had he seen
a more hostile, inhuman place. Maybe stars were worse,
but you couldn't even imagine the surface of a star. He
could more than imagine Colossus; he was here.

For a terrified moment he thought that his implants were
going to kick in and expose him to the kami of Colossus. If
the kami of Dis had whispered Michael's insignificance,
those of this place would bellow it. They would snuff him
out by sheer indifference.

But he didn't need the implants to feel time stretching
out into a long, impossibly vivid moment. Michael felt balanced on the rim of eternity here, in the presence of vast
forces it would have been presumptuous for him to capture
and name as kami. The moment seemed overflowing with
power and import, and he suddenly heard Rue's quiet voice
saying, "How would you have to feel, to want it all
again . . . ?"

In seconds he might die, incinerated on Colossus—yet
after infinite time maybe he would come round to exist
again, and he would be here again, balanced on this moment. Even as he had in the fathomless past, an infinite
number of times.

Everything—every instant—was infinitely significant.
Even the most fleeting moment, he realized, was permanent.

And then a new voice spoke, calm as an angel.

"Prepare for transfer."

And an instant later the crushing pressure was gone and
the swirling orange was replaced by the calm blackness of
FTL travel. Michael floated freely in his straps.

Beside him Herat was laughing. Unsure of what he had just experienced, Michael started laughing too—and he was surprised to find as he laughed that a great weight had somehow lifted from his heart.

LEAVING FTL HAPPENED without drama. Suddenly the inscape window Rue had positioned by her g-bed showed stars. The pilot turned around in his seat, grinning, and gave a thumbs-up.

"Here come the others," he said. Rue looked, but could see nothing. She cloned the radar display he had in front of him and sure enough, one by one tiny needle shapes were popping into existence around them. One, two, five, eight, eleven . . . She held her breath while the call signs came in and let it out in a *whoosh* when Mike's ship signalled its presence.

Twelve, thirteen, fourteen . . . And no fifteenth. They waited tensely for almost half an hour, but the last ship didn't appear. Finally the pilot turned to her and said, "Ma'am, I don't think they made it."

She had been thinking this, but hearing him say it made Rue feel sick anyway. She let out a ragged sigh and said, "Bring everyone in. If we're secure, we'll inflate a balloon-hab and hold a ceremony honoring them."

Sola, the tactician, nodded. "Good idea."

"Meanwhile, unfurl the telescopes. We need to know where the hell we are. Passive sensors only—no radar yet, please."

She waited while the scopes came on line, then started them scanning. These instruments were infinitely better than the one Max had bought for their first trip to the *Envy*. Thinking this reminded her of him and his endearing fallibility. She felt a sharp pang of loss, which threatened to blossom into worry about what had happened to Rebecca and the others.

After meeting Mike's kami, Rue no longer believed she had to let her emotions lead her. She still loved her emotional life and had great sympathy for her own feelings; but it had become clear to her that she needed to be unsympathetic to the urges that came with many emotions.

Worrying meant that she cared about her people; but right now, worrying would not help bring them back. She returned her attention to the view.

Even though they gave no light, there was no missing Apophis and Osiris. Their convoluted magnetic fields swept the black sky like invisible hurricanes. Rue's ship felt those fields, though they were millions of kilometers from the Twins. Noise from the fields made the dwarfs the brightest radio emitters for light-years.

She soon had a visual fix. The dwarfs must be ancient, for they gave no visible light at all—not the gold of Colossus nor the coal-red of Erythrion. These worlds were older than the Lasa; they appeared in her scope as round holes in the starscape. They orbited one another at a distance of fourteen million kilometers; unbelievably close, considering each had a diameter of a million and a half kilometers.

No—they did give light, she realized, as she turned up the gain. Both dwarfs sported crowns of flicking auroral light around their poles.

Rue had never thought of the halo worlds as lonely before, but the Twins were different. This was a forbidding place, like a frozen tomb. The feeling reminded her of the fractured plain of Dis.

"Ambient temperature is six kelvin," said the pilot. "The Twins register at about three hundred K. But . . . we're picking up pinpoint infrared sources. Lots of them!"

"Show me one." She waited while the telescope realigned.

What swam into view was a long thread of light. In infrared and speckled with dimness and distance as it was, it looked to Rue like a road, winding gently through space to infinity.

"A tether." She and the pilot had spoken simultaneously. Rue laughed. "It's a power tether." It was strange to see something so familiar and homey in this place—especially knowing that humans had not created it. Then again . . . "How many are there? Are they broadcasting standard position data?"

"It's like . . . a whole galaxy of them in orbit. Around both Twins. Thousands. Tens of thousands. But no signals. I don't think they're ours."

"Well. Not a Cycler Compact colony, then . . . But that's probably their energy source for launching cyclers. Where are they beaming the power?"

But she could already see the answer. As the light-enhanced view pulled back, she saw the dwarfs as gray cutouts encircled by Saturnian rings composed of thousands of tiny scintillas of light. Both dwarfs were surrounded by such rings.

And right in between the dwarfs, at the fixed but empty point in space about which they both orbited, a brilliant flare of infrared shone.

Dr. Herat's voice came over the radio. "Of course! The only stable place in this system, other than low orbit around the dwarfs, is at their orbital center. It's like the axle of a wheel, gravitationally speaking. There might even be asteroids or a moon there. Let's take a look."

The telescope zoomed dizzyingly in to that bright spot. Things swam in and out of focus for a second. Then Rue saw everything she had hoped to find here—and everything she had feared to see.

THE INTERCEPTORS WERE clustered in a wall formation, pointing at the distant Lasa construction site. Behind them, a balloon habitat had been inflated and inside it Rue held a ceremony honoring the pilot and gunner whose ship had not made it through from Colossus.

As a cycler captain, she was the traditional choice to perform such a memorial. She had learned, on the *Envy* and in the depths of Oculus's ocean, that she was truly a captain when she forgot to doubt herself. Today, she could let the voice of tradition and centuries-long purpose speak through her. The authority was not originally hers, but it became hers through her acceptance of the role.

"We see before us the reason why sacrifice is necessary," she told the assembled fliers, who were clustered in a loose ball in the center of the habitat. "This is the origin of *Jentry's Envy*. It may be a Lasa colony or a machine intelligence, or something else entirely new. It appears that resources are being skimmed off the Twins and shunted to that central point—whether to build a new cycler or to feed an alien civilization, we don't know. But the starship *Banshee* is moored there. The men who have made themselves our enemies have come to steal from us the prize that *Jentry's Envy* hinted was here. If this is truly a construction shack for new cyclers, then this system is infinitely precious to us. Such new cyclers may be our last chance to restore our civilization to the greatness it once had. Our comrades, Julia Daly and Harald Siever, fell in the course of trying to guarantee a future for their children and ours. They exist now as part of the kami of this place. We will remember them, always."

In an ancient gesture, the assembled bowed their heads for a moment of silence. As the memorial broke up, Rue saw Mike hanging out at the edge of the crowd, uneasily glancing back at her. After the effort of speaking the eulogy, she felt strangely disconnected and so she felt it easy to go over to him. At the same time she was cringing inwardly at the thought that her need to save her crew had gotten two people killed and she was calculating whether the speech she had given would result in greater morale and respect for her. Her distraction allowed her to smile at him warmly, and say, "Thank you for being here."

"It's not like I had any choice," he said stiffly.

"Still. I need you with us, Mike. I . . . need you with *me* on this. We went through a lot to get to this point, and I'm sorry about the deception of the past months. But my people were—are—in danger. It was necessary."

"Yes, Captain."

Now Rue's carefully built mask crumbled. "Oh, Mike, I'm so sorry." She reached out tentatively. "Have the past months changed you so much?"

"No." He jammed his fists into the pockets of his jumpsuit. "It's you who's changed, Rue. You . . . don't need me. There was a time when I thought you might."

"Need you? Like Herat needs you? No, Dr. Bequith, I don't need you that way," she said hotly. "And I hope I never do. I'm not looking for a servant, I'm looking for an equal. Somebody who's with me not because of what they can do for me, but because of what we can do together." She turned away, shaking her head. "Once upon a time I imagined we could do great things together."

He flushed with anger. Rue regretted her sharp words, but damn it, none of this was her fault. She shook her head and floated over to Dr. Herat, who was floating nearby in a flock of inscape windows. "What are we faced with, Professor?"

"Crisler's here all right. And he's right at the source." Herat pointed to a window where a false-color image of the Lasa construction site glowed. "This place is pretty complex. From what I can tell, they get their raw materials from tethers that hang down into the dwarfs' upper atmospheres. They skim the elements they want off the top, which must take a long time. These tethers are powered by electrodynamic ones higher up. They bundle the scavenged materials and toss them at the orbital center of the system. There, the Lasa use something like a multilobed ramscoop to pull the packets in and feed it all into this." *This* was a cylinder, a kilometer long and almost half that in width, that radiated infrared at about 300 K. The *Banshee* was moored right next to this cylinder.

"So are they building a cycler there?" she asked, nervously twining her hands together.

"Actually, I don't think so. At any rate, I don't think they could launch a cycler using beam power. The total number of power tethers they've got in orbit around the Twins will produce trillions of watts of power, but that's not enough. It's kind of a puzzle, actually," he said happily. "The tethers produce far more power than they'd need to construct a starship or run a sizeable colony, but not enough to launch much more than a cycler cargo. There's no colony. If there's a starship, it's hidden inside that cylinder. So what are they doing with all that power? I don't know."

"What about the *Banshee*? Are you sure Crisler didn't detect our arrival?"

He nodded. "It's got a very low-level radar ping going. They're not expecting visitors—why should they? These ships," he nodded at a window showing their interceptors, "are not supposed to exist."

"The R.E. discounts the halo as a threat," said Sola, who'd come to hover nearby. "We're seen as bumpkins. It's our biggest advantage."

Rue nodded, contemplating the interceptors. Michael had come to examine the windows as well; secretly she was glad he was putting his anger aside, if only for the moment.

The interceptors certainly looked exotic, and Rue'd had the engineers emboss their diamond hulls with ruby lettering: Lasa script. They had copied fragments of writing found on a wrecked Lasa ship. Nobody knew what the words said; the point was not to fool the Lasa, but to convince Crisler that these interceptors were native to this place—part of the machinery.

Sola, the tactician, pointed to a top-down map of the Twins' system. "We can send teams A and B around the dwarfs, so that they ride in to the construction site in the pellet streams from the scavengers. Two ships at first, so as not to alarm Crisler. They'll dock opposite the *Banshee* at the construction site and we'll disembark as quickly as we can. If we can employ countermeasures to their inscape or sensors, we'll do that. The two squads will look for any control center, as well as looking for your crew, Captain." He shook his head. "That will be the tricky part."

"You don't have to remind me," she said coldly. "Then what?"

He shrugged. "Then the other interceptors approach. We'll see how close we can get to the *Banshee* before we have to open fire. But all we have to do is take out a critical system, like her engines and she'll have to surrender. If she's caught unprepared, it should be easy. Immobile, she has no options, because we can slide in behind the 'construction shack' to avoid her weaponry. We'll board her and secure your people."

Rue nodded. "Sounds good. Prepare everyone. It'll take a couple of days to orbit the dwarfs, so we'll head out right away. Communication is to be by laser only. We'll leave this outpost and one interceptor to act as observers."

"So who's on the in-teams?" asked Mike, his expression neutral.

She hesitated. Rue didn't want to send Mike into the fray, but if she left him here as an observer, he would be furious with her. "I'm going," she said. "With one squad, to bring my people out. Dr. Herat will go in the other ship, and . . . and since you control that autotroph thing, you'll go with him. We need to know what's valuable and what isn't, here. Do we need to secure the whole system to be safe? Or just the new cycler? Only you and Herat can make that assessment."

He nodded, his expression neutral.

The Klaxons sounded and everyone began to suit up to return to their ships. Rue watched Mike as he talked to Dr. Herat. His eyes often drifted back to her; he knew she was watching. But they were separated by meters and an impossible gulf of duty, for now. She tried to fix his features in her mind, in case she never saw him alive again.

HERAT WAS NOT one to let fear get in the way of his enthusiasms; so Michael was surprised at how subdued the professor seemed as they began their run around the back side of Apophis.

As soon as they were coasting on the aerobraking trajectory the pilot had chosen, Herat ordered the telescopes out and began silently studying the face of Apophis. Michael checked on his autotroph companion, and when he was certain the swarm's systems were all working, opened a connection to the ship's telescopes for it.

As he worked he brooded over what Rue had said. Was it true that he knew no other way to relate to those he cared for, other than service?—to place someone else's needs above his own, and ensure that those needs were met? Wasn't that what love was?

Or was it possible that love was sharing your own goals with someone else? In which case . . . just what were his goals? He didn't know anymore.

"Something's happening," muttered Herat. "I was right."

Michael climbed through the maze of pipes and struts that was the cabin of the interceptor and settled beside Herat. His shoulder brushed the hot carapace of the autotroph's capsule.

"What are you talking about?"

"It's been bothering me since we arrived. Why didn't the Lasa notice us? Acknowledge our presence?"

Michael shrugged. "Maybe they weren't looking. Or maybe we didn't send the right signal to wake them up. Or they haven't noticed us either, which is quite likely."

"Maybe they weren't looking. If they weren't, that would suggest that this installation is running on autopilot. Maybe it and its ancestors haven't encountered a sentient species in a billion years. It could have evolved away from its original purpose and then *Jentry's Envy* would be an accidental mutation—a throwback.

"But if it was expecting us to know how to signal it? That would imply that this place was not meant for us. But I believe *Jentry's Envy* and, by extension, this place, was a gift. Meant for anyone who wanted to take it."

Michael saw his point. "The lack of a greeting is ominous."

"I was hoping that the system had signaled Crisler when he first arrived. Now I don't think it did. Look." He gestured to a long-range infrared view across the horizon of Apophis. Michael could see the faint thread shapes of the orbiting tethers and a vague pink glow that the window legend said was a retreating cloud of small packets bound for the construction shack.

Herat read Michael's look of incomprehension and scowled. "Look at the packets, man! The closest ones are days away from their origin. The whole stream stretches from a million kilometers above Apophis all the way to the shack. It's a long continuous flow of building material— but *it's been cut off*."

He was right. The last packet of building material sent from the Twins had gone out days ago. Michael saw where Herat was going with this: "The system started to shut down as soon as Crisler arrived!"

"Yes." Herat scowled at the display. "The question is, why?"

"But that's great, Professor. It's a major clue. We'd better laser this back to the fleet."

Herat glanced up, shrugging. "I suppose."

This wasn't like the professor at all. "What's wrong?" Michael asked.

For a moment Herat looked exasperated. Then his shoulders slumped and he said, "I know that it was right for me to join the halo. The Compact, I mean. The R.E.'s rotting from within. My career was winding down anyway; the Panspermia Institute's a farce, always has been . . . I just miss my children. I don't know if I'll ever see them again, Bequith."

"After this," Michael nodded to the Twins, "you can still go home. You're not a wanted man in the R.E., Professor. Crisler thinks you're safely dead."

"It's not that. I . . . sometimes I just feel my age, Bequith . . . Michael. After this . . ." Herat gazed sadly at the displays. "What will there be after this? This place is a treasure world, for sure. And it's the climax of my career.

The end of a long search. It's funny. After all these years, I'm sorry to see the search end, maybe because I'm old enough to know that it's all downhill from here."

He laughed. "Never mind. Look, maybe the Lasa machinery is supposed to run on its own until someone intervenes. Then it hands control over to the newcomer. It's an instinct of the machine, it's designed that way. So maybe the shutdown means this place is functioning the way it was originally designed to: It won't eat up the resources of new colonists. It will only turn back on when they allow it, which would be when they are not competing with it for resources.

"Or I could be wrong. Anyway, send our observations to the fleet."

Later, when they turned the lights red for a sleep period—their orbit of Apophis would take several days—Michael found his mind whirling on about Rue, about himself, and about Laurent Herat. The last time Herat had acted like this was on the shores of Kadesh. Hard to believe that was over a year ago. At that time, the professor had come face-to-face with his own version of the kami of Dis. His lifelong enthusiastic chase after the alien had turned up worse than nothing. It seemed he had pursued ultimate answers for himself in that search and those answers weren't there. For a while, *Jentry's Envy* had convinced him it could be otherwise, but he was now coming again to face the same reality.

Thinking this made Michael sad and yes, he heard that whisper of the kami, saying *it doesn't matter, nothing matters*. To hold an artifact millions of years old in your hands and realize that every being for whom it had held significance was long extinct—that would rattle anyone who thought about it too long. And Herat had thought about such things his whole life.

This whole place could be a vast machine running senselessly on after the deaths of its creators. The Lasa must be extinct and if Rue Cassels had not stumbled upon *Jentry's Envy*, perhaps no one would ever have found this place. It would have gone on about its ceaseless activity, a kind of guardian of the underworld, of the tomb of interstellar space.

Time swept all away and it would sweep Laurent Herat away soon enough. Also Michael Bequith and all his cares and loves. These thoughts jumbled together in his mind, bringing him a confused, unpleasant melancholy, as he drifted off to sleep.

So they traveled on in their circuit of the giant failed star. All around, as they passed, the Lasa machinery that surrounded Apophis was changing. Over the next days Michael spent hours staring at the cloudscapes of the brown dwarf. Ancient and incredibly cold, they flowed like oil, a spectrum of icy blues visible only under extreme light amplification.

Apophis had been stillborn. It had never attained enough mass to burn hydrogen and so like all brown dwarfs it had glowed in its brief glory by gravity and magnetic forces alone. After billions of years, it had almost exhausted the heat of its birth. Only very rarely did the dwarf's magnetic field pull a twist of energy up through the atmosphere; then, wan arches of light would shimmer above the cloudscapes, only to flicker and collapse, exhausted, after a few minutes.

Nonetheless, bright things moved down in that realm, where flat, viscous thunderheads moved like charging armies across dark plains of dense cloud. Fusion-powered aircraft wove in and out among the starlit thunderheads, like birds at play. And in some places, great dark balloon cities drifted, tethers unreeling for hundreds of kilometers below them to tap the cloud decks. In the telescope, these balloons looked more like ancient battleships than craft of the air; to withstand eighteen gees of gravity, they were buttressed with squat girders and plated with titanium.

Were there windows in those floating fortresses? And did some entity, part of the mechanical ecology of Apophis, pause sometimes to gaze out at the stars?

Every now and then, sun-bright engines would kick into life atop one of those balloon cities. Stark nuclear light brought the gunmetal-blue cloudscapes into sharp relief, somehow making Apophis seem even colder and more alien. The tanker carrying lithium, beryllium and other hard-won treasures would climb laboriously for hours until it rendezvoused with a passing orbital tether.

The orbiting tethers grazed on whatever rose from the depths. They passed cargo packets up and past their orbital centers and flung them off their outermost arms. Each became a little world on its own, negotiating its position with the Twins through the music of gravity. After flying a million kilometers, each and every packet of cargo would arrive at a spot a few meters on a side, there to be caught by another tether in a higher orbit. This one would fling the cargo on its ultimate course, to meet with the invisibly distant construction shack that was the ultimate reason for all this activity.

Now, though, these intricate systems were falling silent. The jets cruised aimlessly. The floating cities withdrew their arms and hung silent. A few last cargo rockets clambered to the top of the atmosphere, but as they fell again they disintegrated in seconds. Stillness spread slowly, but unstoppably across the dark continents of air.

Michael's interceptor brushed the upper atmosphere of Apophis, briefly becoming a meteor before bouncing back into space. They shot silently through a province of motionless tethers and after another day lined up right behind the final cloud of packets heading for the shack. The cloud would act like chaff to the *Banshee*'s radar; they would be invisible until they were almost to the shack.

There was really no preparing for what they might find there. They could only contemplate the world they had come to and, when they slept, let its dark kami whisper in their dreams.

RUE WAS EXERCISING to counteract free-fall weakness when the call came. The message, encrypted and sent by laser, was from the remains of their fleet, which was now spiraling toward the construction shack as unobtrusively as possible.

"Captain, we've got new reconnaissance pictures of the *Banshee*," said the young woman in the inscape window. "We think you should look at them, stat."

Images popped up, familiar at first: the twin balloons of the *Banshee* were now in full bolo configuration, swinging at opposite ends of a long tether. They appeared as twin glowing beads standing out from the long dark cylindrical body of the construction shack. Other photos showed close-ups of the habitats, which had been rounded can-shapes when Rue had ridden in the ship. One was still shaped that way; the other was smaller, spherical now, with a number of gathered bunches of fabric knotted at one end.

They had a catastrophic hull breach, Rue realized as she flipped through the rest of the images. Finally she came to one that showed the ramjet section of the starship. It was lit by six arc-welding torches. The tiny stars shone on long black scars and hairlike bunches of fullerene jutting out of the hull.

The scars were in lines, such as lasers would make. But where between here and the *Envy* could Crisler have gotten into a battle? It didn't make sense—unless Rue's crew had done something?

For a moment her heart leapt at the thought—but she knew the resources they'd had to work with. Unless they attacked the gunnery stations and took over the *Banshee*'s own lasers . . .

Anxiously, she forwarded the images to the other vanguard interceptor. This ship, which contained Mike and

Laurent Herat, was now almost directly behind the construction shack relative to her. They were approaching from opposite sides, according to plan and so far the *Banshee* didn't seem to have noticed. Indeed, the *Banshee* wasn't really scanning, which implied that they felt there was no threat here.

It took several seconds for round-trip messages and she didn't want to risk an open laser link, lest the beam overlap one of the *Banshee*'s sensors. So Rue waited for long minutes while, she presumed, the others pored over the images. Finally Dr. Herat's face popped up in a little window.

"It looks like laser fire. The ship's badly damaged—I don't know if she'd be able to start the ramjet with the condition it's in. If Crisler's not expecting reinforcements, I'd say he's in pretty dire straits at this point. We may not need to fire a shot to take the *Banshee*."

This news should have cheered her, but Rue didn't like not knowing who had crippled Crisler's ship.

Her answer came six hours later, as she was eating. They had just completed a braking maneuver and were lining up for the final deceleration to rendezvous with the construction shack. Rue had an inscape window open over her plate, the shack, now floodlit from the *Banshee*, visible in it.

Suddenly the window went gray and the words SIGNAL LOSS appeared in it. Rue blinked at it in puzzlement for a second. Then she heard a sound like snakes hissing and the interceptor seemed to shudder under her.

The pilot shot past her, cursing loudly. He yanked himself into his seat and now Sola was yelling orders like there'd been a hull breach.

Hull breach! She dove for her own g-bed, waiting for the confirming spike of pain in her ears as pressure dropped. It didn't come, but she felt the ship turning under her. She reached over and punched the tactician's arm. "What's happening?"

"We lost forward sensors. We're flipping over to use the aft set."

"Did we hit something?"

"Don't know . . . no, it wasn't like that." Sola looked a bit gray. "I think it was a laser. The *Banshee* must have spotted us."

"I'm setting up a dusty plasma shield," said the pilot. Rue's window came back on-line, showing a turning starfield. A glowing orange haze appeared and slowly thickened until the stars vanished.

"How am I supposed to see through this?" said Rue.

"Telescope's off-line," muttered the pilot. "Hull registered a two thousand degree temperature spike. Definitely a laser."

"What's the *Banshee* doing?"

Sola had a bunch of windows open. ". . . Nothing," he said, puzzled. "It hasn't varied its radar ping. No movement, no heat signature from weapons fire."

"Incoming transmission," said the pilot. "It's from IR 21." That was Mike's ship.

Doctor Herat appeared again, this time looking flustered. "Rue, we've been fired on! It's not coming from the *Banshee*. It might be an automated system, probably an asteroid defense. It's pretty persistent, we've taken three strong hits already."

She tapped the window to reply. "Find out why! Are we too big or something? I thought we were supposed to register as one of those cargo packets 'cause we're part of the cloud. Why didn't that work?"

The time-delay to Herat's nod was almost imperceptible; they must be close to the shack. "Maybe there's some characteristic of the packets that we—" The window went gray, as the shuddering hiss happened again.

"How much of this can we take?" she asked Sola. He shrugged.

"Probably a lot," he said. "These ships are designed for reentry into a brown dwarf's atmosphere, after all . . ." Another hiss and the lights flickered. "But that's different," he said less certainly.

Herat reappeared. "Captain! The cargo packets are all broadcasting a weak transponder signal. We didn't notice it before because of the interference from the Twins. Each packet seems to be broadcasting a unique signature, but of course we don't speak Lasa so—" *Hiss.*

Now Rue's ears did pop. "Depressure!" shouted the pilot, even as the clamshells folded up over their g-beds and Rue found herself alone in the dark, flickering gray inscape windows her only company. She sat paralyzed for a second, then swept her hands out to open a series of diagnostics, as well as an intercom line to the others.

". . . the hull's intact," the pilot was saying. "But we lost a seal around the airlock. We can grow a new one, but it'll take a few hours. The hull's acting like a lens, concentrating the laser light in a few spots."

"What about the shields? Aren't they working?" she demanded.

"Yeah, they are, or we'd have been vaporized by now."

This is the same battle the Banshee *fought,* she thought. Another hiss came and more indicators turned red.

"—the call signal." Herat had reappeared, his image distorted and full of static. "Our autotroph AI deciphered it. It's a—" the signal cut out for a second. "—manifest. You have to send the following string . . ."

"Are you getting that?" she shouted to the pilot.

"I think so." Silence—she pictured him retransmitting the signal Herat had provided. At least, she hoped that was what was happening.

"We've missed our scheduled burn," he said abruptly. "I'm going to have to expose our engines to the laser in order to decelerate. If I don't we'll overshoot or hit the shack—"

"Just do it," she said. "If this doesn't work, we'll be roasted anyway."

Crushing weight enveloped Rue. She pulled her hand up to close her fingers around the Ediacaran pendant. *You've come this far,* she thought at it. *You can go a little further.*

The burn ended. "Coasting in," said the pilot. "After all

the fireworks, the *Banshee* sees us now. But we're coming in on the opposite side of the shack. It'll take them a while to get someone out to us."

"What about the others?"

"Other ships copying our maneuver. They're okay," said the pilot.

"Get ready to disembark," she said. She wanted to feel relieved that they had survived and were here, but she was out of time. Rue reached into the storage bins under the g-bed and pulled out the components of the army pressure suit they'd fitted for her.

She dressed quickly; as the helmet snapped in place with a satisfying click, Rue looked down at the weapons that dangled from the suit's belt. No time for relief now; no time for fear. Only time to take the most direct route to her crew and woe to anyone who got in her way.

25

RUE STEPPED INTO familiar darkness. The stars surrounded her and for a few moments they were all she saw. It wasn't until she turned around that she made out the black absence that was Apophis and, looking opposite that, saw the corresponding silhouette of Osiris. Her interceptor was gliding away, a ghostly knife-shape. It had dropped off her squad of six and would now take up station near the construction shack. That too became visible as she continued turning; it was much closer than she'd expected, a vast rectangle of darkness that must be only a few kilometers away.

Sola and the rest of the squad were feverishly setting up countermeasures to avoid detection. The interceptor had dropped them off in the middle of a cone-shaped zone of space where the cargo packets coming from the Twins were funneled inward. For a few moments, she and her soldiers would appear as part of the cloud. By the time they left the cone, they must be invisible.

While the soldiers unfurled stealth shields and started spraying a mist of liquid helium around to blot out infrared, Rue turned her attention to the shack. Behind it lay the *Banshee*. Crisler's starship would likely have strewn sensors all around the shack; their arrival on its other side was not so much a sneak as a way to shield the interceptors from attack.

Though not visible, she knew the other interceptor would be arriving as well. Mike and his team would be hanging in space just as she was, preparing to enter the alien structure.

Sola handed Rue a secure comm line and she plugged it into her suit's shoulder. "Good so far," he said. "Insertion as planned?"

"Yes." The squad grouped up, attaching lines to one another, then fired reaction guns to take them over the curve of the shack. Now they would find out if their countermeasures were working. Rue's mouth was dry, but she was surprised at how calm she was, now that they were finally here. She had thought about this moment for months, but in the end, her worries and nightmare scenarios were a distraction. She needed to focus on the moment and only that way would she get through it.

They'd spent a lot of time debating whether to go to the shack first, or the *Banshee*. Her people could be in either place, but were most likely to be aboard the starship. Even if they were somewhere in the shack, the *Banshee* was a better place to make a stand. Crisler could not destroy his own ship to get at them.

There was no sense of movement, of course; the stars were simply rising, slowly and gently, over the short horizon of the shack. After a few minutes something new began to rise: a bauble like a paper lantern. It was the larger of the *Banshee*'s two balloon habitats, swinging on the end of its invisible tether. A kilometer away from it, below the shack's horizon, the smaller habitat would be swinging the other way.

She had only that one glimpse, then Sola raised one of the radar shields and blocked her view. That was okay; Rue didn't need to be reminded of the layout of the *Banshee*. The two six-story balloon habitats had similar internal plans and swung opposite one another from the central axis pod. The heaviest component of the starship in view was a pair of flowerlike assemblies of tungsten plates that petaled out from the cables halfway between the axis and the habitats. At the rotational axis of the system was a can-shaped weapons pod much smaller than the balloons. It held a fusion reactor and various supplies as well as missiles and lasers. Another tether trailed off at right angles from it, ending sixty kilometers away at the ramscoop and engines.

"EVA cart at Long-thirty, Lat-forty," said one of the soldiers. Rue oriented herself and looked in that direction. One of the *Banshee*'s familiar raillike carts came into view; it must have just launched from the starship's axis.

For a tense few seconds nobody breathed as it approached. Rue was peripherally aware of one of her soldiers slowly bringing his laser rifle up to aim at the space-suited figures on the craft.

"No," she said. "They're headed for the shack."

"Agreed," said Sola. "Let them go; they're five less men for us to worry about at the *Banshee*."

They continued to watch as the cart lofted gently over the black surface of the shack and disappeared into the mist of stars beyond.

"They're checking out the interceptor," someone muttered.

"Good," said Rue. "It's supposed to distract them."

They had drifted far out from the shack now and were coming in line with the swiftly rotating habitats of the *Banshee*. Each swept past once per minute, which meant they were traveling at 180 kilometers per hour relative to Rue.

There had been spirited argument about their next maneuver. Like any spaceship, *Banshee* had micrometeor defenses, including automated lasers. Unlike other ships, though, its systems were of truly paranoid power and accuracy. *Banshee* was designed to be able to withstand deliberate attacks by missile and laser weapons. If *Banshee* had been at alert, they would have been spotted and targeted instantly. They could all be vaporized in a second by the ship's countermeasures.

Banshee was also designed to resist being boarded. According to Sola, such a rotating ship was usually designed to detect the sudden addition or subtraction of mass at either end of its tethers. It could literally feel the weight of an arriving man.

Normally one boarded a rotating spacecraft at the center and then moved down an elevator or drop-shaft to the rotating portion. But if Rue's squad were successful in approaching the weapons pod and began rapelling down a tether from there, they would be doing so in full view of the targeting and weapons systems and they would be felt and pinpointed instantly.

The alternative was a much more scary maneuver. For the next few minutes, their lives would depend entirely on the largely untested equipment they'd brought. Rue tried to breathe regularly, watching the tiny screen in her heads-up display. It showed them drifting directly into the path of the swinging habitats. She looked up in time to see the larger one flash past, disturbingly close. She could practically count the oxygen tanks hanging off it. It swept majestically away, arcing up gradually until it was rising vertically, then it was cut off behind Sola's shield. Invisibly behind that shield, the smaller habitat was racing down to meet them.

"Form up," ordered Sola. He took Rue's arm and that of one other man. They put their feet into the loops of a two-meter long cylindrical rocket and clipped their waist tethers to it as well. "Lean back," said Sola. The rocket twisted under them, little jets firing, as it figured out the distribution of their mass.

"Commit," said Sola tersely. The rocket was in control now; this would either work, or they would be dead in seconds.

Rue braced herself as she'd been coached to do. Suddenly the rocket lit and they were surging forward—it felt like *upward*. They'd left the countermeasures behind and here came the habitat. Rue had a strange perceptual moment when she felt as if she were standing on some high peak on Treya; someone had put glowing Erythrion on a chain and was swinging the whole halo world at her.

The habitat seemed to leap at them—then it faltered and stopped, barely meters away. Rue gaped at it. Suddenly the wall of translucent plastic began to rise, as if yanked up by some capricious child god. But by then Sola's man had leapt across the intervening space and slapped a sticky patch to it. Another man had performed the same maneuver from the other rocket.

A tether attached to the patch zipped up with the wall and yanked Rue and Sola and all the others off the rocket. The metal cylinder tumbled away while Rue swung wildly and in gravity now with nothing but stars below her.

A brilliant flash lit the wall, casting a long crazed shadow upward from the dangling soldiers. "They're on to us," said Sola tersely.

"What was that?"

"The rockets. They lasered them."

Rue clung to her thin rope, heart pounding. She was disoriented by the stars spinning past and the odd feeling of looking down at them. She could only watch as two soldiers glued a transparent emergency airlock to the hull. Once it was inflated, they entered it and began lasering a hole through the hull itself.

"Incoming defenders," somebody said. The others raised their weapons; Rue craned her neck up to see things that looked surprisingly like *Jentry's* mining spiders clambering down the side of the habitat. They were having trouble getting around the bunches and folds of material

that had been tied together after the habitat was holed,
days or weeks ago, by the construction shack's lasers. In
surreal silence, the robots glowed and exploded as her men
targeted them.

"We're in." Sola tugged Rue's tether. She looked down
to see two of her men entering the *Banshee* through a
ragged hole in the hull. Glowing flinders plummeted past
her; red-hot droplets splattered on Rue's shoulder, hissed,
and went out. A whole spider fell past, its legs scrambling
and one flailing limb caught Rue's tether. Feeling oddly
detached, she saw the tether part.

She was falling. Rue screamed and reached out, catching Sola's ankle. For a wild second she hung above the
wheeling stars. Bright flashes pulsed below her as the
lasers in the *Banshee*'s weapons pod targeted the falling
spiders. If she let go, she would share their fate.

Then strong hands pulled her up and she flopped over
the resilient lip of the airlock. Sola fell onto her and the airlock gulped closed. In another moment she was being
dragged into bright calm light and landed on all fours on
the familiar decking of a corridor in the *Banshee*.

Rue needed a moment to compose herself. She sat up,
watching her men fan out in either direction. They were in
one of the ring-shaped corridors that ran around the outside of the habitat. About five meters to her right was a T-
intersection; the hallway there would lead to the hub of the
round habitat.

In the other direction the smoothly curving wall was interrupted after a few meters by a tightly wadded and stapled bundle of hull material. The decking and ceiling here
had been cut away and sections of the inner wall removed.
The habitat was basically just a big plastic balloon and
here was a spot where the balloon had been gathered and
twisted to make it smaller.

"Countermeasures," directed Sola. One of the men set a
squat gray cylinder on the floor and flipped a switch on its

side. The solid-looking can hopped, its sides bulging and smoking slightly. Rue heard a series of loud clicks, that seemed to originate *inside* her head.

"What was that?" asked Rue.

"We're using optical networks and coms exclusively," said Sola. "That was an EM bomb. It made a burst of microwaves that should have fried all the electronics in the vicinity. Hopefully it'll shut down their intercoms and sensors."

Somebody had dumped a satchel full of little buglike things onto the floor. They rose on buzzing wings now and swarmed off down the corridor. "Hunt bots," said Barendts.

Rue thought she recognized where she was. "They should look one deck up, northeast quadrant from our position," she said. "There's storage spaces there that could be used as a brig."

"Come on." Sola waved his men into motion. They trotted to the nearby intersection. Before they got there, Sola raised his hand. "Hostiles!" His men crouched back against the walls; a second later, Rue did likewise.

Pure crimson light flashed out of the intersection. She saw one of the little hunt bots twirl, flaming, out of the axial corridor.

Sola pitched a grenade around the corner; Rue was thinking *no that can't possibly be one of the explosive variety*—and then it went off and blue-black smoke poured back. She let out a *whoosh* of relief, though naturally Sola wouldn't have used an explosive in here; the blast could have torn the hull open.

The smoke made normal vision impossible, but her suit's HUD display showed a sketchy view of her surroundings, rendered from laser or sonar. It wasn't an inscape display; she and her men had their inscape temporarily disabled as a precaution against spoofing.

Sola's men were diving and rolling into the side corridor

now and she heard taser fire. She hurried after them on wobbly legs. She had just rounded the corner when somebody swept her legs out from under her and she fell on her back. Bright flashes and the sound of gunfire surrounded her. Rue righted herself and looked ahead—catching confused sonar glimpses of man-shapes wrestling in the smoke. Somebody's discarded taser lay near her and she picked it up before thinking to unholster the one on her belt.

One of the fighting figures went down (others running away from her beyond it) and just at that moment a powerful gust of wind blew through the corridor. The smoke glided away in a single solid mass as though suddenly reminded that it should be somewhere else. Rue sat up.

Two spider robots and three space-suited men lay on the deck. The prone men's suits were all R.E.-issue. Rue's own men were already moving on toward the hub of the corridors.

Rue got to her feet unsteadily. She couldn't help looking down at the faceplate of the man nearest her.

She recognized the face behind the glass. This was a man who had sometimes joined her crew at lunch in the cafeteria. He was quite a joker. Now he was unconscious and turning blue as he tried to breathe.

"Captain!" Barendts was waving at her to hurry up. Rue knelt down and undogged the man's faceplate. Jared, that was his name. As soon as the glass was open he sucked in a deep breath.

"Come on!" She stood indecisively. There was no time to examine the other two. Rue ran after Barendts, feeling sick at what they were having to do.

The others were already going up the spiral staircase at the hub of the four spoke corridors. Rue caught up to them at the top of the stairs. There had originally been two more floors above this one, but now the staircase continued up in its cylinder past two sets of sealed doors. The ceiling visible through the opened doors on Rue's level was bunched and bundled. The walls had been partly dismantled, so that they only rose to head-height now, like partitions.

Rue nodded when she saw this. "If they're on board, they'll be here," she said. "Crisler wouldn't house any of his own people in such a dangerous spot." One pressure leak and the whole level would be in vacuum.

"We lost our hunters," pointed out one of the men. Sola shrugged.

"Search the old-fashioned way, then," he said. "Two men stay here; you two take that way and we'll go this way. Clockwise when you get to the ring corridor." This was Rue's chance to show she had learned her infantry-tactics lessons well; she covered Sola while he ducked through the doorway, then he knelt and waved her through. She ran past to the first door and flattened herself next to it.

The door was shut; Sola ducked past her and she hit the switch then dropped to a crouch. The door snicked open. Sola had it covered and nodded curtly to her. Rue poked her head around the corner.

The odd billowy ceiling made this wedge-shaped room look like it was half-filled by a solidified cloud. It must be cold up here: Icicles hung from the folds of hull fabric. Boxes were stacked around the room's periphery and the single table held two plates with half-eaten meals on them. There were no chairs; but another door beckoned on the far side of the room. Rue eased inside and Sola followed.

This time Rue took up position behind a stack of boxes and Sola went to the door. He was three steps from it when it flew open. A crimson flash caused her faceplate to polarize momentarily; then she saw Sola tumbling backward, his chest smoking. Another flash and the boxes in front of her exploded.

Rue rolled across the floor, firing her taser as she came back to a crouch. Sparks flew around the doorway, then someone leaped through it. The man was in a pressure suit and held an antipersonnel laser.

The laser looked just like the one she'd seen dangling from an arm of the submarine back on Oculus. This might even be the man who'd shot Max.

Rue jumped to one side just as he fired. She fired back, raising another cascade of sparks from the boxes where he now crouched. Even a near miss with the taser might short out his suit's systems, leaving him helpless—but she was having no luck.

Fire engulfed her hand. The taser exploded and the slap against her palm spun Rue around. She fell back against the smoking remains of the table.

He stepped out from behind the boxes, between her and the inner door now. The door opened and another figure dressed in an R.E. suit entered.

He glanced back, then casually took aim at Rue with the laser. She flinched and scarlet light blinded her.

There was no pain. As her faceplate depolarized she saw the man in front of her collapse to his knees and then fall on his face. The back of his suit was a blackened mess.

The soldier who had fired stepped over his body and knelt in front of Rue.

"Are you all right?" The voice was that of a woman. Rue shook her head in confusion.

The soldier reached up and undogged her own faceplate. "It's me, Mina!"

Mina. This was the woman Rebecca had begun seeing when they were aboard the *Envy*. She was one of Crisler's people, but obviously not on his side.

Suddenly Rue understood why Rebecca had left Oculus with Crisler. "She came back for you," she stammered.

"Come on," said Mina. She extended her hand to help Rue to her feet. "I've been managing to swing shifts so I could be with your people," she said. "It paid off, I guess."

Rue stooped to examine Sola. His eyes were open and lifeless.

She forced herself to turn away. With difficulty she

made sense of what Mina had just said to her. "Are they here?" she asked.

"See for yourself." Mina pointed to the inner doorway. She could see two people standing on the other side. Rue ran to the door.

Rebecca and Blair both ran forward when they recognized her. They were alone in this small room. Both began talking at once and Rebecca grabbed onto Rue's gloved hand like a free-faller reaching for a safety line. A hot stab of pain in her hand made Rue pull back. She looked down and realized with a shock that her right glove was burned and fused. Waves of pain were radiating from her hand.

"I've been shot," she heard herself say. She had to keep her priorities, she reminded herself. "Where are Corinna and Evan?"

"They're aboard the cycler mother," said Mina. "Crisler's using them as explorers."

The room was spinning. "Rebecca, my people are outside," Rue said. "Get them . . ." She couldn't manage the rest, as everything blurred and roared together. For a few seconds she was sure she was going to pass out and she sat down heavily on the deck waiting for it. The tide slowly receded and she looked up to see the four remaining members of her squad crowding into the room.

This place had been set up as a prison cell. The walls were cut off near the top, as elsewhere on this level, but here they'd been stapled into the folds of hull material. There were four cots, a small table and a footlocker.

Blair was grimly rummaging through the locker. Rue's men clustered around Sola; he was obviously dead.

Rebecca was crying. "Rue, you're alive," she said. "They told me you'd drowned."

"How did you get here?" asked Blair. He was filling a satchel.

"It's a long story," she said, trying to smile. "Are those your records, Blair?"

He nodded to Rue, looking grimly relieved. "They were

going to wipe it all. All my work." He had recorded everything, from the day they left Erythrion to Rue's discovery
of the Lasa habitat builder at *Jentry's Envy.*

"What do we do about Sola?" asked Barendts sharply.
"Leave him?"

They had discussed this before the mission. Casualties
might have to be left behind; these men were here because
they had accepted that risk. Now that they were in the situation, though, Rue found herself shaking her head.

"We take him as far as we can," she said. "If we have to
abandon him to escape, then that's what we'll do. But I'm
not leaving anyone behind if I don't have to."

"Have you taken over the ship?" asked Rebecca.

"Not yet," she said. "That's next on the agenda."

Mina nodded sagely. "So those are your ships out there."

"Yeah." Rue waved one of her men over. "I'm hurt, can
you give me something?"

All four of them were suddenly looming over her,
scrambling in their belt pouches for analgesic patches.
"Your glove's been wrecked," Barendts pointed out. "We'll
have to seal it."

"Go ahead."

He sprayed the glove with a plastic aerosol that hardened on contact. Meanwhile Rue fumbled her faceplate
open with her other hand and let someone apply a patch to
her forehead, which was the only exposed piece of skin
large enough. She was sure she looked like a dolt now,
with a military-black square on her brow like a little target.
But there was nothing for it and anyway, the pain was receding now like a half-remembered dream.

"Crisler'll have to surrender now," said Mina. She took
Rebecca's hand. "You're sure the halo'll have me?"

"Of course."

"I know you must have taken a cycler to Maenad," said
Mina. "What I can't figure out, though, is how you managed to bring a big enough force with you to be able to take

over Crisler's other ships. And you faked the transmissions perfectly—I mean, you even got the voices and faces right."

Rue and all her men turned to stare at Mina. "What?" said Rue.

"Admiral Crisler relayed the chatter through inscape," said Mina. "Half an hour ago—we watched the video feed from here, from the freighter and the other cruisers . . ." She stopped. "Why are you staring at me like that?"

Rue got to her feet. "What freighter? What cruisers? How many?"

"The . . . the three cruisers. You know, the old decommissioned ones Crisler had refitted and moved to Maenad."

Rue looked at her men. They looked back expectantly.

Sola was gone. It was up to Rue now; she would have to improvise. "Plans have changed. Everybody, get ready to abandon ship. Mina, tell me more about these ships."

Mina looked confused now. "They came out of hyperdrive an hour ago, just twenty thousand klicks away. Like I said, a freighter and three decommissioned cruisers. Crisler managed to get the rights to them after they were liberated from the rebels a couple years ago. They signaled us right away. I thought you must have been aboard them, I mean that you faked out Crisler . . . But if those aren't your ships, where did you come from?"

"Ma'am," said one of the soldiers, "we can't abandon ship. We'll be fried as soon as we leave the hull."

"Maybe not," said Rue. "I have an idea. Anyway, Crisler's got reinforcements coming. If we stay here . . ."

"But our boys will take them out," said the soldier.

Rue checked the time in her suit's HUD. "They appeared much closer to here than we did," she said. "Crisler's ships may reach us before our interceptors reach them. In which case, he's got both us and the construction shack as hostages. No, we've got to get back to our own ship and get out of here."

But we'll go through the shack if we can, she told herself. *I won't leave Corinna and Evan behind if there's any way to get to them.*

TEN MINUTES LATER they crowded into an airlock above the collapsed levels of the habitat. They had encountered no more resistance on their way here; it seemed that Crisler's people were spread out, perhaps mostly in the construction shack. If there was a way to get up past the hub and down to the other habitat without being lasered, they might well have been able to take over the *Banshee*. The hardened defenses of the starship were too strong, though.

Rue undogged the cover over a small quartz window and gawked up through it. "Yeah, there they are. See?" She stepped back and let Barendts look.

"Big black plates," he said. "Halfway up the cables. What the hell are those?"

"Antimatter generators," said Rue. She'd heard all about this stuff from a scientist who'd chatted her up shortly after they embarked for the *Envy*. "The *Banshee* can direct the particle stream coming in from the ramscoop through those tungsten plates. The radiation mostly just heats the plates on the way through, but a tiny fraction gets converted to antimatter and collected with magnets. That way, the *Banshee* can replenish her antimatter supply just by, say, orbiting close around a star and turning on the ramscoop."

"So?" said Barendts. "What's the point?"

"The point is those plates are designed to be put in the way of energy beams. The *Banshee*'s lasers aren't going to get through one."

Barendts nodded. "So if we cut one loose . . ."

"Exactly. Do you think we can get there outside?"

Barendts shook his head. "We'll have to go up the elevator shaft." The shaft was an inflated tunnel that paralleled the cables, joining the habitat to the central hub of the ship.

"All right, let's do it."

They piled out of the airlock. A set of elevator doors faced the airlock in the attic of the habitat. Two of her men set to prying the doors open.

Blair was pacing up and down, trying to get comfortable in his suit. They'd taken suits from the tasered R.E. soldiers for both Blair and Rebecca. Blair's was too small.

Something behind the doors broke and they slid open. Barendts jogged over and stuck a mirror on a pole out into the shaft. He examined it for a few seconds, then said, "There are autoguns in there. Antipersonnel tasers, I think."

"Can we take them out?" she asked. If not, they were stuck here.

"Simplicity itself," said Barendts. He laid the mirror pole down on the deck so that the mirror was inside the shaft, righted it so the mirror pointed upward and unslung his laser rifle. "Guys, come here. Sight off the mirror."

Rue was amazed at their ingenuity: they proceeded to shoot up the shaft by bouncing their shots off the mirror on the pole. The tasers inside the shaft had no way to shoot back, except at the pole itself. Several did just that, sending cascades of sparks back along it. Barendts and his men were standing well back and they ignored the jolts.

Sparks and bits of flaming metal fell down from above. After a minute, smoke drifted down as well. Then there came one of those rushes of air like a god inhaling and the smoke vanished. The pole twirled and would have fallen into the shaft if Barendts hadn't grabbed it. He peered into the mirror for a long while, then said, "That's all of them. Let's go."

Climbing the shaft was simplicity itself. There was a ladder inset into the wall. Barendts and two of his men went first, then Rue, with the others behind her.

The shaft towered up to a seemingly infinite height. It was almost half a kilometer to the hub from here. But as

Rue climbed, her weight lessened and it became easier the farther she went. About halfway up, Barendts said, "Elevator coming."

The other men swore. "What is it?" asked Rebecca. "Reinforcements?"

"Probably," said Barendts. "Captain, may I have your permission to get ugly on this wall here?"

"I thought you were going to put up one of those inflatable airlocks and drill through inside it."

"The elevator would run over it. Yes or no? It's coming!"

"Yes!"

Barendts swung out from the ladder and slammed a disk-shaped charge against the wall of the elevator shaft. It stuck and he swung back. "Everybody hold on!"

The explosion was deafening, even through the suit. The ladder shook and tried to throw Rue off. She held on and looked up again to see smoke swirling and disappearing into a miraculous gale that had sprung up in the shaft.

Above, the elevator car had stopped moving. Rue could see the shapes of hatches in its floor. If those could be opened from the inside, then she and her people were about to be lasered.

"Come on!" shouted Barendts, his voice way too loud in Rue's headphones. He swung out and around again, but this time he was holding onto a line that he'd tied to the ladder. He disappeared into the gale. The man behind him followed an instant later.

There was no time to think. Rue grabbed the line and swung out. The wind caught her instantly and pushed her straight at a ragged black hole in the side of the shaft. She fell sideways out into night.

Barendts had calculated perfectly. As the wind vanished into vacuum around her, Rue fell against the outside of the shaft. Looming over her was one of the petallike tungsten plates. It hid any view of the hub above—so the lasers there could not touch her. One by one the others shot out of the bright tear in the side of the shaft and Barendts's men caught them. When they were all hanging from the lip of the tear—not so hard, since gravity was much reduced here—Barendts clambered up and began gluing handholds to the underside of the plate.

Rue could hear several persons' ragged breathing coming through the com lines. She said, "Everybody up now. We're going to have to use our suits' reaction jets to fly this thing. When Barendts cuts us loose we're going to fall, but coriolis effect will take us away from the habitat. Our main task is to keep the plate from spinning. If we cut loose at the right time we'll be aimed at the horizon of the shack and if we can get over that, we're safe." One after another, they climbed up. "No, don't grab with your hands," said Rue as Mina clutched at one of the new grips on the plate. "Put your feet through them. The plate is going to be our new 'down' when we cut loose. We'll fly it like those guys on Earth used to fly on ocean waves. What did they call it?—surfing."

She demonstrated. Soon they were all hanging feet-down off the plate, with the glowing habitat below and the stars streaming past under that. "Ready," she said to Barendts.

He had attached another charge to the gimbal joint that connected the plate to the shaft. Now he unslung his laser again and prepared to laser the charge.

"Ten, nine, eight, seven . . ." Barendts was counting down. As the *Banshee* slowly spun, he was lining up so that centripetal force would throw them at the shack. ". . . three, two, one—"

He fired the laser and a silent explosion silhouetted him. The plate shook over Rue's feet—but nothing else happened.

"Oh, shit," said Barendts. It hadn't worked.

"Everybody shoot the joint!" shouted Rue. The others unslung their lasers; she saw one rifle fall away; it arced out over the stars for a few seconds before vanishing in a flash of light. Destroyed by the hub lasers.

"Wait," said Barendts, "We have to line up another throw at the shack. We'll miss it if we drop now!"

"Too late!" Rue saw shadows moving inside the ragged hole in the side of the shaft. Whoever had been in the elevator car, they were out now and coming.

Bright spots appeared on the gimbal joint and in a few seconds the metal was flaring intolerably bright. *I hope the joint's not tungsten, too,* she thought.

Without warning they were falling. Everybody seemed to be shouting or screaming, up turned down, the habitat whipped by and the stars were tumbling past—

"Jets forward!" shouted Rue as she brought up her own reaction pistol. She fired and several others did too. The plate wobbled under her feet, the *Banshee*'s cables and shaft came into view and then the hub was peeking over the edge of the plate.

Light flashed and someone screamed. Rue was momentarily shrouded in smoke but she kept her feet braced in the straps and fired her pistol. After several agonizing seconds, the hub crept down over the plate's horizon again. Just as it did, the edge of the plate began glowing dull red, then orange.

"Who did we lose?" asked Barendts.

Silence for a few seconds. Rue looked around, but visibility was limited in her suit and in this dark.

"N-nobody," said Mina finally. "The laser caught my reaction pistol—blew it out of my hands. I've got a little leak in my glove, but nothing I can't seal."

Rue was watching the stars turn. "Jets back," she said. "Two second burst." They all fired and stabilized the plate again.

She could see the construction shack. It was above and to her left, but it was hard to know if they were headed in that direction. The plate they were riding was massive; she doubted if they could change its trajectory easily.

The metal under her feet glowed again, then faded. At least it looked like the plate would hold.

There was a long silence, as it sank in that they ha͏̱
now anyway, escaped. Then Blair's dry voice filled Rue͏̱
head.

"Well, Captain, this may not be the best ship I've crewed
for you, but right now I wouldn't trade it for anything."

26

MICHAEL GRABBED THE autotroph canister by its handles,
peering momentarily through its little window at the spiral-
shaped thing inside. "You asked to be here, here you are,"
he said to it. Then he hauled it to the airlock and cycled
through. The others were already outside, preparing to
jump off the interceptor as they approached the construction shack.

The only light source outside was the stars, but the shack
glowed in infrared and his suit helmet translated that into
an image. The shack was huge and its quilted surface un-
dulated slightly in places, like the fabric of a hotter-than-
air balloon Michael had once seen on Kimpurusha.

"It's that ferrofluid again," said Herat. "These Lasa are
nothing if not consistent." Likely there was no solid hull
under that liquid, only a moveable matrix of powerful
magnets. The shack's size and shape were a matter of con-
venience. Right now, it was a cylinder over a kilometer
long and almost half that in thickness.

They slid behind the shack relative to the *Banshee*; as its
glowing habitats vanished behind the horizon of the shack,
their pilot said, "Fire," and the rail-shaped cart they hung
onto pulled away from the interceptor. Michael had little
sense of movement unless he turned to watch the interceptor depart.

Harp, their squad leader, pointed back along the surface
of the shack. "I can see Captain Cassels's group. They're
headed for the *Banshee*."

The cart drifted to a stop a meter from the shack.

Michael switched off the infrared view and turned on his helmet light. The ferrofluid was a dull black, and until he reached to touch it, he wasn't sure he was seeing it. The surface indented slightly under his touch, but he couldn't penetrate it with his glove.

"No surprise we can't get through here," said Harp. "They'd want to control the placement of doors. Where's that photomosaic, Professor?"

Michael waited while they located an airlock. He was scared, in a completely different way than he was used to. This alien artifact was potentially more dangerous than any he and Herat had investigated—but the chief danger here was Man, not the alien.

Still, he told himself, *this is what I've been waiting for.* Ever since Kimpurusha, he had been wandering, waiting to come full circle. Now, finally, he had his chance to strike at the conquerors of his home. This time he would get it right.

Harp drew them over the curve of the shack to where one of the Lasa's distinctive airlocks sat nested in the spiky black skin of the shack. The soldier unclipped a hunt bot from his belt and pushed it through the resilient liquid. Michael tried to open an inscape window to it by habit; of course that didn't work in this military situation. He brought up his HUD and peered at the tiny image it projected ahead of him.

The inside of the shack was mostly one open space, lit by red laser light. For a moment Michael thought he was looking at some kind of computer-generated cartoon, however, because the interior of the place was overlaid with layers of ghostly image. Three dimensional ghosts shimmered as the hunt bot moved from its position by the airlock. It was as if some ectoplasm had been shaped into the cylinders and planes of giant machines, all faint and trembling. Through these vast ghosts moved tiny objects similar to the hunt bot.

"No hostiles visible," said the soldier who was piloting the bot. "Shall we go through, sir?"

"Standard penetration maneuver," said Harp. Two of the soldiers flipped through the lock, then Harp and the last soldier. Without comment, Herat followed. Michael grabbed the autotroph's canister and was the last through.

Now he saw with his own eyes what the bot had reported. He could see all the way across to the other side of the shack, but hazily, as though a giant hologram were projected inside the shack. The hologram of a colossal, intricate machine . . .

As he watched, one of those little Lasa bots swept by, not four meters away. As it passed, the contours of a half-visible girder swayed, and seemed to gain solidity.

"What . . . ?" He appealed to Herat. The professor chuckled in delight.

"You've never seen the inside of a three-d printer before, have you, Bequith? I believe we're looking at a new cycler, or part of one. It isn't being built, so much as *condensed* atom by atom. The bots used a combination of magnets, laser holography and vapor deposition to create the entire thing as a single object. Incredible."

He couldn't tear his eyes away from the sight. Over the weeks or months, the elemental material harvested from the Twins would be breathed into this space and manipulated by subtle forces to come to rest here, there; to join with neighbors to become solid, or form the boundary of such a solid. The whole cycler was a single thing, so much more tightly integrated than humanity's modular machinery that its structure rivaled the organic.

Or exceeded it . . .

"There's air," said a soldier. "Not great, though, and low-pressure. A mix of helium, hydrogen, and oxygen."

"Keep helmets on," said Harp. "Which way, Professor?"

"Um?" Herat too had been staring. "Ah. To our left, I believe. I think there's another chamber there." Where he pointed, blackness shimmered beyond the phantom machinery. Another wall of ferromagnetic liquid? They drifted in that direction, hunt bots roving ahead.

"I still don't understand what they're building here," Herat muttered. Michael didn't take the verbal bait; he was too busy trying to keep his flight straight while hauling along the autotroph canister.

"I mean, the tethers around Osiris and Apophis won't produce enough power to launch a cycler," the professor went on. "So then, what is this?" He gestured at the slowly coalescing machinery in the center of the shack.

"A colony," somebody else said. Michael was startled at the thought—but maybe it was true.

"They might have spent most of their energy to launch the *Envy*, and then this is being provided as a home for whomever the *Envy* manages to find on its ring," Michael suggested.

"Halt," said Harp. They were approaching the wall that separated this half of the shack from the rest. Michael could see circular airlocks at regular intervals around the wall. The rest was ribbed and spiked ferrofluid, all conforming to the invisible shapes of the magnetic fields that held it in place.

He knew there were no living beings here, unless the other half of this structure held habitats. If it did, this would be the only settled spot in the Twins' system, which made no sense.

The hunt bots reported no human presence here, not even that of other bots. Crisler's people must have decided to leave this gestation chamber to do its work without interference. That was a lucky break.

They sailed up to one of the airlocks, and Harp repeated the procedure of sending a bot through it first. Michael was nervous—expecting at any moment that some trap of Crisler's would be sprung on them. Nothing happened, and the bot proceeded to beam back pictures of the new space.

The second half of the shack was a single large space, like the first. But while the first contained only the ghostly shadows of machines materializing, here the objects were fully made. The entire space was crammed with a giant, bulbous, and somehow insectile thing. It was vaguely egg-shaped, Michael thought, with circular holes in the end closest to the bot. Those could be weapons . . . or engines.

The entire white skin of the thing was covered in intricate, multicolored lines of text—but not, Michael realized with a shock, the spiky red writing of the Lasa.

"That's Chicxulub," said Herat. Michael could hear disbelief in the older man's voice, an echo to what Michael himself felt.

"It *is* a cycler," Michael said doubtfully.

"It can't be," insisted Herat. "Look at it, it must be incredibly massive—built with all kinds of unnecessary metal plating and girders . . ."

"It's a drop ship!" exclaimed Harp. "Like our interceptors."

"No . . . Too delicate for that. And way too big. I have no idea what it is," Herat concluded. Normally mysteries excited him, but he seemed more uneasy than pleased at this particular one. "But if not Lasa . . ."

Michael laboriously turned the autotroph canister until the little window pointed toward the cycler-or-whatever. "Translate that," he instructed the autotroph being.

The bulk of the giant machine obscured whatever else might be in the chamber. Harp took them through the airlock cautiously, but so far there was no sign of hostiles. But as the hunt bots shot away to explore, Michael spotted something far down along the curve of the ship. "White light," he said to Harp, pointing. "There."

Harp deployed countermeasures, and they began crawling slowly along the inside wall of the chamber, flat invisibility shields held overhead. Gradually, the source of the white illumination revealed itself.

Here was Crisler's base of operations. Two small balloon-habitats had been inflated inside the shack, one against its outside wall, and one half-encircling the nose of the giant machine—which Michael stubbornly decided must be a cycler, regardless of what Herat said. The habitats were a patchwork of white, made of the same stuff as the *Banshee*'s habs. In several places each was transparent; Michael recognized the material the soldiers used for temporary bubble airlocks.

The habitat attached to the shack wall was small, probably subdivided into no more than two rooms. The one encircling the cycler's nose was much larger; it looked like it held as much volume as two floors of the *Banshee*'s habs.

"Guards visible," said one of the hunt bots. "Cameras on habs."

"Seen." Harp gestured to two of his men. "Auto-aim on the bot's signal. Get ready to take out those cameras."

"Whatever you do, don't hit the artifact," said Herat.

Michael had to laugh. "Have you deciphered the writing yet?" he asked the autotroph.

"That which I have seen," it said. "There is much that is not visible from this point. I must be allowed to circle the vessel—"

"Not now—" Michael forgot whatever else he'd been about to say. He was looking in the direction of the habs, and had noticed a change in the white glow coming through the plastic.

"Sir," he said, "parts of the hab are *pulsing*. Pulsing red."

Harp cursed. "It's an alert! They've seen us. No more time for subtlety, boys. Fire."

"Wait!" shouted the professor. "Maybe it's not us they spotted, but Rue's party."

At that moment they lost the feed from the lead hunt bot. Michael looked around his shield, to behold a very strange sight. Where a moment ago the air within the cavernous space of the shack had been empty, now a long line of tiny glowing beads lay strung between the balloon-hab on the shack's wall, and the mangled smoking wreck of the bot a hundred meters closer. In the second or so Michael stared, he saw some of the little beads vanish, while others seemed to split in two, or begin to drift.

"Behind your shield, Bequith, that was a laser shot!"

shouted Harp. A moment later the black hull material next to Michael exploded into vapor before splashing back to heal itself. "We're under fire! Infrared lasers! Target and fire, men!"

Around him, Harp's men popped up to shoot, then retreated behind their shields. The shields began to smoke and shake, but there was no sound, and nothing to see—except, when Michael looked down by his foot, where that second shot had hit the hull he saw a little constellation of glowing blue spheres, none bigger than his thumbnail. They drifted, serene and self-contained, like newborn stars.

Fire. He was seeing fire. The laser shots were igniting the hydrogen/oxygen mix that filled the shack. But what would have become a Hindenberg-class inferno under gravity behaved quite differently here.

His shield warped; he felt the heat through his gloves. Michael felt a surge of fear and adrenaline as it finally hit home the kinds of energies that were aimed at him. He drew his laser and cleared a window in his shield to shoot through. He had been dreaming for months of what his first combat against the R.E. would be like; now that it was here his mind was fixed only on the moment.

Behind him, the autotroph being was speaking, but he had no time to listen as glistening, mirror-clad men began flipping into the air from the balloon-habs, and more threads of flaming air converged on him.

"PREPARE TO ABANDON ship," said Rue. The tungsten plate under her feet was glowing hot in places, and its edges had become ragged from laser fire. The constant battering by the *Banshee*'s laser defense system had knocked the plate past the construction shack, and Rue had gotten her people to focus their hand jets on firing tangentially to their course. The trick had worked; the construction shack was eclipsing the *Banshee*. After a last few agonizing seconds, the lasers of the *Banshee* vanished behind the black curve of the shack, and they were safe.

"Everybody kick off," she said. "Head for the shack." They dove for it: Rue, Rebecca, Mina, Blair, Barendts, and the three remaining soldiers. One of them was waving his sensors at the black hull.

"I read energy discharges," he said. "A firefight, looks like."

"Any way to tell who's who?" she asked.

"One group is small, appears to be pinned down by one wall. The other group is near the airlock where we saw a bunch of men headed earlier."

The shack was just a big blot to Rue. "Which is closer?" she asked.

"We're equidistant. But we need to get to an airlock anyway, Captain."

"No, we don't." Rue sighted along the quilted surface of the shack. The material's bubblelike surface clearly showed the patterns of magnets that underlaid it. "Target your lasers on the exact center of the dome of hull material directly ahead of us. We'll make ourselves an airlock there."

"Ma'am?"

"Just do it!"

She couldn't see the beams, but four glowing spots appeared on the hull, quickly converging into one. Then suddenly the hull wasn't there anymore. In its place a blast of black droplets was spewing into space, revealing a three-meter hole in the shack's hull.

"Quick! Before it heals itself!" She jetted through the black rain and found herself in a vast space lit by red light and galaxies of little blue stars. Air was rushing around her, trying to push Rue back through the gap, and spiraling with it came thousands of those little stars. She and Jentry had played with flames like this when she was young and she knew what was about to happen: As the beads were sucked into the moving air they merged and became tongues of fire. For a few moments Rue was licked by a passing inferno.

Her people were through, and just in time as the array of magnets supporting the hull shifted and the ferrofluid reached out to close the wound they'd made. The long tongue of flame halted, became a large irregular ball shape, then died from the inside out. Its outermost skin fractured into hundreds of tiny beads, which began drifting away as if nothing had happened.

New lines of stars appeared—one, two, four, all lancing through the space around her. Rue and her people were floating, vulnerable, in the crossfire of a battle.

"Where?" shouted Barendts. "What the hell is all this?"

The swirling clouds of firebeads made it hard to see, which was probably good just now, she thought. One thing Rue did make out was a standard balloon-hab, attached to some kind of very large machine dead ahead. "Make for that!" She jetted toward it.

One of the marines screamed as his suit jetted white fire. Barendts whirled and fired back along the telltale line of firebeads joining the dying man to a blurry figure near a balloon-hab attached to the shack's hull. He was rewarded with a jet of fire at that end. "We're dead unless we get inside now!" he shouted.

Rue reached for the white surface of the balloon-hab. No time for niceties this time: She shot the material with her laser, burning a long ragged tear in it. Despite the pain in her hand, she used her gloves to force the tear in. Pushing against the air that was coming out, she climbed through.

Big flapping white sheets were flying at her. She dove to the side, cursing, and dragged at the things to keep them from covering the breach. Balloon-habs were a bit too efficient at sealing leaks, sometimes. The others clambered through her hole one after the other, then rolled out of the way while the white panels slammed against it and glued themselves into an uneven patchwork.

"This—this is the new ship," panted Mina. "They've attached this hab to the nose of the new cycler as a place for the crew during takeoff. The theory is that once the cycler's at speed it'll calve off a bunch of its own habs, the way *Jentry's Envy* did. At that point they'll have it make up a human-friendly one, like you did. Then they can move out of the habs."

They hung in a small pie-slice of a larger doughnut-shaped structure. This chamber was crammed with crates of supplies. "Who's *they*?" asked Rue, eyeing the lack of space. "Crisler can't be moving the whole *Banshee* crew in here."

"Some of the science team, and marines loyal to Crisler," Mina said. "He'd be returning on the *Banshee* with the real prize."

"Real prize?" Rue gestured around to indicate the whole vessel they had come to. "This isn't it?"

"No. There's something else—but I don't know what it is. Only that it's small enough to be carried by one person."

"We'll worry about that later," Rue said. "If Corinna and Evan are here, we have to find them." She pointed to a pressure door that separated this tiny room from the rest of the hab. "We go through that. Now."

THERE WERE A good ten of Crisler's marines hunkered down next to their balloon airlock on the far side of the shack. Even with the nose of the cycler between them, there was little cover here. Michael was wreathed in a gas of bubbling black ferrofluid; laser shots had half destroyed his shield and he had several burns on his suit. Both sides were laying down a covering fire to prevent the other from getting out of sight behind the cycler.

"*The ancient pact is turned on its head,*" said the autotroph. It must have completed translating the rest of the Chicxulub script covering the outside of the ship.

"What have you learned?" Herat asked it.

"Professor, this is hardly the time," said Michael incredulously. Their little squad was outmanned and outgunned, and Crisler's men might get reinforcements through the airlock at any moment.

"No better time," said the professor. "Now, tell us what those inscriptions say."

> *"The ancient pact is turned on its head*
> *The hermit who carries the lamp now hands it on*
> *The god who devours his children comes now for*
> *those who sought to defy him."*

"Ancient pact? Hrm, don't know about that," said Herat. "But the hermit who carries the lamp? Lamp Bearers? It's talking about the Lasa!"

"Fascinating, professor, but—"

"Whoa, what's that?" shouted one of the soldiers. Michael peeked out from behind his shield, in time to see several space-suited figures explode through the shack's wall, to the accompaniment of gouts of fire.

"It's our boys, back from the *Banshee*!" One of the newcomers took a direct hit from a laser, flailed, and went still. "Give 'em cover, men!" shouted Harp. They all began shooting.

Michael didn't fire. He was too busy puzzling out what had just happened. Somehow, they'd targeted one of the magnets holding up the ferrofluid. As he watched, the lattice of magnets rearranged itself, and the whip of fire that had been exiting into space choked as the wall reappeared.

"That's it!" He leaned out, and aimed carefully—not at the mirrored shields of the marines that the others were targeting, but at a square black block several meters above them. Though his heart was pounding and he was sure he would be hit at any second, he waited until he was sure he had the shot, then pulled the trigger.

The magnet unit flared and exploded. Instantly, the ferrofluid wall behind Crisler's marines bubbled out and exploded. With a visible *whoosh* of firebeads and flame, they all went spiralling out into space.

"Good work, Bequith," shouted Harp. "But they'll just come right back through the airlock."

"Not if we mine it," he said. Without a word, one of the soldiers took a smart grenade from his belt, programmed it, and threw it in a perfect free-fall straight-throw. Moments later it reached the purple airlock disk, and stuck.

"They can still come through the wall like Captain Cassels did," said Harp. "So move it! We need to secure the habs on that cycler!"

They dove through constellations of firebeads, and now Michael allowed himself an instant to appreciate what he was seeing. It was as if he had become a giant, flying through the stars, batting suns out of the way with the back of his glove. The blue sparks seemed to have become more intense in the past few moments, indeed they were floating alone in a new velvet darkness . . .

"Hey," he said. "Anybody else notice that the lights have gone out?"

He flew on through a vision of stars, as in his ear, the words of the Chicxulub whispered:

> *"The sword we forged has turned upon us*
> *Only now, at the end of all things do we see*
> *The lamp-bearer dies, only the lamp burns on."*

Rather than go through the door, Barendts had gone around it, tearing a long rip in the flexible wall material. He'd tossed a bot through that, and a moment later signalled all clear. Rue stepped through after him.

This room was larger than the last, but equally crowded. Floor, walls, and ceiling had coffin-shaped hibernation chambers clamped to them, the only open space a kind of tunnel through them. Even here, pieces of equipment floated, tethered by cables to the walls.

A face popped up from behind one of the coffins. It was the senior member of the science team, Katz. He looked wan and nervous. It would only take a few laser shots through the hull to evacuate the place, and kill him.

"Who the hell are you?" he demanded. He'd have a hard time seeing Rue's own face through her helmet, and probably wouldn't have recognized Barendts. She decided to take a chance: Clumsily with her one usable hand, Rue undogged her faceplate and levered herself past Barendts.

"It's me, Professor. Rue Cassels."

The flight of emotions across Katz's face was amazing and gratifying. "Captain," he managed to stutter after a moment, "how did you get here?"

"Rue?" Two more faces emerged from behind the hibernation tanks, and this time Rue's own face must have betrayed her; Evan Laurel and Corinna Chandra bounded over, laughing with amazement.

"Is this a rescue?" Corinna asked incredulously. Rue could only nod. Corinna hugged her tightly, tears starting in her eyes.

"But how?" muttered Katz, as he drifted to the side. Now other people were emerging from hiding: It looked as though the whole *Banshee* science team was here, and they all looked as stunned as Katz at Rue's arrival.

"So much for the halo-worlders being backward," said Evan proudly. "But really, Captain, how did—"

"Later," she said. "We need to get out of here. Where are your suits?"

"The marines in the next section have them," said Katz, nodding through the tunnel of coffins. "They stuffed us in here a few minutes ago, no explanations. We didn't have a window to look out, but we saw a couple of flashes—"

"Okay," said Rue. "We need those suits, so we need to get into that chamber. That means all of you get back into the storage room behind us, now! We don't want you caught here if the pressure goes."

They crowded past her, and Rue led her men forward. There was another stout pressure door at the end of the hibernation chamber.

"So," said Barendts, "how do we handle this one? Straight through, or stealthy?"

"I think we . . ." She forgot what she was going to say, as the pressure door slid open. Rue found herself diving behind one of the hibernation chambers, like everybody else.

Three of Crisler's marines emerged, one by one, into the chamber. They all had their hands up, gloves pressed against the sides of their helmets. There were no weapons in their belt loops.

Rue relaxed and straightened up from her hiding place. "Good work, Lieutenant . . . Harp, is it?"

The men from Michael Bequith's team filed in after their prisoners. Mike himself was there, and safe, though his shield and the autotroph canister he towed were a bit laser-scarred. Rue couldn't help but grin at the sight.

"All safe and accounted for, I see," she said. "We were . . . not so lucky. We lost two."

"There's still a squad of Crisler's boys out there," said Harp. "They'll be closing in on us right now."

"But we have hostages," she pointed out.

"With respect, ma'am, we had no trouble breaking in here and capturing these men. Why should it be harder for them?"

"Because these fellows weren't expecting us," she said. "They had no idea who was attacking, or what we were after."

She turned to wave at Katz, who was peering through the slit in the far wall. "Everybody come and get your suits! Then we're getting out of here."

"May I be so bold as to ask who is getting out of here?" asked Katz as he pulled himself through the maze of coffin-shapes. "Have you come to rescue all of us, Captain, or just your crew members?"

Rue frowned at him. "I wasn't aware that you needed rescuing, Professor. You joined this expedition of your own free will."

Katz shook his head angrily. "None of us are here by choice, Captain—not any longer. Once we learned what happened on Oculus, there was a general revolt. Crisler had us all put into cold storage, and we were only awakened a few days ago, then put to work building this." He waved around at the balloon-hab.

Now that she had her people, Rue's plan had been to call the interceptors. They would be able to pierce the shack's ferrofluid hull easily, and come alongside the hab. Each could hold two or three extra people during normal flight—but Katz's staff numbered fourteen. There was no way they could pack them all into the two interceptors that were here.

"Pardon, Captain, but we've fulfilled our mission," said Harp. "These people are under no threat from the admiral. We can negotiate for their release later."

Rue looked around at the faces of the science team. She saw a lot of apprehension there. "I disagree," she said. "I think these people are pawns now that Crisler has what he wants. I think," she said to Harp, "that now might be the best time to negotiate—while we have everything he wants."

Harp scowled, and seemed to be about to say something; Mike Bequith moved forward and said, "There's a defensible point in here that looks as though it was set up as a command post; maybe it's time to make a call?"

She found herself smiling at him. "Show me this spot."

The next chamber had an airlock, and numerous lockers that the science team now proceeded to plunder for their suits. The inner wall of the chamber was not made of the ubiquitous white plastic of the other surfaces, though. It was white metal, glistening like it had been oiled. Scrawled across it in eye-hurting colors were the odd loops and dots of Chicxulub writing. And in the center of the wall was a purple disk-airlock.

"Chicxulub," said Rue. "Not Lasa writing?"

Mike shook his head grimly. "We may have been mistaken about the origin of the *Envy*," he said. "This writing covers the entire outside of the ship."

"What does it say?"

"It doesn't make much—" Mike started to say—but the autotroph interrupted him.

"Only the Phoenix persists," it said.

There was a momentary silence; even the members of the science team who had been cramming themselves into their suits stopped to look over.

"Well," said Rue. ". . . where does this lead?" She pointed to the airlock.

"Come," said Harp. He entered, and she followed. She noticed that Mike was right behind her.

The airlock led to a large spherical chamber, reminiscent to Rue of the interior of the Lasa habitat on the *Envy*—or, she thought now, what she had taken to be Lasa at the time. An inscape unit had been set up here, and Rue was about to activate her inscape link when she saw something else. Near one side of the white metal space floated a very familiar object: a round, diaphanous chamber similar to the one she had crafted to control the *Envy*. The chamber was pulsing blue right now, and various holographic vectors were interpenetrating it, like the petals of a ghostly flower.

"You guys built an interface," she said as Katz and the others crowded in behind her. "I'm impressed."

"Well," smirked Katz as he moved beside her, "you bragged about how you did it enough times that we knew what to . . . do . . ." He was staring at the glowing sphere in shock.

"It's come alive," he muttered. "What . . ." He reached out to touch the wall of the sphere; Rue did likewise, and felt a faint vibration through her glove.

"What's happening?" asked Rue.

"I don't know, but if I had to hazard a guess, I'd say that all the fighting outside has woken this lady up."

"Then we'd better get out of here." Rue popped up her private inscape and keyed in the command sequence that would summon the interceptors. Before she could execute the order, though, Barendts came flying through the airlock and tumbled through space, trying to maintain his aim on the purple disk. Others of the science team were leaping and scrambling through after him; there was pandemonium in Rue's earphones.

"What's going on!"

"—Attacking!" Barendts stabilized himself against a large egg-shaped object that jutted out of the chamber's wall. He kept his laser aimed at the airlock. "There were too many—and the civilians were in the way . . ."

Rue took quick stock of her people: They were all here, plus most of the science team. She looked back at the airlock, in time to see a bare hand thrust through the surface. The hand was waving frantically, as if in warning.

Slowly, the rest of a female member of the science team emerged through the lock. As her head broke the surface of the ferrofluid, it became clear that there was a laser rifle butted up against her jaw. Her eyes were wide with fear.

Several other human shields appeared, and behind them, marines from the *Banshee*. "Lay down your weapons!" commanded one. "We have more hostages in the other room, and we'll kill them one by one unless you surrender."

Barendts and Harp looked to Rue. She made her face into a neutral mask to hide her outrage, and nodded to them. Reluctantly, they and the other soldiers let go of their weapons.

The marines holding the hostages moved aside to let another figure through the airlock. This man steadied himself against the edge of the lock, faced in Rue's direction, and depolarized his helmet to show his face.

"Hello, Captain Cassels," said Admiral Crisler. He was smiling. "I don't know how you managed to get here, but

now that you are I'm sure you'll have plenty of time to explain it all to me." More marines entered the chamber, and
he gestured to them to take the weapons from Rue's men.

27

RUE STEELED HERSELF. She would not flinch away from
this man; he was not Jentry and she was not a helpless child
anymore. "Admiral Crisler, I was just about to call you."

He smiled ironically. "Considering your situation, I believe you." He shook his head. "I honestly admit, I'm
amazed to see you. How did you manage to follow us
here?"

Rue had been ready for that question. "Living in the
halo worlds, we've had to spend a lot more time and re-
source building slower-than-light ships than you. It was
easy to fix up a couple of rendezvous ships with antimatter
rockets; after the beams launched you back to the cycler,
we had them launch us. We used the antimatter rockets to
decelerate down here, and we have another set ready to
boost us out."

"A desperate gamble," Crisler said, his eyebrows raised.

"Not really. Because of *why* we're here . . . it's simply
that I came to get my people," she said. "As you see I have
found them." She gestured around at her crew. "Looking at
the state of the *Banshee*, and the number of berths on
this new cycler, it doesn't look like you've got enough
room for them anyway. Why not let me take them off your
hands?"

Crisler looked surprised, then laughed. "A tempting offer—if I believed you about why you're here, which I
don't. Or rather, I know you came for your crew, but what
about them?" He pointed at Mike and the professor.
"You've arrived with soldiers and scientists, just like I did.
I doubt your little expedition's as small as you make it out

to be. Regardless of what you want, I'm sure these people want the cycler mother."

"The what?" asked Herat.

Katz hung his head. "Self-reproducing starship technology. It's what we suspected we'd find here. When we got here and saw this place, we knew: *Jentry's Envy* was not made by the Lasa. It's a Chicxulub ship."

Crisler nodded. "Renegade Chicxulub—who would have thought? Katz here tells me that the Chicxulub were wiped out by their own planet-killers. But apparently not all the Chicxulub were loyal to the extermination program to begin with. There was some kind of splinter group toward the end, and they adopted the goals of the Lasa. They made the cycler mothers, and so here we are." He frowned suddenly at the glowing control sphere. "Katz, why is that thing on?"

"Sir, it seems to have come on by itself. The gunfire, maybe . . ."

"Well, shut it down." Katz obediently slipped into the control sphere, and began gesturing at the holographic spires and disks inside it. After a few moments he emerged, shaking his head. "Some kind of sequence has started. I can't shut it down."

"Get inscape going," snapped Crisler. "I want to see what's happening here."

Rue switched her inscape implants to receive, and watched as windows blossomed throughout the sphere. As this was happening, she noted Herat moving over next to Katz, and Mike going the opposite way, towing the autotroph canister. Crisler's men had examined it then given it back to him after deciding it wasn't a weapon.

"So what's a cycler mother?" asked Herat casually.

"This place," Katz said. Seeing that Rue was listening, he said, "All human societies have outlawed self-reproducing machines. You know the disasters that happened the few times the things were made—ecological catastrophes, nanotech-based diseases . . . Most other sentient species also ban them. But not the Chicxulub. They raised their creation to a fine art. All the machinery around Osiris and Apophis is part of a full-grown cycler mother— a machine that gives birth to cyclers."

"This is all very well," said Rue to Crisler, "but it doesn't get you very much, does it? Your cycler mother is stuck around a pair of brown dwarfs. How are you going to adapt it to launch FTL starships? I take it that's your plan."

Katz looked mournful. "He doesn't have to adapt it. He can just take—"

"That will be enough, Professor," said Crisler. He turned to look at an inscape window that showed stars. He frowned, and waved a hand to adjust the picture. "I thought this camera was mounted on the outside of the cycler?"

Katz glanced over. "It is." He did a double take. "Oh, that must be the fires you see . . ." No, those tiny pinpricks were not the luminous blue dots of the ongoing fire, but the real firmament.

"Get a bot out there!" shouted Crisler. "What's happening?" Meanwhile, he gestured to swivel the view in the window he did have open. Not surprisingly, after a moment the *Banshee* came into view.

Crisler popped open another window. "*Banshee*, answer! What's happening to the shack?"

"S-Sir . . . We were watching the other ships coming in, it must have just happened—"

A new window appeared, either from the bot's perspective, or the *Banshee*'s. Rue could see the long black cylindrical shape of the shack. It appeared normal except at one end, which was flattened, belling outward a bit even. And extruding through the ferrofluid was the nose of the cycler. As she watched, the balloon-habs emerged.

"It looks like we're launching," said Herat with a smirk. "Unplanned, I take it?"

"Shut up," said Crisler. "You, and you! Take one of the seeds back to the *Banshee*. We can't afford to risk keeping them all in one place."

Some marines began levering one of the two large egg-shaped objects out of its socket in the wall of the chamber. As they did Herat turned to Katz, eyes wide. "Did he just call those . . ."

Katz nodded unhappily. "Cycler mother seeds. We think so, anyway. Each one can regrow a complete construction system like this. These are the real treasure here."

"Well, it seems that we're out of time," said Crisler briskly. "I don't understand what you hoped to achieve here, Rue, with this little band of pirates. But as you can see, our cycler's launching, and so we've got to get her crew secure, and get ready to follow in the *Banshee*. The newly arrived ships will remain to study the cycler mother.

"But as to you . . ." He scowled at Rue. "You're quite right that we don't have the resources to support you. Nor can we let you escape with word of what we found here." He nodded to two more marines. "Escort Rue and her people outside, and kill them."

"Admiral, this is insane!" Katz pushed forward, his face red. "It's murder!"

"Dr. Katz, you still have some limited usefulness," said Crisler coldly. "Unless you'd like to join your friends outside, you'll keep silent and do your job."

Rue's heart was pounding, but somehow she didn't feel fear—just fury. She looked around at the people in the sphere. The scientific team were cowed, all pressed back against the walls as Rue's crew reluctantly drifted forward.

Then Mike Bequith caught her eye. He jerked his head almost imperceptibly toward the inscape screen that showed the shack. Then he winked and reached behind him.

Behind him was the canister containing the autotroph life-forms.

She had no idea what he was planning; anything they did now was just likely to get them killed. But Rue looked Mike in the eye, and he looked right back. That mysterious smile he sometimes got was hovering around his mouth.

Rue looked at the inscape window, and her heart leapt as she saw what he'd been indicating: two smudged absences of stars hung there. They would be easy to miss unless you knew they were there.

Rue caught Mike's eye and shook her head very slightly; then, using her link, Rue issued a command to the interceptors. Mike looked incredulous. He frowned and nodded back at the autotroph canister. She shook her head again.

The two marines carrying the seed were blocking the exit to the chamber. People's eyes were momentarily on them, so no one but Rue noticed as two sleek gray shapes shot out of the black smoke in which they'd been hiding, like Earth squids leaving clouds of ink. Here they came, looming closer and larger, she could see the Lasa writing on them—

"Admiral!" It was the *Banshee* calling. "What the hell— are those part of the cycler?"

"Admiral," cried Rue confidently, "I think you should look to your ship."

Crisler whirled to look at the inscape window. He was just in time to see two spindle-shapes, glowing brightly from the *Banshee*'s lasers, smack into the axis assembly of the starship. Amazingly, the interceptors *bounced*, tumbling unhurt away from the wreckage before each regained its poise. Then as one they turned their antimatter beams on the damaged core of Crisler's ship, and the flash of light overwhelmed the camera. The inscape window went black.

"Perhaps it's time to talk terms," said Rue in the most self-assured voice she could muster. Out of the corner of her eye, she saw Mike Bequith's eyebrows shoot up, then he smiled dazzlingly at her.

"Captain Cassels," Crisler said in a tired voice, "were those your ships?"

"Indeed they were, Admiral," she replied. "But not *all* of my ships. If you or one of your men could find an external camera and aim it at your own newly arrived allies, you might see something more."

Crisler gestured impatiently to one of the marines. The man narrowed his eyes, and another inscape window opened.

Moments later a new inscape window bloomed. This was probably transmitting from one of the cameras on the outside of the cycler because the picture was grainy and ill-focused; the camera was at the limit of its zoom. Still, it showed enough to make Rue feel a rush of relief.

There were the rest of Crisler's ships. Three were mirrored spheres, each twice as large as the Lasa habitat of the *Envy*. The last was little more than a girder framework with dozens of cargo balloons attached to it.

And closing fast on the ships were all thirteen of Rue's remaining interceptors.

"My men have just taken out the *Banshee*," she said. "Unless you and your men surrender immediately, the rest of my ships are going to cut yours to pieces."

Crisler looked terribly weary. "Just how *did* you get here? Those aren't like any ships I've seen before. And is that Lasa writing on them?"

"I'm afraid I can't tell you anything, Admiral. But as you can see, I'm not just here with a little band of . . . what did you call us? Pirates? As you saw, we've got some short-range interceptors. Obviously, they had to come from somewhere . . ."

The admiral glowered. "No deal," he said finally. "I've accomplished my mission here already. This ship appears to be leaving, and so we'll be leaving with it. Once the cycler is underway, we'll have it create a habitat large enough to house all of us comfortably. Then we'll steer her back to Chandaka. Those little interceptors of yours can't stop us—this entire system is full of laser defenses. They hit anything that threatens the construction cylinder—and what do you bet they protect this cycler as well?"

He shook his head. "Regrettable that I have to lose my other ships. But it's an acceptable loss."

To Rue's surprise, Professor Herat raised his hand. "Admiral, this might be the time to mention that there isn't enough power in this system to actually launch a cycler."

"Of course there is," snapped Crisler. "They launched the *Envy* from here. And this ship, as you can see, is on its way."

One of the inscape windows showed the glowing wreckage of the *Banshee* dwindling behind them. Rue noticed that everyone had begun to drift toward one wall of the sphere: They were starting to accelerate.

"Sir," said the marine who had been controlling the inscape windows. "I've located a signal originating from Captain Cassels."

"Disable her suit radio," said Crisler. "That's it then," he said when the marine had finished. "Cassels, I am going to bring home the means to end the rebellion. I'll have the Chicxulub weapon adapted to hunt the rebels anywhere they go. After we let the ships loose, we grow, they whither. It's as simple as that."

"But the rebels use alien technology," said Katz. His voice was strained. "How can you target the rebels without also hitting the aliens?"

The admiral shrugged. "Collateral damage. The professor here should know," he said to Herat, "that all our overtures to them failed anyway. Humanity has no friends in this universe. If they won't be our allies, then they're vermin."

"But once the genie's out of the bottle, how do you stop it? The ships will continue to breed, they'll always be out there . . ."

Crisler shook his head. "That's where R.E. technology comes into it. We intend to adapt the ships so that they and all their systems are reliant on microtransactions with a Rights Owner. In order to breed, they'll have to contact us for permission."

Mike laughed humorlessly. "And you'll be the Rights Owner . . . of an entire fleet of warships."

The admiral nodded. "Any good plan has room in it for both altruism and self-interest, Dr. Bequith. This is a good plan."

He waved to the marines by the door. "Take the prisoners outside. You can use them for target practice."

Rue caught Mike's eye, and nodded. He reached behind him.

"No!" shouted Katz. He jumped at Crisler and for just a second he had the admiral by the throat. Then his own momentum carried him past. There was a bright flash and he screamed. When he hit the far wall and bounced away, he was limp.

"If anyone else tries—" Crisler started to say, but at that moment a swarm of hissing, buzzing things rose from behind Mike Bequith and flew straight at the marines.

"Bots!" shouted one marine, as he tried to bring his laser to bear. Four flying beads landed on the laser itself, and began vibrating madly. He shouted and let go of the smoking rifle.

Then Michael Bequith was struggling with him, trying to get the taser at his belt. Rue saw Barendts leap forward too, and the small chamber erupted into combat. Rue dove out of the way of a laser shot, only to collide with one of the researchers.

"Tasers only!" shrieked Crisler as a stray beam burned a line down the leg of his suit.

People were boiling everywhere, kicking each other in their haste to escape the chamber. Rue found herself propelled in the direction of the control sphere. She grabbed its crystalline edge, and pulled herself inside.

Instantly stars bloomed around her. Since crafting the controls systems of the *Envy*, Rue had spent many hours in her own cycler's cockpit, so she was instantly familiar with this one. Quickly, with one eye on the mayhem outside, she zoomed the view out.

Osiris and Apophis made twin walls on either side of her. At her navel was the cycler, and a meter away the construction shack had returned to its normal cylindrical shape. Next to it a tiny version of the *Banshee* was drifting, gutted and dark. The two interceptors waited near it.

She moved her hands within the hologram to call up the cycler's flight plan. The Twins zoomed out, becoming small spheres, and now a curved line showed the cycler's course. It was going to whip closely around Osiris, and then accelerate outward . . .

In exactly the opposite direction to Chandaka. If somehow the machinery here were able to accelerate this ship up to the same velocity as the *Envy*—eighty-five percent lightspeed—it would take it a decade or more to cycle back to Chandaka. No, Crisler would choose another destination. There must be another lit world closer on this course . . . In a moment, she had it. She knew where Crisler would abandon the cycler and return to High Space.

An arm reached into the sphere and dragged her out. She started to fight, then saw that it was Mike. "Come on!" he shouted. "We've got to get out now!"

Smoke had filled the chamber, which was still full of struggling forms. She followed Mike to the exit and out, to find herself with the rest of her crew, and most of the science team, in the balloon-hab. Herat, of all people, was standing over the entrance, firing into the smoke with a laser rifle.

"This way!" It was Harp, gesturing from an airlock opposite to the one that led to the hibernation cocoons.

Rue grabbed Herat's arm. "Professor. Laurent! We have to go!"

Herat whirled. His face was a mask of anger. "—Shot Henry. Just shot him down!"

"I know. Come!" She hauled him through the door after Harp.

"Status," she said to Harp as the door closed behind her. Rue found that as soon as she stopped moving she drifted to one wall of this new chamber; might as well call that direction down, she decided. This new room was packed with supplies like the one on the other side of the hibernation chamber.

"They seem to have wrapped hab chambers like this

around the nose of the cycler," said Harp. "That'd mean there's about ten of them—"

"Twelve," interrupted Corinna Chandra. She was actually smiling, a rarity for her. "We're continuing to accelerate, Captain, and not all of these people were able to bring their helmets." About half the science staff had made it out.

"Anyone want to stay and take their chances with Crisler?" shouted Rue. No one moved. "All right. These balloon-habs are anchored to the cycler somehow. We're going to detach this one and float away. Got it? Get moving!" She clapped her gloves together, and was rewarded by a wave of pain from her injured hand.

She could see shadows of movement on the other side of the door: Crisler's marines. They could have cut through the wall separating the two habs in a second, but doubtless they or Crisler had realized that this little ring of balloons was their only chance of survival if they were to ride the cycler out of here. They couldn't afford to damage it.

Rue's crew were swarming over the floor and staring out the hab's one small window, looking for the points where the balloon-hab was attached to straps glued onto the cycler's skin. Harp turned his laser on the lowest setting and at Evan's command, made several quick cuts through the floor. Rue's ear's popped as air hissed out of the hab for a few tense seconds before the hab's skin repaired itself.

"Now we're only held by the doors," said Evan. They set to work on those.

Mike Bequith had been huddled with Herat in one corner. Now he floated over to Rue. "I count twelve. We should be able to get everyone safely into the interceptors . . ." He trailed off, looking around in obvious puzzlement. "Rue . . . where's Barendts?"

"Your little rebel friend? I don't know," she snapped.

"But he was one of the first ones out," said Mike.

She sighed. "So?"

Mike took her by the shoulders—she was about to protest, when he said, "Rue. *Where is the cycler mother seed?*"

"Look, I think we have more important things to think about right now."

"No, Rue, I don't think we do," said Professor Herat, who had come up behind Mike.

"The seeds are the key—they're the real treasure of this world, Rue. With them, Crisler might learn how to make his self-reproducing warships. And with them, you could make any number of *Jentry's Envys* . . ."

Corinna and Evan had detached their side of the door through which Rue had entered this hab. The whole hab shifted a bit; it was now hanging from the cycler only by the other door.

"Barendts took the seed," said Mike.

"Took it?" Rue laughed wildly. "Took it where?"

Mike looked at her. A look of shocked comprehension dawned on his face. "Of course!"

He dove for the hab's other door, elbowing Corinna aside as he closed his faceplate. Before Rue could react, he had opened the door and swung through.

The door hissed shut. Rue turned, gaping, to Professor Herat. Herat had put a hand over his mouth, fingers trembling.

"Laurent? What is it?"

"Crisler's not the only one who might be able to resurrect the Chicxulub weapon," said Herat. "The rebels could do it . . . if they too had a seed . . ."

Suddenly the hab let loose and began to tumble. Rue barely felt the motion. Barendts was making for one of the interceptors with the seed in tow. And Michael Bequith had gone to join him.

MICHAEL FOUND ANOTHER airlock and cycled through it. He was too busy inventorying his supplies to think about what would happen next. He had a laser rifle, reaction pistol, and those autotroph bees that had survived their diversionary attack. Those huddled in one of his belt pouches now as he opened the outer airlock door to hard vacuum.

Osiris loomed above him. Below he saw nothing but

stars—no, that wasn't quite true. One bead of the necklace of habs had fallen from the cycler. He watched it tumble, intact so far, away into the dark.

Between them, he knew Rue's crew and the science team would be able to find a way to signal her interceptors. They would be all right, he told himself as he braced himself, preparing to leap into the void.

Funny—not too long ago, he had stood on Dis, facing just such an empty sunless sky. Then, Michael had made sure he was tethered at all times; the prospect of drifting off into endless space had terrified him.

There was not a whisper of that old terror now as he stepped off the cycler into the void.

The cycler shot up past him, a moving graffiti-scrawled wall visible only by faint starlight. Michael got the light-enhancers in his helmet working, and turned away from the now-bright starship.

The stars were sharp points; as the cycler passed, the exhaust from its engines was blinding. He jetted away from twin columns of light that speared into the night. As he turned again he saw the oval glow of an aurora crowning Apophis.

He knew in general where he was going, so began jetting toward the ruins of the *Banshee*. Barendts wasn't visible yet; he might never be unless Michael got a lucky glimpse of his reaction pistol firing. Uncomfortably, that suggested that Michael might miss him and go to the wrong interceptor.

He couldn't afford to think about that. Michael recited a mantra to calm himself as he flew through the darkness. All was silent, and he had no sense of motion at all. Only the faint whirring of his suit's systems, and his own breathing, told Michael that he was still real, a physical man and not a spirit drifting in the void.

Part of him was bracing for an onslaught of despair from the kami of Dis. Surely they were still there? But no, they had gone silent. Michael realized this with a kind of shock—when had that happened? When had his constant companions, who had dragged him down all these months, evaporated?

It must have been his decision to rejoin the rebels—to take back Kimpurusha, or die trying. Was that it? He tried to remember his days on Oculus . . . but no, they had been there then.

Perhaps it was the battle that had just passed. The immediacy of it, the adrenaline. Wasn't this his natural environment now? The battlefield?

Michael frowned, and shook his head. He was no soldier. He might make a credible spy, but he'd had no stomach for hurting anyone, even the marines who had tried to kill him today. Barendts, a trained fighter, had carried most of the attack that got them out of Crisler's clutches.

Far ahead of him a tiny star flared to life, then died. That must be Barendts. Michael lined himself up and made the difficult course correction that would take him that way.

They were approaching the construction shack now. In enhanced light, he could see the white spindle-shapes of the interceptors. Barendts was making for the one on the right. Good.

If both Crisler and the rebels had the secret of the Chicxulub ships, at least there would be a level playing field. Maybe the ships would clash among themselves, ignoring the humans until there was a victor in space. Maybe they could spare lives, not take them that way.

Sadly, though, the halo worlds would lose either way. Without more *Jentry's Envys*, they were doomed to increasing isolation and irrelevance. Rue's civilization, which he had been born into and still loved, would come to an end.

Barendts was a faintly visible star-shape struggling with a cylindrical white seed at the airlock of the interceptor. The marine hadn't spotted Michael yet.

He knew he shouldn't have left Rue and the others helpless in the balloon-hab. He cast about for something to take his mind off of that in these last minutes of free fall. Fear . . .

Yes! He still couldn't remember when the kami of Dis had left him. He tried to focus on that. It hadn't been in battle, he knew that now. Before that, then . . . and he had it.

When Irina Case told him that his kami might be the means for reviving the spiritual life of New Armstrong, something had changed in Michael. He'd had no time to think about it then; he'd been arrested immediately afterward, but his kami were powerful and despite what he'd said to Irina, he now believed that he had not simply found them, but had created them; they were not real entities with lives of their own, they were his Art. With them, he had somehow strengthened Rue through her grief. Maybe his kami really could heal a whole world.

And then, as the interceptor fell into the fiery maw of Colossus, he'd had a momentary flash when he thought he understood Rue's Supreme Meme. Somehow, in that moment of insight, the dark whispering voices of Dis had departed for good.

This realization was so astonishing that he almost missed the interceptor. He made a frantic last blast with the pistol, and was actually able to touch the magnetic soles of his boots to the hull of the interceptor and grab the back end of the seed, before Barendts noticed him.

The marine whirled, laser raised.

"It's just me," said Michael. "Brilliant move, skiving off with this thing."

"Bequith!" Barendts laughed shakily. "Quick, let's get it inside. I think I know enough to pilot one of these through the drop; say, how'd you like a holiday on Kimpurusha?" He holstered the laser again.

Michael felt his heart leap at the name of his homeworld. "Kimpurusha? Is that where you're taking it?"

Barendts laughed again. "You never knew, did you?— That's where I was trained. Years after your people tried their insurrection—but they still knew you. I knew who you were when you first came on board the *Spirit of Luna*!"

"How?" Had rebel cells continued to exist on Kimpurusha after Michael's own uprising failed? No, that wasn't possible; they would have tried to contact him, surely.

"We had the same mentor," said Barendts. "You remember Errend, don't you?"

Michael's stomach turned over.

"He sure remembered you. You were . . . how did he put it? One of the pawns he had to sacrifice to convince the R.E. that Kimpurusha had gone quiet. But he always hoped you'd kept your allegiance and that we might activate you again. A farsighted man, Errend."

"Indeed." Michael looked over the seed to where Barendts was trying to wedge his end into the airlock. "Need a hand there?"

"Sure, buddy." Michael went around the seed and crouched by the open airlock next to Barendts.

"Why don't you just grab it there, and—"

In one motion Michael unholstered Barendts' laser, and kicked the marine off the interceptor.

"What the hell are you doing!" Barendts tumbled over twice before he got his reaction pistol in hand and steadied himself. "This is our only chance now, don't you get it? If Crisler gets away with the other seed, he'll be able to build a weapon we can't stop! Hell, one that even *he* can't stop! He'll win the war, Mike. Kimpurusha will have fallen for all time, and it'll be your fault!"

Michael regarded him calmly over the edge of the airlock. "What war is it that you're talking about?" He had to laugh at his own thick-headedness during the past months. "I know all about that war, I just spent the last five years of my life uncovering its victims with Professor Herat.

"Out there in High Space, the war is of all against all, and it goes on forever. No one needs anyone else if they can simply pull up roots and move a few light-years to get away—which works great until you run up against someone who's there already. That's the great lesson of the

Chicxulub, isn't it? No matter how big the galaxy, its resources are finite—but with FTL, mobility isn't. Barendts,
the result is always—always—the disintegration of the
species into thousands of subspecies that war among themselves and with their neighbors. Permanent war. In all the
lifetime of the galaxy there's only been two exceptions: the
Lasa and the Chicxulub. The Lasa opted out of FTL travel
completely; they discovered an environment that encouraged cooperation rather than competition: the halo worlds.
No halo world can stand on its own. They need one another, and war between them isn't possible because of the
barrier of lightspeed."

"You're crazy," said Barendts. "Put down the laser.
Can't you see what's happening here?"

"More clearly than ever. The Chicxulub are the only
other solution, Barendts. The only other solution is to keep
yourself pure, and wipe out every competitor. That's what
the R.E.'s all about, isn't it? It was created to force humanity to stay together.

"The lit worlds are lost no matter who wins, can't you
see? Whether you and I bring this seed back or not, the
R.E. either wins, and goes the way of the Chicxulub, or it
loses, and we end up with every world for itself. A thousand wars where before there was only one."

"You want the R.E. to win!" accused Barendts.

Michael shook his head. "Actually, I want the Lasa to
win. Now you'd better find something to hold onto out
there, because I'm shutting this hatch and then we're going
after the rest of our people."

From inside the hatch it was easy to pull the cycler
mother seed inside. Michael could see Barendts waiting
just outside, but he had no weapon. He continued to rail
impotently at Michael until the hatch was shut.

"DON'T MIND THE COLD, guys," said Rue. It was only about
-50 Celcius in here so far, which brought back memories of

her escape from Allemagne. "Just breathe through your
noses." At least everybody had their suits on; it was just the
scientists who were missing their helmets that were having
trouble. So far everyone had been calm, sitting along the
walls silently while the techs worked.

The lights of the hab flickered. Now *this* they didn't
need. "What's going on?" She moved to where two technicians were trying to rig up a transmitter.

"Looks like the emergency supply was just a superconducting loop. It's bleeding out pretty fast, ma'am. I'd say
we've got about ten minutes of power left."

When the power went the cold would really start. Those
without helmets would develop severe frostbite around the
face and ears, then their lungs would start to burn.

She would have to fix things before then. "Okay, how
about reserve oxygen?" The techs pointed to a set of panels
under the floor. Rue opened one and examined the tanks
there.

"Listen up, people! We're going to do something haz-
ardous. I'm going to fetch one of our interceptors." *If Mike
Bequith hasn't stolen both,* she thought bitterly. "I'm going
to have to cut a hole in the wall and exit through it. There'll
be a huge pressure drop, but it'll be temporary. Once the
patches are on, you'll be able to breathe again. Is everybody clear on that?"

Several of the exposed faces went white, but no one
protested.

"Better for two of us to go," said Harp. "I'll come."

"All right." Rue pointed a laser at a section of wall well
away from the vulnerable scientists. "Rapid, deep breaths,
people. Get ready to plug your noses." She aimed.

Clunk. Something big had struck the hab a glancing
blow; Rue found herself and Harp tumbling like dice in a
cup. Moments later the hab stabilized, but not its inhabitants: Everyone was shouting at once.

"Wait, wait! Shut up everybody!" They gradually quieted. Then Rue heard it: a tapping on the door. She flew over to it and looked through its tiny window.

Michael Bequith grinned back at her. He was holding a large and cumbersome inflatable airlock, trying to attach it to the door. After a minute he gave her the thumbs up, then she heard hissing.

The door opened. Mike filled the doorway, his suit covered in smoking frost.

She grabbed him and hugged him tightly, despite the cold that seared through her cheek as she laid it against the breastplate of his suit. "You came back."

"Of course." He seemed a bit offended that she had doubted him.

"But the seed . . . the rebels . . . don't you want to fight the R.E.?"

Mike sighed, and reached up to smooth back her hair with one icy glove.

"I don't want to destroy, not even destroy the R.E." he said. "I . . . want to build."

A DAY LATER, Rue joined a large crowd that had gathered around a big inscape window in the larger of the cruisers they had captured from Crisler. The scientific team was here, all talking excitedly about the spectacle unfolding in the window. Someone had found material to make black arm bands in honor of Henry Katz.

"I knew there wasn't enough power in those tethers to launch a cycler!" laughed Herat. "But never in a million years would I have imagined they'd do that!"

That was bright enough to illuminate both Apophis and Osiris like a minor sun. The thousands of conductive tethers that orbited around Osiris normally just drew power out of the brown dwarf's magnetic field. Somehow, they had orchestrated a vast current flow back into the dwarf—and the result was the biggest flare Rue had ever seen burst off a dwarf. It stood out of Osiris's equator like an incandescent spear, and though they weren't visible from here, she knew that a vortex of tethers was amplifying and aiming that flare. The full power of Osiris's magnetosphere was pouring power into an energy beam of astonishing power.

Crisler's cycler rode the crest of that wave of energy like a leaf in a hurricane. The acceleration was enormous; Crisler and his men were either in their hibernation tanks now, or dead from the pressure. The cycler was thriving, though, soaring on wings of magnetized plasma faster and faster, trying its best to catch up to light.

Rue made her way over to the professor, and Mike who was as always next to his mentor. Rue reached out and touched Mike's arm. He turned with a wide smile.

"And so," Rue said very softly, "the halo worlds become able to launch our own cyclers at last." Mike took her hand in his, and squeezed it.

She'd barely had a chance to talk to Mike in the whirlwind of activity that had followed Crisler's escape. When he arrived to rescue her team and she realized he had abandoned the rebels, Rue had felt a rush of happiness that had carried her through the whirlwind. Now, with Crisler's ships secure and dispatches ready for sending to Colossus, New Armstrong, and Crisler's probable destination, she could finally relax for a moment.

The scientists cheered the cycler launch like they were watching a sporting match. Herat turned away, smiling fondly, and said, "Hello, Rue. Are you getting ready to leave?"

She nodded. "There's much to do. Are you staying here, Laurent, or are you going back to High Space? Now that we know they exist, I'm sure you'll be able to find the Lasa themselves."

He shook his head. "No—or rather, we already found them. They are that." He gestured to the vast machinery of the Twins visible through the window. "That and no more. The original Lasa—the species that gave us the name—realized that no species is permanent. Only the ecological niches, the environments friendly to one or another kind of life, have any kind of permanence. They saw that they would rise and fall like every living form. So, instead of trying to extend their existence, like so many other species before and since," he sighed, "they looked to ways of preserving and nourishing an environment that would encourage the birth and growth of species similar to themselves. Cooperative, farsighted peoples."

He turned back to contemplate the view. "I'm going to stay here, and make it my life to study this place. The Lasa, you see, aren't a species. They're an environment—an ecological niche. Bequith, here, explained that to me. And I'm coming to agree with him that humanity would do well to expand into and nurture this niche."

As usual, Rue didn't completely understand Herat. But he smiled at her, and turned back to watch the cycler launch. That smile was enough to tell her he was content.

She turned to Mike, and now her throat was tight again. "And what about you? You came back for us, when you could have gone with Barendts and become the greatest hero of the rebels."

He shrugged. "I just realized it would never stop. We might get Kimpurusha back, but what then? It would never return to what it was when it was part of the Compact. And . . . and I realized that freeing Kimpurusha wouldn't satisfy me. There was something better I could do."

Rue bit her lip, avoiding his eyes. "So where will you go now?"

He had that mysterious smile again. "I want to help revive the Cycler Compact. Right now, there's nowhere I'd rather be than wherever you're taking the cycler mother seed."

"Why, Mr. Bequith," she said, grinning back at him. "Where else would I take it? It's coming with me to Erythrion."

He hesitated. "And your crew will go with you. That's six, including Rebecca's girlfriend; there's no room in the interceptor for one more . . ."

Now she laughed. "Evan is staying here. He wants to return to High Space."

"And that means . . ."

She took his hand and smiled into his eyes. "There is a berth on my ship, Mr. Bequith, if you would like to have it."

28

RUE STOOD AT a window, and the view from it was real, neither holographic nor inscape. Treya shone close by, a sphere of pearly auroral light transfixed by one circle of purest white radiance where the artificial sun was shining today on clouds. The orbital colony where Rue stood had once been the property of the Cycler Compact; it had seemed a fitting place for her to stay, for now.

"You see?" she said to Michael, who stood at her side. "Sunlight, of a sort. Too bright for me, but you'll like it."

Michael rested his hand on hers. The cuffs of their shirts were an identical black; she wore her captain's uniform, and Michael had accepted the high-collared clerical counterpart. He looked good in uniform, especially now that he seemed to have overcome his demons. He radiated authority.

Sounds of debate came from behind them. A long oak table filled the other end of the room. A group of men and women, mostly elderly, were going over a complex set of plans and edicts. They all looked slightly shell-shocked. A week ago none had suspected that their lives would be overturned by the arrival of Rue.

There were fourteen people here; fourteen in all Erythrion who had once held positions of power in the Cycler Compact and who might still be trusted by the people. On Oculus, the Compact had been a living thing, a vast and ancient order that encompassed both government and religion. Oculus had been vibrant, forward-looking. Well, Rue was determined that Erythrion would become so too.

Only the monks of Permanence and a few holdouts from the old days had responded immediately to Rue's summons. On her arrival she had exercised the prerogative of a cycler captain in ordering a special session of the Compact executive. The first replies had been angry accusations that she was playing some trick; she had been called disrespectful to the glorious past that the proud few still revered.

Her response to that was to transmit substantial excerpts from Blair's records. The discovery of *Jentry's Envy* and the proof that Rue had learned to control it was enough to yield a second round of responses. These were respectful and curious. She claimed to come bearing great news, and yet she had not arrived by magsail. Had she come from High Space? And what was this news?

Her first meeting here, a week ago, had begun inauspiciously. The men and women who filed into this office were just civilians—albeit rich and powerful, some of them. They had long ago retired their uniforms and rented out the offices of the Compact to local businesses. Ten people who might have been here had refused to come, citing more important business of one kind or another. Rue suspected that they simply believed the Compact was dead or not worth reviving.

She had not minced words during that first meeting. "The Cycler Compact has been reborn," she told them. "Erythrion is requested to restore its institutions to the standards of the Compact. In the months and years ahead, you will have the opportunity to return to your traditional roles in the administration of the Compact. In fact, Erythrion is critical to the rebirth of our great civilization. For we will be the first halo world in decades to begin launching new cyclers."

They had begun to come around, gradually. Then, as the news of the cycler mothers sank in, skepticism had changed to enthusiasm, then almost feverish excitement. The scattered worlds of the halo *could* be reunited. The shared experience of living in the interstellar fastness could reach everyone, no matter how remote. From being isolated colonies with no belief in a future, they could become explorers and settlers again. The offer was almost unbelievable; in a kind of desperation to prove it real, they were working day and night now to lay the groundwork for the return of the cyclers.

The argument behind Rue and Mike now reached a fever pitch, then broke in laughter. She turned. Corinna Chandra stood at the head of the table, waving to the text in a holo window. "That's it, then," she said. "The monks of Permanence will take charge of the cycler mother seed. We will see to its nurturing and growth."

There were nods around the table, some reluctant, some enthusiastic. Rue smiled at Corinna, who seemed to be beaming all the time, these days. Corinna had adopted the seed as if it were her own child, and she was fiercely protective of it. This new agreement was a good one; people still respected the monks, and they alone still controlled the myriad launch beams and power tethers that orbited Erythrion. The launch beams could double as weapons in a pinch, everyone knew that, so the monks' possession of the seed would not be threatened.

Everyone sat back, relaxing and talking excitedly. The cyclers could come again, and the psychological isolation of Erythrion would be ended. Even now Blair was in an editing suite preparing his records for broadcast. Rue had no doubt that they would be the most highly watched documentaries on the net for the next six months. By the time they had finished airing, the impact of what was now possible would have begun to sink in; Erythrion would begin to thaw from the long winter of the soul that had gripped it.

"Ten minute break," said the abbot of Treya's Permanence monastery. "Then we need to discuss Brother Bequith's dangerous new theology."

"Dangerous?" murmured Rue to Mike, who grinned. They headed for the door with the rest of the crowd, but the abbot stopped Mike.

"You have seen more of the universe than any of us, Brother," said the abbot seriously. "We know the grave discoveries you made about the life and death of civilizations. I just don't understand why such proof of the fragility of life hasn't convinced you that Permanence is our only hope. I mean . . . what can we possibly offer the people of our worlds that would be better than an eternal civilization?"

Mike looked the abbot in the eye and said, "Children. We can offer them children." Then he politely stepped around the abbot and into the hall.

Rue grabbed his arm as he walked, and laughed. "You're learning fast," she said.

"Learning? What?"

"How to be a prophet. Cryptic utterances are an essential part of the role, aren't they?"

He blushed slightly. "I just didn't want to get into it all right then."

Michael now believed that the theology of NeoShinto was incomplete. "It tries to make us one with the universe—and it succeeds. But I got lost in that oneness, and I suspect many people do. Your Supreme Meme taught me that the little inconsequential details of my everyday life are as real and valuable as everything else put together. In science they have a principle called *complementarity*: mass and energy are the same thing, but you can only have one at a time; a particle has momentum and position, but you can only see one of those at a time. So it is with our lives. We need to honor our sense of unity with the world, but we also need to honor our individuality. Both are true. Both are absolutes, and we have to nurture both if we're to survive on these worlds."

He had tried to explain the theology of it to her, but Rue wasn't really interested, and he knew that. "It's just . . ." he had said after a half hour's discussion, "just a new way to both accept mortality and throw yourself into life. Nothing's permanent. But everything can hand what's unique, what's best about itself, to what comes after."

"Like the Lasa?" she'd asked.

He nodded. "And like the Chicxulub."

They walked upstairs and into the gloriously hot artificial sunlight of the colony cylinder. This tiny world was a cylinder twenty kilometers long and four across. The land wrapped itself above to become sky, with an intolerably bright fusion lamp at the axis providing daylight for the parks and forests that dotted the inside of the cylinder. Rue and Mike went to sit on a bench under a shady tree, and after fumbling out her sunglasses she draped herself over the back of the seat and drank in the air. It was nearly as natural-smelling as that of Chandaka. Things were peaceful here; among the distant clouds, people glided and swooped on diaphanous wings.

"One more meeting," said Rue. "Think they're ready to go it on their own for a while?"

"They'll have Corinna and Blair to keep them inspired," said Mike. "And we should be back in a few days, if all goes well."

"*Excuse me.*"

Rue looked around. A rather officious looking woman in a gray suit stood on the path. "Are you, um, Meadow-Rue Rosebud Cassels?"

Rue stood up. "Yes, I am."

"My name is Alita Strong. I represent . . . your family."

"Represent?"

"I'm their lawyer." Rue continued to stare blankly at the woman, who finally said, "Surely you know that there are lawsuits outstanding against you, and . . . financial matters to be settled . . ."

"Financial . . . ?"

"It took us a while to find you," continued Strong. "But I told my clients that a face-to-face talk with you would probably be the best way to resolve things. Have you got a few minutes?"

"What? Now?" Rue felt a strange flutter of nervousness. Politicians and generalissimos didn't scare her anymore, so why was her heart pounding at this development?

Strong was walking toward one of the campus buildings near the one Rue had rented. Rue turned to Mike, appealing to him for something, any sort of guidance.

He took her hand and said, "Let's go see, shall we?"

They followed Strong inside the building and down into a lounge below the surface. Two people were sitting on low couches there. Both stood as Rue came down the steps.

"Good morning, dear!" gushed Aunt Leda as she minced forward.

"Hi, Sis," said Jentry, who slouched with his hands in his pockets, not moving from his spot near the back of the lounge.

Time seemed to stop for Rue. There he was, and damned if he didn't look older. Shorter. Skinnier. Jentry was dressed in his usual station gear, rather gauche in the plush environment of the lounge.

There was no way to look him in the eye and not remember all the times he'd beat her. Rue remembered now, though, that there had never been any occasion when she hadn't fought back. And it was with a cool tingle of pleasure that she realized that after her military training on Oculus, she could beat him in a fair fight any day.

"Brother," she said in a sweet voice; she felt Mike's grip on her arm tighten. She extricated herself from that hold and went to embrace Aunt Leda. "Aunt Leda. How are you? I'm so sorry about Max."

"Yes, we only just heard the news." Leda contrived to look weepy. "That is—it was a few days ago. We didn't know you were here, the news came from our dear friend Colonel Jackman . . ."

Rue nodded. Jackman had been one of those who had refused to come to her meetings here. He must have called Leda with the news—Leda and who else? Ah, now the intrigues would start!

Rue turned from Leda to Jentry. "How are you, Jentry?"

"I'm okay." He hesitated, then stepped forward, hand out. To her own surprise, Rue shook it. Then it came to her how she must look to these two: imperious and proud in her uniform, with a sharp-eyed monk standing, arms folded, at her shoulder.

She laughed, and plunked herself down on one of the couches. "Well, who of us would ever have expected this!" She patted the seat next to her; after a moment Jentry sat cautiously next to her. "How's the station, Jen? Still racing those mining bots?"

He looked shifty, and said, "It's okay. Yeah, I, we . . . We got a bit of a debt problem right now, so—"

The lawyer cleared her throat. Jentry looked at the floor. Rue appraised her, with a raised eyebrow.

"There's two little matters we need to get behind us," said Strong, coming to sit opposite Rue. Leda remained standing, a rather fixed smile on her face. "There's the matter of the inheritance from Max of course, and then the—"

"Inheritance? What inheritance?"

Leda and Jentry looked at one another. The lawyer sighed.

"I gather you haven't been informed. Max Cassels made you his heir."

Rue sat there with her mouth open for a bit too long, because suddenly Mike was sitting next to her holding her shoulders. "Are you okay?" he whispered.

"Okay? Okay?" She tilted her head back and laughed. "I'm great! Oh, Max, why'd you—" Then she realized something. "But—he must have done that before we left . . ."

Strong nodded. "Yes, the night before your departure from Treya, he registered a new will. You were to receive his entire estate. Of course, what with taxes, litigation fees, and monies owing to certain plaintiffs . . ." and here Leda turned pink and tried to look smaller, "all that's left is the house. And contents. And this." She held out a data card. "Keyed to be unlocked only by you."

Rue took the card numbly. She had tears in her eyes, she realized. It was simply that by this one gesture Max had brought her into the Cassels family. Since her parents died, Jentry had done everything in his power to make her feel like she didn't belong. And Leda had been no help. It was only now that Rue realized how deeply the wounds had reached. Bereft of family, she had run from world to world, across years and through adventures that had made her into something quite new. A cycler captain. A woman of power and influence.

And now, Max's gift to her was to affirm that she had been a Cassels all along. That she had a home.

There was a respectful silence while she pulled herself together. "Well," she said at last, "I will open this in good time and," she glanced sharply at Leda, "in private. Thank you."

"There is one other thing," said the lawyer.

Rue stood. The inheritance had been quite enough, she was thinking. "We need to be getting back," she said to Mike.

"It concerns a certain family heirloom, entrusted to Jentry Cassels and stolen by you."

Rue whirled. *"What?"*

"The ediacaran pendant your grandmother had," said Leda. "It was never rightfully hers. But Jentry has been so kind as to reveal its existence to us, and as provenance was never certain on it . . . well, it's legally his now."

"Come on, Sis," said Jentry. "I need that thing to pay off our debt. You wouldn't want us to lose the station, would you?"

She stared at him. Possibly a million things came to mind that she might say right now, but none seemed adequate.

Finally, in a kind of daze, she said, "I traded it on Oculus for supplies. Sorry."

Strong cleared her throat. "Then you are liable for the—"

"Take it up with the Compact," snapped Rue. "Bill the Cycler Order. I assure you we're good for it."

Then she turned on her heel and stalked out of the room.

A FAMILIAR COUNTDOWN was ticking away in the background. Rue floated once again in oxygenated liquid, watching Mike adjusting his G-bed through the wavery liquid that filled the interceptor.

"I hope this is the last time we have to trust our lives to one of these things," he was muttering.

She smiled fondly at him, and lay back. In just a few minutes they would fall into the brooding red cloudscape of Erythrion, and if the gods and kami were kind, they would survive the transition to FTL flight. In a few hours, they would be at New Armstrong.

Michael was going there to teach Irina Case's people his new alternative to Permanence. And she . . . she came to take back what was hers. She would see *Jentry's Envy* in her control again, and the men who had taken it would find justice, or die.

They would arrive at New Armstrong well in advance of the *Envy*. Rue would make her case, buttressed with plenty of evidence from Oculus. New Armstrong would be threatened with sanctions by the Compact if necessary, should they not comply. But they would. They would take Mallory and his people into custody once they rode down the beam, and a new crew, handpicked by Rue, would replace them. Then, finally, the *Envy* could be brought back onto her original ring and, in a few years, she would return to Erythrion.

Maybe by then Rue would be ready to captain her again.

She had been putting something off, she knew. A little holo window showed Erythrion approaching, like some baleful god. With a sigh, Rue took out the card Max had left for her, and pressed her thumb against it.

The card darkened, then a tiny holo of Max appeared in it.

"Don't ask," he said with a shrug. "I couldn't very well leave it all to the old bat, could I? You deserve it, Rue, you do."

But why? She mouthed the words.

As if he'd heard her, Max paused. "You came along at a time when I'd started to lose hope, Rue. I didn't believe there were good people in the world anymore. But you came stomping into my life, all oblivious to the little jealousies and intrigues of the family, as though you'd somehow been kept in a crystal jar somewhere, pure and unsullied by the rest of the stinking clan. At first I couldn't believe it. But I believe it now. So I'm going with you to Chandaka, and maybe we can make this family stand for something again—or maybe for the first time. Because I wasn't able to do it on my own.

"But if you read this, then I didn't make it back. And maybe it will have been my own doing; I hope not."

"I hope you thrive, Rue. I know you will. And take my stuff and use it well . . . and keep it out of her clutches." He grimaced.

"Thrive, cousin. Thrive."

Rue raised heavy fingers and thumbed open a pouch on her suit. She brought out the little ediacaran medallion, and held it up for a moment, arm shaking with the effort. She could see the delicate galaxy-shaped spiral of it on the siltstone.

"Brace yourselves," said the pilot. "We're starting the dive."

Rue could feel the hand of Erythrion begin to press down upon her. The interceptor swayed from side to side, and her heart began to hammer.

Across from her, Mike grinned a stoic grin and said, "We'll make it. We have a house to come back to now."

"And so much more," she replied with a smile.

We have time.